Dancing With Donal
Bad Boys Book Four

Christine Young

Chapter One

Fall 1825
Glasgow, Scotland

"Well, I see nothing if anything has changed in these parts. It's still raining and the wind whistles through the trees. I'm chilled to the bone." Graham Chamberlin, Donal's little brother walked into the front door, taking off his hat and the raincoat he wore before striding into the downstairs office.

"What are you doing back from Maryland? Didn't expect to see you this soon. Why did you come home? You weren't due back until next month." Donal sat at his desk, a pen in hand, finishing correspondence to be sent to his brother who was supposed to be in the States overseeing the tobacco plantation.

"Came home to look for a wife. Seems there are not many women in the states, only married women and black folks; of course there are the natives. While the nights aren't as cold there, it's still nice to have a woman to welcome into my bed and warm me. A wife is what I'm needing these days, a good Scottish wife."

"Daryl MacTavish is off limits to you." Blessed hell that's just what he needed, his brother chasing after all the eligible skirts in Glasgow.

"I suppose everyone else is too. Fine by me. Knowing you, she is most likely uptight and a prude as well. Prim and proper is not what I like in my women. I want wild and unrestrained passion in my nights, velvet softness beneath the lacy frothy trappings."

His brother had never met Daryl, thank god, and he truly didn't have one clue as to what he yearned for in a relationship. What he did know was that Daryl was far from uptight and a prude. "Where do you ken you'll find a suitable mate? Not at the balls and recitals, I doubt. I ken, debutants don't seem to be your sort of woman."

"Don't know yet, perhaps the markets. A lass who is not afraid to get her hands dirty with a solid day of work, one who will be warm and passionate in bed. One, of course, has to give this family an heir. You certainly are not accomplishing the job. What has you digging in your heels, if you ken who it is you want?"

"Yes, well, I've given that a great deal of thought, and it won't be long before we have an heir." Donal scribbled a few more lines to the message he was working on before sealing it and setting the letter aside. Even though Graham would not be on the receiving end of the missive, someone needed to see to the information written here.

"Has the little MacTavish lass agreed to go along with your proposal? She's a tiny slip of a woman and you're a great brute of a man. Do you ken if you'll fit? You might just rip her apart." Graham belly laughed, seeming to enjoy the cruder side of his comments with his staid and stoic brother.

"Are they all so uncivilized and unpolished in Maryland or do you have a first priority in that department." Donal handed the letter over to his valet. He stared at his little brother, wishing he knew the real reason Graham was in Scotland. Nothing was obvious where Graham was concerned. While he had the reputation of a bad boy, Graham was the real bad boy in the family. A few years ago, he'd heard rumors about Gray, but one should never believe gossip.

"I'm the first," he laughed, helping himself to the brandy. "The premier. Like to say I just tell it as it is."

"How many bastards do you have?" Donal confronted him, a grim look on his face thinking about the hearsay that floated around his brother's comings and goings. "Hope you are taking care of them yourself and not with Chamberlin funds. It's likely you'll go broke if you don't learn to keep your sizable man parts in your pants."

Graham grinned from ear to ear, "You jealous, big brother?" He sobered. "I've no bastards. While I lived with the Cherokee, I almost had a child. The boy died in childbirth as did his mother. You don't have to worry about anyone soaking up the money. "There was another woman, and a child as well, but they are gone too."

"I'm sorry about your children, the women as well." He paused momentarily, thinking there was more to these stories than Gray was willing to tell. "Our business is doing better than ever, but I will admit to you the largest part of our strength comes from the production of the tobacco here in Scotland and the change into usable forms. Our factories out shine the money we take in from the crops. So, how many blacks do we have who are still slaves?"

"None, all the blacks I buy are given their papers, a choice as well. They are allowed to stay and work for us on our land and we take a percentage of their profits or they may move on. We provide quarters that have been updated and the ones who have learned to speak English have relayed to the others what their choices are. Whatever children they have will gain their freedom. After that they are given their papers and they can decide what it is they want to do with the rest of their lives."

"And how many stay?" Donal asked, concerned they would have to continue to buy workers. Buying people for slave labor was abhorrent to him, but in order to keep the plantation a working one, he needed farmers. "Are we still offering a plot of land to those who stay?"

"Most remain on the plantation. They don't have much choice. There is nowhere for them to go except north to Canada and that is a risk most don't want to take. The journey is long and hard, fraught with untold dangers. If they can keep their families and earn an honest day's living as a free man or woman, they are happy. I am constantly on the lookout for more land, but I have to keep traveling west. Don't know how long we'll be able to keep up the practice."

"Good, good, let's keep doing what works for us. I do understand we won't make as much money, but I don't believe in slavery. I want our plantation to run smoothly with working people earning an honest day's living."

"There are those who resent what we are doing. Their slaves grumble about the fairness of it all. They point to us as a symbol of bad luck and anarchy. They don't want to see their way of life interrupted, and that's what they fear we are doing." Graham sat down, sipping his brandy and seeming to enjoy the comforts of home.

"Good, good, I suppose you plan on staying until you find a mate who wants to follow you to Maryland."

Donal always wondered how long Graham would want to stay in a foreign country. Now he knew. Graham tied all the knots in the states that needed tying and was most likely back to stay. He had mixed feelings about Graham's return and understood he would have to find someone he could trust to replace him, "You're not going back, are you?"

"Don't plan on it. We've an amazing overseer. He thinks the same as us about slavery, that is. I don't believe it will be too many years before slavery is abolished all together. There are growing trends to do just that, especially in the north."

"What will you do here? Laze away the days and play with the willing skirts?" He paused a moment. "Ah, you say you want a wife. I wish you all the luck in that endeavor. We are not getting any younger."

"No, I only stopped here to say hello and perhaps let you feed me for a day or two. I'm off to my inheritance. The land grandmother left me in her will. As you well know, I was gifted with land in the highlands. A crumbling estate if I recall. One that is large enough to keep me busy for a while. Perhaps I'll find a suitable lass there."

"It is settled then. Dinner and in the morning you will be off to new inspiring adventures."

Donal was pleased with his brother. He seemed to be growing up and taking on more responsibilities.

"You will be left in these vast spaces to woo your darling Daryl MacTavish. I really do believe she is too tiny for you. You should look for someone who will match you muscle for muscle, height for height." Graham laughed, pouring himself a second glass of brandy. "I'm going to miss all this. Suppose I'll have to make sure there are all the necessities where I'm going put down roots."

"My brawn or her lack of it is not the point. She is the woman I want and will wed whether you think we will fit well together or not."

His words had never been spoken truer. Something about the little lass with the bright and unruly red hair always intrigued him, as he

4

recalled some of their past encounters.

He rose from the desk where he'd been sitting, thinking of Daryl and wishing he could see her this very moment. Striding to the window and trying to forget his brother was intruding on his solitude when he wanted someone else to be doing the same thing, he stared at the countryside. The rain must have stopped, but the wind still did more than rustle the leaves on the trees.

He smiled, his grin widening as his brother rambled on about something, he wasn't sure. In any case he didn't care. He now had plans for this afternoon. It was high time he said hello to his future wife. He was ready to begin to initiate her into the ways of a man and a woman. It seemed to have been eons since that night he kissed her. What age had she been? Possibly sixteen. The kiss made a lasting impact, but for the second kiss she'd only been a few months away from eighteen.

"Do you mind if I leave? Make yourself at home as I'm sure you planned. It seems I've an important errand to run."

His heart raced at the idea of an encounter with the little spitfire as well as in anticipation of the kiss he envisioned.

He cleared his throat, turning then to speak to Graham. "I don't plan on returning until later this evening. Close up the house and I'll let myself inside. Enjoy your evening. If you're hungry Justine will make sure you are fed well."

Donal strode from the room with single-minded purpose and a primitive need he'd never felt before. He'd seen Daryl and he assumed Lacie racing across the grounds toward the tiny pond and waterfall Daryl often visited. He was looking forward to a spirited and passionate confrontation, but first he had to get rid of the youngest sister.

There were so many possibilities.

The afternoon was before them in all its glory. He couldn't have asked for anything better.

In the stable he mounted his favorite stallion, Achilles, and urged him to run. They rode toward the MacTavish estate, hoping to see Daryl. In any case he would begin his pursuit of her today. He pulled Achilles to a stop, staring at the apparition in front of him.

Blessed hell, but even from this distance she was beautiful, strands of her wild red hair flying around her face and behind her, her small torso moving in perfect rhythm with her horse. His body tightened with need, thinking how well they would move together in bed. Good god admit it, sexual need was at the forefront of his mind.

If she wasn't a virgin and innocent, he would ride after her and take her wherever they ended up. He would pull her from her horse and onto his lap. Lord, but he imagined what it might feel like if she straddled him as they made love while they rode. That fantasy, he supposed, would be nearly impossible. Still, it was a thought worth pursing one day if he dared.

He couldn't remember the last time he felt this way; eager, enthusiastic and full of lust.

Lord, he had to retrieve at least a small amount of the control he was famous for. He had plans and he wanted to stick to them. Frightening her today with his thirst for her was not part of the strategy.

He grinned. Unexpectedly, Daryl MacTavish fell into his plans. He would have to be careful here, not too much persuasion, just enough of a taste for an innocent lass such as the young MacTavish girl to follow him willingly into marriage. This could turn out to be one of the best days of his life. From this moment on, he would diligently pursue Daryl in the guise of courting.

She was on his land. Trespassing. The thought gave him reason to smile, perhaps a favor in return for allowing her to enjoy the property.

His smile grew as his heart felt lighter for the first time in months. He'd been waiting for just this type of opportunity. She had been harder than the devil to get alone. It seemed she worked day and night in her bakery. He'd stopped by a few times, had coffee and a pastry of some sort. He never knew what he was eating because he couldn't stop watching her.

Ah, this was indeed Saturday afternoon. She was taking a much-needed day and a half of rest. He knew first-hand the shop was closed on Sundays. Perhaps he could spend some time with her tomorrow, too, continue the courtship, the wooing of Daryl.

When they married, he'd remedy that. She didn't need to work six days a week. Lord knows Flynt should have made sure his sisters were better taken care of. None of them should have the need to work. When they wed, he would give her everything she needed or wanted.

Having seen the direction she rode, he followed the path to one of the most beautiful scenes on his property, a place perfect for the first stages he planned, a kiss, a taste of Daryl. Again, all he needed now was to figure out how to get rid of the little sister, prompt her to leave of her own accord. Yet somehow, he felt she would oblige him. There was something amazingly astute about the littlest MacTavish. Only one year younger than Daryl, she would make some man a wonderful wife.

The ground flew beneath the horse's hooves. He tried to formulate a plan in his head as he raced forward. He had followed her here numerous times and watched from afar as she would wade in the pond on hot summer days, showing her delicate slender feet and ankles. Today was not one of those.

He was ready for this encounter, more than ready.

When he finally reached her, she was sitting by herself on a rock, watching the waterfall that fed the small creek. Sunlight filtered through the budding trees. The light was meager but it danced and played on the ground as well as on her vibrant hair, creating a myriad of shimmering colors. He was sure the strands would burn his fingers if he touched them.

He stopped and for a few seconds watched, trying to commit the scene to his memory. Lacie was nowhere to be found and he delighted in that fact. Daryl would be alone with him for the first time since that unusual encounter a couple of years ago and the one at the beach house that sent his blood boiling. Lord, both were so long ago he couldn't recount exactly, but he remembered the moments as if they happened yesterday.

The chase, the catch then the kiss.

The bad boys, Flynt, Broc, Cam, Leslie and himself had been in Flynt's house on the third-floor drinking as they played cards. Flynt's sisters were hiding in the room spying on them. Each man gave chase to one of the sisters. He didn't know about the others, but he caught Daryl and kissed her. It seemed Leslie must have chased after Lacie.

He would remember that kiss forever.

She was too young then, but the kiss haunted him over the last two years. Well past eighteen years of age, Daryl MacTavish was no longer too young to pursue and conquer, to chase, catch and kiss. He was the man to do just that. He would court her in his own manner, taking his time with her. There would be no way he would give her a chance to say no to any of his proposals, including marriage.

She turned to look at him then, her eyes wide with surprise he hoped and not fear. He had been quiet. "Hello, Daryl. Mind if I join you? Nice day, don't you think?" he asked, stepping forward, not waiting for an answer.

He stood beside her. She rose, pressing her hands down her skirts.

The smile on her face brightened, and he thought she might be pleased to see him although she appeared a tiny bit anxious. He wondered if she also remembered the kiss as well as the beach house confrontation.

"I didn't invite you here." Her voice held a nervous ripple as she spoke.

"It's my land," he told her, cocking an eyebrow while he took her measure.

She was wearing a light green riding habit, a bit of lace showing at the neckline. The hat she wore was tossed on the ground beside the boulder she'd been sitting on and the green plume appeared to have wilted in the sun. Her soft pink lips were slightly parted as her huge blue eyes shimmered with some unknown emotion, hopefully passion.

"No, well, of course you're right. So, I was just thinking it might be time to leave."

As if undecided, she stood then sat down smoothing her riding habit then she stood again. For a few seconds she gazed at the waterfall before turning her attention back to him.

"Don't ken what you want to do?" He laughed, keeping the sound behind his teeth.

"No." She smoothed the fall of her skirts again.

"I wouldn't want to be the cause of your departure. You are always welcome to come and go on Chamberlin land."

Once more he moved closer and as he did, she stepped back, bumping her legs against the large rock she'd been sitting on. She moved one step forward.

"Of course not, it's just that..." She swallowed then he watched as her breasts rose with the deep breath she inhaled.

"There is no need to be nervous. I thought I was your friend."

At this moment he was a man well pleased, her expressive blue green eyes lending good reason for the quick impression. He stepped closer and it seemed with each step he took she stepped back then she turned away from the rock.

"I'm not." She moistened her lips before sucking the full bottom one into her mouth. "Nervous."

Liar. Her lips were moist now, ready to be tasted. He grinned at the notion. "I watched you fly by on your horse. You were a bit reckless. I assume you don't ride that way every day."

When he became her husband, he needed to put an immediate halt on all her careless behavior.

Now and with little effort on his part, her back was against a tree. There was nowhere for her to go. "I ride that way when the mood hits." She closed her eyes for a few seconds, long sooty black lashes resting in the pale hollow around her eyes, her breaths tiny and ragged. "Flynt doesn't care so I do whatever I please."

Now he stood in front of her, so close he could feel her tiny and very rapid breaths as they whispered across his face. He wanted to see if her heartbeat matched his.

That, the racing of her horse, would end with their marriage.

"You remember the day I kissed you?"

Lord, but he hoped she remembered as clearly as he did. He recalled the heat and the sweet velvet of the inside of her mouth.

She nodded her head, more mahogany strands of hair coming lose from the pins, spilling around her shoulders. He picked up a strand, holding it between his fingers. "Silken fire," he murmured, hoping someday the length would touch him with fire and she would respond to him with the passion he knew she possessed.

"I don't ken what you are talking about."

Slowly, and unbeknownst to her provocatively, she swept her tongue across her bottom lip, her eyes shining with raw hunger that someday he meant to unleash.

"Chase, catch then kiss, that is what I did that evening and if I recall, you wanted my lips to caress yours just as much as I did. Would you like that today?"

Once more she moistened her lips, gazing at his mouth, and he had the most disconcerting feeling she knew what she was about then suddenly she looked away, breathing thinly again, her breast rising and falling.

"You did chase me when I ran from the room," she agreed with him.

"You wanted me to catch you." His grin, he was sure, reached from ear to ear. "I ken the fact as do you."

"I would never admit to such a thing. I ran because I wanted to get away." Her body quivered slightly and he hoped the trembling was the thirst for his kiss rising within her slight frame.

"Whether you admit to it or not, the fact remains I caught you. Just as I've caught you now. You do recall what comes next."

"Don't ken why you say that," she murmured.

Once more, her tiny pink tongue swept across her full bottom lip. "I've no idea what you are talking about."

"If I'm not interpreting all the signs wrong, you're wanting me to kiss you again, just as you did that night."

He bracketed her head between his hands, smiling, waiting for her to acknowledge the truth of her feelings. His mouth was close, her erratic breathing as well as the fluttering pulse at the base of her neck told him all he needed to know.

"You would be wrong." Her breasts rose and fell again then again, with the blatant lie.

"Sweet little liar, but I will not kiss a lass who says no." With his thumbs he created tiny circles on her neck. "Do you want to say yes or no to me? Don't think too long as the opportunity to kiss me could pass. I might change my mind."

She closed her eyes, her breath quivering as she waited. Then finally, "Yes, please." She opened her eyes then, her gaze focused on his mouth, her question shook him to his core. "Are they as soft as I remember?"

She unmanned him with those words. Soft?

This was what he sought, her compliance and willingness to kiss him, but he meant to prolong this as long as he was physically able. His voice shook now with his need, "Please what? You must say the words if you want that kiss and Daryl, I don't think there is any part of me that is soft."

"Your lips are," she said steadfastly, trying to make her point. "I wouldn't say so if it wasn't true."

He bent close to her ear, shaking off her comment. "Say the words, lass. Tell me how much you hunger, no yearn for my kiss."

Next to him he felt the slight shuddering of her body, her breasts now pushed against his chest, their rounded firmness enticing him to take more than he intended today.

"What?" she looked startled, confused yet she still stared unrelentingly at his mouth.

He felt the hesitant touch of her fingertip on his lips. "Ach, lass, you cannot tease a man this way. It is not well done of you." At the slight stroke his body jerked awake.

"They are soft and wet, just like I remember."

He groaned, the gist of her words going straight to his groin yet still waiting for her to say the words that would allow him to kiss her. "Chase, catch, now I'm still waiting for the last part. Tell me you want me to kiss you or we will be like this forever."

"Please," she sighed, his lips nearly touching hers. He felt her breath and nearly kissed her.

"Please what?" He continued knowing she wanted but seemed afraid to give permission. "Why do you hesitate so? What is it you're afraid of?"

"I cannot say." Her hands ran through his beard, curiously exploring. "Your beard is soft too. I like the way it feels on my hands."

He groaned. He was sure she was remembering another time when she granted him more than a kiss. He'd been hell bent to teach her a much-needed lesson and went too far, even though he didn't regret it.

"You must," he said, wishing he had not started this game.

He knew she wanted the kiss, the caress of his mouth against hers.

Giving what he knew she wanted should have been easy, but he needed more, craved her permission.

"Donal, I do want you to kiss me more than anything."

He had heard enough. His mouth fashioned itself across hers. He forgot everything but the sensations the kiss evoked within him. The tiny sounds undulating from her told him she enjoyed the kiss even while her fingers sifted nearly frantic through his short beard and hair. He kissed her again and again, his tongue sweeping across the velvet heat of her mouth. He needed to find a way inside her, to touch the satin heat within.

He pulled away, slowly, one by one withdrawing all the pins from her hair until its massive unruly length curled around her shoulders and down her long slender back. He ran his finger through the strands. She was so beautiful he could barely inhale a breath. "Open for me, open your mouth and let me inside."

Staring at him again, ignoring his words, "Your lips are soft and so is your beard. You didn't have a beard two years ago."

"The last time I kissed you and held you in my arms."

He meant to remind her of other intimacies they could share if she was willing and would agree to be his wife.

She inhaled a sharp gasp, her eyes widening with the comprehension of that day and what she allowed him. "That is not well done of you. In any case, there are parts of you that are soft. Even if you are unwilling to admit to the fact," her words indignantly whispered from her lips.

So affected by her sweet words, he could barely contain the passion and hunger warming his body. He needed more from her, "Part your lips, lass. I need to feel the warmth and taste the sweetness only you can offer. I need to be inside you in more ways than one, but I'll settle for this small intimacy right now."

"You didn't do that last time." She sounded confused but when he set his lips on her, she parted for him.

Before he took advantage, he whispered, "You were too young and I really had no business kissing you. The time after that..." He didn't finish simply because he didn't wish to remind her of the events at the beach house. If he did, she might run from him.

"You did."

"So true." He was inside her now, touching her teasing and exploring every sweet part of her. Her tongue met his with all the sweetness and heat he remembered. This was a heaven made in hell to provoke him and tempt him to toss her skirts right where they stood.

When she responded with a passion and hunger as primal as his own, he knew waiting for her had been right and positive. They would do well together as man and wife. Together they would share passion and sensual delights of the body. He would give her whatever leeway she desired, and he would pamper her even let her run the bakery if that was what she wanted. Even so he needed to hold back. This was uncharted territory for her and there had been no commitments between them.

It seemed he could not help himself. His hands cupped her breasts. The tips hardened beneath his caress. Her head fell back, instinctively giving him more access to her body. She was untried, inexperienced yet it seemed she knew what to do.

"Should you be touching me there?"

Surprised, he smiled at her. "Should you be allowing it?"

He didn't wait for an answer, understanding he needed to claim her. Daryl MacTavish was a prize men would covet, and it might be some time before she would agree to a marriage or Flynt would agree for that matter.

He partially unbuttoned the shirt she wore so he would have access to her neck and perhaps steal a look at the valley between her breasts. Sucking and licking, teasing with his teeth, he slowly put a mark at the base of her throat. It was his claim to her and he decided he would make sure it remained until he could put a ring on her finger making their path together official.

Pressed against her now, his sex was hard and throbbing against her belly. Never before had he stopped when his rod felt as if it might burst. Everything with this woman was a first. He wanted her to feel him. If he guided her hand to him, he wouldn't be able to stop.

Chase, catch, and kiss.

He drew away, having accomplished that as well as a bit more. When she opened her eyes, they were glazed, stunned, simmering with the sexual pleasure he introduced her to.

"Is that all?" she asked, fumbling with a button on her shirt and to his delight managing to undo one more.

The soft curve of her unveiled breast called to him. Taken with a brief moment of chivalry, he buttoned her shirt. "You need to keep your garments closed all the way to the top."

The shimmer in her eyes changed to fire and he was sure it was anger, her tiny hands fisted as her sides, "I will button and unbutton my clothes the way I want them, when I want."

Stepping back, his arms crossed in front of him, "Very well, what is it you want? Unbuttoned or buttoned?"

With his calculated words her eyes seemed to cross as she stiffened. "Unbuttoned of course. It is hot out here." She finished with those words as if she needed an excuse.

"Please allow me. How many, two three or all of them? You must tell me when to stop." He felt as if someone else took over his mind. He was a besotted fool for egging her on this way. If she continued in this vein, he'd be hard pressed to keep his promise to himself, but he would enjoy the view as long as she presented it to him.

~ * ~

Daryl unbuttoned the three he'd undone then the fourth she'd nervously fumbled with. "I won't allow a man to dictate to me. I will do as I please."

She understood she was stubborn to a fault and this could have serious complications if she continued on this path. She wanted those kisses and more. To her dismay, he stopped, grinning at her.

"So." He began eyeing her open blouse with a soft chuckle that both enticed and irritated her, "If I tell you to do one thing then you will immediately do the opposite?"

"No, I will weigh the consequences of both choices."

In this case she didn't, she just reacted to him. Her head was muddled. She had dust for brains.

"Ah, I see what you're about. Good thing I'm a gentleman. The result of your actions just now could have me tossing your skirts and coming inside you with my sex not just my tongue, although my tongue would be nice too. I would like to taste you. Is that a complication you've considered? I suppose it would also be an invitation to any man you might run across."

She pursed her lips together, her body shaking. She was thinking about what he said and not understanding most of it except the part about him coming inside her since she liked what he did with his tongue. Her expectations wouldn't go any farther than that, "I might like you tasting me. You, not any man," she amended, smiling at his lips, "tossing my skirts. You did something like that before and..."

His scowl and the deep breath he inhaled led to him saying, "Do you have any idea what you just suggested?"

"No, not really. Maybe you could explain."

What she did know was that she felt things in certain parts of her she'd only felt once before. Those sensations were at his hand. Also, she remembered, Hope, one of her friends, had tried to explain things to her but she still didn't understand all of it, all Hope tried to tell her. Most of what Hope said came from the women she'd known in the Turkish harem where Hope's mother had been taken when she was captured.

"I'd rather show you."

He moved closer to her, his hands clenching and unclenching at his sides. Yet the grim expression on his face told her he wasn't pleased. His silver blue eyes were drawn together. They looked like smoldering steel.

"You won't because I'm too naïve and inexperienced to understand. I ken it but I was hoping you would be the man to change that circumstance."

She wanted him to deny her words. More than ready to find out what having her skirts tossed would be like with this man, she wanted to challenge him to the point where he would indeed show her. Being told as well as threatened about the things he was going to do was no longer enough.

"Not until we are wed." His words were gritted out in a husky voice she'd never heard from him before. "When the vows between us are said..."

"Well then," she paused, a fingertip pressed against her lips, "I will never have the experience of you inside me except of course your tongue. Is that what you want?" she tried to take a different route.

For a moment, he seemed puzzled. "Why is that? Of course I want more than my tongue inside you, but..."

"Because I'm never marrying. As I think I said before, I'm never marrying you or anyone else. If you want to have me, it will be only with me remaining in control of myself. You, or any man, will never own me. I'm not chattel to be bought and sold to the highest bidder."

"I've no intention of owning you or buying you. The last thing I would ever want to do is sell you. That notion is absurd. I will change your mind concerning marriage but obviously not this afternoon." He extended his hand. "Come, it's getting late. I'll take you home."

She understood she was defensive, but she needed to make her point before time went on and he wouldn't believe her. "I can get home by myself. No need to waste your time on me."

"Of course you can. If I believed otherwise, I wouldn't have chased, caught and kissed you. A woman who cannot take care of herself, I wouldn't be interested in, if they could not find their own way home." He still extended his hand, expecting her to take hold. "Now, I would love to hold your hand in mine while we walk to our horses. If you don't want to then..." He seemed to be waiting for an answer.

She was too astounded by his words to think clearly. When he cleared his throat, his arm still outstretched and waiting for her to take his hand in hers, she accepted. His hand circling hers was big and warm. She felt overwhelmed as if he consumed her, yet the feelings were good and right for her.

The feminine part of her was pleased.

In silence they walked to the horses. He gave her a boost up and she waited for him to mount, watching the play of his muscles as they stretched his shirt as well as his pants. Touching her swollen lips with a fingertip then looking his way, she wondered if he felt the same as she did.

It seemed he read her mind, "Yes, the kiss was good for me, too, so good I'd like to try again after I see you home. Would you like that? Another kiss? Perhaps in the stables or maybe in the kitchen, or we could take a glass of wine to the parlor and kiss on the sofa."

"I'd like that. Any place would be nice. I like the way you taste," she spoke slowly, watching him as he pulled up beside her. It was difficult to remove her gaze from his luxuriously soft moist lips as she recalled how they caressed her, but she would try.

It seemed he needed to change the subject though, "Would you like to race to that tree down the road. It's far enough to challenge your mare, but not so far my stallion would have the advantage of his great strength and size."

He was referring to himself comparing them in a way she didn't want to acknowledge. Yet a strange exhilaration filled her. She would race and win, showing him she was faster, more than equal despite his great size. Nodding, she nudged her horse forward, knowing she would need a fast start to even have a chance of beating his stallion in this short bout.

"Cheater."

His words were loud as was his laughter. She bent over her mare, close to her neck as she urged her forward and faster. "Go fast. Don't let that brute beat us. You can do it." But she heard the pounding of the hooves behind her, closing the distance.

The tree passed her by just as Donal did. She didn't know if he staged the tie or if they really did finish dead even. In any case, she didn't care, pulling her horse to a slow walk.

"Did you plan that or was the race a tie?" she asked, smiling sweetly as she flirtatiously tilted her head to one side, understanding by the look in his eyes she would never know the truth.

"I beat you fair and square even after you started too soon." He laughed and the sound filled the air. "You had to cheat to even come close to a tie. If you did not start early, I would have passed you sooner."

"I like the way you laugh," she sighed softly, wondering if all men were so obtuse. "You won't tell me the truth and we both know you didn't win."

A cool evening breeze caressed her flushed skin. Donal

challenged her. She liked the way the challenge felt. He baited and teased, still he never laughed at her or the conditions she was beginning to set for their relationship. It seemed to her he let every demand she made go by the wayside, giving her her way in everything. She reminded herself, he was a man set in his manly ways. He'd never let her have her life as her own or tolerate her disobedience when the stakes were different. This was just a game to him. It was too bad, because he was exceptional to look at and his kisses left her mind reeling as well as butterflies dancing inside her stomach.

Lifting his manly and very broad shoulders he continued to say, "I'm a man, of course I won. It goes without saying."

The sound of his warm chuckle sent a little thrill down her spine. His words were another test he was sending her way.

He captivated her, enchanted her and aroused her to such a degree she couldn't think straight. If he wanted, he could do anything, caress her anywhere and she would not say no to him.

What to do, because he understood the power he possessed.

"Men don't win everything just because they are a man. Women are just as smart or smarter than men. We are quick and strong, strong enough to give birth. Could a man do that?"

She grinned, believing she held the best argument. He could not refute childbirth or deny a woman's strength in that matter.

"Perhaps some are as smart. I'll give that to you but as to decision-making, they are sorely lacking in said skill. If you recall, you were riding hell bent across the field, not a wise choice when there was no reason."

"Nothing untoward happened and it never has."

"Call it luck," he said as he arched one perfectly shaped eyebrow.

"Why?" She was shocked by his comment.

"Women usually think with their heart not with the logic that comes from rational decision making. You were lucky your horse did not step in a hole and throw you. Worse, your mare could have broken a leg and you would have been forced to put her down."

She chose to ignore the latter part of his words in favor of her strength. "If they didn't, no woman would have more than one child except those like my sister Bliss who had twins."

She would not let down her argument, knowing she was right.

"As long as the man gives his woman a choice. There are those who don't wait, holding their breath for the woman they are courting to give them permission to kiss them. There are some who take that which is not freely given."

"Some men take. I ken it."

Once again, she was thinking about Donal and his strange behavior today. He did wait for permission. She longed for him to do so much more than kiss. While she had ideas, she just didn't know exactly how they would actually play out. So, she could not tell him what she wanted. When she used his words to say she would like him to do something wicked, he said no and he would wait until they were wed.

"As to men giving birth," he paused as if searching for the right answer. "Maybe, maybe not. That does not make a woman stronger."

"When you hear your wife's screams as your first child is born, then you will understand what I'm saying. When you watch her lose her food for the first few months, then you will ken how strong she is. There is so much more to a woman that few men understand. I don't care to elaborate." She pointed, "Look, we are almost home. You have my permission to kiss me again."

"Are you truly ready for another kiss or do I need to chase and catch you first? There is something nostalgic about the chase as well as the kiss."

"I believe you've already caught me, at least for today. My body thrums with a need I don't understand. I want things you plan to deny me unless we wed. It's not fair, you know."

"Tell me..."

She looked down for a moment unable to explain the sensations to him, didn't know what she should say and what she shouldn't. She was shaking her head, "I cannot." Embarrassment consumed her as heat rushed to her cheeks.

"Why?" He persisted, a silly grin on his face.

"Do you always pursue things so tenaciously? I cannot. That should be good enough for you."

He sighed deeply while his eyes narrowed suspiciously, "Sadly, it is not enough. Why can't you explain to me how you feel?"

She glared at him, understanding he would not let up until he had the answers from her he sought. "Because I don't have the words. Even if I did, it would embarrass me."

"I will help you with the words," he told her as he brought his horse closer to hers.

She nudged her horse forward, wishing the conversation into oblivion. Heading into the stables she dismounted, ignoring him the best she could. A stable lad approached but she waved him away, wishing to take care of her horse and hoping he would forget the conversation in the ensuing moments.

Before she could even give the horse water and food, he was leaning nonchalantly against a wall, watching her with his hooded eyes, seeming to study and evaluate everything she did. When she looked at him, he smiled, a masculine all-knowing grin.

He didn't say a word, just waited, his expression unchanging while she brushed her horse. There was nothing more she could do, nothing to take up time. "You can go home now that you've seen me to mine."

"I would be remiss if I did not accompany you into the house. Perhaps your cook left food warming and we could share a meal. I do understand you've not invited me inside to share food, but I would accept if you did. And," he paused, "you asked for a second kiss."

"I'm sure there is food. What I'm not sure of is if I can eat anything."

She knew she could not. Nothing would sit well. The butterflies in her stomach just would not settle as they tenaciously somersaulted around.

"I assure you that you would be able to eat if you explained yourself. The omission is lying heavy on your breasts, rattling your nerves and making you irritable. Your stomach is now taking the brunt of all your confusing emotions. I like all sides of you though."

"Perhaps you would like something to drink," she murmured, latching the stall door and heading for the main house, still trying to ignore his presence so close to her.

"Only if you imbibe as well. A little alcohol would ease your mind and you would be able to divulge those feminine secrets I would love to learn about. Wine will help you relax."

She didn't look back. Her pace quickened. She'd never been so embarrassed. Heat flooded her cheeks at just the thought of explaining anything feminine to him.

"I'd prefer brandy."

"Whatever you wish."

She could not walk fast enough to distance herself from him. His footsteps echoed behind her. He was allowing her escape for now. Well, she decided he commanded and would expect anything he wanted, but she didn't have to comply with his wishes. Wasn't it after all her wish to have the control of her body, mind and thoughts?

Inside the kitchen, she sat down at the table, letting him decide whatever it was he was trying to decide. She wasn't going to eat because she simply wasn't hungry. He poked around, finally finding the meal cook left.

"Bangers and mash, perfect for a cold spring evening, don't you think?" He dished up two plates. "Since you didn't send me packing. I assume you would like to eat with me. Or is it the next kiss that has you in anticipation, unwilling to send me away?"

He poured glasses of wine instead of searching for the brandy before setting the bottle on the table.

"I don't want to explain anything to you."

"Eat up." He waved his fork in the air, a manly grin stretching across his face. "You will need your strength for the good night kiss I've planned." he paused again, "if you be tellin' me yes when I ask." He was enjoying every moment.

"You no longer want me to explain?" she felt a moment of relief.

"I didn't say that now, did I? I will have my explanation before I leave tonight." He sat back, washing his food down with his glass of wine then pouring another and topping off hers. "A man my size has big needs. Eventually, you will learn that and in time you will fill mine just as I will take care of yours."

"I don't think so."

Slowly, she sipped her wine, scrutinizing him over the rim of her glass. Automatically her gaze slipped to his full lips as she recalled how soft and warm they were. She couldn't stop the tiny mew of pleasure that sighed softly from her, nor could he hold back the manly grin on his lips as he realized she was thinking about that kiss and the ones to come.

"We shall see." He lounged in his chair, tilting it back so it was settled on just two of its legs. "Should we continue this conversation in the parlor, perhaps a more fitting place for two adults to have intimate discussions about feminine things as well as another kiss."

"I'm quite happy here."

She wanted to put off said discussion, hoping the ensuing darkness would prompt his departure.

"Your very feminine ploy is obvious, and it won't work this evening. If I have to stay all night, I will hear you out and teach you that you don't need to feel embarrassment with me. You can say anything you want. I'll never judge. You will learn that you can talk about feminine conditions and I will listen with grave interest." His words were softly spoken but to Daryl very believable.

"It's no ploy." She was adamant and meant to stand her ground.

"No kiss then." He challenged further. "By the way, your sweetly tasting pink tongue moistening your lips tells me you are anticipating my mouth over yours. You want to be inside me and taste me. Am I right or wrong? Be honest now, lass, or I might never trust you again."

"Right, of course you are correct." She rose then and walked to the parlor. Give him what he wants and embarrass him, she wanted to say.

He followed her, so close behind her she was sure she felt his manly warmth penetrating through her clothing. She waved a hand in front of her in a feeble attempt to cool her body and not beg him for that kiss.

"Are you hot?" he asked.

She felt his breath on her neck where he pulled her hair back. "No, no, never that. It's just..."

He turned her then. His lips and teeth caressed her throat, teasing while creating a wild havoc the same sensations he wanted her to explain, exploding inside her.

"Little liar, don't' you know you must always tell me the truth. Your face is flushed, and it is your thoughts about me, us that cause the unusual brightening of your cheeks."

"I don't mean to lie, it's just that I can't think when you look at me that way. At times I'm not at all sure I even know my name. You do things to me. Don't you think you should leave?"

While he was studying her, she sat down in a wing chair, folding her hands in her lap to keep them from fumbling with her buttons. What she needed was to sit on them, but that would prompt another discussion she didn't want to have.

"Another glass of wine?"

He filled hers before she could tell him yes or no, before she could even figure out if she wanted one.

"I..."

"I've left you tongue tied again? Did you want to unfasten another button? I didn't request for you to fasten them. At least I can't remember such a demand when I'm enjoying the lovely view you are giving me. Your breasts are quite beautiful. I believe they would fill my hands and I've large hands. Also, I believe you would like the way your breasts will feel when I hold them and touch the velvet soft nipples."

She looked down then and saw what he was seeing. Her gaze went to his, her eyes she knew were wide with surprise. Yet she didn't move to fasten them or cover herself. "I..."

"Again, nothing or very little to say?" He chuckled softly and it was an easy laughter, one that exuded confidence and male comfort.

Unlike herself he was at ease with this banter. It left her scrambling for words, her mind in a coil. She could not help but wonder at the lack of gray matter in her head. At the moment her brain must be filled with dust or cobwebs.

When she looked up and noticed his silver blue eyes seem to darken, she couldn't help the words tumbling out. "You do things to me, things..." She inhaled long and deep, searching her mind for the words and came back to the explanation she didn't want to give him in the first place. "Things I don't know how to explain."

"You have unfastened so many of the buttons I can almost see the dusky pink circles surrounding your nipples. I like it that you are not wearing a corset. Oh dear, but if I say that, will it mean every day in the future you will wear one of those horrible contraptions?" He paused, a fingertip to his chin. "I tell you honestly, you have to wear a corset. There is nothing more to it. Yes, a corset it is. They are so much fun to take off a lady, the right lady anyway."

She nearly laughed at his posturing and wondered if she was indeed the right lady. "I will don a corset when it pleases me. You may have all the fun you wish to have taking it off. When it pleases me and not a moment before."

"Ah, lassie, feminine wiles. I'm surprised you are not tilting your head a bit sideways and demurely lowering your splendidly dark lashes. I so dearly love to render them useless. I will make sure the notion of unlacing your corset pleases you when it pleases me."

She stiffened, feeling the imaginary brunt of his hand against her face. He needed to go home as she was near total exhaustion, which was the reason why she could not stay a step ahead of him in this conversation, the verbal game he played.

"I would like that kiss now then you can leave."

She turned prim and proper, needed a night of sleep so she could think clearly tomorrow not that she needed to because she probably wouldn't see him. The breath she inhaled was not enough as she choked on the sip of wine caught in the back of her throat.

"I believe your words were, and I quote, 'My body thrums with a need I don't understand.' You still need to explain that to me so I can stop doing those things to you if that is what you desire. My manly sensibilities need to know the truth as I only mean to please you."

"You can't really expect me to say what I'm feeling. You're a man and you would never understand anything about a lady."

She held her breath, praying for him to say she didn't need to expound but knowing he would never give in. He would either get what he wanted or he would stay."

"Ah, but I do want to know about feminine things only a lady

24

knows. I'm always curious and eager to learn. How will I discover these truths if you don't enlighten me? One cannot expect to learn without a teacher."

"Can't I just have that kiss and say goodnight? We really don't know each other so well as to say the things I'm thinking. I know you don't really mean everything you are saying. Do you?"

"Every day we are going to know each other better. Now, perhaps I can help with this difficulty you are having. What part of your body thrums with need?" He folded his hands in front of him, appearing to be waiting patiently as one roguish brow arched skyward.

She didn't trust him in this. No, she didn't trust him in the least. Her fingers went to the buttons on her shirt as she tried desperately to calm herself. For a moment she looked down then back to his eyes. "Parts I shouldn't talk to a man about. Lady parts. Things men aren't supposed to know about."

He smiled, "We've made progress. Now how do they thrum?"

She moistened her lips before looking to the sky for divine intervention. Nothing happened. "They pulse and I'm hot, swollen. I need to..." She looked at him afraid she might die from mortification. "I want you to touch me, I think, and perhaps wet. I dinna ken anything else, but I believe you can fix my problem or make it worse. I'm not too sure."

"Very good, you have earned your kiss. What you have told me is that your most beautiful feminine folds, the soft petals that will embrace me after we are wed," he paused, "once we are wed, they will be ready for me to come inside you. Do you want that? Do you wish for me to come inside you?"

He drew her onto his lap. Once again, the kiss was long and sweet, so very deep and hot that she was swept away on the magical enchantment he created. "Donal..." she sighed into his mouth.

"Are you hot and wet, ready for me?" he asked as one hand cupped her breast and the other her waist drawing her closer.

She nodded, her hips seeming to move of their own accord, desperately trying to get closer to him, begging him to explore and plunder her most private feminine parts. She arched her back as she seemed to lose what little control she had from the beginning. "Yes, will you give me relief?"

"Not until you become my bride." He kissed her again and again, his lips finding the mark he made earlier, enhancing the tender spot so it would stay there until he had another chance to sip in that beautiful place. His spot. "Your feminine folds are swollen and hot. Your body is slick with your cream. If you were not a virgin, I would delve inside your sheath, but you are and I want more than that from our relationship."

"Please." She wanted more than that too. "I will never be your bride," she whispered with no conviction, "So you can show me what it is I need. You can come inside me now. You can have me whatever way you want to have me, you can have it with me. I willnae object."

Abruptly, he pulled away, gazing at her, studying her. "Will you meet me tomorrow at noon by the waterfall? We can kiss again and perhaps I'll introduce you to another part of lovemaking then we can go into town together. I would once again like to see you safely to your home above the bakery. If you'd rather go by yourself and have no one to talk to, I would not consider interfering in your peace and quiet. You would also risk the dangers of the road."

With that said, he set her on the couch. For a moment he stood by the door, then with a nod he left.

Daryl leaned on the windowsill and watched him ride down the road. Her knees were so weak she could barely stand. He left her confused, disoriented to be sure. If she wasn't mistaken, aroused significantly to be uncomfortable. Hope told her kisses would do that to a woman and that is why men kissed them. She touched her breast as he had. It was a light caress and all he did was hold them in her hands.

When she touched herself intimately, she was wet, slick with moisture just as he told her she would be. She wondered what it was he would do, how he would caress her to take away this strange ache. Hope told her things but not nearly enough. What he did at the beach house came to mind. She wanted him to do those things again.

Tomorrow she would tell him what she did.

~ * ~

The night before he left, Graham slept fitfully. He'd not wanted to tell his brother about the real and very threatening activities in the states and the talk that could set families against families. Leslie advised him against saying anything prematurely and told him he would look into the problem. He had emissaries he would send, but all that would take time. Leslie told him his brother Link would take care of everything.

No need to worry Donal.

"Well," he murmured. "I'm on my way to the Highlands."

He had no idea what he would find there or if there would be a wife for him. He would just have to see what developed. The crumbling estate, he mused, rubbing his chin thoughtfully, didn't exactly sound like a place where one could make a home and raise children. Even so, he was going to try.

Graham pulled Draco to a halt just as the large drive to the Chamberlin estate began. He'd spent too long in Edinburgh, enjoying the sites as well as the women. With luck on his side he made it to his ancestral estate, gifted to him by his grandmother, just before the first snows of winter would start. What he discovered in the city was that the life of leisure and balls he was invited to didn't suit. Neither did any of the debutants he met there.

As he studied the lane and the row of trees leading to the front steps, he noticed three different heads poking out from three trees along with spindly arms and legs waving at him. He laughed outright, remembering days long past. Times when he and Donal played in the same trees, usually not in the dead of winter though.

After watching for a few minutes, he nudged Draco forward, keeping his attention on the lads, wondering just how old the boys were and to whom they belonged. Clearly, they appeared to be at home in his trees. He pulled up beneath the first trees.

"Come down, lad. All of you present yourselves. Front and center," he called out in his sternest voice, hoping they would obey but not having any illusions.

They seemed to take his order to heart, all three dropping to the ground in almost perfect unison. Urchins, to be sure, landed sure-footed on the grass beside the lane. They all needed to be scrubbed from head to toe, possibly twice but they would clean up well. He needed to laugh but didn't want the laughter to come at their expense.

The threesome lined up in front of him, straight faced and stiff as boards.

The tallest and he assumed the oldest of the trio spoke. "We were told to watch out for you and welcome you home. Heard you were coming just a week or so ago." He inhaled a deep breath, obviously meaning to say more but was interrupted.

"No one told us we'd have to be here on the lane for two weeks. Did you know it's cold out here?"

"I was never informed I had a deadline." Graham's laughter was unchecked this time.

"Well, someone should have done just that or you could have sent a message." The tallest said indignantly. "Not like it's summer."

He'd just been properly chastised by the boy and meant to proceed with further introductions lest they think it okay to reprimand an elder. "Do you have names? I'm Graham Chamberlin." He waited for acknowledgement and perhaps some information if they were agreeable.

"I'm Dodge," the tallest said as he cleared his throat. "Been called that for a long time now."

Graham reckoned he must be nearing nine or ten years. He directed his attention to the next in line.

"I'm Ollie." The lad nodded, his hair falling in front of his face before he looked up and pushed it away with his hands. It was hard to tell Ollie's age, but he was pretty sure the boy was younger than Dodge, perhaps eight or nine.

"And you?" This lad was small and seemed to need at least three good meals in his belly. The others must have helped him into the tree because he wasn't tall enough to reach the lowest limbs.

"Midget," he grinned, "Please to meet you, sir. We're supposed to make sure you have everything you need and show you to the house."

"Who sent you?"

From what Graham heard about the estate, he didn't think anyone here would care if he was greeted or not.

The boys looked at each other, sharing glances several times before they seemed to come to a silent agreement.

"Ria sent us."

Graham found himself nodding his head, rolling all the names around in the cobwebs that made up his brains right now and could not come up with one person on his list of employees who was named Ria.

He dismounted, intending to walk with the boys to the stables and discover a little bit more about their truths and how much more they would be willing to tell him. "Who is Ria?"

As he walked past them, he wondered if they intended to stay on the lane. Looking over his shoulder, Ollie was drawing circles in the dirt and Dodge was tugging on Midget's hand. Once again, seeming to reach some form of silent agreement all three started walking.

"Ria's no concern of yours," Dodge said, his voice gruff and taking on a prickly edge. "We protect her as does Miss Millie, so you don't have to worry about her or go near her."

Protect her? Bloody hell who or why would she need protection from. For a moment he thought to ask them for more information. By the slant of their lips he didn't think any more material about this mysterious Ria would be forthcoming. Instead, he decided to let them lead the way to the stables and give them time to become accustomed to him. Clearly, they had trust issues.

A few minutes later, Graham stopped in front of the stable doors. "Do you know how to take care of a horse? Draco needs a brushing down then food and water. Any of you want to do that?"

"Don't know nothing about horses," Dodge said, looking at him as he had mush for brains. "Don't know how to ride."

"I'm afraid of the huge beasts," Ollie said, once again his gaze directed to the ground below and what he was doing with his foot.

"I'm not," Midget volunteered. "Don't think I'm big enough to brush him."

"Then perhaps at least one of you should learn. What do the three of you do around the house besides wallow in the dirt?"

The words were uttered harsher than he'd intended but nonetheless he meant what he said. Everyone would have to do something in his household if they expected to be fed and clothed.

Once again Dodge, the apparent spokesperson for the trio, said, "I'd like to learn how to take care of your horse. As far as I know it's the only one in the stable now but don't have the time. Have to protect Ria and right now she could be in trouble. We've been away too long watching for you."

His words were said defensively and to make a point of telling him he was at fault if anything happened to the mystery lady.

The boys looked at each other for a few seconds. Once again it seemed the silent conversation between them was understood. They took off at a run, and Graham watched them speed around the back of the house where the servants' staircase would be found emptying into the scullery.

If there were no horses in the stable, would it figure there was no stable boy? Graham led his horse around the house, resigned to the care of Draco. Entering the outbuilding he searched for anyone who could help him.

"What can I do?" A man strode from a room at the far end of the building.

"Draco needs to be brushed down then fed and given water. Is that your job?" Graham asked, handing the reins over to the man, impatient now to discover what was going on in the main house and establish himself as the owner. Apparently, there were things that needed tending.

"I'll take care of anything, sir. Nice to have you back in residence, sir. You staying this time?" the man asked.

Graham stared hard, his eyes narrowing. "Shamus, is that you?"

He held out his hand in greeting. As lads Shamus played with him as well as his brother and the Duke.

"It is and you're a sight for sore eyes, I tell you. It's about time someone arrived here to right the wrongs going on in this place."

Graham clapped his old friend on the back, thinking he might have to take a few minutes more to find out a few things. "Got some questions if you're up to answering them."

Shamus looked over his shoulder as he rid Draco of his saddle and blanket. He took a few seconds to start brushing the stallion. "What do you want to know?"

Graham positioned himself against the stall, crossing his arms in front of him. "Let's start with the lads. Who are they and why are they here?"

Shamus grinned as he stroked the horse several times. "The lads, so you met them. Not surprised that Ria sent them to greet you. What did they tell you?"

"Not much, just that their job is to protect this woman, Ria."

He waited then, studying the man.

Shamus hauled out a bucket of water and once Draco had his fill gave him his food.

"Dodge do the talking?" Shamus laughed.

Graham nodded, his brows drawing together as he waited impatiently for Shamus to be a bit more forthcoming.

"He's the oldest and if you were looking closely without assuming anything, Ollie is a little girl and Midget, of course, is the youngest. They came with Ria one day and they've stayed, although Ria keeps herself scarce with good reason. Not exactly sure why they stayed, but the house is shelter for them."

"Where did they come from?"

"If Dodge can be trusted the worst streets in Edinburgh. Had to do things, if you get my drift, just to eat. I'm surprised they let on that Ria is a woman."

"I'm beginning to understand a few things. Why does Ria have reason to keep herself scarce?"

He didn't like the direction of his thoughts, although there were a myriad of reasons why the lady might not want to be found.

"Around these parts the main reason is well known and I'd be hopin' that your first order of business would be to get rid of Leod, your manager of the estate. Don't recall his last name, whether or not I was ever told I can't be remembering. Think the lady is hiding from something that happened to her in the city, but that's just my gut telling me things. There's no evidence I could be right or wrong."

"And why would I want to get rid of this man?"

He didn't like the fact the questioning and answers began with

Ria and ended with Leod. Again, his mind travelled in a direction Graham didn't appreciate nor would he allow.

"He's turned Granville Manor into a whorehouse. Pretty simple. Don't think it's what you would want for your home. Now, is there anything else I can do for you?"

"Answer more questions when I have them."

"Whatever you like."

"Millie still here?" he asked, as he pushed away from his position, meaning to see for himself at the main house.

"Only because she keeps praying either you or your brother will show up and set this mess to rights. Suppose her prayers have been answered."

"Suppose they have."

Determined, Graham strode to the manor, walking up the broad front porch steps. When he stepped inside, a man stumbled drunkenly down the stairway from above. His pants were unfastened and his shirt hung loosely from his shoulders.

This must be the man Shamus was alluding to a few minutes before. He spread his legs, his hand at his side. "Who are you?"

"I believe the better question is who are you. I'm the owner and didn't realize anyone was living here. The home, I was told, is empty."

"Leod is the name. I took up residency here when it seemed no one was going to claim the land and the crumbling home. Didn't ken why it should go to waste. So many in these parts are homeless."

"I see, well, you'll have to move out."

"How do I know you're tellin' the truth and you are who you say you are?"

He stumbled a bit then hanging on to the back of the chair, the man stared at him, his eyes narrowing in seeming concentration.

"You don't, except for my word as a Chamberlin." Graham couldn't imagine anyone living here unless they were desperate. "You haven't seen fit to make improvements?"

The man shrugged, his body seeming to relax. "No funds. If you'd sent money, I would have done something."

"Most likely drink it away," Graham mumbled.

A woman ran down the steps naked but holding a dress in front of her.

"You use my home as a whorehouse?"

Anger began to simmer inside as he perused the rapid flight as well as the woman's backside.

"She wanted it. I was just obliging her wishes."

The man's grin was nearly toothless, and what Graham could see of teeth they were yellowed and brown.

"That's why she was naked and racing away. Get out." With a shaking hand, he pointed to the door.

"My things..." the man started up the steps.

"I'll have them put on the front lawn. You can have them picked up when you please."

Arms crossed in front of him, both impatient and angry, he waited for the man to leave.

When Leod finally exited the house, he let a long sigh of relief from his lungs. Striding through his new home, he examined every part of it, every nook and cranny. He was just about finished on the third and last floor when he noticed a movement, a tiny shadow push back against the wall and the softest whimper.

He reached the spot in two quick strides then hunkering down, he peered behind a lose wallboard. What he saw surprised him. Two huge blue eyes peered at him from behind a set of knees drawn to her chest.

"Who are you?"

She pushed back farther. From beneath her ragged skirts two sets of dirty, bare toes caught his attention. She pushed grimy and disheveled hair from her face, but the terror he saw in her eyes lingered.

"Cat got your tongue?"

He almost laughed but held it not believing for a second, she was seeing anything humorous in this situation.

She was shaking her head, clearly terrified of him. In all his life he couldn't recall any woman every being frightened let alone terrified when he was present. His thoughts travelled back to the man, Angus.

"Did Leod hurt you?"

He would have the man tarred and feathered if he hurt this tiny delicate woman.

She was shaking her head no.

"Good then. Come on out and tell me your name."

He held out a hand to her.

She pushed back farther.

"I promise I won't hurt you," he paused, realizing he wasn't getting anywhere with her. "At least tell me your name."

"Ria."

"That's a fine name, Ria. Now tell me why you are hiding here on the third floor?"

"Leod." Tears slipped from her eyes.

"Blessed hell," he muttered. One look at the man and he knew trouble surrounded him. "You told me he didn't hurt you."

"Aye, but he wanted to rape me."

Chapter Two

Donal sat on a huge boulder tossing rocks into the pond and watching as the ripples expanded before reaching the bank. While he had not expected Daryl to be prompt, she was now almost an hour tardy. He supposed it was her way of protesting some of what went on yesterday. He challenged her more than what could be considered prudent. She would never be easy to deal with, he realized, hoping he would do things a bit better today.

Reluctantly, he admitted to his highhandedness. It wasn't well done of him so soon into the courting of a wee and very innocent lass. At the time he believed it to be important. Actually, still did. Recalling the way she unconsciously fiddled with her buttons giving him a view of her he never expected, gave him good reason to grin.

The pounding of horse hooves caught his attention. He smiled to himself as he stood to watch her. As usual her hair was slowly coming lose from the pins. Good god, but she attracted him as no other woman. Her beauty seemed to shine from the inside out, more so each time he was with her; learned new things about her every time they spoke.

She reined up in front of him, gloriously disheveled. He understood she would appear something like that after their lovemaking. His gut tightened, his body hardening with barely controlled need.

"I'm glad to see you."

He helped her dismount, his hands around her waist, delighted with the feel of her feminine curves beneath his hands. A man could get used to this heaven in a short time if he allowed it.

"Sorry, I know I'm late. I guess I wasn't coming then changed my mind. If I'm honest, changed it again as well as one more time after that. You did tell me you wanted me to say the truth whenever I could."

Her steady yet fake contrite smile nearly made him laugh.

"I would have waited another hour. I might have gone to see what the trouble was. You did tell me you would be here. Lass, if you don't want to see me all you need do is say the words. Don't ever pretend. If you canna say it to my face, send a message."

This time her repentance didn't appear fake.

"You make me nervous and excited, that's all. My thinking nearly nonexistent, muddled as well when you are present and I swear that when you are with me, I've cobwebs for brains." She breathed slowly in then out. "I wanted to be here."

"Making you nervous is not my intention. Come let's have a bite to eat. My cook packed us a basket of food."

He needed Daryl to relax and enjoy the afternoon whilst he could be with her. While the sun was shining there was also a slight breeze, cooling the air just the right amount to make the weather pleasant. Today she wore a sky-blue riding habit, her eyes a matching color.

"I haven't eaten all morning." Yet she didn't move, her hands held tightly together beneath her chin. "I'm thinking I should have ridden straight to town."

He sat down on a blanket, patting a place beside him. Her look was wary as he watched her inhale a ragged breath. He poured two glasses of wine then held one out to her. "Look through the basket and see if there is anything you like."

She sat down without a word, watching him before accepting the proffered drink. "I suppose I should. Eat something. It will be a long night and morning if I don't."

He smiled when her gaze remained on him and not the basket of food. "While you might like me, you cannot eat me."

The tiny start of surprise amused him. "I forgot what I was about. Like I just told you, when I'm around you I can't think straight." She turned her attention to the contents of the basket. "Why there is more here than either of us can eat in two days."

"Thought we should take it with us when we head home. There will be enough for dinner if you would like or I could take it all home with me. Your choice of course. I would never presume to know what you are wanting."

"You are too solicitous by far."

She picked out one of the ham and cheese sandwiches his cook made.

"Good choice and I didn't realize one could care too much."

For a few minutes they ate and drank.

"Why?"

"I cannot read your mind. Why what?" He topped off their glasses.

"Why are you being so nice? I've made it perfectly clear what it is I don't want. For you, courting me is a waste of time."

Her hand holding the glass trembled, wine sloshing from side to side.

With passion he hoped. "You haven't convinced me of anything. Your arguments are feeble, have holes in them and lack much needed logic. In short, Daryl, I don't believe you or at least I believe your mind can be changed."

"My arguments are sound. It is you who are confusing."

She finished her glass then poured herself another.

He wanted to tell her not to drink too much but he knew she would do the opposite. Perhaps he should assume she would finish the bottle. Ah, but thinking was growing too difficult. He needed to be three steps in front of her and understanding what she would say.

"You are wearing face paint today, some color to your eyelids and cheeks as well. It's a new look for you," he said, a need to send the conversation in a new direction. "I like it."

"Does that mean you didn't like the way I appeared yesterday with nothing to enhance my feminine features?"

She posed for him a well-practiced smile on her lips as she tilted her head a bit sideways, looking at him beneath her lashes.

In this he could dig himself a hole deep enough to be his grave. "I adore you both ways. When your face is devoid of feminine enhancement, I can see the slight dusting of freckles across your nose."

"Like I said far too nice." She stood, walking to the pond, glass still in hand. "What are you about?"

When he followed her, she handed him the glass of wine before sitting down on the rock. Pulling off her shoes and stockings, he watched the pink toes emerge. Then, surprising him she lifted her skirts and walked into the water.

"What are you doing?"

"What does it look like?" She pulled her skirt higher as she walked farther into the pond. "You should try but you should also know it's freezing. Oh, they are getting wet."

She was certainly right. The lace edging on her underclothing was definitely getting wet, and the water was soaking higher. He laughed, "Come here and I'll be happy to fix it."

Slanting him a puzzled look she obliged him. In seconds he reached beneath her skirt and pulled the underclothing down to her ankles. "What?"

"All you need do now is step out of them." He laughed at her look of chagrin and once more was surprised when she did as he asked. Stuffing them into a pocket, "Now you can wade up to your knees.

"I can, can't I?" she grinned at him, clearly delighted and seeming to ignore the fact she was now naked beneath her skirt.

When she hefted the fabric higher, he enjoyed the view and once in a while he saw a flash of thigh. Her legs were long and slender, well-muscled for a woman. He supposed it was because of the riding. He certainly looked forward to seeing more of her.

Content, he sat on the boulder, his glass of wine in one hand, hers in the other. She would soon be freezing but he wasn't about to tell her if she had any sense at all, she would come out of the water. If he did that, she would inevitably stay in until midnight or beyond.

"I can't feel my toes." She was walking slowly toward the bank. "I'm freezing."

"You should stay in until they freeze and crack off," he told her pleasantly knowing she would do the opposite.

"Now you are being perverse. You said that just because you want me to come out. I'm not stupid, you know. I ken when to come out of freezing water."

She sat on the same rock now trying to dry her feet with her skirts, showing all kinds of delicious white skin.

"Of course, I didn't. I would never try to second guess you."

He picked up the cloth that had covered the food. Kneeling beside her he dried her feet then held the stockings she removed. Very slowly he drew them up each leg then tied the ribbon holding them. He could barely stifle the groan rumbling from deep in his chest as his fingers moved over her. He was doing this to himself and he was not used to being left in need.

After the intense physical desire of last evening, he'd meant for today to be lazy and completely the opposite. Not now, when he touched her legs, the action of undressing then helping her dress was so sensual, he was hard pressed to contain himself. The ever-present knowledge that she wore nothing beneath her gown did nothing to ease his own needs.

"My underclothing?" Her hand shook when she held it out. "Where?"

"Not today. Seems I've misplaced your silky drawers." He knew his grin was shameless, but he had no intention of giving them back to her. The knowledge she was naked beneath her skirt delighted him, arousing him more than he intended to admit even to himself.

"You lost... I don't believe you." She was defiant and angry, her eyes blazing, hands indignantly on her hips.

His brows rose, "You will believe or not believe what you want. You can look for them. When you find your frothy underclothing, I'll put them on you just as I did your stockings. They are very pretty stockings, the tops embroidered with tiny pink flowers. I would have picked out blue flowers for you."

"Why?"

"Are you always so suspicious of everything I say? It's simple really, because blue flowers would go with your eyes."

She sat down, her lips pursed together. "That doesn't make sense. You can't even see the flowers on my stockings."

"I could if you removed your dress."

Now her brows drew together. "I want my underclothing."

"You are welcome to look." He held his arms out wide.

She stood in front of him. He spread his legs so she could come closer then held her by the waist. This could be torment from hell then he held out his arms again as an invitation for her to search him. When she was wading, he'd put them in his saddlebag and now he meant to enjoy her fingers touching him as she looked for something she would not find. Although she might find something else.

"I will then." She touched his shoulders, patted him down from beneath his armpits to his waist.

"Nothing. What did you do with them?"

He shrugged but refused to say a lie so he said nothing. Then he repeated, his voice husky, "Nothing."

"Well, I wouldn't say nothing." She inhaled a sharp quick breath. "Your shoulders are so broad." She ran her hands across them. "May I?"

This time she was fiddling with his buttons not hers and he couldn't be more delighted to see where this would go. In seconds his shirt hung open, his bare chest welcoming her explorations as her fingers flexed against him.

"Do you like what you see? You can touch me anywhere you'd like."

Her hands roamed across the expanse of his chest, stroking and lingering on his male nipples. "You are nothing like me."

"I ken that fact. Do you like what you see?" he repeated.

"I do," she told him as her fingers traveled lower to stop just above his waistband.

"I'm glad but..." He cleared his throat. "You should stop now."

"Ah," her eyes shone with merriment as well as passion. "I thought you understood what to say in times such as this one. You should have told me to keep exploring and touching you. I don't obey a man's commands."

He started to say the words but she stopped him with a gentle touch of a finger to his lips.

"Too late. You already told me what it was you wanted. Of course, as I just said, I refuse to obey any man."

"Then I should have the same liberties as you. Should I undo all the buttons and touch your nipples. Oh, but I would suck them into my mouth and gently bite the velvet tips, worry them until I hear tiny ripples of pleasures. Would you do the same to me?"

"Like this?" she asked as her lips touched his nipple and she bit slowly worrying the tip.

"Blessed hell, yes."

He gritted out, unable to stop himself and in any case he planned before they left but not this soon to do just what she was doing. His nimble fingers in seconds had all her fastenings undone.

"You didn't ask. Are you now a bad boy and no longer a gentleman? I will have to decide which Donal I like the best"

He was mesmerized by her alabaster skin as well as her breasts tipped with tender pink nipples begging for his attention. "You will be the undoing of me." His lips found one breast his fingers the other. He touched, caressed and sipped the exquisite pink flesh as her hips moved against him, against his hard arousal, beseeching him for more. They fit together perfectly.

He kissed her again, pulling her so close her naked breasts pressed enticingly against his chest. He closed his eyes, willing his body to find the strength to end this precious torment.

Drawing away he opened his eyes, lightly touching the tip of each breast. "I do want you, lass, but I'm going to take you home now." He covered her and almost as quickly as he unfastened her bodice, he had it fastened.

"I want you to finish what you started. You should ease the pulsing and heat that has me very nearly mindless. I want you to fix what you started."

"I don't dare." If he looked at her, touched her again, he would surely lose what little control he possessed.

"I don't please you." She turned away from him.

"If you pleased me more..." He couldn't finish the words and he sure as hell couldn't touch her again. He set her to the side and strode away, gritting his teeth and understanding he needed to convince her she wanted marriage because he couldn't take much more of this.

It would take such little effort though to relieve and ease her arousal. She was already naked beneath her riding habit. If he let his imagination run wild, he saw her flesh, the cream as well as swollen folds she wanted him to caress. Another groan escaped him.

"We should go now."

He gathered the food and wine, placing what they didn't eat into the container.

She didn't move then crossed her arms beneath her breasts, pushing them higher to further entice him. If he didn't know better his jaded heart would think she did it on purpose. "No. I don't want to leave yet. But don't let me stop you."

He did stop then, midstride before turning to her. "You know I won't do that."

He whirled and continued packing up. He tied the reins of her horse to the buggy he came in, trying to regain control of his mind as well as all of his senses.

"You wouldn't dare leave and take my horse with you." She was striding toward him, her smile having changed to blazing anger.

She provoked him to a point where he was going to have to go, get as far away from her as humanly possible. He supposed sitting next to her in the buggy and recalling everything he saw today would not help his condition. He would never leave her alone without some way to return home.

"Perhaps you have the right of it. We should give ourselves to each other. Come here." He smiled and watched her starting to retrace her steps, to back away from him.

Her spine stiffened. Her eyes widened. "No." She was backing away from him. "No, I don't think so, not today. How dare you assume I would allow you privileges?"

He called her bluff and realized she wasn't as willing as she let herself think. While she was curious, she wasn't ready for the next step, just as he suspected. Rushing this was not part of the plan.

"Am I supposed to take your words at face value? If I said those, you would do the opposite." He stepped toward her. "Chase, catch and kiss is that what you want, or do you want more?"

He pulled her into his arms, pushing aside her hair so he had access to the tiny delicate lobe he so adored. "I believe we should go home. What do you say? Would you like to ride in the buggy with me? We've taken this sensual game between us as far as it should go at the moment."

She leaned into him, holding tightly to his arm, her sigh of relief reverberating through him. "I'd like to ride in the buggy with you if you'll have me. I didn't mean to tease or make you think I wanted more when I'm really terrified."

"I ken you want more but I also know today is not right. Ah, lass, we are just getting to know each other. Trust my superior knowledge in this game of love. While I love to play and tease, I understand your innocence and don't mean to ever take advantage of it." He did once but he did not mean to repeat that event.

"Thank you, I think, but I don't want to lead you on. Can I ride home with you tonight in the buggy? I ken it's not safe at night on the roads. I would have left earlier."

"That's why I brought the buggy but tell me true. Do you want me to relieve you of your discomfort?"

"Yes and no. We should wait, I suppose. My sisters would yell at me if I gave in to your gentle but sweet coaxing so easily. Hope would be disappointed her lectures weren't listened or adhered too."

"And what are her lectures about?"

He was curious and sure it had something to do with the sensual need Daryl felt when he kissed her.

"She said never let a man touch you below the waist." Daryl seemed to be reciting from memory.

"You let me take off and put on items that couldn't have happened if I didn't touch you in the wrong places according to Hope."

She was still in his arms, unprotected and appearing to like it He knew if he held her much longer, he might not be able to keep his promise to himself or to her.

"I didn't want to get all my clothes soaked through," she told him, a prim air about her. "You did a good deed."

"That was certainly a good plan," he told her, swirling his tongue around the shell of her ear while she shivered in her arms. "Shall we leave?"

"I suppose so, as it is the sky will start to darken before you get me home."

She smiled, looking happy, even content.

They started on their way, her horse tethered to the buggy. "Tell me about your days. I'd like to help you make sense of your bookkeeping if you'll let me that is."

"Lacie will figure it out," Daryl said with confidence.

"You already told me she couldn't make sense of anything you'd done."

He watched her back stiffen and understood she didn't like what he was saying to her even though he just repeated what she explained to him. "I think I can help."

She turned to him then, a distinct glare in her eyes. "How?"

"You told me you forgot to label receipts. No matter how hard you try that is probably not going to change. We can begin with setting up two boxes for you to put receipts or bills in. One can be for the products you buy to make the breads the other can be for the rent of the building, and perhaps personal items you purchase for yourself. Try to write what it is but if you forget, Lacie will have enough information to put the money in the correct columns."

"What about my income?" She smoothed her skirts, grimacing as she seemed to think about what she would say next. "I don't think I have any money left over after the bills are paid. Flynt complains that he has to give me money every month."

"He should give you an allowance. You're his sister after all. He has responsibilities."

"So true, but everything he gives me I use to pay my bills. I wanted to be like Bliss. She makes money and it's all in the bank even though she doesn't do well with the bookkeeping."

"Bliss is the artist?"

"Yes, and she makes a lot of money. She could be independent if she wanted but she fancies herself in love." Daryl leaned back on the carriage seat, closing her eyes

"You don't believe in love?"

"Interesting concept but I don't know how I feel about it. Never have been in love." Her slim shoulders lifted a bit then, "Maybe it exists maybe it doesn't. I'm more inclined to think of Hope's and Flynt's version of lust. Is that what we have between us, lust?"

He choked, clearly shocked by her words. He didn't know how to respond. He thought for several seconds then began, "What is between us right now is probably not love. I do lust for you and clearly." He brought her hand to his lips slowly kissing the palm then each fingertip. "You lust for me."

"Perhaps you are right."

It seemed she thought about what he said.

He felt the quivering of her body and smiled, meaning to direct the conversation one more step, "The pulsing need you feel when we kiss, the swollen slickness of your most feminine parts, in my opinion, that is very definitely lust. You do lust for me just as I lust for you."

"You're right of course and I'm not going to pretend I think differently. We can agree on things, and I don't think you said those words so I would go off on a different tangent. Don't know what that would be anyway."

"So, we have a way to help with your bookkeeping. How do you spend the rest of your day?"

"I get up about four o'clock and get ready to go downstairs," she began, smiling at him and placing the hand he let go on his knee. "Are you really interested or are you just pretending?"

"Interested."

"Okay, I fire up the oven and start mixing bread dough. I usually have at least one loaf ready to bake from the evening before."

"How many loaves do you make?" His hand rested on top of hers, tracing lazy circles with his thumb."

"I don't know. Don't think I ever counted."

"You should know what your production is so you can adjust to the number of customers who come into your store."

She looked at him, a strange expression in her eyes. Her entire body seemed to go limp. "I've no idea how much I sell, how much I make or how many customers come into the store.

"You must have some idea."

She ran her free hand through her hair in a feeble attempt to get it away from her eyes. "I like to talk to them and I have about ten regular customers who come in every morning. I sell to a cook who doesn't like to bake bread. She comes in first thing as soon as the store opens and buys three loaves."

In a very endearing and feminine gesture she shrugged her delicate shoulders again, leaving a tiny breath of air as she did so.

"Do you have bread and pastries left over at the end of the day?"

He was wondering what she did with the day old. There were any number of places she could sell it, and he wondered if she threw it away.

"Yes, I don't throw it away."

"Good, then you can tell me if you sell it the next day at a lower price or..."

She stopped him mid-sentence, a glint in her eyes. "I give the loaves to the needy."

His heart nearly stopped when she said the words, a slew of scenarios racing through his head. "How?"

"Weel, you're not going to be liking what I'm saying but I don't care. I take the bags down to the slums, and I give it to the homeless and the beggars. There is a lady there who I always go to first. She is down on her luck. Her husband died, leaving her with three babies all under eight years old and one newborn."

"You're right. I don't like what you are doing although my heart agrees with you. You are putting your life at risk every time you go there."

"I ken it, but they need help."

Well, they were in agreement about one thing. She knew it was dangerous. "Could the young mother who has the three children help with the baking in exchange for the free bread?" He held his breath while she thought it over.

"I could use the help. I'll ask her tomorrow night."

"Looks like you've got company." Donal nodded toward the window of the bakery.

~ * ~

"Oh my, I forgot. We were all going to meet at two for tea and some conversation." Lacie was staring at her, making faces as if she knew she'd been with him.

"Conversation? About what?"

"They talk about their husbands and what they do to get their way. Their men fall right into line no matter how many horrible things they threaten them with." Fascinated by the play of expressions across his handsome face, she watched. His brows drew together for a few seconds then he smiled.

"I'm not sure you do but obviously I don't talk about my man because I don't have one."

"Only because you don't want one. You can talk about me all you like. I don't mind at all, since I'd like to be your man."

"What fun would that be. I couldn't tell them anything about us and how I get my way with you."

He pulled out his watch, "You're about two hours late. Your sisters have patience. I'll give them that and," he whispered next to her ear, touching the lobe lightly with the tip of his tongue. "I give you everything you want."

Daryl grinned at him, ignoring the heat he sent through her as well as his words. "They know I'm always late. They just didn't expect you to be with me."

"Ah, something that is nice to know. I'll remember that next time we plan an engagement and suggest you arrive an hour early." He helped her from the buggy. "I'll leave your little mare at the townhouse if that's what you would like. Right now I would very much like a good bye kiss."

He helped her from the buggy, letting her slide down his long length. By the way she moved against him, he knew she felt every hard angle and plane of his body.

"With everyone watching?" Heat rushed to her face then her hands in a belated attempt to hide the color.

"The blush becomes you." He pulled her into his arms. "Is that a yes?" he asked as his breath whispered against her cheek.

She turned to meet his lips, touching his with her tongue. They danced and played, arousing and tempting while his hands cupped her bottom as he pulled her against him. Pushing against him, she needed to feel him, all of him. He kissed her and kissed her again, the dance primal and demanding.

She didn't want it to end.

He drew away with a groan of passion and desire she was beginning to recognize. He touched her lips with a fingertip. "They are swollen and ripe for more. Your sisters will understand and know you kissed me as a woman should kiss her man. Alas, we have prying eyes and you will have questions you might not want to answer. I have to go to Dumbarton tomorrow morning, but I'll see you the next day."

She nodded, her breaths still coming in tiny little gulps from the heat of the kiss. "I think I'll miss you," she whispered.

"Good, and I will send someone to help you deliver the day-old bread. Don't protest yet, just think about it and you can send him away tomorrow evening if that is what you would like." He kissed her again, once more tantalizing all her senses before stopping. "If I had the time and you would let me, I'd carry you up the back steps to your home and make love to you."

"Ah, but if I remember correctly, you told me not until we are wed."

"Too bad you have such an excellent memory. I'll see you as soon as I can."

She watched him leave, her hands clasped beneath her chin while her heart pounded desperately wanting more from him. Letting a few more seconds pass before she entered the room full of her sisters and their questions, she waited for her heart to stop pounding so hard.

When he finally disappeared from her sight, she inhaled a deep breath resigned to answer the inquiries waiting for her inside. They would want to know everything but she was determined to tell as little as possible. This relationship was too new and way too special to share just yet. She wanted to keep it to herself.

When she closed her eyes, it seemed she could remember every caress, the sensation of his lips against hers and the way he demanded a response. He didn't need to demand though. She would give him anything he asked for.

Except control of her.

Chase, catch, kiss, perhaps she was doing the chasing and catching.

She turned then, walking confidently to her bakery. When she stepped inside, she gave a tiny shrug of her shoulders. "I forgot."

"Seems you didn't want to remember," Bliss said, laughing at her truth. "You were having too much fun with your new beau. Do you like his kisses?"

"That's true. We were kissing and I liked them, yes."

They witnessed the kiss and Donal didn't hold anything back. They would all ken something more, except Lacie. She didn't think Lacie would know what they were about.

"You've got to tell us everything," Chelsea said, grinning broadly. "He kissed you. What else did he do? I never wanted Cam to be a perfect gentleman but he tried so hard. It went against all his natural instincts."

"I think that's between Donal and me."

She poured herself a cup of tea and sat down. The warmth of the hot water mingled with the slight bitterness of the tea tasted good.

"She is absolutely right," Hope said, watching her as if she could see into her mind. "But we do need to know if you used protection like I taught you. If you didn't, we need to think about the possible consequences and what Donal will expect from you if you carry his child."

Shocked, she spilled the hot liquid. "What? I, we..." She swallowed then and mopping up the spilled liquid she tried to gain a sense of equilibrium."

"Now Hope," Lacie began, addressing their sister in law. "Daryl would not be so stupid as to make love with Donal Chamberlin. She barely knows the man. Today must be the first day they've done anything together. A person doesn't share intimacies when they've only known each other a short time."

"By the way they kissed, she knows him better than we think," Bliss said then leaning forward. "How well do you know that man? For that matter how long and how many times have you been together in secret?"

"Bliss!"

"Do we have to send our husbands after Donal Chamberlin to make sure he does the right thing by you?" Chelsea asked, her voice quiet then she laughed, easing some of the escalating tension in the room. "Just as Flynt made our husbands wed us."

"Flynt didn't have anything to do with the fact Broc married me. He came to his senses, that is all. He did it all by himself and with no coercion."

"Two minutes before the twins were born," Chelsea reminded her.

"No one can make a man do something he doesn't want to do, at least not a real man," Hope said, a silly grin on her face.

"I'm not marrying anyone." Daryl held her cup in her hands. "He did ask me, you know, and I told him never. Won't let a man control me."

"That's the way of it then. He will either leave you or get you pregnant then you will have no choice. The man is always in control," Lacie said, her tone so matter of fact it startled Daryl. "No matter what you think or how you behave, the man makes the decisions."

"You're right, Lacie, and that is why I won't wed, ever."

"You're to jaded to just be eighteen," Bliss spoke softly. "I hope your mind changes before it is too late for you."

"No, I won't let anything like that happen." Daryl was shaking her head, repeating her words while she tried to convince herself. "That won't happen."

She remembered pleading with him to do something to ease the burning ache he created. Was that something that would make her pregnant? She made a mental note to ask Hope when they were alone.

"By the blush on your face," Bliss began, "he's done more than kiss you. Now I should understand better than anyone how men can have a way of making a lady witless, unable to form a rational thought. Everyone knows I carried the twins and almost gave birth before Broc had the good sense to marry me. His touch, well, I couldn't say no and I don't think I ever wanted to."

"No one here is judging you," Chelsea said. "All of us," she looked at Lacie for confirmation, "except for maybe our youngest sibling have allowed our men to take liberties before we were wed. It's just the way of things. I wanted Cam so bad I practically begged him, and he tried so hard to court me properly the way a debutant is supposed to be courted. I made it very hard on him."

"We aren't judging. We would like to make this easier for you," Hope said with a tiny shrug and a sigh. "Unfortunately, nothing is easy when it comes to men."

Needing to change the subject, Daryl cleared her throat as she looked pointedly at her little sister. "I'm going to do better with the books. Donal and I talked about it today. I can't pay you though until I start to make a profit."

Lacie laughed, "You know you are going to try, but I don't have any expectations of the sort. If you don't ken what is coming in and going out you will never know if you are making a profit or not."

"No really, Donal suggested a few things and I think he truly wants me to succeed."

"Imagine that," Bliss chuckled knowingly. "Just like Broc wants me to do well with my art. Make sure when the two of you get married, he lets you keep your money in your name. He could take everything."

"At the moment there is no money. And," she paused, "we are not ever getting married.

"Me thinks you protest too much," Chelsea said with a sideways glance and a smirk.

"If I'm correct, Flynt is giving you money every week so you can keep the bakery open. It might be some time before you turn a profit."

"I know but Donal gave me a couple of ideas."

She knew she was repeating herself but really did want to earn money her own way. Selling bread though was nothing like selling paintings.

"What did he suggest?" Chelsea asked.

"First thing is that I need to know exactly what I sell and that I don't make too much just to leave it all sitting on the shelves at the end of the day. I'm going to have a ledger and mark down when a person comes into the store as well as what they buy. I do ken that I often have muffins left over but I truly like to make them."

"You have loaves of bread leftover that you give away. You're not going to make money giving away your product," Lacie said pointedly while she shook her head at her older sibling.

"I like to eat your muffins," Hope said. "I should send someone to pick up a half dozen every morning. That way Flynt will contribute but he will also get something in return for his efforts."

He gives me more money than a half dozen muffins but thank you. It's very thoughtful of you. I will take any help I can get."

"Well, our cook hates baking bread. I'll send her down in the mornings for a couple of loaves. That way she'll only have to bake on Sundays," Bliss said, and she paused in thought. "I'll make up an advertising flyer for you to pass out at the shop. Maybe I'll even go to our neighbors and let them know what you are doing and that you would appreciate their business. I can vouch for your skills."

"I'm overwhelmed. Do you think I should start to bake more?"

"No." They all chorused.

"At least not until you run out of product by the end of the day," Lacie put in her advice. "Since I'm still living with Flynt, I'll ask for a loaf of bread as well as the muffins Hope is ordering. I adore the bread you make."

"If you do start to do better, you can increase what you make. None of us really understood how serious you were about making your endeavor workout. We can all pitch in," Chelsea said.

"Maybe I can find out where our cook buys the main ingredients for what she makes. Perhaps there is a place where you can buy for less," Hope said.

"Make a list of what you buy the most of like flour and sugar." Lacie paused. "Butter and eggs too."

"Milk," Daryl added.

"We all have chickens. You shouldn't have to buy eggs," Bliss pointed out, "although we have more in the country."

"We have a milk cow too but can't really bring the old girl into the city. She would probably stop producing and of course we have nowhere to put her," Chelsea said. "I can just imagine the roll of Cam's eyes if he saw a cow in the backyard.

"I will make a list with the prices as well." Daryl grinned, feeling as if this day might well be a turning point for her. It was good to have her sisters helping her and Donal as well.

"More tea," Lacie asked, "and a cookie or two? Chelsea brought them. I hope you have something to eat for dinner. You're starting to look a little thin. Are you eating anything at all?"

She looked to her upstairs rooms then back to the girls. "No, I rarely eat dinner. I'm so tired by the end of the day all I want is to go to bed. Today though Donal and I had a picnic of sorts by the waterfall on his property. I had a huge ham and cheese sandwich and two glasses of wine. So, I don't need anything else to eat."

"That's why you forgot about us and were two hours late instead of the usual one. What else did you do besides eat and drink?" Bliss asked, tilting her head a bit as if trying to see into her mind.

"Oh my god, I hope you weren't doing that. In the last few minutes, you've managed to unfasten three of your buttons," Chelsea said, her mouth dropping open. "You know you have always fidgeted with your buttons when you're nervous."

"He probably told you to keep doing it," Lacie laughed her grin huge. "If he did, you would button them right back up if I know you, thank god."

"No, he told me to fasten them," she blurted, covering her mouth, her eyes nearly crossing. The heat on her cheeks would be evident for everyone to see.

"So you kept unfastening them," Lacie added laughing, seeming not to see the horrified stares of her sisters. "Has he learned you will do the opposite of what he tells you?"

"What does that mean?" Hope asked.

"It means he's learned to phrase statements so they don't sound like a command then he adds, it's up to you of course. And then he says do you think it best. If he really wants her to do something, he will tell her the absolute opposite and form the words in a command. That way she will really do what he wants her to do," Lacie said.

"Wise man," Bliss said laughing softly as she stared at her younger sister. "He is slowly and artfully winding you around his little finger in case you haven't noticed. You need to be careful or you will find yourself mindlessly doing everything just as he wants."

"It's not like that," Daryl protested, realizing it could very well be exactly like that. "He always gives me a choice."

"After he's presented you with things he doesn't want you to do. Cam is just like that," Chelsea said. "He can always find a way to make me cross eyed when he's trying to make me see his reasoning."

"As does Flynt."

"How do you get around it?" Daryl did not want to lose her autonomy so easily. While Donal could be right some of the time and what he proposed was a good idea to her, she decided she would still do the opposite. Just to keep him on his toes and not conceding to his wishes all of the time.

"Stand up for yourself," Lacie said. "I know I will if anyone ever wants to court me. I won't let a man have his way in everything."

"You've not turned eighteen yet, although you're close. There is plenty of time to be courted and fall in love," Bliss said. "Don't rush your life away."

"And all of you are so old," Daryl said. "Lacie just wants Leslie to notice her."

"As I'm sure he will in time," Chelsea said, slanting her a critical look and a voice of concern as she fastened her gaze on the littlest sister. "You are absolutely popping out of your corsage. Is that all you have to wear?"

Lacie visibly colored. Daryl reached out, touching her hand and knowing her little sister's breasts seemed to be getting larger by the day. "She wears the dresses that fit when she is going out to see other people. Today it was just us girls, so she chose something more comfortable."

"That top cannot be comfortable," Bliss succinctly pointed out. "It's so low and so tight..."

"If I can remember, I'll say something to Flynt but Lacie needs to be more assertive." Chelsea turned to speak directly to Lacie, "I'm sure Flynt will give you money for clothing."

"Anyway, we should be going now. Broc will want me home for dinner and to take the twins off his hands. I dread seeing what the three of them have done to the house. Most likely if he didn't keep them in the nursery, which he never does, everything will be in a shamble."

"We all have to leave, but first we'll see to the dishes," Hope said, gathering as many cups and saucers as she could carry.

A few minutes later, Daryl sat in her living room upstairs, gazing out the window. Her thoughts were on Donal and what her sister said about him. She was wrapped around his little finger and they had only spent a few hours together.

What to do?

Chase, catch, kiss, that was certainly what he did and now he plotted to make her his wife. Except for that one thing, marriage, she really didn't have any objections. She wanted the closeness, the touching and kissing. No other would do for her. So, it was him or no one.

Damn but she was fiddling with her buttons again. She had to change anyway. Wandering into her bedroom she managed to ready herself for bed and lay out her clothes for the next day. She inhaled on a ragged breath then letting the air out slowly, she touched herself.

In bed that night her sleep was filled with dreams, such real dreams she woke in a sweat, her body thrumming with the pleasure she imagined. It must be close to four. She groaned, rolling over in her bed.

She had plans today and she would do her best to keep track of what she made, what she sold then what was left over at the end of the day. When she reached the kitchen, there was a light on and the oven was hot.

"Who are you?" A woman she didn't know stood in her kitchen, grinning.

"I'm Justine. I'm here to help, that is if you would like my help. Donal sent me here since he wasn't going to be home anyway. Said you were too tired at the end of the day. You shouldn't have to work so hard."

"I can't pay you and he knows that for a fact."

Daryl realized the truth of her sister's words but this was a blatant offer by Donal to control her. She couldn't just let that be.

"Told me you'd say that. Truth is I'm getting paid whether I work or not. I'd rather work."

"I won't except charity." She was going to recount every objection she could think of to this lady.

"Said you'd say that too. I can leave if you like, but I'd rather be here. It's your choice. Wouldn't you like to have someone to talk to?"

"Yes and no," Daryl tied her apron. "You've already put the first batch in the oven. You are efficient."

"I did and I divided the dough into five sections. Marked it down over here. Figured that was what the ledger was for."

"You're right, of course. I forgot about that and it's only been one day. I suppose I do need help."

"I am good and organized so I ken that you are not. We will work well together and if you don't want me back tomorrow, you be sure to let me know. I won't come if you ask me not to."

"Won't Donal need you tomorrow?"

"Oh my, now I forgot." She reached into a pocket and pulled out a letter, handing it to her. "He asked me to give this to you."

My dearest Daryl,

Daryl rolled her eyes. She could hardly be his dearest yet although the word sounded nice.

I didn't have the heart to tell you I'd be gone for more than a day. The work at the shipyards will take a couple of days at best and most likely close to a week. I will come to see you as soon as I return home.

Looking forward to the chase, the catch and most of all the kisses. From now on it will be more than one.

Donal

"Well, that is that. He won't be home for likely a week, but I'm guessing you knew that already."

"Just like you, he left me a message. So I knew this morning and I'm guessing he departed last night so he could get home to you sooner."

"I don't know about that."

"It's the truth. I've been with him for the last five years. Never seen him smitten before. Never seen him write a note to a lady to explain how long he'd be gone either."

A few enjoyable hours passed. Ten loaves of bread sat on the shelves as did four dozen cinnamon muffins. True to their words her sister's cooks visited the store and bought bread and muffins.

"If you like I can pick up some of the essentials for you tomorrow before I come to work. I know of a little place where flour and sugar along with some other things are very cheap. I buy a lot so I get a lower price than if I buy a small amount."

"That would be nice."

Daryl wondered if the noose Donal slipped around her neck was tightening. She accepted the help with little to no argument. Justine was coming back tomorrow and probably the next day.

"Do you have other customers?" Justine asked, just as the little bell over the door chimed again.

"A few." She tried to count in her head the number of people who usually came but today she was seeing new faces. By nine o'clock she was very nearly out of everything and she had people who like their pastry at noon.

"We should probably bake at least one more batch of bread as well as rolls and muffins. Don't think you've got enough for the rest of the day."

Two o'clock rolled around. She sat down with Justine and the ledger as well as the receipts from today's sales.

"You did well. Donal will be proud of you."

The words hit her funny. She liked what Justine said, but it seemed it put too much emphasis on what Donal felt about her work and what he personally helped her with. It wasn't what she wanted.

Was it?

"You only have two loaves of bread left. Two of your amazing cinnamon rolls and four muffins also. Are you going to sell them as day old tomorrow?"

"No, I plan on taking them to a woman I know who has too many children to feed. She can't afford much. I usually have more leftover. The others will be disappointed."

"I ken. I'll go with you if you'll have me."

"I'd be pleased. Donal said I should ask the woman if she wanted to work for me. That won't offend you will it?"

Justine waved her hand in the air. "Of course not. It will give you time to teach her what you want her to do while I'm still here. I will have to return to my duties at Mr. Chamberlin's home soon enough and if today is any indicator, your business will pick up with a little organization.

~ * ~

Emilia tucked her baby in beneath her coat, holding her breath as she watched the baby's father pace back and forth in front of her house and praying the child would keep sleeping. She thanked whatever guardian angel was watching over her that she had not been there when he knocked on the door. Her other children were huddled behind her, warned not to make a sound lest he hear them. The oldest a lad of eight understood the dire consequences if the man discovered them.

She knew they were hungry and she prayed the nice lady from the bakery would not stumble on to this scene. Emilia didn't know what the man would do if he discovered someone was giving them food, helping them. He wanted them to need him, but she didn't need any man. Vowed she'd never again give in to temptation of sweet honeyed words that brought her to their bed only to discover the man would abuse her.

Her first husband, the man who sired her first and second, had not been like that. He'd been true and kind but some sickness took him. He worked at the tobacco plant for his entire life and smoked the smelly weed too. Joshua kept telling her of all the medicinal properties of the plant and how he would live forever but she thought better, seeing him waste away, coughing and spitting up blood in the last of his days.

She was alone then with two children to feed and no money. While she was not of the privileged class, her family lived well. When she wed, she'd never thought her marriage would end with the untimely death of her husband.

"No," she whispered softly but too loud she kenned.

Her son tightened his grip on her shoulder in a silent warning she should be quiet.

The sweet lady and another she'd never seen before was knocking on her door, and it didn't seem she would leave. Now her husband was talking to her. This just wouldn't do but she had the children to protect. She bit down hard on her lip to remind her to remain quiet.

She held up the loaves of bread but the man grabbed them and threw them into the street.

"My woman doesn't need charity." His yelling carried across and down the street. "I take care of her."

It seemed the pretty lady said something else that angered him. Don't stand up to him, she wanted to yell but it was too late.

He slapped her across the face. "Get out of here and don't come back."

The two women spoke to each other, one racing off and leaving the pretty lady behind to fend for herself. That didn't seem right, but she knew neither one of them could win against him when he was in a drunken rage.

The lady spoke to him again, seemed to try and reason with the man. She knew he could not be reasoned with. Emilia knew it was coming yet she didn't dare warn her. In any case she didn't think it would do any good or that she would be in time. If she showed herself now, not only would he take the baby but he wouldn't leave without hurting her.

In his care the child would die. She didn't know why he wanted this girl child. Then she realized, he would whore her out as soon as he could. Her body started to tremble, tears threatening.

Once again, her son's small hands on her shoulders reassured and comforted. He was so much like his father. No, she mouthed the one word when she watched that horrible man fist his hand and hit the lady square in the face.

She dropped to the ground as if she was weightless then she didn't move. The man kicked her hard before he stumbled toward a nearby tavern.

Emilia watched him, terrified he would turn around until he

vanished inside. Still she waited, watching for him. She should go to the pretty lady.

Handing the baby to her son. "Whatever you do, protect the children. Don't let him find you or take the girl from you. He has planned bad things, unimaginable things for her. I'm going to help this pretty lady, have to you know. It's the right thing to do. Pray for all of us and maybe for once our prayers will be answered."

The boy nodded and with a quick kiss to his forehead, Emilia left staying in the street shadows.

When she reached her, she said, "I'm so sorry. I'm going to help you."

She moaned softly and that told her she was alive. "Good, where do you want me to take you?"

"Home."

"I kenned that. Where is home?"

"The bakery, you know, the one on..."

"My god, what are you doing?" A man stood over them, a gun in his hand. "Leave her be."

"She was only trying to help." Her son stood in front of her, the baby in his arms and the other two children beside him.

"I see. Why don't you move away so I can see how she is doing?"

Chapter Three

"Sir, Sir!"

Donal watched Ashford run toward, him waving his hands and yelling something he couldn't understand. His expression contorted with fear. A sick feeling in the pit of Donal's stomach told him something was terribly wrong. His valet and friend since childhood would not be here unless something happened to Daryl.

Quickly he strode toward him, his fists clenched tightly at his sides. He knew this would be bad news. "What is it?"

"Got here as fast as I could sir. Daryl is hurt, hurt bad but she's alive, just in a lot of pain. A man hit her a solid punch on the side of her head after he backhanded her. Thought you would want to know."

"Blessed hell, where were you?"

He understood the question was ridiculous but the gut-wrenching pain he was feeling at the news rendered him senseless irrational at best.

"Keeping an eye on her a safe distance away so she wouldn't know I was following her and she wouldn't know you didn't trust her judgment. Just like you told me. Justine was by her side." His breathing had just about calmed. "Rode here as fast as I could. Know you're upset, understand the fear for your little gal."

"Good, where is she now?"

He was nearly to the stables, his strides lengthening every second until he broke into a run. It would take him most of the night to get home. He needed to see her now.

"Sir, I took her to your house and she's in your bed just as I was sure that's what you would have done. Didn't think you want her somewhere she wouldn't be safe and protected."

"Justine?" The lady was also supposed to keep an eye out for Daryl. Justine had the most level head of any woman he knew.

"She's sitting beside her trying to keep her awake like the doctor told her. Don't want her to fall asleep, concussion and all."

"Now, start from the beginning and tell me exactly what happened. It was those damn loaves of bread she's giving away, wasn't it? If I could, I'd put a stop to all this nonsense."

No, he wouldn't do that. Her independence was a lot of the reasons why she found a way into his heart. She was his heart. *"Mo chroi."*

"Yes, it was but she didn't find Emilia. Instead she found a mean old drunk who was also looking for the woman. He didn't like it when Daryl told him she didn't know where she was. He was looking to hit someone and Daryl was an easy target. In the wrong place, so to speak.

"Emilia's a little slip of a thing, down on her luck. I showed her the door of the small cottage I live in and told her to make herself at home. Hope that's all right with you. Didn't know what else to do. She couldn't go back to the place she and the children were living in. That man would find her for sure."

"Good, good." He inhaled a deep breath as he saddled his stallion. "It's your home, yours to do with what you like."

As much as he wanted to race home, he wasn't going to risk his horse. Ashford had everything under control along with Justine. Daryl was in good hands. He steadied his emotions. Wouldn't much do to overreact.

"Do you want me to stay here and oversee the cargo or come home with you? I'll stay wherever you need me," Ashford asked, his arms crossed over his chest and a determined look on his face.

"Stay here. Your horse is winded and you'd need a new mount. I'll take all three horses here and change up every so often. I want to make it home by morning."

Good lord, but he needed to be home right now, this instant. "Steady, steady, calm your nerves," he murmured yet his heart raced and calming himself at this point seemed unmanageable.

Every possible scenario flew through his head. The only thing that would give him peace was to see her, hold her hand in his. This was so wrong. He risked her life when he gave her the leeway to make decisions for herself. How could he be so stupid?

What to do?

He'd been a fool but he thought it had been the only way to hang on to her. Instead, he risked losing her to a drunken sod who put her in danger. He understood the situation could have been far worse.

The night wore on as Donal made his way back to Glasgow. The morning sun was just beginning to rise when he handed the reins to all the horses over to his stable boy. "Take care of them. They've been ridden hard."

He set his steps straight to his house and to Daryl.

Taking the stairs two at a time he raced to his bedroom. In the doorway he stood for a few seconds looking over the scene in front of him. Daryl's fiery red hair was spread on his pillow, her face pale and when he stopped next to her to remove the cooling ice pack from her cheek, he choked back a sob at what he saw. "Blessed hell, I didn't even imagine this."

"It will look worse tomorrow and probably the day after before it finally starts to heal," Justine said, her voice a steadying calm as she rose from the wing chair she'd been sitting on. "Why don't you wash up a bit, splash a little cold water on your face before you come sit with her. Emilia and I are going to go to the bakery, keep it going for her. The doctor said she needed to stay in bed at least three days."

"I'm going to have a hard time making her stay in bed. She's going to want to go to the bakery, and she is going to insist she is fine."

He gently pushed her hair from her face, thinking there should have been something more he could have done to protect her.

"You couldn't." Justine was shaking her head, reading inside his mind. "She was determined and she almost didn't let me go with her. When I knew we had to get out of there, she sent me to get Ashford. The man hit her hard. She dropped with a tiny cry and that was all, nothing more. When Ashford and I got back to her, Emilia was bent over her."

"Emilia is a good sort?" he asked wondering about her and why Daryl wanted to help her so much. "The man would have hurt the other lady. I need to find him, make him pay."

Justine shrugged, "Guess we'll find out. She's coming with me this morning but she has to take the baby. Her eight-year-old said he'd take care of the other children. The little boy is stoic, seems to take on all the cares of his family. Guess he needs to step up and be the man."

While Justine talked, Donal shrugged out of his shirt, cleaning up and donning a fresh one. He sat down on the big chair next to the bed, picking up her hand in his. She looked good in his bed, black eye and bruised cheek. He should be grateful the attack had not been worse. She was alive and that could possibly be a miracle.

Justine placed a hand on his shoulder, "She's going to be fine. I ken it. Just stay by her side and she'll know how much you love her."

Love her? Did he love her? If he didn't, he had no idea why he reacted this way. Tears slid down his cheeks. "I could have stopped this."

"Just from knowing your little lass one day, I'm telling you short of hog tying her there was nothing you could do. I'm going to get Emilia now. If you need me, send her boy to the bakery. He promised to wait downstairs. I left food in the warming oven. When she wakes up there's some chicken broth. Don't think she could chew anything, at least not for a few days."

"Thank you."

Love, he kept rolling that over in his brain. He didn't know. He just didn't ken how that would feel, only that Daryl meant more to him than his own life.

"Before I leave, I'll bring up a tray of food for you, something to drink too and if I get a chance later on this morning, I'll send someone to the house with bread and coffee, a pastry or two."

He watched Daryl then he dozed, nightmares whirling in his head, worse scenarios as terror seemed to take over his mind. She moaned softly, bringing him to attention, turning then her eyes opened.

"Donal?" She moved her hand slightly as if she tried to touch him.

"What is it? You're hurt. You have to lie still. Just tell me what you need and I'll get it for you."

"Where am I?"

She tried to sit up but failed, her hand touching her bruised cheek then a little cry of pain.

"You're in my bed, lass."

He smiled at her knowing she would want to make some false claim or use feminine wiles to try to get whatever it was she was thinking about. He couldn't let that happen. Had to be smarter than she was. In her condition that shouldn't be hard.

"What happened? All I remember was that I was talking to this obnoxious man about Emilia and now I'm here."

She grimaced as it seemed the pain became more and more real.

"The obnoxious man punched you."

To her, he needed to make light of the situation. Didn't want to terrify her more than she already was.

"I'm in your bed... thirsty." She looked to the nightstand. "I don't have..."

He reached for the glass of water and supporting her head, he helped her drink.

"So just what are you thinking about?"

He knew she wore very little, just her chemise. He assumed Justine would have made her comfortable and he'd seen her bare shoulder beneath the covers when he looked at her cheek.

"I don't know. It's just, well, I didn't wake up this morning thinking I would be in your bed tonight." It seemed she tried to laugh but she cringed instead, closing her eyes.

"I didn't expect to see Ashford and have him tell me you were hurt. It wasn't well done of you. I don't like it when you're in pain and this seems more like agony. I want to strangle that man with my bare hands."

"Well done of me?" She appeared astonished then closing her eyes grimacing before another little cry of pain, "My cheek hurts, my entire head hurts. Why are the walls moving?"

"Because you have a concussion. You really need to learn how to take better care of yourself. Like I just said, it wasn't well done of you." He wanted her to acknowledge the fact that perhaps going into that part of Glasgow at night, hell anytime, alone was not a great or prudent idea. All he wanted from her was to act with common sense and think about her actions.

"You did warn me..."

Her eyes were still closed and a tiny moan of pain seem to emerge.

"I did, lass, but you wanted to do good deeds."

The trait was endearing but she needed to find a way to help those less fortunate in ways that wouldn't put her life in danger.

"Now the doctor said you mustn't go to sleep, but it has been quite a while since you took that beating. I doubt if sleep will do you harm since you woke up fine just now. I'll stay right here."

She tried to sit up again and this time she was a bit more successful. "You need to sleep too. How did you get here? You must have... You rode all night, didn't you?"

"For you, yes. Ashford stayed to see to the business."

"I'm in your bed so you can't go to sleep."

Through all the bruised coloring on her face, he actually saw a slow rise of color.

"I could join you but I won't. I've a feeling we'll be having company in a few hours, and I don't want to compromise your reputation."

He suspected from what Justine told him, Daryl's family was beginning to help her with the bakery. They'd spread the word about her shop. He knew first-hand the product was good. If Flynt showed up here and he was in bed with her, her brother would demand a wedding. That was exactly what he wanted, but Daryl didn't, not yet. He still had a lot of work to do to convince her to his way of thinking.

She blushed again. It was endearing. He did want to be in his bed with her, but the repercussions would have a ripple affect he didn't want her to have to deal with.

"Company?" she queried, seeming to mull over the idea for a few seconds. "Oh goodness, I've got to go to work."

"No, you do..." he stopped himself once more, seeming to leave everything up to Daryl when he wanted to quash that impulse.

She tried to stand and before he could stop her, she swung her feet out of the bed and promptly melted to the floor. His heart leapt to his throat. For a second his fear for her froze him to the spot.

"Daryl." The one word whispered from him.

He knelt to pick her up, cradling her in his arms, wishing he could absorb her pain into him.

Such fear for her. He'd never felt anything like this. It was debilitating.

"What happened?" she asked. "I..."

"You what?"

"I have to go to the bakery. They will need me."

Justine has everything under control and Emilia is helping. Her son is waiting for messages of some sort. I was so very concerned about you, I don't remember everything Justine told me. I think he is in the parlor."

"He is very protective. Donal," she paused, once again her hand on her head, "I really don't feel well."

"If you want to go to work, I will take you in the carriage. Dress yourself in whatever you wore yesterday that Justine must have left somewhere. I will not help. If you cannot do it by yourself, why then you are not strong enough to bake." He looked around for the clothing but could find nothing. "Justine must have guessed you would try this too soon. She has hidden your clothing, either that or sent it to be washed. She is very efficient."

"Not just yet. I might run off customers if they saw me looking like this. You've convinced me with all your manly preening."

"What makes you say that?"

She did need to be aware of how she looked, but he wasn't going to use scare tactics.

"By the way you look at me." She reached out, touching his beard. "I've never seen you stare at me quite the way you are looking at me now. You appear petrified then it seems as if are going to cry. I know it's because of the bruise that I'm sure is even now growing. Can I go to sleep? I do believe I'd like to do that, go to sleep."

"Of course, *mo chroi,* you have become my heart."

He pulled the covers over her, tucking her in as if she was a small child, once again realizing she was more important to him than he ever thought possible.

How to convince her now that she actually wanted to become his wife?

He truly wasn't sure how to go about the enormous feat. He rested his head on the bed beside her, closing his eyes for a moment only. She touched his head with her hand. Perhaps he should join her and to hell with the repercussions. It would result in what he wanted. Flynt would make sure they were walking down the aisle before the week was done.

She didn't want that and she would resent him.

What to do?

She slept fitfully for about another hour and sure enough, the first one into the room was Flynt. He scowled but didn't say anything right away.

Then, "What is my little sister doing in your bed?"

It seemed to Donal he was not angry just needed to let him know it wasn't at all proper of him to put her here. He was doing things with his sister that society wouldn't approve of, and Daryl would pay the cost. He didn't intend to let that happen, but Daryl would have the last say. Perhaps Hope and his marriage changed Flynt. He seemed less judgmental realizing they were all human.

"Healing." Donal smiled as Flynt strode into the room. "That's what her body has to do right now is heal, nothing else and I intend to let that happen."

"She's coming home," Flynt said. "She still has her old room. The one where she stayed before she moved out."

"I don't want to," Daryl said, her voice soft. "I'm not going to go anywhere. This is where I want to be."

Donal shrugged, his grin growing larger, in his mind repeating her last phrase, *this is where I want to be.* "It is her choice after all. Doctor said she should rest. This is the best place if that is what Daryl wants."

"You're letting her decide because she is doing what you want. If she said the opposite, you would argue."

"Never." He felt smug and arrogant. He chose the right words and he knew it as fact.

"Would you two please stop it? My head hurts just listening to the bantering going on." Slowly she sat up, prudently keeping the covers pulled above her shoulders. She glared at her brother. "You didn't even have the decency to ask me how I am. You waltzed in here demanding things you've no right to demand. You don't care about me. Your concern is how other people see you or me. I'm not really sure which it is."

Flynt ran his fingers through his hair, seemingly disconcerted and with a loss for words. "Well, how are you?"

"Weel now that you ask, horrible." She closed her eyes, grimacing for what Donal was sure dramatic effect, which he thoroughly applauded. "Donal road all night so he could see how I was doing. Now I'm not going to let you bully him. If all you're going to do is goad Donal into disagreeing with you, you can leave. I don't need you here even if you are my brother. I'm over eighteen and can answer for myself even if you don't like my decision."

"Would you like some hot tea? One of my servants delivered a fresh pot while you were sleeping. Flynt, you can even have some if you can find a way to curb your tongue."

Donal smiled as he offered Flynt refreshment knowing he made the right decision.

"Prefer a glass of brandy," Flynt muttered appearing clearly disturbed at what was transpiring right in front of him. One would think he would have learned a lesson with the first two sisters. No, he still meant to tell his siblings what they could and couldn't do.

"I am thirsty. I'd also like a robe or something to put on for our visitors. Has Justine brought any of my things here yet?" Daryl smiled at her brother before turning her attention to him. "Do you know?"

"No, while I'm sure Justine will do just that, she is busy with the bakery and your customers. I'll get you one of mine. That should cover you up just fine." He sent a grin Flynt's way just to see the creases on his forehead get deeper. "But you need to pace yourself, *mo chroi.* If your body is telling you that you need to sleep, well then, you should tell your well-wishers that it is time for them to leave." He looked pointedly in Flynt's direction.

"I do like the way you phrased that." She smiled and turned her back to the men when she slipped Donal's robe over her shoulders. Then, "It smells like you. It pleases me. Is there anyone else downstairs to see me? If not, then Flynt, you should leave, I'd like to sleep until someone else comes to call. Maybe they can space the visits so I can sleep between each one. I know Donal needs to sleep as well. He did ride all night to see how I was doing."

"You must be feeling better. You're beginning to sound just as you always do." Flynt kissed her lightly on one cheek before leaving.

"Your brother has vanished and hopefully he won't return anytime soon. Now, what would you really like to do?" Donal sat on the other side of the bed. He'd not slept for over twenty-four hours and he was hoping she would want to sleep. If so, he'd curl up on the other side. He really didn't expect her sisters to visit until this afternoon.

"There are dark circles under your eyes." She reached out to touch his face. "Now I'm sure they don't match my superb coloring, but I ken you need to sleep as do I." She smoothed the pillow beside hers. "I don't have any qualms sleeping with you and I'd find your company much more entertaining if you had all your wits about you, but I think it fitting you sleep on your own bed, one I might add that your feet don't dangle off the end."

"I didn't hear one groan of pain in your entire discourse. I'm pleased at that. Didn't like it when you were moaning all the time. You are well on the way to mending." He inhaled sharply.

She tossed her pillow at him and immediately winced. "I should not have done that. Indeed, I need to wait at least another day before I cosh you with your pillow." While she didn't smile, her eyes seemed to twinkle with humor.

That was good.

"You're tiny and very weak. The cosh was well done of you even though it hurt you. Your wince and groan were not as big or loud this time. I think I will lie down beside you, but I'm going to send Emilia's boy to inform all your sisters they are not to visit until after two o'clock this afternoon."

"What is so special about that time?" she asked, falling back on the bed, a tiny wince of pain ensuing.

"Five hours is the number of hours sleep I'm thinking I need to function properly. If Flynt, or when Flynt informs them you are sleeping in my bed, I need to defend my actions with clarity and to the point of course. Although I ken you can defend yourself about my very manly actions, I also don't want to put undue stress on you, particularly at this time. If you were healthy, well then..."

"You don't need to defend yourself. I do. Could you please get my pillow for me?" She slipped her arms from the robe, allowing the covers to fall to her waist. She was almost naked. He saw her breasts sway provocatively beneath her shift as well as the fact that as he watched her, her nipples hardened. He inhaled hoping for the control he was surely lacking. She is still in pain, he reminded himself, even though Daryl was the woman needing that reminder.

"When you are in pain you shouldn't tempt a man so. Seeing you so scantily covered does please me. No, it pleases me immensely. It's a shame we can't pursue this blatant invitation of yours more thoroughly. I would love to teach you something new about the ways between a man and a woman."

Blessed hell, but she was staring at his mouth again. While he understood it was what Hope advised to arouse a man, this was no time to be doing such a thing.

Not when a single kiss would have her crying out in pain.

"I ken what you're saying, but my feminine parts do not." She looked wistfully at him, in a way daring him to relieve the ache she was experiencing. "Could you help me without kissing my mouth. Perhaps you could kiss other parts of me."

"I would do more harm than good, *mo chroi.*"

He was rethinking his earlier words that they would wait until wed. He needed a means to bind her to him and if she was agreeable, they would make love sooner rather-than later. In any case, whether they made love or not, he would remind her of a woman's pleasure as soon as she was not in pain. He began to make plans.

Not tonight though.

"You forget, I decide about my needs, about my body," she told him reluctantly though and with an added wistful sigh. "I'm too tired.

Will you hold me in your arms while we sleep? I think I would like that."

He ignored her request for the time being. "Well then, if I were to kiss you, not a chaste peck on the lips but as I've done before, would you be able to enjoy the moment and let your feminine petals unfold with pleasure, grow swollen and damp in anticipation of receiving me?"

She blushed as he hoped but she was also thinking about what he asked her then she was shaking her head. "I don't think I can even chew without pain. I'd like more tea though laced perhaps with headache powder. Perhaps after the tea we could try to kiss."

"You will of course let me know when there is no more pain so we can give and receive pleasure again. Of course, if you don't want that you don't have to tell me," he finished on a chuckle. "A mere man does like to ken what his woman wants. It's truly hard to be thinking one thing only to discover you've been doing everything all wrong."

She looked as if she wanted to hit him again with the pillow. He'd allow that because it told him her spirits as well as her body were healing nicely. The doctor told her a week but he didn't think it would be more than one day before she was up and about, working at the bakery and asserting herself.

He was pleased, very pleased and decided a strong man could let his woman make decisions for herself. Yes, that was the way of it. A woman, just as a man, should learn from experience. In time though he prayed, Daryl would come to accept his advice not just ignore it. She would learn to take needed protection with her into the parts of the city that were not safe.

She yawned, closing her eyes now and snuggling into the covers. Sleep, and he hoped a deep sleep, would encompass her with only good dreams. He didn't want her to remember what happened or to think about the things that couldn't happen. He didn't want the pain to be all she remembered about the good deeds she attempted. In fact, she had been successful in helping Emilia. He should tell her as soon as she woke.

Chase, catch, kiss, he meant to pursue that mantra as soon as she was able.

~ * ~

This was the first day she did more than sleep and eat. She wandered around the house for a while, looking at things, picking them up thinking about a possible life in this home with Donal. The idea pleased her. Yes, it might just be a fine reality. They got along well together. He seemed to want her as much as she did him.

Smiling and not for a minute pretending she would obey him if he said no, she decided to ask him if he would agree to let her go to the bakery today. She was bored to death. Needed to do something with her time.

"Donal, you're back." She ran to him, her arms spread wide hoping for a huge hug and a kiss as well.

"I am." He wrapped her in his arms, kissing her then seeming to need more he kissed her again, his teeth tugging gently on her bottom lip. "You should go into the bakery today, don't you think? Only if you want to though."

Staring at his mouth, she suddenly decided other endeavors between the two of them might be much more fun than going to work. "Perhaps we should do something else, you know," she said, gently touching his lips, caressing, delving inside with the tip of her finger, knowing she enticed him.

"You want my manly parts now? I can tell you are trying to seduce me. I'm not going to allow that. No, we will take some time soon, just for ourselves but not at this moment. When we have as much time as we need..."

It seemed he meant for her to finish his sentence, at least in her mind if not by answering him. "I see, you want to get rid of me." She sighed deeply, trying to appear offended then turned away. "I do need to go to work, see how things are going. I know you've reported to me but first-hand knowledge is always better than second hand. My bruises are almost healed. I might not frighten all my patrons away."

"At four o'clock I will be there with the carriage and you should be ready for a new adventure. We're going to the country for three or four days, possibly more. Would you like that? Justine will not be needed. Can you cook?"

For a moment she thought that was a silly question but baking wasn't cooking. "I can. I've always liked to be in the kitchen. We can do better than just fend for ourselves. I'm a very good cook." Silently, she cringed at the small lie she told. How hard could it be?

"I will see you then at three?" she asked, needing to assert herself and be part of making the plans.

Even though she'd been in his bed for several days now, he didn't touch her except to kiss her good night. She needed him to be more like the man she knew before she was hurt. He laughed easily and smiled more. Now it seemed he was always worried about her.

"Two o'clock and earlier if I get everything done by then. I can't wait to see how you will respond to my plans."

She was beaming. He would see the smile stretching across her face that she could not hide even when she put her hand in front of her mouth. "I will be ready. You've already packed my things?" She paused then thinking, "What plans?"

He nodded, "Last night when I first thought about leaving with you for a little holiday and having you all to myself, I made a few decisions." Then he bent closer to her whispering, his breath feathering across her cheek. "I have packed no underclothes for you. You will be provocatively naked beneath your dresses. I will be thinking about that fact every moment I'm with you."

She wanted to appear surprised but couldn't quite manage it. So, instead she said the words, "I'm shocked."

Her hand on her breast, eyes wide. She found her heart thundering with all the possibilities she could only imagine.

"Little liar, of course you are not surprised. You please me and the tiny fib pleases me as well. If you like I will be content to remove what you're wearing beneath your dress right now and you can think about the wonderful things your man will do when we are alone."

He winked and it sent another shiver up her spine. His hands were on her waist and moving lower as if intending do what he suggested right now, here in his parlor.

"I wouldn't know. You've never done anything but kiss me. I don't know anything about other wonderful things you might do to my woman's body." She wanted that and so much more. "You will have to chase me first. I don't know if I'll let you catch and kiss me though. Perhaps it will be the opposite this time. Maybe I'll kiss you first."

"Catch you." He nipped at her earlobe. "I will and I'm sure that feat will not be too hard since you seem to fall willingly into my hands."

"Kiss me."

She very nearly groaned when his tongue explored her ear before he nibbled and kissed his way down her chin until he found her mouth. He was very good at kissing, she thought as their tongues danced and played. A tiny wave of jealousy swept through her as she thought of the other women he'd done the same and more with. It was quite possible that if she asked him sometime, he would tell her how he knew so much about pleasing ladies and the lady parts that were beneath her gown.

He is a bad boy.

"Best you leave before I can no longer contain myself." He patted her on the rear, chuckling as he let go of her. "I've got business to take care of before I can leave the city. This is not helping when all I want is to toss your skirts and explore every beautiful inch of you while hearing the tiny little cries you make when I please you."

"By the way," she told him, skipping backward and so very proud with herself for figuring out a way to tease him. "I've nothing on beneath my dress." She lied but meant to remedy that before he picked her up at the bakery.

He groaned then. "Perhaps noon. We can explore so many promises in the carriage before we even reach the waterfall. If you're amenable that is. I will begin your seduction then. You will swell and get slick with moisture then you will want to cry out, moaning with the deliciousness I create inside you."

"Maybe, maybe not," she said softly as she headed out the door. "I want to have a say in what and when things are done. So perhaps not the waterfall, we should wait a while to make everything so much more..." She had no idea what to say then.

"Of course, I wouldn't have it any other way. Ashford is waiting to take you. I will bow down to your female sensibilities and do whatever or whenever it pleases you. Everything will be your choice; time, place, how and anything else you think of."

"See you soon," she called out over her shoulder, feeling light and carefree. She did want to marry him, did want to spend her life with him. Even so, she was terrified of not having a say in what happened in her life and to her. Perhaps she could teach him.

"Ashford, you've come to my rescue again. You are such a dear. I just don't know if I could walk that great distance to the bakery. It might take me all of five minutes."

She laughed as she stepped in front of the carriage, looking forward to the intimate time she would spend with Donal. Her brother would certainly have something negative to say about it if he knew.

He helped her into the vehicle. "Always want to be of service, ma'am."

"And the boss told you to take me, that I was still healing and weak as a kitten or some such thing. Am I right?"

"Pretty much so. Believe he has plans and wants you rested."

A few minutes later she waltzed into the bakery. "Hello." She waved at Emilia who was in the front of the store. "Is Justine in the back? I want to talk to her." She kept right on going without waiting for an answer.

"She is. You are better?" she asked. "I'm so sorry that happened to you all because of me."

She stopped, turning to speak to Emilia's comment. "My injury was not your fault and you know it. That horrible man is responsible. I am fine and nothing hurts anymore. Donal and I are going to the country for a few days to do nothing except learn about each other. Just wanted to tell Justine but she probably knows, most likely knew before I did.

"Justine, there you are." She opened her arms to hug her. "You have been wonderful and now we are asking you for more things while we play."

"Truly, I've enjoyed this much more than cooking for Donal. All your new customers are an absolute delight. When I have to go back to cook for your man, I'll be disappointed. Come, let me show you what we've done."

Justine led the way into the back and the ovens. "I'm making cookies now. We've added your grams favorite ones."

"Ginger cookies?"

"Really. Your gram puts in an order every morning for a half dozen and we do cinnamon rolls as well as three different kinds of muffins. Emilia says she can add shortbread cookies as well to the menu. What do you think?"

"That you're not going to need me."

She was honestly feeling a bit depressed about this when she should be elated the bakery was growing and perhaps making money for the first time. Now she was going to be gone for another three days. Well, if that was true, Flynt would be pleased he didn't need to fund her endeavor, but he'd be furious when he discovered her at Donal's home in the country.

"Of course we will. You've started to gain customers, and your family has done so much to advertise. Most of it is by word of mouth, but the flyers Bliss made are wonderful too. That's why it is growing. No other reason."

"What can I do to help?"

Here she was, asking in her shop, but there was nothing else to do.

"You're still recovering. Off with you now, go in the front and enjoy some tea and a scone. Oh, we have scones too. You can visit with the customers and they will be pleased."

"I see..."

"Wait for Donal to pick you up." Justine waved her away again.

She nodded and did as told. The tea was hot as was the scone. Justine gave her some strawberry preserves and butter.

"How are you, lass?"

The deep voice rumbled behind her and gave her a little start then pleasure. His hands on her shoulders, lightly pressing gave a signal as to the tenor of the rest of the trip, evocative, sensual in nature. "Donal, you're early." She could barely speak.

"I wanted to be here sooner." He placed a gentle kiss on the back of her neck then another before biting gently. "We've a couple of hours to explore more intimacies between us, teach you knew ways to give and receive in a relationship. Would you like to learn?" He extended an arm before he waved to Emilia. "Remember to close up early and if you are taking leftover bread, go in the morning hours after the first batch is baked. I'll send Ashford back to town tonight and he will escort the two of you home."

"Donal." She wanted to clear the air, tell him the lie she told because he had not given her the needed time. "I didn't tell you the truth this morning. I'm admitting to it now so don't be angry."

His brows drew together, "About what Lass?"

They were sitting in the carriage and it was slowly moving, picking up speed. "That's just the thing. I meant to fix the lie. I forgot and you came too soon. I only told it because I wanted to tease you."

"Now you're worrying me. Best you tell me before I start thinking a host of things that are not true." His voice sounded husky and different somehow. "I don't like you lying to me."

She swallowed unable to figure out what he would do or react. She tried to smile, "I am wearing my undergarments."

He let his head fall back and roared with laughter. "Then you'll just have to remedy that. I do enjoy taking them off you. Almost more fun than imagining you without wearing any."

"Now?"

She wasn't going to strip right here in front of him. Doing so would just be too embarrassing, but wasn't that better than having him take them off as he did before.

"Yes." His grin seemed to stretch across his face and he was patting the seat beside him. "You can come here and I'll help with anything you might need."

She sucked her lips into her mouth. "I don't think I can move." She really did feel frozen to the seat.

"If you cannot come to me, I'll be pleased to come to you."

Once again he patted the seat.

She should have waited to tell him, should have just not told him. He reached across and pulled her onto his lap.

"Donal!" she squeaked, closing her eyes at the sensation of his arm rubbing across her breast.

"Now, how should we go about doing this?" His hand rested on her ankle, massaging tiny circles. "Should I take your stockings off too? I think I'd like that. Would you appreciate this more? All of my manly parts are saying I should touch you everywhere and that your lady parts will adore me for it. They will grow hot and swell with more need and even more until I give you what they are literally crying out to receive."

"I can do it myself." Her hands were quivering she was so confused and stimulated just hearing him talking. "What? Oh? Crying out for what?" She panted there was no other way to explain the short fast breaths of air.

"You were frozen to your seat a few seconds ago. Now I believe it would be more fun for me to do it myself. What do you think? Will you give me your blessed permission? It's your choice you know. Do you want to or do you want me to?"

He was teasing her. He wasn't really going to do this in the carriage. Was he?

"I don't think I can think."

She closed her eyes as the hand that was holding her ankle roamed up her leg, massaging and caressing, playing behind her knee. He moved slowly and the dance of his fingers against her thigh was divine, enchanting in every way. She squirmed and she wasn't if it was to bring him closer or to push him away.

"You should open your eyes. I want to see them when I touch you. Really, Daryl, I couldn't have thought of a better way to spend our time travelling to the country. This idea of yours was exquisite. I'm pleased you thought of removing everything but your dress."

He found the top waistband and pulled. "I..." She nearly jumped from his lap when the back of his hands touched her belly.

"You're squeaking. If you want me to understand you, you will have to enunciate your words properly."

She scooted a bit as his fingers found sensitive flesh, feminine skin and she yearned for so much more but she didn't know what it was she needed.

"How?" she croaked now. "How can I do that when you are doing those things to me? I never thought..."

She couldn't finish the sentence and even while she was trying to form words, her legs were opening for his exploration.

"No, that's good, very good just the right amount of tenacity." He ran his hands down her legs as he slowly moved the silken fabric down to pass over her feet. "Now I have two pair."

They were off and he was holding them as a prized possession. "I won't have any underclothing left if you continue that way."

"As far as I'm concerned, you don't need any. At least not when I'm around to be intimate with you and imagine what is beneath your skirts. Why I believe you will always be weeping for me. I much prefer you this way, but of course I wouldn't want you to blindly obey my wishes. You must do only what pleases you."

"Weeping for you? I don't understand what you're saying, but you do ken I wouldn't do that, blindly, obey."

He was playing with the ribbons that held her stockings up. Once more, his fingers danced on her legs exploring more of her. "Oh," and the word was very nearly a moan. "How is that? That?"

Her heart raced and it seemed she thrummed with need only he could give her a release from what he was doing but he refused to do that, refused until she agreed to marriage. This was blackmail, she decided.

"How are you feeling?"

His voice was soft, butter soft, almost a wicked delicious purr yet there was a gruffness about it that stimulated her even more.

"Hot."

"Good and you will feel hotter before we reach our destination. I plan on making sure of that." One silken garment slowly and sensuously came off then the other. Once again, he held them as if they were prized possessions before stuffing them in another pocket.

She tried to move back to the other side but he held onto her. "You got what you wanted."

"Not yet, not even half of what I've wished for." His kisses along her neck continued as did the teasing of his fingers on her legs and belly.

"What do you want now?"

Good lord, he was touching her belly and she couldn't help but move her hips, seeming to ask him for more and more and he seemed willing to give.

"Your hair down. I want your hair falling down your back and curling around your shoulders. The need to run my fingers through it is very nearly undoing me." Slowly he began by taking one pin at a time from her hair. Each pin, he slipped into his pocket and every strand that fell lose, he rubbed between his fingers, smiling. "So soft just like the rest of you. I do believe I can get used to this. Your softness pleases me as do all of your sinful curves."

"Sinful?" her voice quivered.

"Sinful because they tempt me."

She was sure at least an hour passed before he had all the pins out. "You ken this is pure torture."

He sensuously ran his fingers through her hair. "It feels like silk. Ah lass it is torture for me as well," he murmured, touching his lips once more to her neck, sipping and biting.

"The same as your beard, so soft, soft as a kitten's fur," she murmured, closing her eyes again. "What are we going to do when we get there? More of this?"

"If the sun is shining, we will go to the little pond and waterfall. Justine made up a dinner basket for us. Would you like to continue investigating and discovering how we can be together, all the different ways? How you and I will fit perfectly after we are married."

"A, yes I believe so but can we change the subject?"

"What would you like to talk about?" he asked but his hands and lips continued their dance of pleasure across her body.

"How does she manage so much?"

"Who?"

Daryl was trying to keep her mind off his hands and lips. "You ken I'm a bit jealous of the woman. She ran her bakery, made food for them and now she was probably delivering the leftover bread."

He shrugged his so broad and masculine shoulders then she realized his fingertip trailed slowly across the bodice of her dress, dipping lower with each pass, tugging on fabric, lowering the corsage to only one end.

"This is very low. I don't like it you know, other men seeing the soft curve of your breasts. They will be tempted to do this." He tugged a bit on one sleeve then the other.

She watched as the entire bodice slowly slid down her body. One breast was free then the other. He kissed her, sucked the nipple into his mouth then bit gently worrying the tip with his teeth. His lips rose to the mark on her neck as he sucked there also.

In his lap, she squirmed again, her body seeming to disobey her commands to ignore what he was doing. "Donal, you are making me so..."

"Ready for me? If you hold real still, I'll take your other nipple into my mouth, but you can't move."

She did move, "I can't help it, please."

"Not until you sit really quiet."

He kissed her on the lips then, his tongue creating even more evocative rapture. He held her head in his hands not allowing her to move but deepening the kiss with each second, but her hips continued to beg for him as she arched against him. She couldn't stop because everything he did created a deeper and deeper ache between her legs.

"I can't."

She moved again, opening her legs for him yet she didn't know why. Then abruptly he brought her dress up covering her.

"We are almost there." His breath whispered across her cheek. Even that sensation created more havoc within. She was sure she would burn if something didn't happen to relieve the fire soon.

"I can't move and if you expect me to ride, you will be displeased." The heat from his explorations singed every part of her. "You are burning me alive."

"We will take the buggy. Ashford is going back to town and he will leave the carriage and use one of the horses in the stable. When we reach the waterfall, should we continue what we started here?"

He set her on the other side. "The buggy, that's good but you can't think to drive and..."

Too bad she couldn't think. Her brain was filled with mush.

"You spread your legs for me just now. Did I please you so much you wanted me in more intimate spots, places no other man has touched before? I felt the movement against my lap. You are a naughty girl for a bad boy. You want my fingers there in the hottest, dampest part of you."

"I didn't."

She knew she did just that, and she wasn't positive why but she had a guess.

"Little liar, but I don't mind this fib. Soon enough you'll understand why and know that when I touch you, you will always want to open for me because you ken, I want to be inside you. Tell me you understand."

"No, I don't yet but I'm willing to learn."

"I suppose that will have to do for now."

When the carriage rolled to a stop, he helped her out. Even his hands on her waist thrilled her more than she wanted to admit.

"The stable lad will take care of everything," he told Ashford. "We are going to leave now. Don't feel obligated to wait for us. We will be a while. Go on home and see to the ladies and their deliveries."

He turned to Daryl. "Do you want to drive or would you like me to?"

She was definitely surprised at his query. "You should. Why did you ask me?"

"I was feeling lazy and thought you might like to take the reins, be in control. Isn't that what you are searching for? Power over your man? I'm quite willing to give it to you."

His wicked grin told her that wasn't the reason.

"What were you going to do if I did?" She crossed her arms in front of her, thinking, "You wouldn't be keeping your hands to yourself, would you?"

"To tempting, no I would kiss you and do other delicious things with your beautiful body."

"I thought so. Now, while I like everything you do, I'd probably end up driving us right off the road. You wouldn't want that and neither would I. I ken it's much better for us to be safe this afternoon. Are we going to stay to watch the sunset?"

"Weather permitting. There are clouds on the horizon though. A few dark ones so I hope it won't be raining and if it does, well, we will probably get drenched. If that happens when we get home, we can remove all of our clothing. I would like to look upon you naked. Would you like to see me?"

She truly didn't want to think about those words. The buggy was moving at a fine clip, breezes sifted through her hair. It would be in a fine tangled mess by the time they got back to the house.

"What did you do at the bakery? Hope you didn't work."

"You trying to make small talk?" she asked, finding a bit of humor in the sudden change of conversation.

Perhaps he was just as aroused as she was and not so subtly trying to keep his mind off what he started in the carriage.

"I am, just admittedly attempting to keep from thinking about what we are going to do once we get to the waterfall. If I don't, I might just stop the carriage here and continue what you began."

He seemed to study her while she felt the heat of his gaze.

"What I began?"

"Yes, as you told me about the lack of underclothing and your lie. That was quite some time ago and I haven't forgotten."

"You have me there," she told him grudgingly.

The small talk wasn't helping her. She knew he would carry through with what he started in the carriage ride then advance it one step further. "I thought we would have a glass of wine and talk about your day. What you did before we set out on this spontaneous holiday. What I did at the bakery."

"That's not at all what I've planned. We are going to..." He turned to her grinning again. "I almost told you what we were going to do. That wouldn't be right," he murmured, "Not right at all. It should be a wicked surprise. Don't you think?"

"Tell me. I don't like surprises. They rarely turn out the way you want them to," she said with a soft sigh.

"It's got to be a surprise. Nothing else will do and this, I promise, will change the way you think about surprises."

"Why?"

"Just the way I planned things, but if you put your agile mind to thinking you'll figure it out." He playfully touched the tip of her nose with his fingertip. "It's something you've been asking for."

"You're finally going to make love to me." Her breath hardly made it from her lungs. "I want that, you know."

"Told you, I don't intend to do that until we are wed. Wish I felt differently." He shrugged then, his broad shoulders lifting slightly.

"You will teach me how to make the thrumming go away."

Lately it seemed she was in persistent need. She ached when he touched her, when he looked at her and even when he didn't look at her. Her thoughts were always on his kisses and the smooth, warm glide of his tongue across her lips.

"Looks like we are here and just in time. Remember my mantra chase, catch, kiss." His eyebrows lifted as if she would know the answer.

She got down without his help, tapping her toes, arms crossed in front of her. "I'm waiting."

"Very well." He strode to the boulder then sat down, resting his back against the huge rock. "You must do the catching, if you like that is. I'm not going to be very hard to catch though. All you have to do is walk over here and you've caught me."

"No, I don't suppose you are difficult. Indeed, it appears you are verra easy. Yet you seem to me to be smooth as glass." She started walking toward him then stopped abruptly. "What have you got planned? Is this the surprise?"

"You're a suspicious little thing, now aren't you? You want to chase and catch me, I ken it. You sometimes fashion yourself in a man's role, so now I'm giving you the chance. Come to me then and fashion yourself as a man would in this circumstance."

Slowly, she walked toward him. Very slowly and now she stood in front of his feet, his long legs stretched out. "I'm not trusting you much right now. You've got this wicked, no, devilish look in your eyes. I've no idea what you're talking about. Fashion myself as a man?"

"If you do what I ask you will be well pleased as will all of your beautiful lady parts. I'm going to give you a woman's pleasure. After you catch me that is."

She moistened her lips, then, "What do you want?

"Only," he paused then gesturing with his hand, "a foot here and

a foot there. Then you may kiss me and we will begin the next journey."
He patted the ground on both sides of him.

"Why would you want that? I don't understand anything at all."
She inhaled a long and very shaky deep breath.

"Don't be asking so many questions. I promise you will be
pleased as if you were downing a sweet glass of wine. Preferably a fine
red Bordeaux."

She did as he said then he reached up, taking her by the waist and
brought her down so she was sitting on him, her legs straddling his body.
"I don't understand any of this."

She felt like a ninny, nothing making any sense what so ever.

"You will. Now let's start where we left off in the carriage."

He slowly pushed the sleeves of her dress down her arms until
her breasts were free. "They are beautiful you know, soft yet firm. The
velvet tips taste wonderful and they come to such a hard-tight bud."

She watched as he uncovered her, as his eyes glimmered and he
bent to suck a nipple into his mouth. She ran her hands through his hair,
the ends curling just above his collar.

He continued to say, "I'm going to kiss you again. Here and
here."

He touched each nipple with his lips and tongue. He kissed each
corner of her mouth and his hands roamed her upper body, fondling her
breasts, teasing them until the nipples were tight, hard peaks.

She was hot. Her body continued to move against him as tiny
sounds rippled in languorous waves from her lips, sounds she couldn't
stop. Didn't want to in any case. "Donal, you are doing it to me again.
I'm hot and wet. It's not fair, you can't just continue to torment me."

"Spread your legs wider, *mo chroi*." His hand roamed her leg all
the way to her belly while he continued to kiss her and explore other
places. "You are so soft, soft everywhere."

She moaned again and felt more heat spiral into her. "I want your
shirt off." With fumbling fingers, she was unfastening the buttons until
she pushed the fabric off his shoulders. Her breasts touched his chest and
the sensations were sensual and delicious, primal in nature. She moved
against him until she heard him groan. It seemed her smile reached to her

toes before settling in the most sensual and hottest parts of her.

"You need to hold back or I might just explode."

He laughed. Blessed hell, but the last thing he wanted was to hold back her passion. "You want me almost as much as I want you, *mo chroi*."

He touched her in her most intimate parts with his finger. "You," she swallowed hard. "You are touching me and I don't think I ever want you to stop but I ken I should tell you no."

"I am and there is this tiny satin bud right here."

He caressed the knot, smiling when her hips jerked in response against him while she arched her back and her breast pushed so close to his lips he could almost taste them. "You like this?" he asked as he massaged it over and over while her body moved with pleasure.

"I," she licked her lips, "Yes."

"Good, don't close your eyes."

He slipped a finger inside her body." Your tight sheath is soft velvet heat to my finger." He whispered as he bit her ear worried the tiny lobe. "I touched your maiden head. I'm not going to break through it today but soon, *mo chroi*. Very soon if doing so pleases both of us. It will be your choice."

"Donal," she started to feel spasms engulf her but he stopped. Held so very still, she believed he was now frozen in time.

When she began to spin out of control again, he drew back, "Not so fast, you are slick so very wet. I'm enjoying this almost as much as you are. The ever-changing expressions on your beautiful face fascinate and enthrall. Bringing this to its culmination too soon would be an injustice. This exquisite delight for you should be prolonged for as long as possible."

"You seek to plague me. I can barely breathe and I want you to finish this. I remember how it will end."

"Ah, but I want you to know the greatest indulgences by bringing you to the brink over then over again when you finally find your release it will be all the sweeter, a painful pleasure, you will want me to gift you with all the time. There is no way I can just finish."

He kissed her again, sucked her nipples into his mouth, massaged the tiny knot that he told her was the source of all her pleasure. Then it seemed he allowed her to begin the spasms. He pulled back two more times, that had begun so many times before and now they kept coming and coming.

"Donal!" After the longest time, she fell against him, spent and unable to move. Closing her eyes, she tried to calm her body. He touched her again and still she responded. Not like the first time but again feeling the incredible release pulse through her.

He laughed, rubbing her back, calming her body even as it seemed he wanted to start this all over. "Was it good for you?"

"You have no idea," she said.

"Oh, but I think I do," he laughed again, looking smug. "We should have some of that wine and the food then we can do this all over again." He paused for a few seconds. "Only if you like."

She swallowed as she felt his fingers on her. "That is not well done of you. My feminine parts are pleased but I think I will die right here, sitting on you if you start this again."

She stood and he let her go. "The chase was good, but the kiss next time will be even sweeter. I will kiss you there where my fingers were."

"You will kiss me? With your mouth? There?" She knew her eyes were huge.

~ * ~

Ashford made it back to town before the women began their charity rounds. "You said you would be doing this in the morning. Didn't believe you for a minute and neither did Donal. He turned to Emilia. "What if you were to see that man who was looking for you and hit Daryl? What would you do? The two of you cannot fight him off or stop him from hurting you in anyway."

She held her head high. "I don't trust the man and I ken he is dangerous, but I cannot always be waitin' for you, now can I? You have a life of your own. A very busy one I ken."

"You've got to wait for me. It's not safe for you on the streets. It doesn't matter that your intentions are good. You know the man will be hurting you if he finds you and what will that wee babe do for a mother if he gets his way?"

She gently touched his face. "I have to help my people, the ones in need and who are starving. Just a few days ago I was one of them. Besides, I knew you would be back in time. Didn't we, Justine?" She turned to look at her new friend, seeking confirmation of her words.

"I guessed as much. I..." she paused thoughtfully. "You two think you can handle all this on your own then go on with you. I'll start the batches of bread to rise for tomorrow then I'll go home and set out dinner for the two of you, after that I plan on going to my room to sleep." With that said, Justine turned and walked back to the kitchen.

"Come on then, I grabbed the buggy from the stables so we don't have to walk."

He helped her into the vehicle, enjoying her company.

"You really don't mind doing this? Justine and I could—"

"Hush now, we just talked about a few things that could go wrong and that doesn't even include the ones we haven't thought of. Besides, I like you, lass. Don't want anything to happen to you."

"You like me?" She turned to face him, her eyes wide.

"I do and one of these days soon, if not today, I'd like to kiss you."

He knew she would protest but hoped it would only be because of her past life. The one he needed to learn more about.

She stared at her hands, which rested in her lap before she seemed to take a breath for courage. "It's been a vera long time since a man has kissed me. I wasn't all that sure I liked it then, but I wouldn't mind trying with you."

"You wouldn't say no if I kissed you now?" He stopped the horses, reins still in hands to watch her.

She moistened her lips and he grinned. "A kiss would be nice. I think."

Keeping his gaze focused on her and placing one hand beside her head, he kissed her. She tasted sweet and innocent despite her past life. She had not been kissed well and truly, so deep it would render her senseless. He wasn't going to do that today.

When he pulled away, "Did you like the kiss?"

She nodded, her face a tiny bit red. "I will be pleased to kiss you again when we are done here. Now, do you know where it is you want to take these few leftovers?"

"I do." She pointed down one of the streets. "There are a couple of homeless men who are usually under the bridge, taking shelter this time of night. Not only would they like the food, but they would also find a job appealing. They want to work."

Sure enough the two men approached smiling. "Thank you again. You're a gift from God, lass, that you are."

Ashford had to agree with the men. He was sure he fell into her spell the first time he saw her. Then and there he decided he would court her. The biggest problem was that she already had four children. He wasn't sure she would want more and he really did want a child of his own.

What to do?

He would have to figure that out when the time was right. There were always solutions to problems if one searched and considered all the obstacles.

"Now where?" He urged the horses forward, unable to keep his mind off the kiss.

"Down that street there is an elderly lady. While she has a roof over her head, she doesn't have much. She has a sweet tooth so we give her the cinnamon rolls if we have any left."

They continued in that vein until everything was gone. "Now, time to get you home and to your four children."

"Justine took the baby home. It's so much easier now that she can eat some solid foods."

"Are all your children from your first husband?" He didn't want to pry yet he did want to know everything he could about her and try to figure out what she might want in her future.

"Just my oldest." She turned red. "Now, I ken what you must be thinking but it's not true. I don't do that kind of thing."

"Just what am I thinking?"

He was thinking of things he shouldn't be. What should he believe then?

"Like a man would and I'm going to speak honestly the way I've heard men speak. You think that after my husband passed, I spread my legs for any man who came along. Particularly after I just let you kiss me. Well, I'll tell you right now I haven't been kissed in seven years until just now. I've been counting the years since my boy was born and my husband killed. I haven't had sex with anyone, at least not sex I wanted."

Ashford paled and wasn't sure what to say. Emilia obviously had a story to tell and he hoped she would speak it to him. They pulled up to the stables and after handing the reins to the stable lad, he escorted her to the house they were now sharing.

"You can tell me about the children if you wish. I've been told I'm a good listener." He put a kettle of water on to heat. "You hungry?"

She sat down, watching him. "You know I planned on cooking dinner, but Justine said she would leave a meal for us."

"Seems you've been in the kitchen long enough for one day. I purchased some meats and cheeses today, two loaves of bread from the bakery if you remember. You can cook dinner on Sunday when you don't work. Ah, I see Justine set a tray for us."

He brought out the food then sitting next to her, he held her hands in his. "If you talk to me, I promise I won't judge. Tell me about the children. You just said the oldest boy is the only child from your marriage."

Tears were welling in her eyes while she nodded. "I found the two little ones on the street, the boy and the older girl. They are brother and sister but their mum and da are dead."

"The baby?"

She was sobbing now, her body shaking as if every horrible memory was emptying from her. When she looked up her eyes were red, her skin blotchy but to him she was never more lovely and vulnerable. He wanted to enfold her in his arms and vanquish all the pain.

"I was..."

"I think I ken what happened. You don't have to tell me if you don't want. Your boy is taking care of the younger ones."

"I think I have to tell you, speak the words and perhaps the pain of those day will vanish."

"You might be right about that."

He did agree with her, always believing that when you spoke about your problems you would feel better.

She closed her eyes. When she opened them again, determination seemed to shine from them, "I was raped. The first time I was coming home from working as a seamstress. He was beside me, talking and pushing me into an alley. I tried to get away from him. The next I knew he had me pinned to the wall and he was..."

"Hush, everything is fine now. He's not going to hurt you ever again."

"Now it is but it wasn't just that time. It went on for weeks until I got pregnant. Now he wants the little girl so he can pimp her out when she is old enough."

"That's not going to happen."

Chapter Four

A point of no return was quickly approaching. Despite his vows, he would be hard pressed to keep them. He wanted Daryl and he was going to have her and the sex might be the only thing that would convince her to wed him. Yet he didn't want a bastard. He needed a legal heir.

He didn't like his thoughts much right now.

Pouring the wine and setting out the food he watched her closely, wishing he could be inside her head. Well, that would never happen. To him she was an enigma impossible to comprehend. Nothing she did was ever what he anticipated.

"Here, are you all right?"

He sat down beside her, sipping the wine, wondering and hoping for their current relationship to change to an engagement. At least with a commitment, he could give in to his harsh vow that they would not have sex until wed. The agreement to marry would have to be enough.

"Different." It seemed she studied the landscape. "I've never, you didn't really tell me... It seems I forgot..."

"No, there is no way to explain and if you think about it, I've never experienced what you just did."

He was at his wits end. It seemed she'd withdrawn from him and he needed a way to pull her back into this reality instead of the one she'd withdrawn to. "Tell me. What is it that has you looking at the horizon?"

She set the wine on the boulder before walking to the pond and tossed a pebble into the water. He stood beside her, his arm around her waist, making a huge effort to garner the much-needed patience to deal well with Daryl MacTavish. He never thought courting would be this difficult.

A kiss, a touch here and one there should have been enough, but it wasn't. He wanted her to speak first.

"Is there a man's pleasure?" She turned in his arms. "And if there is will you teach me how to give it to you?"

He couldn't stifle the groan. "A man feels pleasure every time he makes love to a woman. That's not true for a lady. The man needs to make sure she reaches her climax before he spills his seed inside her."

"I see but maybe I don't. You didn't feel any pleasure from what we just did."

She was asking questions he didn't want to answer but he had to be honest. The answers to her questions were solely his responsibility. "It seems to me you should have been groaning and moving as I was."

"I felt joy with every caress and touch I gave you. The pleasure I felt when you touched me nearly sent me to a place I cannot go right now." He groaned just reliving the experience in his mind.

"But it wasn't the same as what I felt."

He wasn't at all sure where this conversation was going to end up. "No, it wasn't anything the same or as intense. I did feel enormous gratification."

Silence settled around them and he was intensely aware of the changing weather. His plans for the rest of the afternoon and evening were rapidly fluctuating.

"Will you teach me how to give you pleasure? The way you just did for me," she asked him. "I'd like that. Make you groan and make all kinds of noises when I do it right?"

The thought of her mouth on him did cause him to groan. He imagined so much they could have between them. "I can but you might be shocked."

"I've been shocked every day since you started kissing me. Today was the biggest surprise of all."

"Pleasing you pleases me," he told her, his voice growing husky with the passion building deep inside once more.

"Then teach me. I could give you your man's pleasure right now. I want to hear you and see you when you find release. Isn't that what you said to me? You will keep your eyes open, right?"

"Are you begging? You don't have to do that you know. But..."

"But nothing. I want to see you, touch your man's parts like you did me. I want to know what you look like. You said you would kiss me there. Can I do the same to you."

Blessed hell what did he just unleash? A passionate woman, one he desired more and more with every passing second. "Yes, you can kiss me anywhere that suits your fancy."

She looked as if she was waiting for something else, but he didn't understand. Then, "Don't you have to be naked? I can't lift your skirt to reach you, you know. It's not quite that simple."

"That's your job if you're going to pleasure me. You must figure it out."

He tossed out a challenge and wondered just how long it would take for her to undress him. She didn't have a problem with his shirts and she liked to fasten and unfasten buttons. He held out his arms. "How do you think you will accomplish this, undressing of me?"

She pursed her lips while she stared as his waistband. "I know nothing about what we do is proper but this isn't something I ken. Do you need to be standing or should you sit down as you were before? Maybe you should lie down. I know I could not have stood while you did those strange and marvelous things to me. My knees would have given out. You unraveled me, you know."

"I don't know. I do ken that standing wouldn't work for me, at least not in this instance. Once we are wed, I'm sure we'll do it lying down and standing with you against a wall as well as on the kitchen table and..."

She stepped back, blinking her eyes several times, seeming to seriously ponder what he told her. Her innocence enthralled him. "You would make love to me on the kitchen table and against the wall?"

"No, not make love. I believe you might call the act having sex or even a good fuck."

He shouldn't want to divert her attention from giving him pleasure, but he loved to watch her eyes widen when he said something outrageous.

"A good fuck," she whispered softly the sound of her voice

continuing to arouse. "Whatever does that mean?

"Yes, yes that's true. What that means is for you to learn, eventually." He grinned at her, unable to repress his feelings. "We could discuss this, but we also wouldn't make progress in this man's pleasure you want to give me. Where my gratification is concerned, I'm not always a patient man."

"Flynt used to talk about a good fuck and he'd laugh. It always had to do with his mistress. Never Hope. With Hope the word was always lust."

He watched her fiddling again, but she didn't have buttons. This time it was the tiny string tying her bodice together. He smiled understanding her apprehension and all the things she was now needing to mull over.

"We are a tiny bit off topic, and I'm thinking that was my fault. Perhaps we should go back to the question of how I should be. I'm thinking sitting would be nice. I'll lean against that boulder again."

"Alright," she paused then, "what do I do then?"

Well, he knew he hadn't been thinking straight when he agreed to this. "I suppose you should be next to me. You could straddle me like you did when I gave you your release. Yes, that is the best course. I do believe we have mastered this situation and come to all the proper conclusions."

She did then, and his hands rested on her waist. "You started by kissing me."

Her lips found his, innocently at first then as if she remembered all he did with her. Now her tongue swept the seam of his mouth where she nibbled and licked before tugging on the bottom lip with her teeth. She drew back, her brows creased together in a picture of perplexity, "Are you going to open for me?"

He did and the sweetness of her soft tongue sliding inside his mouth sent his heart spinning out of control. Her taste was pure honey, heady and intoxicating. She was his. She would understand that soon, he prayed.

She brushed her hands across his nipples, touching them. Suddenly, her lips and teeth closed over one. He planned on doing nothing, of letting her explore and entice at will. Swallowing hard, his hands settled on her waist as he fought for control that was quickly slipping away.

The groan rumbling from his throat surprised him, as did his heavy arousal with such innocent and shy contact. "I must be doing this right." She pushed away smiling at him. "I ken the groan means I'm pleasuring you at least a little bit."

If you were doing any better..." He stopped.

Her hands were on the fastenings of his pants. This was it then. She would be shocked, he understood that, but he didn't want her to shy away from him if this was too much too soon.

"I'm not sure."

She fumbled and fiddled as well. This wasn't her blouse. The backs of her fingers touched bare skin. He sucked in a breath of air, realizing they were about to go down a second new experience for her.

"Just unfasten them," he gritted out then sucked more air when cool air hit him and she ran a fingertip down his long hard length.

She looked at him then focused her gaze on his sex. Her eyes were huge simmering pools of blue. Her tiny pink tongue traveled slowly across her mouth. "You are huge," she whispered in seeming awe, but he heard no fear or apprehension in her voice

"Only when I'm aroused to this point." *Of no return.*

"Can I kiss you?" All teasing and talk of man parts vanished.

He was nodding his head but she wasn't looking at him. Then her lips touched him and his hips jerked as he burned beneath her hesitant touch. The kisses were tender and oh so tentative. Blessed hell but he needed her to take him inside her mouth.

"Caress me with your entire mouth," He told her his voice raw with desire. "Take me inside you."

She looked at him then, "Are you sure? Will it hurt?"

"Only if you don't."

He nodded as she bent over him, taking him into her. The moisture and the heat of her lips and the inside of his mouth was burning him inside. His hands were around her head as he encouraged her and his hips bucked each time she sipped and nipped his aroused flesh.

He reached beneath her skirts, finding the velvet nubbin that brought her so much pleasure. A tiny mew caught his attention as she began to move in the rhythm he set.

Waiting for her to reach her own climax tested him in every way. He knew the second the pulses began and the tremors ruled her body. "Use your hand on me, *mo chroi*."

She looked at him then, "Donal!"

"That's it, let it all come. He gave in to the pleasures she created in him. He cried out then as his seed lay outside not inside her. He knew he was well and truly damned.

She rested on him, her breathing harsh. "You did it to me again," she finally whispered. "This was supposed to be about you, not me."

"I couldn't let that happen."

He was smiling at her, gently caressing her in an attempt to calm both of them.

She sighed softly, her breath whispering across his chest and he yearned to know if any of what was going on here would change her mind about marriage to him. He prayed it would. More of this might kill him. If her brother knew they were alone together, he would insist on marriage. Good thing he was preoccupied with Hope.

He stroked her hair, ran his fingers through it, giving her a chance to recover. *I think I'm falling in love with you, mo chroi.* "Do you feel that?"

"What?" Her breath whispered across his chest once more. "The rain is starting."

"Rain. Rain?" She sat up, pushing tangled hair from her face.

He fixed her dress, "Go to the buggy. I'll grab everything."

"Just leave it," she said as she ran.

"Never." He tilted his face skyward, rain sluicing across his skin as he secured his pants and pulled his shirt together fastening one button.

"Hurry."

He had the basket packed. With the blanket over his arm he set everything inside their vehicle. "We are going to be drenched by the time we get home."

The top of the buggy was meant for shade from the sun not a

pounding rainstorm with the drops swirling in all directions. He was right. By the time they left the buggy with the stable boy and ran hand in hand to the house, they were both soaked through to the skin. He swept her into his arms, carrying her up the steps to his room.

"I'm dripping all over the floor."

She shivered and he was suddenly worried she might get sick.

"You need to get out of your wet clothing." He was unfastening her dress, slipping it down over her hips. Then she was naked in front of him. He wanted to look at her but she was already trying to cover herself with her hands. Her blush seeming to reach from her face to her toes.

"Wh-what about you?"

Her shivers affected the sound of her voice. She was shaking and at the same time turning from him.

"Don't hide from me," he said while he strode to his armoire. His shirt fell to the floor. He grabbed a robe. "You need to get warm. Put this on."

He finished undressing. For a few seconds he stood before her, naked. He wanted to show her what he looked like and who he was in every way.

"You're beautiful."

Her hand rose, momentarily reaching out to him.

"We need to get your hair dry."

He built up the fire that had been started by servants.

She laughed then and the sound was good for his soul. This day was unique and uncomfortable in many ways. New challenges and she met each one head on with curiosity as well as passion. They would do well together if he could convince her that she would be better off as his wife than his lover.

"It will take forever to just comb my hair out let alone dry it. But you can try."

"It will please me to try. Sit here." He was on a fur rug in front of the fire. "Do you have a comb in your things?"

She lifted her very slender shoulders then tugged at the opening that was slipping down. "I didn't pack." She sat down. "You did."

He found her valise then rummaging through the contents he

pulled out a comb, holding it up. "I'm looking forward to this." He sat down behind her. She was right. Her hair was a tangled mess. "Let me know if I hurt you."

"I've a tough scalp," she said, turning her head to look over her shoulder at him.

He hesitated a moment before he began to run the comb through hair that wouldn't allow anything to penetrate despite his attempts. "This isn't working."

"The thought of you combing my hair was appealing but it takes some expertise." She laughed then and took the comb from him. "Like this," and she showed him a few tricks.

"I'll try again." The task took far longer than he thought yet he loved her hair at its wildest. "Are you warm enough?"

She was hanging onto the front of the robe. "I am. The fire feels good, but I think I would like to get dressed."

He'd expected this sooner but was reluctant, needing her to become more at ease with her near nakedness. "Probably not such a good idea, lass. It's almost time for bed and you would just have to let me take everything off you again."

"We're going to sleep naked? In bed? We didn't before." Her eyes wide, she was now looking from his bed to him then back again.

"I think I've touched and kissed every beautiful inch of you and we've shared each other's personal self intimately. I know I'm going to sleep naked." He never wore anything anyway. "What you do is up to you. I would never expect something from you that you weren't willing to give."

"I'll think about it, maybe if you make... well, just maybe."

"The lovely expressions sweeping over your face are enchanting, and I swear your eyes are crossing."

He was grinning inside, loving every beautiful moment she was gifting him.

"As I told you earlier today, you shock me every day and this day you've managed to surprise me more than ever before. I never know what outlandish thing you are going to do or ask me to do." She ran her hands through her hair. "I think my hair is nearly dry." She turned around, her back no longer to him. "I'm hungry. Can I have some wine?"

"Deflecting from the question. I like that but it would please me if you slept naked with me."

He rose then and brought the tray of food and bottle of wine to set on the floor by them.

"Isn't that just for a husband and wife?"

He poured them glasses. "I want you to be my wife but no, many people who care even a little for each other sleep naked. I care for you a lot. Do you care for me?"

Her hands clasped beneath her chin, "You know I do. But..."

Donal was slowly and she perceived expertly changing her mind about marriage. Since they'd been together today, he'd never once told her what she should or shouldn't do. With every new breath she needed him more than the one before, and she could never imagine a life without him by her side. Literally, he stole her breath and when he touched her, she burned.

A few minutes ago, he left her at the door to the bakery with a sweet, deep kiss and the words he would see her tonight after the bakery closed. She grinned, touching her lips with a fingertip cherishing the hot intense sensation his lips on hers created.

When she walked inside, the tables were filled, the patrons seeming pleased. The shelves were still full with delicious pastries. Apparently, Justine and Emilia added to the menu again.

How did they find the time?

She continued, unpinning her hat and shrugging out of the lightweight shawl Donal placed around her shoulders before they left for town.

Her wrist was grabbed. "Daryl MacTavish?" The words seemed to be whispered with a harshness she'd never heard before.

She tried to jerk her hand away, but the woman held on. "Let go!"

"Excuse me, I just wanted to talk to you." Her words were saccharine sweet. She removed her hand. "Have a seat."

"I don't know you." Daryl stared hard at the woman, unexpected fear settling in her stomach. "We couldn't possibly have anything to talk about."

"I carry his child." She smiled as if she had just said something important. "You should know your Donal is not loyal to you. He has bedded me and I bear the fruits of the love we have for each other."

"You expect me to care, why?" She turned to leave, not wishing to spend one more moment in this woman's company. Not wanting to believe her she tried to exit the room, but the woman continued to lay her filthy words in public.

"I know he wants an heir and I'm going to give him one in seven months, give or take."

A sick feeling swept through her. She could not be speaking of Donal. Had he truly slept with this woman only two months ago? "Who?"

"Ah, I see I've got your attention now. Donal's child, this child will be the heir he so wants that he's willing to take up with a little bitch such as you to get it. You cannot give him what I can. This baby," she placed her hands on her stomach, "will be the first born."

The sickness disappeared replaced by a raging anger. She had been confident in her relationship with Donal, and this lady should not be able to put doubts in her head. "Only if it's a boy and he acknowledges you. Otherwise your child will be born a bastard."

"He will. He cannot deny that we were together two and a half months ago." She broke off a piece of a ginger cookie and delicately placed the tiny morsel in her mouth. Her feral cat eyes burned with hatred.

That was before Donal began to court her, poured his heart out to her, telling her he wanted marriage. Was she just a replacement for this woman? Moisture clogged her throat.

"By the way, I'm Katrina Madison."

"You seem to know who I am."

She stiffened, trying to sort everything she knew against what she didn't know. Honestly, she didn't know what attracted Donal to this woman or why he would sleep with her.

"I do. Saw him kissing you through the window. That will have to stop. I can tolerate a mistress when we are wed, but it must not be so obvious. You must understand you're just his last bit of muslin." Katrina continued to eat as if this was a daily occurrence.

"Rest assured I will never be any man's mistress. Can you say the same? I know of Donal's reputation as a bad boy so nothing that pops up in the future about his past behaviors will surprise me nor will it change my mind about him. If he slept with you, which I sincerely doubt, it was before he started courting me." Her words felt like bravado, no meaning or substance in them.

"It is what he does in the future that is important. Rest assured he loves me not you," Katrina told her smugly.

"Time will tell." Daryl rose, walking into the backroom then leaning on the counter she sucked in a deep sob as tears began to fall.

This was not how she wanted to proceed, not what she expected when she entered her bakery.

She didn't want to have doubts about Donal, didn't need any more insecurities. Wiping away the tears with the back of her hands, she stood up straight. With a difficult swallow she smiled, deciding she would ask Donal about this woman the first chance she got. If this was his child...

What to do?

This would have to be discussed with Donal, but of course the discussion would have to wait. They were both at work and she had so much to think over. She needed to decide how she would approach the news of the day.

He would tell her the truth. She was sure of that. Donal was a man who wouldn't lie about a past or present lovers. What she didn't understand was why he pursued her when there was a woman he'd already bedded who could possibly be giving him what he wanted. Why didn't he ask this lady to marry him?

The reassuring hand on her back helped relax her.

"Now tell me, what is it that has you in tears when you should only be about smiles this morning?" Justine stood by her side. "I'll listen. Did he treat you wrong? If he did, he'll have me to answer to."

She wiped more tears away, trying not to sniff but failing

miserably. "No, of course not and while I won't say he was a perfect gentleman, he didn't do anything I didn't want him to do."

"I can assume your troubles don't have anything to do with your man."

Justine stepped back, arms crossed in front of her. She was studying her and Daryl felt as if the woman could read her mind, see right through to her verra soul.

"No, you can't assume that," she said, wishing she had the answers and wondering too if Justine might know something about Katrina Madison.

Daryl didn't want to say anything to Justine until she confronted Donal. She wasn't going to be anyone's last piece of muslin, nor was she going to spread gossip or lies.

"Riddles are not my best. A plain-speaking person like myself can't solve them easily," Justine pointed out. "Tell me exactly what happened."

Daryl raised a shaking hand, directing Justine's attention to the main room of the bakery. "It's that woman."

"Does that woman have a name?" Justine walked to the door to take a look into the restaurant.

Daryl heard the sharp indrawn breath of air and knew she was in danger of losing Donal. "Do you know her?"

"Katrina Madison. She's back and with more evil directed at you and Donal, I'm sure. Don't give her a moment of your time. Donal has been trying, obviously without success, to get rid of her." Justine's voice held a hint of concern as well as anger. "She is an evil, selfish woman."

"She told me she is carrying Donal's heir and that he would marry her." Her voice shook with worry and fear. She had never realized until Katrina showed up unexpectedly the intensity of her feelings for Donal.

"This won't do," Justine said, "I'm going to go out there and tell her to leave."

"Don't." Daryl put a hand on Justine's arm. "What you say to her will not do any good or sway her in any way. The only person who can tell her to leave is Donal, and at this moment he doesn't know she is here."

"I ken it but it doesn't make this easier," Justine hugged her. "He doesn't love her. If he did, he wouldn't be courting you."

"Tell me what you know about her." Daryl sat down, unable to function at the moment while Justine brought them both a cup of hot tea and a chocolate cookie as well.

Justine inhaled a long deep breath, her eyes roaming heavenward as if searching for the words. "What I know about that lady is that she has no one's interest at heart except her own. She is a pariah to all who know her."

"I understood that the moment I saw her. There is something truly evil about her, but what is his history with her. He obviously made love to her or she couldn't claim to carry his child." And only a few months before he started courting her.

"I'm sure he will explain everything to you. He loves you. You must know it's not my place to tell tales."

"He's never told me he loves me, but I haven't told him either."

She didn't say anything because she didn't know if what she felt was lust or love. Hope always told her what she felt for Flynt was lust, but that was because Flynt didn't want to hear the word love. She didn't know if Donal thought the same as her brother.

"Well, you wanted to know about Katrina Madison. She grew up with Donal. Lived just down the street from him a few blocks away. I wasn't working for the family then but I've heard a lot from Ashford who sees through the woman's ploys. Ashford and Donal were also childhood friends."

"Unlike Donal who only sees the good in a person." Daryl said, wondering how true that was. He never struck her as being naïve.

"Donal wants to see the good and I daresay he gave Katrina so many chances I wanted to cosh him over the head in hopes it would knock some sense into him." Justine laughed then.

"You don't think I've anything to worry over where Donal is concerned." But she knew the truth. If that woman set her sights on him with the promise of a possible heir, perhaps she had been too convincing about never marrying. "He told me he didn't want an illegitimate baby."

"Do you keep telling him you won't wed him? If you don't want to lose him to Katrina or even someone else, best you say the words he needs to hear. You know you don't want to lose the man."

"No, I don't but I'm, well..." she paused, "I'm afraid of marriage, terrified I would lose myself."

"I ken you are afraid of the wedding bed even though you've Hope and your sisters to explain things to you. You can't let that deter you."

Daryl felt the heat rising to her face as she remembered all they'd done the last few days. "Not as afraid as I was," she whispered, barely able to speak a word as they seemed to catch in her throat.

"You've made love with him then. Did you take precautions? Perhaps it would be best if you didn't think that far ahead. If you were to carry his child, he wouldn't give another woman a second thought."

"No." She was shaking her head but she could tell by the expression on Justine's face she didn't believe her. "We." She tried to swallow again, "We did—we gave each other pleasure but he wouldn't make love to me. Won't until either I agree to marry him or we are wed."

"I'm not sure that was a good decision in light of who showed up in your store to torment you today. We'll have to make do with this situation best we can."

"We will, but why, if he doesn't like her why would he make love to her?" Daryl asked, puzzled by all that had been said.

"She's a woman who knows how to seduce. I'm sure she wasn't a virgin at the time because Donal would have been more concerned about her if she was. You need to ask him if you want an answer."

"I think I'll go talk to her."

Daryl felt resigned to discover as much as possible before she confronted Donal or even agreed to wed him. He had explaining to do. A lot of it. She stopped suddenly, realizing she had no right to explanations of any sort.

"That might not be prudent. Why don't you pull those cookies from the oven and mix up another batch? It will give you the time to decide if confronting her is a good idea or not. If you decide to speak with her, what will you say?"

She was nodding her head, understanding she should not be

impulsive, something she tended to be. "Alright then, as long as you promise to tell me anything you might remember about her."

"Of course, lass, I just wish I'd been around when they were in their teens. Ashford could probably tell you more about the pair. Ashford watched as Katrina ran him around his little finger. At one time I think Donal was head over heels in love with her."

"I ken it but Donal would never admit to something like that." The thought gave her reason to smile. "What happened?"

"If the rumor was true, she cheated on him more than once and with more than one man. He can't abide dishonesty from anyone."

Thinking about what Justine said, she read the recipe in front of her, mixing the ingredients for the cookies then tasting them. "Do we get all our eggs now for free?" It was a good feeling to bake, a sort of catharsis for her. She needed to purge Katrina Madison from her mind.

"We've managed to do just that as well as convince a few people to bring in milk. I've started churning the butter."

"So, we are making a profit?"

The bakery was still full of people and the time was nearing two o'clock. In the past she'd been putting chairs on the tables and getting ready to clean and close the shop when two rolled around.

Hands at the small of her back, she stretched then walked from the kitchen. Katrina still sat at the table, sipping her tea. Daryl poured herself a cup before sitting down beside her.

The silence between them seemed to echo in the room. "You're a cocky little bitch," the words certainly poured smoothly from Katrina's lips.

Daryl wasn't at all certain what to say, she cleared her throat but said nothing, unsure now why she was sitting here staring at her teacup.

"Well, if it isn't my dear friend, Katrina," Bliss said after giving Daryl a kiss on the cheek. "What are you doing back in the city?"

Then she turned to Daryl. "Did you know that Donal and Katrina were once good friends? Katrina messed things up though when she slept with..." Bliss was tapping her fingers on the table. "What was his name? Angus? No, it must have been Adam, no, it was both of them and he found out later you slept with someone named Stewart."

"You have a lot of nerve speaking of such things," Katrina said, clearly agitated by Bliss' words.

"Do I now? I've only slept with one man, my husband." Bliss smiled at Daryl then winked.

Daryl felt that at least someone was supporting her when she was walking around blindly.

"But you were pregnant before you were wed. Heard the vows were barely said before you were in labor giving birth," Katrina seemed to need to hurt Bliss.

Bliss smiled. "At least I am wed. A rumor that you started says you are carrying Donal's child. Can you prove it? Are you even pregnant? This wouldn't be the first time you lied about a pregnancy to get your way."

She shook her head, "He slept with me a little over two months ago," she said smugly. "I conceived then."

"Who else did you sleep with a little over two months ago?" Bliss smiled prettily then pointedly said, "You do ken your reputation and all. If Donal denies the encounter, no one will believe you."

"Oh, there you are Bliss. Why, Katrina, I didn't know you were back in town," Chelsea said as she pulled out a chair and joined them. "Emilia, can I get a cup of tea? I stopped by to help close up the shop. Didn't know Daryl had returned from her outing with Donal."

"Is Ashford going to help deliver the leftovers today?" Bliss asked Emilia as she poured the tea.

"I believe so. He is protective and would be angry with me if I went alone, after what happened to Daryl."

Emilia's voice trailed off as she looked over the women sitting at the table, seeming to notice the unique expressions on their faces.

Daryl understood she still blamed herself for what happened. There was nothing she could have done to stop it. Protecting herself and her children was the most important thing to do.

Justine walked from the kitchen and turned the sign over the door to closed then set about closing the shop. Most of the customers were finished and left. Those who weren't done continued to talk. This was just exactly what she wanted her little bakery to be like.

"I'm going upstairs to rest. I'll be down tomorrow bright and early for a full day of work." She was going to say she was meeting Donal but stopped herself. It wouldn't do for Katrina to learn that. She would probably follow her.

She went up the inside stairs, unable to remove Katrina and the possible child from her head. She didn't want to think about Donal doing those deliciously wicked things with that woman. Yet she also wasn't sure how she would bring up the topic, fearing he would forget about her and take up with Katrina.

Walking into her parlor she flopped down on the sofa. Her head resting on its back, she closed her eyes. She was desperate and worried sick. Her body shuddered every time she thought about Katrina and Donal being together.

"Daryl, is that you?" A comforting voice asked from her bedroom.

She couldn't help but smile. Donal was here. He wasn't with Katrina. Probably didn't even know she was downstairs, pregnant and in her bakery. Fiddling with the shirt buttons she walked into her bedroom.

"What?"

"Do you like it?" Donal's grin was wide.

"It takes up the entire room," then she paused. "How did you get in and how did you get that inside?"

She was now pointing at a huge bed. One his feet wouldn't hang over.

"I figured that if I was going to be spending time with you and in this bedroom not my own, I needed a bed my size." His lazy grin followed the offhanded remark.

She was still smiling even though she knew a serious conversation was coming after he answered her questions. "First, how did you get inside my apartment? I locked it just as you wanted me to."

Even while he was patting the bed beside him, he told her, his smile widening with each second. "I had a key made."

She wasn't shocked or even surprised. "Without my permission."

He shrugged not bothering to try to appear contrite. "I didn't think I needed it."

"No, I suppose you didn't. So how did you get it inside? There is not enough room to get any one part of it through the door."

"Come here and let me hold you."

"How?"

Standing her ground, she didn't intend to do as he bid until he answered her.

"If you give me a kiss, I'll tell you," He patted the bed again.

Plain and simple she could no more tell him no than the sun would stop shining. "Alright, then we have to talk about even more important things, well one really important person."

His grin changed slightly while she climbed onto the bed then into his arms for a long, slow, heart-stopping kiss. Then, "How?"

"While we were in the country I had it built in here. Right in here." He looked proud of himself. "What is it you want to talk about?"

"Katrina Madison."

His face grew hard, his eyes shimmered with anger. "What about her."

"I met her this afternoon." She waited for some sign of admission or knowledge of what she was about.

"And..."

"She says she is two months pregnant with your child."

"I have to go."

~ * ~

"Ah, lass, you're so beautiful." Ashford said running a fingertip along Emilia's jawline. "May I kiss you?" he asked. "Know I will never do anything without your permission."

"I like your kisses. They make me feel hot and strange at the same time. Do you feel the same?"

"Yes, to your question and is that a yes to mine?" he asked, now touching her lips with a fingertip.

"Yes," she closed her eyes, breathing deeply then, "Yes and yes again."

He groaned softly. Emilia watched Ash's head lower to hers and his black eyelashes close. She felt the brushing warmth of his warm, moist lips over hers all the way to her toes and back. She sighed and shivered at the same time, realizing she'd never felt anything such as this. This was nothing like the way her husband kissed her.

"Are you cold," he asked, his voice husky, his eyes darkening. "You're shivering. I should get a quilt or something to warm you."

"I'm not cold."

How could she explain the sensations coursing through her and tantalizing every sense she possessed? How did she tell him the shivering was from the inferno he was building inside her, reaching all the way to her soul?

"You're shivering."

"No, not that way. I just felt quivery and good all over when you kissed me. It's not like anything I've experienced. You make me feel alive and vulnerable all at the same time."

She both felt and heard the quick ragged breath he inhaled.

"If you like, I'll kiss you some more." He whispered close to her ear his breath against her cheek sent more shivers streaming through her.

His lips moved over hers again, and again she trembled slightly in response. He nuzzled the corners of her mouth, the edge of her jaw, the delicate lobe of one ear. sipped at the pulse beating quickly in her neck.

With each motion of his head, his soft beard stroked her skin, gently, teasing, bringing her body to a wild, shimmering life. More heat rushed through her as she let him have his way with her.

"You sure you're not cold?" He chuckled, seeming to enjoy this, his light mood seemed strange to her also.

Nodding her head, she made a murmuring, purring kind of sound, a tiny mew of pleasure. "I'm sure."

"Do you like this, lass?" he asked. "Do you like the way I touch you here and here?

"Oh, yes," she whispered, her voice shaking with desire.

"Good, then slide your arms around me. We're going to do a lot of kissing tonight." His hands were at her waist as he pulled her ever closer. She liked the way his big body felt against hers as well as the warmth emanating from and seeming to slide into her.

"You know I'm not cold."

"I am." He quickly kissed her nose.

"Oh, I didn't know," she said apologetic. "I didn't think you could be cold because I'm so hot and you feel warm to me."

Emilia slid her arms around Ash and nestled in close. Her breasts pressed against him. She was surprised to find that her nipples were sensitive again. Not hurting, just... alive, responding to his kisses in ways she'd never imagined possible. Her breasts were swollen.

When she moved subtly against his chest, the odd, shivery feeling rippled through her from her breasts to her toes. It felt so good that she arched her back slightly and rubbed against him again, more slowly.

"Is there a broken spring in the couch, lass?"

His voice held a hint of amusement and she liked the way it sounded.

"No, I just like..." Her voice splintered into silence because she just didn't know how to say the words, to explain what she felt and didn't know if it was proper or not.

"What is it you like? I should know so I can do it again and again. You can tell me anything you like."

She licked suddenly dry lips and tried to swallow but found no moisture in her throat. "I..." she tried again.

"From the color of your cheeks," he said, "I think I know what you're trying to say. Let me help."

She shot him a startled look. "You know what I'm thinking and feeling too?"

"First, I want to loosen your gown a bit. I won't hurt you I promise and if you don't want me to do something then tell me. Will you do that for me, lass? Talk to me?"

She nodded, giving her permission.

His long fingers spread wide across the top of Emilia's back. As she arched into him, he dragged his chest slowly against her breasts.

Heat pummeled through her.

"Oh!" she said, startled.

"Did I hurt you?" he asked.

Only then did she realize his movements had been anything but accidental. Curious, she stared at him.

"Little lassie?" he said. "Was I too rough? Remember you said you'd tell me."

She shook her head watching him. "Blessed hell," he whispered, "You are the most beautiful woman I've ever known."

"I am?" she asked, surprised once again, astonished by his words.

"Yes, you are," he said.

The look in his eyes made Emilia's mouth go dry. She licked her lips then tried to swallow.

He watched her tongue.

"You're right," he told her. "It's time for you to learn more about the way a man and a woman should be together."

"I don't understand."

"After tonight you will. Just another kiss, that's all."

She nodded again, "Very well."

"We're both going to like this."

"You too?"

The heated glide of his mouth over hers scattered her thoughts. She forgot the question she had been going to ask. All her attention was focused on her lips and the havoc he was creating inside her. Her lips were vividly alive, hot where his tongue was touching and cool where it had passed on.

Her arms tightened around Ash until she was pressed hard against him. He helped by arching her back and rubbing her breasts over his chest again, bringing her even closer.

Her breath came in brokenly as she opened her mouth for his questing tongue. His tongue dipped beneath her upper lip, gliding, probing, circling. His teeth caught her lower lip. He tugged gently.

She made a ragged sound and opened her lips wider. His tongue was hot inside her mouth, and the taste of his kiss was sweet beyond bearing. She didn't want this moment to ever end.

She sought to tell him how good it felt, but she didn't want to end the sweetness. So, she gave him back the kiss, sliding her tongue over his, probing the sultry corners of his mouth then catching his tongue delicately between her teeth.

His breath came out with a hoarse sound.

Instantly, she released him.

"I didn't mean," she said quickly. "I don't know anything about this kissing stuff. You're the only one I've ever really kissed. I'm beginning to think my husband doesn't count. Are you all right?" she asked unhappily. "I didn't intend to hurt you."

"You didn't."

His voice was husky and his eyes were a smoldering silver-green between his nearly closed lashes.

"You groaned." She accused.

"You've been making sweet little noises since my lips first touched yours."

"I was?"

"Yes."

"That was the same?"

"Hush now," Ash said, lowering his mouth over hers again. "Tonight, we're just going to kiss."

"Mmmm."

After a few moments she forgot all about what was and wasn't kissing. The feelings cascading through her were delicious and so new. So was the taste of Ash, his heat, the textures of his beard and lips, tongue and teeth.

It was kiss for kiss, a longing so intense she could barely breathe. She didn't know he had pulled the sleeves of her gown down her arms and her slightly covered breasts felt the coolness of the air.

"You said just kissing," she accused, looking at her exposed body, yet she didn't want him to stop.

"It's hard to kiss through your gown."

"I'm not wearing a dress over my mouth."

"Kissing your mouth isn't my intention."

She stared at him. His eyes were pale green fire against the dark color of his skin. Each time his head moved, candlelight shimmered over his short black beard. His lips were red from the pressure of their shared kisses.

114

"You want to stop kissing me?"

"No," he said. "I want to keep on kissing you and kissing you until the honey flows and you're as soft as I am hard and we..."

With a sharp breath, Ash closed his eyes, his body tense above hers.

Emilia waited, watching him with wide eyes then she was watching his mouth.

"That's the idea," he said huskily. "Watch me. Watch us...kissing. Watch the way my lips close over yours."

His lips and beard were silky against her ear, her neck, the pulse beating just beneath her skin. When his tongue probed the hollow at the base of her throat, her breath caught. He sucked on her skin, bit her tenderly and shared the ripple of response that swept through her.

She wasn't at all sure what was happening, only that beneath her chemise, her nipples were firm rosy crowns standing up against the thin fabric.

He bent down; his lips parted over one veiled nipple.

"Ash?" she asked uncertainly

"Just kissing," he reminded her, His voice deep.

"Ash?" Donal asked. "You there?"

Donal stepped into the room and almost immediately he backed out.

Chapter Five

"Give us a minute," Ash called out, cursing the man he called friend for longer that he could remember. "I'll be right there."

"My apologies." Donal said as he quickly backed from the room. "Sorry I interrupted but this is important. Too important to put off another minute and especially until morning. I'll wait in the foyer."

A few minutes later, Ashford appeared, a grim expression on his face. "Come into the parlor. Would you like whiskey and what is it that is so important you interrupted my evening."

"Sorry about that, didn't know you were involved with anyone."

Somehow, he wasn't surprised to see his good friend with Emilia. "She's a beautiful lass."

"Emilia, yes she is becoming very important to me," Ash said, heading into the parlor. "It's just as well you interrupted. I was about to take this too far tonight, further than I intended, further than she was ready. Anyway, what can I do and what brings you here?"

Donal accepted the whiskey Ash handed him before sitting down, thinking how surreal this all was. "You remember Katrina Madison? Seems she's resurfaced and is making accusations."

Ash sipped slowly then, his eyes seeming to shutter. "There is no way I can forget that little whore. She's always wanted to sink her claws into you. For a while I prayed daily that would never happen then she disappeared from Glasgow, and I think the entire city breathed a sigh of relief."

"She might have succeeded in that, sinking her claws into me," Donal said, watching his friend for his reactions. "She's in town and it seems she's already putting an edge to her visit which has included

Daryl."

"Why?" Ash leaned toward him, his forearms on his legs, clearly interested in his dilemma. "Why would she still be interested in a man who has made it clear he doesn't want anything to do with her? When she left, I was sure you told her she would never be in your life."

"I did."

Donal finished the glass, tipping his head back, letting the liquid burn down his throat before he grabbed the bottle from the end table and poured another. He wanted to knock down the entire bottle and drown in it. "Told Daryl she was pregnant with my child. Then she implied I would leave Daryl for her and that Daryl was just my latest piece of muslin. She's insane if she believes that would happen."

Liquid spewed from Ash's mouth. "What?"

"Katrina confronted Daryl this afternoon in the bakery. Told her to relay the message to me that she was pregnant and I was the father. Daryl would have told me anyway, but the woman had no business talking to Daryl. I want to make sure Katrina understands clearly that Daryl is off limits to her." Blessed hell, but the woman could create havoc in his life like no other.

"It's not true is it? You didn't sleep with her, did you?"

"Not that I can recall." There was a memory niggling in his mind, something he chose to forget but obviously coming back to haunt him.

"What exactly does that mean?" Ash poured himself more whiskey and topped off Donal's glass before sitting down. "Think I'm going to need this before the evening is over."

"You recollect the night about two months ago when I told you I didn't remember what happened?" Donal asked, staring into his glass, trying for the courage to deal with this new situation. "I was drugged. I know it. We both know I never overindulge and this was different. I remember vague outlines of people and sensations I had no control over."

"I remember. You didn't tell me much though."

"Probably because I was too embarrassed by the one event I could remember distinctly." Blessed hell, but he recalled the evening began at a ball given by one of his best friends. He didn't want to attend the event but felt obligated to support the friend. Why Katrina attended or was even invited he didn't have any idea. Everyone he knew kept her at a distance.

"So, tell me now, everything you remember."

Ash sat back, seemingly relaxed but Donal knew the man was soaking in all he was telling him. Unfortunately, there were a lot of missing details.

"I need to talk to her. Problem is she won't tell the truth," He sighed heavily, thinking he would so much rather be with Daryl in that big bed he bought for her apartment and what he hoped would be many nightly visits. "Need to take the offensive before she can turn this into something that will be devilishly hard to get out of."

"You're awfully vague. What do you remember? Think hard about everything, what you can recollect might save you from this nightmare."

Donal ran his hands through his hair, muttering under his breath and feeling nearly helpless at the moment. He didn't like the feeling. "All I remember is waking up in her bed, both of us naked." He was shaking his head, distressed by the memory he'd successfully, until this evening, been able to put in the darkest corner of his head.

"I see but you don't know if you actually fucked her, do you? What do you expect Katrina to do? Is she wanting you to marry her or just financially take care of the child when it is born?"

"I've no idea. All I know is that I'm not going to be forced into a marriage with her, child or no child." As long as he could put this off, he meant to.

"It's possible she is not carrying your child? Possible she's not carrying any child at all. Over the years she must have taken precautions since she has no bastards," Ash said.

"That we know of. A woman can hide these things if she is smart and if she is careful. You ken as well as I do, they can move to another country, have the child then put the babe up for adoption, no one the wiser."

He thought about the times so long ago that he might have sired a child with her. They were both young and unthinking. He always thanked god there was no baby but now he paused in thought, wondering what the real truth was. He could very well have a bastard somewhere.

"Her family does have the funds to protect her. They also have the power to make your life miserable if you don't wed her," Ash reminded him. "If you mean to confront the woman, you should be careful what you say. Construct the meeting in your mind before you challenge the woman. You can't let her blindside you again."

"That's why I need to see her. I'll know just by looking into her eyes if she is speaking the truth or not. He had always been able to tell when she lied. In this case, lie or not, he would never be leg-shackled to the woman for life. Stopping this before it could take on a momentum of its own was a necessity."

"Not a good idea," Ash said, roughing his hair with his hands. "By going to her you will give her power she shouldn't have. In a sense you will be acknowledging there could be some truth to her words."

"Then what should I do?" Donal asked, understanding exactly what Ash was going to advise.

Something that wasn't going to happen, not because he didn't want it to happen but because Daryl didn't want to commit to him.

"You should marry Daryl tonight or get her pregnant. Either scenario will serve your purpose. Tonight would be the best for both. Go to her, take her virginity and sire a babe. The MacTavish clan has a great deal of power also. That fact could work in your favor. Flynt will expect you to wed her immediately."

"Perhaps that would work, but at the moment Daryl doesn't want to marry me or anyone."

Good lord, how did he come to care so much for a woman who wanted him in every way except marriage?

"And conceivably you can convince her to change her mind."

"So far, I certainly haven't been able to do it."

He understood passion and how it can be used. Daryl's passion was innocent and straight from the heart. Forcing her into something she wouldn't agree to willingly was, not in his mind, the way to begin a life together.

Ash shrugged, looking as if the answer was simple, "Seduce her. I know you can do that, feasibly to some degree you already have."

"You're right. I've already done that."

"So, she could be pregnant."

"You're grasping at straws. No way Daryl is pregnant, much to my regret."

He laughed softly at the irony of all this. A child with her would be heaven sent. It's what he discovered a few short weeks ago that he wanted almost as much as he wanted her.

"Took precautions?" Ash chuckled. "You take precautions with the woman you love and not the whore who has plagued your life since the two of you were teens."

"I didn't take her virginity, not that she wasn't willing to gift me with it. You know as well as I do that isn't the way to treat a woman despite the passion and desire between the two of us. Although the more I'm with her the harder it is to control the things I'm feeling."

"So, back to the problem at hand," Ash said, quirking one eyebrow upward.

"Like I told you, I don't remember anything about that night, just the morning and waking up beside her without a stitch of clothing on my body. I would never have willing done that nor would I have had sex with her."

"Think, is there anything at all you can recall about the morning after or the night before that would be of use here?"

Donal thought, his brain seeming to be in a scramble with no coherent thoughts revealing themselves. He'd spent the last two months trying to forget everything about that night. Courting Daryl helped with that feat. He believed he had truly forgotten the horror and now this.

Now Katrina was back, threatening his future with false accusations, at least he prayed they were false.

What to do?

When he looked up, "The sheets were clean that morning, nothing at all to indicate we had sex but of course if it came to that, it would still be my word against hers. "Who would people believe?" Blessed hell, but he spent his entire life keeping his family name from gossip and scandal.

Now this.

"That's good though. Remembering something like that should give you confidence to move forward. It tells you that even in a drugged state you did not have sex with her."

"I won't marry that woman. If she is pregnant, the child belongs to someone else." He was shaking his head even as his stomach was rolling with nausea at the thought of a life with that woman.

"No, but she can make your existence difficult. Either she is not pregnant at all or she is and is desperate to give her child a father. I don't think under normal circumstances, she would go after you. There must be something else spurring her to act."

"I know, that's the surprise. Even though she seems to lift her skirts for any man who asks, I've always had a soft spot for her."

He did, until now. Now she was threatening a future with a wonderful woman. It was something he'd never foreseen until he first kissed Daryl and now discovered she was as interested in him as he was in her.

Well, almost as interested.

"Do you think you can pay Katrina off? Offer money in return for leaving the country or at least not claiming you are the father when you distinctly are not?" Ash asked, with the hint of a chuckle. He held up his hands. "I ken it's not something to laugh about, but you have to admit there is a tiny bit of humor in this."

"No humor to me," Donal said, still racking his mind for the right words to get himself out of this without further repercussions. "I'm trying my damndest to sweet-talk Daryl into marrying me and haven't had any luck. Then Katrina comes along threatening my future."

"Again, I ask you, have you tried seduction with Daryl? It might go a long ways in convincing her to wed you. I've heard you're smooth and always give pleasure. Wait. Maybe that is why Katrina is after you again. For the pleasure."

"I spent the last three days charming Daryl, and she's still adamant that she will never wed. Does not want a man to control her life, ever. I've never given her any indication that I would tell her what she could do and what she could not, even though I've had to bite my tongue numerous times."

"Maybe you should try telling her that you're just pointing her in the right direction when you tell her how you feel about something. I believe you have done that. I've heard you."

Donal frowned, anger and frustration at both situations began to boil over. "You don't understand what kind of woman she is and neither did I. She's a woman like no other, except maybe her sisters and Hope. They have a confidence about them. Thinking they can make the best decisions, even when said decision gets them into trouble."

"I've heard the MacTavish girls were brought up more like men than women and their husbands coddle them, letting them make choices. They work as well, making their own money."

"You're right. Bliss earns a lot of money with her paintings and now I do believe Daryl's bakery is going to keep her self-sufficient. She doesn't need me for monetary purposes and that pleases me. When she finally comes to her senses and tells me yes, I'll know it's because she loves me and not what I can give her."

"You need to figure out why Bliss married when she didn't have to go that course and try to use that knowledge to reason with Daryl. Knowledge is always a helpful tool to use when debating with a female. Make sure she knows that whatever money she earns is hers and hers alone. Set up a bank account in her name."

"Well, that's a bit ironic. Bliss gave birth to twins just after she and Broc said their vows. I don't want that for Daryl. I won't force her hand that way."

"So, you've seduced her but you haven't made love to her," Ash said a slight smirk on his face.

"I know you. I interrupted but you feel the same as I do and I'm assuming you wouldn't have said what you did if you weren't glad I intruded on you and Emilia. She means more to you than anyone else," Donal said.

"True and she's been through a lot in her short life. I had no idea she had her son when she was only thirteen years old."

"What?" Donal's heart nearly stopped at that news. "I knew she wasn't very old now, but that would make her only twenty-one and she's had four children. Not mathematically impossible but..." He was left with no more words.

"Yes, it's a long story and this is not the time and place to tell it, but I want to marry Emilia. If she'll have me that is, however, she is also negative toward marriage but for far different reasons than Daryl. It isn't control she's worried about. It's the pain of making love. Even her husband used her selfishly for his own purposes."

"Act the gentleman and teach her about love which I'm beginning to suspect she's never experienced and you will have earned her love as well as her acceptance of your proposal of marriage. Teach her there doesn't have to be pain only pleasure."

"I think I've changed my mind. We should confront Katrina. Help her understand that you won't be bullied into marrying her. This cannot continue and the longer she has to spread rumors around town, the worse it will be for you, even though her reputation is anything but stellar."

"What if the babe is mine? What do I do then?"

Despite what he remembered, he didn't want to leave a child of his without a father. He cared too deeply about children.

Ash was shaking his head. "You've no way of knowing that and odds are against it. So, don't even go down that path. If she is with child, it will be her responsibility and hers alone to parent the babe."

Donal inhaled a long and very deep breath of air looking for answers and finding none. "I understand all of that. While understanding doesn't make this easier, I'm relatively sure I'm not the father."

"Do you have any idea where Katrina might be living?" Ash asked, standing then seemingly ready to confront the woman.

"No, not really. My first guess would be at her parent's home, particularly if she's trying to implicate me in her pregnancy. She will go to her parents for encouragement as well as support."

"They kicked her out two years ago. Don't know why but I certainly have my guesses," Ash said. "You believe they will support her now?"

"If she has convinced them I'm the father of the child she carries then..." he wasn't sure how to finish. Then they would make sure their responsibility was transferred to him.

"If they believed you were the father, they would take her back in a heartbeat," Ash said. "Her parents are good and caring folks who have been appalled at their daughter's behavior for years. This would give her a new level of respectability she never had."

"That's why they would jump at the chance to have the rumors about their daughter's behavior put to rest. They would think if she is wed, she would no longer be dallying with other wives' husbands."

"They would," Ash agreed, "but it wouldn't be true. She has this unending need for sex."

"Should we try the Madison residence first?" Donal asked, setting his glass on the end table and standing. With a heavy sigh, "This might be the longest night of my life."

"After that," Ash shrugged, "maybe we can ascertain a clue from her parents."

They rode through town. Donal's heart was in his throat, his hands trembling while his nerves seemed to be on edge, rattling. This might not be in his best interest as Ash pointed out earlier, but what other recourses did he have? He wanted to put an end to this before it escalated into something more difficult to finish.

When they reached the Madison home it was dark, only one light shone in an upstairs window. A brisk wind swayed the tree limbs and the moon sent eerie shadows dancing on the ground. Down the road a dog barked then an answering howl.

"It doesn't appear the family is in residence, but who do you think is in the room with the one shining light?" Donal asked, his guess went to Katrina, "and what is she doing up so late in the evening?"

"My thoughts? Katrina is with a lover. If you catch her with a man in her bed, her case goes downhill from there. The child she carries, if she is pregnant, most certainly could be anyone's. Everyone recognizes that a man doesn't marry a woman on hearsay that she carries his child."

"I have a witness in you. Should we knock and announce ourselves or should we just go inside?"

Donal's gut reaction told him if the door was unlocked, the best course of action was not to announce themselves.

"Under the current circumstances I would say you've every right to walk inside. She has given you that right by claiming you are the father of her child."

Donal inhaled long and deep, searching the home for other lights, an indication someone besides Katrina might be in residence. There was none. For a moment he battled with politeness and the notion of striding into someone else's home without introduction was wrong.

"You ready?" Ash asked a wealth of skepticism in his voice. "Nothing going to happen if we stand out here."

Donal smiled a moment. Ash had a way of getting to the point. "You're right of course. Don't know if I'll ever be ready to challenge Katrina but this has to be done."

He looked to the sky. It was a dark sky dotted with glimmering stars. The moon was nearly a full moon tonight. For a brief moment he smiled, recalling last night on the porch with Daryl in his arms. The weather had been much the same but he had been content, so unlike tonight, his nerves threatening to splinter apart.

Night sounds abounding more of course in the country than here. Still, he recognized the croak of a frog and the hoot of an animal.

"You coming or not?"

"Coming," Donal stepped forward at the front door, his hand raised. He hesitated for a moment. By doing this he had so very much to gain.

The door was unlocked and once inside, Donal looked around. It was much the same as it had been over ten years ago except the furniture looked worn and outdated. There was no one on the first floor, just the one light shining from upstairs. It had not come from Katrina's room but the master chamber, and that thought did give him pause. It would not be well done of them to find Katrina's parents in bed.

What to do?

He didn't think his parents would have the light on this late at night. They were in their fifties, he supposed, or sixties. What were married folk like at that age. For a moment he smiled, hoping he would still be making love to his wife for as long as they lived.

"You going up there sometime tonight?" Ash asked. "Or are you going to stand down here and gaze up the staircase with a strange look on your face."

"I was just thinking about something."

"I'm guessing it has to do with Daryl. Let's get this over with and you can go see her."

"She'll be asleep."

"If you keep stalling, she will be up and baking the first loaves of bread for the day," Ash said, reprimanding him.

Starting for the steps, Donal was now eager to confront the woman who was trying to stand in the way of his dreams. He reached the bedroom door, hand on the knob and having one last moment of doubt. He paused.

He let the door swing open, his mouth dropping in shock at the site in front of him. Unable to form coherent thoughts let alone words, he stood frozen in time for a few seconds.

Then, "Katrina, I see you haven't wasted any time. One man not enough for you now, it takes three to satisfy you?" Donal asked, a chuckle of relief emanating from him.

Ash stood beside him, unmoving and Donal was surprised Ash didn't say something caustic. The site of Katrina in the middle of three men, each doing something erotic to her body, a way of having sex he never imagined.

She was still beautiful, he had to admit, full breast with rosy tipped nipples that would fill his hands and feminine curves that would tempt most men. When he first entered the room, she had been on her hands and knees, two men beneath her touching and caressing, the third behind her, thrusting into her.

Katrina was, as were the men, shameless. He'd never seen any of the men before. Of course, Glasgow was a large thriving town and he didn't know everyone who lived here.

When she realized there were intruders in the room, she sat down between the men who were still fondling her. "I see you came to join us. Five men, I daresay I've never had that privilege before." She turned to her friends, "Do any of you mind additions to our group." In any case she didn't give them time to answer. "Why are you really here, Donal?"

Inwardly, he smiled, pleased he witnessed this. "Thought we should talk but what I'm seeing here speaks volumes."

He laughed, feeling such a weight had just been taken off his chest. No remorse, no more second-guessing where that night with

Katrina was concerned. Cat-like she would land on her feet despite an unforeseen pregnancy. "I'm pleased now. Ash and I will leave so you can enjoy the rest of your evening with your handsome paramours."

She tossed a pillow at him and he laughed so thrilled with the way the evening had turned out. He felt lighthearted and ready to tackle the job of convincing Daryl to marry him.

"This isn't the last you'll hear from me. I am pregnant." She pushed her hair from her face and away from her body. "You will be the father."

He realized just how ugly she was. There was nothing beautiful about Katrina except her face and the ugliness of her mind and inner self overshadowed everything else.

"Perhaps, we've yet to see, but the odds of it being my child are slim to nothing. I didn't even fuck you the night you drugged and disrobed me without my consent. True, I woke in your bed but the sheets were spotless, devoid of my seed or anyone else's. I thank my lucky stars there wasn't another man or two in bed with us."

"Let's go," Ash clapped him on the shoulder, laughing.

As they left the premises, "I'm sure that isn't the last you will hear from her. Now, are you going to see Daryl or wait until the morning?"

Donal pulled out his pocket watch. "It's going to have to wait until morning. I know she wants to go to work and heaven knows we didn't get much sleep the last few nights."

"Weel it's home then. I do need to speak with Emilia about tonight and reassure her that you won't kick her out because of what you saw."

"I couldn't do that. It's your home."

They pulled up in front of his townhouse. Cam confronted him, "Donal, there is trouble. Just thought you should know."

He turned, "What is it?"

"Flynt has gone missing and Hope is worried. It's not like him to vanish without a trace."

~ * ~

Exhausted yet feeling such excitement and anger within her body, Daryl knew she wouldn't be able to sleep. When she received the note inviting her to visit with Hope and her sisters, she decided a chat would do her an enormous amount of good. The night was still young.

She missed her sisters and the talks they always had. While she still had Lacie to visit with, it seemed the only time she saw her youngest sister was when she came to the bakery to work on her books. Her older sisters were all busy with their husbands and children.

When she arrived, the place was in chaos. The men were gone, looking for Flynt who seemed to have vanished without leaving a trace. It appeared the women were done sighing and complaining about the fact they were sitting in a warm room, sipping tea while their men were in the cold hunting for Hope's husband. None understood why they were left the job of waiting.

"Well," Bliss said with a heavy lament. "As usual the men are off doing something while we wait in terror of what news they will bring back. We shouldn't take this any longer."

"What do you think they will say if we venture out on our own? We can take Munroe and the men who are guarding the house," Chelsea said, tapping her finger on the arm of the chair she was sitting on. "They would complain of course, but doing something would be so much better than sitting here."

"If we took the men as our body guards, they would have nothing to complain about," Bliss said with hooded eyes.

"True enough, and I don't have a man who would complain or lecture me about the dangers," Lacie said, grinning. "It will be just like old times when we used to do exactly what we wanted when we wanted. Flynt was usually none the wiser or he didn't care."

"Flynt would order us to stay put and we would head off in whatever direction we thought would be the most fun in complete defiance of his wishes," Daryl said, laughing along with her younger sister.

Her laughter was forced. She did think of Donal and how he might feel. In his head, he would object but verbally he might even encourage her to go in hopes she would do the opposite. It was late and dark. He'd already lectured about the delivery of the baked goods. She touched her cheek where she'd been hit. Second thoughts assailed her. Women were more vulnerable than men, she had no choice but to acknowledge that.

Grams spent the evening watching the sisters and the way they spoke to each other. Daryl was sure there was a wealth of words she needed to say. Yet Grams had a way of letting them make their own decisions where Flynt just bullied them until they did the opposite. She supposed Flynt was the reason she acted the way she did around Donal.

"I'm really glad Cook remembered the ginger cookies. I do my best thinking with cookies and tea. You girls need to stay cautious and alert. Think before you act or even react. Don't assume the fact that Munroe and a few others are with you will keep you safe. Men can fail also."

"What have you figured out, Catherine," Hope asked. "If it's to stay in the house and do nothing, you'll most likely have an argument on your hands. None of us want to sit on our hands when Flynt is missing."

"Don't be obtuse. That's not what I said. You should go in pairs." Catherine waved her hand in the air. You, Bliss and Chelsea, will need to stop home to check on your babies. While you all were chatting, I made sure the stable boy and Cook's little boy were agreeable to going with you. They would love the coin they would earn and that way you can get messages back to me. Don't know how to get in touch with the men though. Perhaps they have a plan of sorts. Most likely they've coordinated between themselves. I'm sure we'll hear something soon. When they find Flynt, I'll figure out some way to let you all know. But if you find Flynt first, you'll just have to get him home and wait for the men to return."

"We have to be back before the men or there could be hell to pay," Bliss said. "Unfortunately, we have no way of knowing when they will return."

"We can always use Hope's tactics to get them off kilter," Daryl said, thinking of Donal's lips on hers and how he caressed every part of her.

"What would that be?" Chelsea asked.

Daryl laughed. She had been using those tactics on Donal the last few days and they did work very nicely, always set him a bit off kilter. "Why, Hope stares at Flynt's mouth and it seems to leave him speechless."

"Yes, and if that doesn't work, I stare at his crotch. He calls it blatant seduction and that my lust for him is always getting the better of me," Hope said with a small chuckle, her eyes shining as if she was remembering things.

Grams bit into a cookie nearly choking from the direction of the conversation. "You girls are going to drive your poor men crazy. Perhaps you should try to be more biddable."

"Crazy with lust," Hope said. "If he never figures out that I love him, I'll always have this lust thing to captivate him. Grams, there is no fun in biddable. We have to keep them on their toes or they will start taking us for granted."

"He won't get bored with you," Daryl said, yet she knew using that ploy would never bind Donal to her if she didn't marry him.

He needed an heir, had told her as much. If she continued to say no to his proposals, he would look somewhere else for a wife.

What to do?

"Better not," Bliss warned. "He'll have you on your back, your skirts tossed before you can say nay. If you mean to keep from marrying the poor man, it's best you don't get with child. He'll have an argument to hold over your head for the rest of your life. He won't want to... well he won't want to give up his child."

"You are playing with fire," Chelsea warned.

"True enough, I need to take care. Not sure exactly what I want where Donal is concerned except that I remain single."

Part of that was a lie. She knew she wanted Donal in her life and as time went on, she wasn't all that sure she did want to stay single. He had never been overbearing or autocratic with her.

"There will be time enough for you to reconsider all your options unless you become pregnant. Donal is wealthy enough and holds more power than you. He could force you to give up the baby. I seriously doubt if Flynt would step in in your defense if you chose not to wed."

"Donal could do that and do you really believe Flynt would be so callused?" Daryl asked.

All of this was so strange. The very idea a man could take her baby away shook her to the core. It wasn't right, simply not right.

"Well yes, Donal could do that as well as make your life miserable if he resented what you're taking away from him, a marriage with the woman he loves. He's clearly smitten with you, and he's not a man who would allow a woman to rule his life. He would do what he pleased and what he deemed right."

Suddenly, the chatter ceased and eerie quiet filled the room. All the sisters seemed to focus their attention on Hope. In these few seconds she turned white as a ghost, her body visibly shaking.

"He's hurt," Hope whispered.

"What is it?" It seemed everyone spoke in unison.

"I don't know, a premonition of sorts. I saw Flynt in a small room, unable to move."

"Where?"

"I don't know. It's cold and he's bleeding. He needs help but we can't do that until we figure out where he is."

Broc strode into the room, his face grim, etched with lines of concern. "Didn't find him." His voice was gruff. "No one I talked to has seen him." He seemed to notice the coats and scarves that had been set out. "You ladies weren't planning on searching for him, now were you?" He looked at Bliss pointedly, "I recognize the guilty expression. Well, it's a good thing I got here before you left."

"She and Chelsea were going to check up on the babes," Catherine said with a stern look pointed in Broc's direction. "You need not be getting high and mighty with your wife. She has hers and your best interest at heart."

"You don't need to defend my wife. She's very good at doing that herself. That might be part of the truth but not all of it. In any case, without further information we don't have a clue where to search. Leaving the house would be a waste of precious time."

"The room was in the seamier part of town, I think. It looked old and a bit dilapidated, dirty as well. We could start by looking in the slums," Hope said. "I want to come with you."

The conversation continued in much the same vein until Donal and Cam entered. They exchanged information before leaving again. Once more the women were left alone. Hope rose walking from one room to the other, picking up things, setting them down until she finally sat down.

"It's time we did something besides sit and wait. It's clear to me the men are getting nothing accomplished," Hope said, seemingly at her wits end.

Bliss stood and asked, "Does everyone have their gun? If so, we are going to implement Grams plan and we're going hunting." She turned to her sister-in-law. "Get the stable boy and cook's son. I'm sure if you think hard enough you can remember some clue that will get us to your husband."

The girls busied themselves, getting everything they needed to make this undertaking safe. This time they didn't split up, deciding to stay together. Daryl and Lacie rode behind, silent, seeming immersed in their thoughts. They wound through the small streets of Glasgow as the evening slowly changed to dawn. Bawdy songs poured out of bars while drunken men staggered down the street and whores posed in hopes of finding a client.

Once again Daryl touched her cheek, recalling the moment where all control of the situation had been taken from her. Her body trembled as a slow glide of fear spiraled through her settling in her stomach. While she understood Donal wouldn't appreciate what she was doing, the choice had been taken from her. Their safety depended on numbers.

She wished now this evening had turned out differently, that she had stayed at home and Katrina never appeared in her life, threatening her future with a man she was falling in love with. Thinking about seeing Donal tonight, well this morning, because it was well past midnight, what would he say or do?

"It's this one," Hope stopped her horse, dismounting quickly. "I can feel him and it's as if some angel guided me here."

Reluctantly, Daryl followed behind her sisters, her nerves

splintering every second they moved forward. She felt as if she couldn't breathe.

When they stepped inside the small room, Flynt was huddled in the back, a man standing over him. Flynt was swigging whiskey.

"Let's finish this and we can be on our way. I'm eager to get home. Need to do that before my wife comes looking for me," Flynt said with a bit of a chuckle if Daryl wasn't mistaken. At the moment Daryl didn't see this man as a threat.

Too late, big brother. Not only did Hope leave the house to search for you without your permission but she brought all of us. She has found you. Daryl's thoughts were in a jumbled mess.

"You're not going anywhere with my husband," Hope said, waving the gun at the pair.

All the sisters stepped into the room, standing side by side in solidarity behind Hope.

"Unhand my brother," Bliss said, the pistol in her hand as she appeared ready to use it. "I'll shoot you."

Flynt grinned then his expression turned to a deep scowl as he began to understand the women had defied any common sense. "He's helping me, Hope, and I've promised Kelly a job. He's earned what I promised, so let him finish."

"My gun is on him."

"As is mine," Lacie said.

"As is mine as well," Daryl said, but her gun hand was not all that steady. She believed her brother, knowing he wouldn't be swigging whiskey if this man was not a friend.

Lacie left with the stable boy to bring a carriage for Flynt.

Hope sat beside Flynt, pulling him into her arms before whispering, "Should I stare at your mouth now or when I get you home? Perhaps your crotch would be a better place to fix my gaze."

"Best do it now. When we get home, I'm going to put you over my knee and thrash you soundly." His mutterings seemed to make Hope laugh.

"Liar, now you owe me a kiss," She touched his face, running her hands down his chest as if trying to make sure he was alive and well.

Daryl smiled inside, realizing more every second about the subtleties of marriage and the seeming control men tried to have over their women. They had unadulterated control only if the woman allowed it. Her sisters and Hope obviously did not give them that power.

"Best we get home now," Bliss said, looking around her as if like the others she was sure the other men would turn up any second. "I for one want to be nestled in my bed when Broc returns."

The girls agreed. They left together, but in time they would have to go their separate ways. Daryl said goodbye to Lacie as they parted at a corner near the bakery. She was proud of the fact they found Flynt when the men didn't but she was also apprehensive about her next meeting with Donal.

When he left her this evening, he'd been withdrawn, aloof. She understood his mood had something to do with Katrina, but he didn't really say how he felt about the woman or her. He did come to help the others find Flynt but she also knew that had nothing to do with her.

Looking up the stairs to her apartment, she sighed. Tonight, it seemed there were a lot of stairs and a long ways to go. She was exhausted. Slowly she climbed, glancing over her shoulder a few times as if she sensed Donal might be there waiting for her.

He wasn't.

Once inside, she slipped from her clothing, leaving her shift on. She didn't have the energy to put on a nightdress. She nestled into her bed, clutching her pillow tightly to her chest. Sleeping was impossible. She punched her pillow turned this way then that.

Nothing she did allowed her to fall asleep.

"Daryl."

"Hmmm..." She turned into the warmth and comfort she knew was Donal.

She must have fallen asleep sometime. She stiffened knowing the lecture would come soon. He was lying beside her, comforting her but this wouldn't end pleasantly, she was sure of that fact.

She bolted upright, her body shaking with urgency. This had been her means to independence and she was slowly failing, leaving the work to other people. "The bakery. I have to go now." Trying to climb from the bed he stopped her. "Donal, please."

"Everything is fine downstairs. Both Justine and Emilia are hard at work. Did you get any sleep last night?" He paused, looking into her eyes. "No, I didn't think so. Neither did I."

"Just do it now. Tell me how stupid and careless I've been. How I put my life in danger and that I should never do such a foolish thing again," she told him, attempting to push away from him.

Yet he held her tight. While he wasn't seducing, just holding, she felt no comfort. In his arms she trembled, worry and fatigue swamping her.

"It's alright, *mo chroi*. I'm not going to lecture you about anything. It seems you understand the danger you put yourself in. I was terrified when I learned what you and the others did. While Flynt was pleased he'd been found, he was also petrified and angry with Hope. We all were."

"I'm sorry. I did think about the other night, but they were all going to be there. I did almost say no, but the more of us the better, don't you think? We would not have undertaken the mission if you and others had been successful. Hope was sure she knew where he was."

"I don't want to talk about any of this right now. Just let me hold you for a few hours. You in my arms is what I need, a reassurance you were not hurt." His voice seemed to break on the words. "No matter how many of you there were, you would never be able to overpower a determined man. Sometime I will show you just how easy it would have been to change the scenario."

She closed her eyes then, felt the warmth of his big body and the security he offered, unsure of what he could show her that would have her convinced that truly one man could have overpowered them. His heartbeats as well as his breaths were steady and strong. There would never be anyone else for her. So why did she resist marriage to this man?

"Donal," she paused, pulling back from him, "What did you do last night? You know, before Flynt went missing."

"Another time." His hand rested on her derrière, pulling her closer. She felt his arousal yet he didn't seem interested in anything but holding her. "We will talk later."

"I should go down to work." She knew he would let her go when he was ready and not a moment sooner.

"You need to sleep. The others understand," he murmured softly. "When I fall asleep, I'd like you to be in my arms. It's something I got used to while you were healing then the days we spent in the country."

Yet the way his hands stroked her there would be no way she would sleep. With each caress she shivered with the growing pleasure. "As do you, I assume." She sighed, touching his beard with her fingers. The softness always amazed her. "We've never been very good at sleeping when you've held me in your arms."

"No, we haven't but that is going to have to change sometime. It might as well be right now, this morning."

"The sun is shining maybe we can take a nap this afternoon. You know, you at your place and me here."

She heard his chuckle. "I don't ever want to let you out of my sight again."

He smoothed her hair, ran a hand down her back.

Even though he wasn't trying, he was reminding her of the fire he stoked within and her soul depth need for him. It was the gentleness as well as the knowledge of what he could do with his lips and hands when he set his mind to the task.

"That's not possible as I'm sure you know."

Even though he didn't want to make love, her body had something different in mind. She would not resist, could never say nay to him and the wonderful pleasure she knew waited for her.

"Doesn't mean I can't try."

"Donal."

"What?"

"I really need to get up now. You don't want to make love but..."

"I've made you want me and I haven't even been trying," he chuckled, rising on his arms to look at her. "Do what you think you need to do. I won't stop you."

Watching, he let her go then. Quickly she dressed, keeping her back to him but when she finally turned, he was lying on his back, one arm over his eyes. He did appear exhausted and she knew this was the best she could do for him.

"Are you staying here?"

She caught her lower lip beneath her teeth, uncertainty swamping her. She needed the knowledge that he was upstairs waiting for her, but with Donal anything could change in a moment.

"If you don't mind. Maybe you can bring some food up in another hour or two. We do need to talk. I don't have the energy to do it now, and it's not just about your early morning adventure that bears discussing. It's more about Katrina as well as the things Ash and I discovered about her. You need to learn everything."

She smiled, realizing he was truly fatigued. She didn't think she'd ever seen Donal this way. Slowly, she walked to him and bending over placed a gentle kiss on his lips.

I love you.

"Sleep then," she turned to leave. "I'll bring up food as soon as possible."

"You do tempt me though." His voice was deep and husky with the desire and passion she was coming to recognize.

Quietly, she closed the door. Downstairs, both Justine and Emilia were hard at work. The scents coming from the ovens were heavenly. Her stomach rumbled. She was hungry and exhausted as well.

After pouring herself a cup of coffee, she grabbed a blueberry scone from the counter and sat down to eat, paying careful attention to the women hard at work.

"Seems I keep showing up late for work and the two of you have just about everything for the day finished. I promise you this will change."

"You should go on upstairs and be with your man. Times too short to waste a second," Emilia said, smiling at her. "We don't have any worries about you getting your hand back into the baking. It's your business and when all the troubles are gone, you will be here right beside us."

She knew Emilia's words were true and if anyone could attest to that, Emilia could.

"You're probably right, but he needs to sleep and..."

She stopped then, realizing she was about to admit to a relationship with him other than just courting. Yet she'd told these two nearly everything, just not any intimate details. She was sure they could guess though.

"It's alright, dear. I assumed you and Donal were intimate. There is always this look in lovers' eyes that tell the world how they feel about each other," Justine said before turning her attention to Emilia, "It's the same look I see in Emilia's eyes when she looks at Ashford and he returns the sentiment. It's obvious to anyone who is paying attention they are in love with each other and no one else in the world matters."

"You're in love with Ashford?" Daryl asked, smiling at the thought. This was something she'd like to celebrate. "I'm glad. He's a nice caring man and he deserves to be happy with a woman such as you."

For a moment, Emilia looked away then, "Yes, I think I am. We... last night Donal interrupted. I'm glad he did but I think Ash was going to make love to me. I dinna ken if I'm ready for that yet. I think it would have been impossible for me to say no to him. He made me feel things..."

"And you like the way he touched you?" Daryl asked, pleased with the news. "That's a very good thing."

"I did, and his kisses they made me feel ways I've never felt before. I would not have told him no. I ken it now."

"Well, he better ask you to marry him soon before he takes any more liberties with your body," Justine said with a huff then a look at Daryl. "Both of you need to take care where your man is concerned. They have nothing to lose but a woman—a woman can lose all she holds dear and sometimes more." Justine seemed to be talking about herself for a moment.

"I think Ash is going to ask me to marry him. He already apologized for going too far. He admitted it was a good thing Donal interrupted us or he would have made love to me then regretted the deed after the fact. Ash also told me he planned on waiting until the wedding night before he introduced me to a woman's pleasure. I'm beginning to think he is a most unusual man."

"So, Donal interrupted," she sighed, thinking of her man upstairs, "well it must have been truly important. I wonder why?" Daryl asked more curious now than before.

She knew Donal had Katrina on his mind when he left abruptly last evening, but what she didn't understand was why he went to seek out Ashford.

Emilia was shaking her head, "I don't know. Ash hasn't said anything, and I doubt if he will. What the two of them did last night is not my business, and I understand that fact. This morning, he was pleased with the outcome though. He pulled me into his arms after he returned home and kissed me."

"I suppose Donal will tell me when he feels like it."

She was counting the minutes until she could bring him some food. He told her he needed to sleep for a few hours. Still, she wanted to learn about Katrina because she was sure what Emilia was speaking about was an encounter with that woman. She wasn't in a hurry though to hear his words about the early morning adventure she undertook with her sisters. From where she stood, the news could be good or bad.

"So, what are you waiting for? Go to him before he leaves. Or is that what you want?" Justine asked as she pulled two loaves of freshly baked bread from the oven then poured coffee into a pitcher. "Go to your man. Maybe tomorrow the day will be normal for a change and you can be part of this wonderful bakery you started. Today you must take care of your personal business."

"He needs sleep."

She glanced upward, thinking of him lying nearly naked in that huge bed he bought for them.

"No more than you do." Justine was clucking a bit. "Go on, go upstairs with the food and wake him up. It is going on two hours since you came down here. He doesn't need any more than that. I doubt if you slept last night after what happened with Flynt and your sisters. Get whatever needs to be said out of the way. Put it behind you and you will both be happier."

"You know about that? About last night and Flynt?" Daryl was astounded. Were there no secrets? "Do you know everything that goes on in the Chamberlin household?"

Justine cackled and there was really no other word for it. "I've my informants. Emilia is right. Mr. Ashford has fallen head over heels in love with her and does want to marry her. They will most likely tie the knot before you do, since she is willing and you don't appear to know what it is you want."

"Ashford is just feeling sorry for me. If he wants to wed me, I'm not going to say no to him. I'm hoping in the process he can keep me safe from that horrible man who attached you the other night. If he doesn't hurt me when he makes love to me, which I don't believe he will..." she looked away for a moment before wiping tears from her eyes. "I do believe the rest of my life will be wonderful. He will take care of the children, and I will give him as many as he wants or the good Lord allows us."

"You want more children?" Daryl asked, surprised. "You already have four." She was shocked by the announcement although she knew some women were never given the choice by their men. She supposed that was something else she needed to talk over with Donal.

"Only two are mine and I know Ash wants a son or daughter of his own, one who can legally inherit. I'm healthy and I had no problems giving birth. So..." Emilia was staring at her rigidly clasped hands.

It seemed to Daryl that Emilia was not ready to share her entire story. "I'm more than a little in awe of children. Perhaps my trepidation is more about giving birth than dealing with the child afterward," Daryl admitted with a bit of hesitancy. "Bliss was so huge. Yes, and I know she had twins, but what if I have twins also. I've no idea what to do with a baby. One can't play with them." She put her hand over her mouth, staring at Justine and the sideways glance she was slanting her. "I'm not pregnant. Couldn't be at any rate. While Donal has not been a perfect gentleman, he wants to save making love for our wedding night."

"By the way, your man needs to take heed when the two of you are together. I'm sure he kens there is always a point of no return and I do believe the two of you, if you haven't already reached it, will be there soon." Justine was wiping her hands on a dishcloth seeming to think of the next few words she might want to say. "Have you decided if you intend to wed him or not? If the answer is no, you should stop tormenting the poor man. If the answer is yes, you need to tell him before another woman catches his eye."

"I was thinking the same way."

She looked down for a second, wondering why she was being so obtuse. Fear, she decided, it was fear that had her shaking every time she heard the word marriage. "I want to tell him today," she paused in thought, "when we talk."

"Yes, the sooner the better, tell the man and put him out of his misery. He's been waiting now for a while, and he's been patient. Patience is not one of Donal's strong suits, and you've taken everything to its limits." Justine seemed to be lecturing her now but the advice was sound.

"I will, I will tell him when we talk, after he gets a chance to eat. I'm sure he is starving." She was making a promise to herself if not Justine even when she didn't really know if she had the courage to carry through with any of it.

"Take the tray to him," Emilia said. "Let him show you how he feels about you. It will be easier then for you to decide and say the words."

She was nodding, all the talk from today spinning through her head. "It won't be easy," she admitted. "Everything seems to be so complicated. I suppose saying the words he wants to hear would be easier if he loved me."

"Go," Justine said, continuing to shoo her from the room with her hands. "Know that even though he hasn't said the words, he does love you. He would have never asked you to marry him if he didn't."

She picked up the tray and started up the steps, wary and excited all at the same time. More than anything she wanted to tell him she would be his wife that she wanted him to make love to her. She wanted a life with him, a future too.

She pushed the door to the bedroom with one foot, turning and backing into the room. "Donal."

When she set the tray down and turned to look at him, her heart stopped.

~ * ~

Katrina paced the downstairs room in her home, walked back and forth, seething inside, her anger boiling up inside. She never lost that which she sought. Now she was on the brink of losing everything. She had been shocked when she looked up and Donal stood in front of them watching her, viewing three men having sex with her. It was not well done of him.

She wasn't pleased.

No, she wasn't pleased at all.

What was she going to do now?

She meant to get even, take her anger out on the man who refused her, made fun of her. Once a long time ago, he was obsessed with her, had made love with her and given her a fine time. Donal had always been a good lover, well-practiced in many different ways to make love. She bet he didn't do some of those things with his pretty little whore.

"Leod, come here." She needed to think and the only way she could think was having sex. "I want you. Do whatever pleases you but make it fast and hard."

He picked her up, seeming to know what she needed. As he strode to the couch with her in his arms, he ripped her clothing. She trained him well. He knew what she needed, night and day. He was the only one of the men here at the moment. A *ménage à trois* would have been nice, but she supposed she would have to make do with a single lover.

A few minutes later she lay replete in the man's arms. She pushed away, gazing at him. "I will have my revenge. Will you help me?"

He was playing with her, his hands still roaming, caressing her intimately, seducing. Of course, I will help you. I seek my own revenge against the Chamberlin's. What will my part be? Will I be able to have the lady in my bed when you're done with her?"

"Of course, anything she is willing to give you is yours, but it's Donal I want to see hurt, not the woman. She is as much a victim as I am and remember, she must be a willing partner. I draw the line at force." She slipped a robe over her shoulders then began to pace. This was the point of it. She wanted payback from Donal, for refusing to believe her. Perhaps force would not be such a bad idea.

"What about the others?" he questioned.

"I don't know, haven't figured that out." She ran her hands through her hair, sweeping it off her eyes. "If I need them, they will also play a part and can have the woman. Seduce her, play with her but as I said, force is not acceptable."

Katrina knew she would have to drill that point home with these men.

"The best way to hurt the man is to hurt the woman he loves," Leod spoke quietly, a huge grin stretching across his ruggedly handsome face. "Let me get her for you then you can figure out what to do next. If you keep her prisoner, Chamberlin will be beside himself."

"I have to think about this. It's all happening too fast. The plan was for Donal to wed me then get me pregnant. He knew I wasn't. He must have figured out that I've never been with child. As to the woman, she's a secondary pawn in this." She stared at him hard, trying to figure out what he was thinking. "I know you want the lass, but I don't want her hurt unless it becomes absolutely necessary." She knew with these men she would have to repeat herself more than a few times.

"Very well, I can kill Donal for you. That would not be a problem," Leod said as he came up behind her, seductively running his hand down her stomach until he reached her most sensitive spots, his fingers finding her softness before delving inside.

She moaned as he continued to charm her to her soul, playing with her body, thrumming the sensitive woman's parts. "You're insatiable."

"No more than you are, but you need to cement a plan a strategy or you will fail."

He was nipping at her neck and across her shoulders, his hands cupping her breasts, toying with the hard peaks that caused her to moan her pleasure.

"We should have sex again. I'll be able to think better."

She turned in his arms before wrapping her legs around him and feeling his heavy sex pushing at her.

He strode to the wall. "Vertical sex is always nice with you."

"I don't want Donal killed. I want him in my bed and at my

mercy."

She sighed then screamed out his name as the sensations began to build.

"You will have to force the man. What I saw of Donal Chamberlin the other night told me he didn't want you in any way."

"A man cannot be forced."

She tossed her head back, giving him better access to her and he moved with her in a primal mating.

"Of course, he can," Leod said and with a grunt he finished.

Chapter Six

"I thought we were going to talk."

She stared at him, her eyes huge and her lips thinned in what Donal could only assume was anger. He understood how to diffuse her fury but didn't have the time, not today anyway.

He didn't want her to be fuming. "Ash was here, bringing me up to date on the men we hired. There is something I need to do before we can talk."

He was out of bed, dressed and slipping on his boots.

"You wouldn't mind telling me what that something is? I can't help but believe you are going to see Katrina." Her voice wavered.

He looked up suddenly intent, watching as her hands shook, guilt rippling through him in dark unanswered waves. At times it seemed something always hindered the progress they were slowly making. He believed Daryl was coming around, would say yes to his proposition of marriage. Might have even done so today, but there was nothing to do about it.

"Don't ever think that. It's not what I want, and I hope you know that you're the only woman I care about."

He watched her breasts move up then down with the heavy breath of air she was dragging into her lungs. "You have to eat. Just sit for a minute and have a cup of coffee and a muffin." Her hands were clasped beneath her chin, brows furrowed together.

She wasn't pleased with him. No, Donal knew she was unhappy and there was nothing he could do to change that fact.

"Did you eat?"

She gave a slight tilt to her head. Sounding miffed, "I have something to tell you and yes I ate downstairs while you were supposedly sleeping."

"Speak up then." He put on his other boot and grabbed his jacket. "You have a few minutes before I'm finished dressing."

Now she was shaking her head, backing from the room, seemingly unwilling to use the time he was giving her. "No, this isn't the right time and it isn't something I want to just blurt out to you then have you run from the room."

He supposed this haste was not well done of him, especially when he told her they needed to talk.

"If that's what you want, I'll concede to your wishes." He kissed her on the forehead. "I'll be back in a couple of days. I promise we'll talk then and perhaps I'll have something positive to say about yesterday's adventures. Right now, no matter what I tell myself I want to put you over my legs and thrash you soundly for putting yourself in danger. What I want and what I'm willing to do are not the same."

"As if you could teach me common sense with violence. At least tell me where you are going. You aren't the only one who worries."

Sometime in the last few minutes she had stiffened her spine and lifted her chin.

"To build a house, that is no secret and no I don't have a secret *rendezvous* with Katrina. She means less than nothing to me."

At the mention of Katrina's name, he felt an instant surge of revulsion.

"Why? Why build houses? And why such a rush you can't take an hour to talk to me?"

She touched his shoulder, quickly turned her and she was in his arms now, his lips seeking hers, tenderly at first then his tongue delving deep into her mouth.

When he pulled away, her lips were red and he delighted in the tiny cry of desire he elicited from her. "Blessed hell, but I'd like to stay and make love to you. This is all your fault."

"My fault?" She blinked several times, her lips thinning again. "What the devil are you blaming me for?"

"And Emilia's, she put the notion into Ash's head. Now all he wants is to please his lover."

"I'm not understanding any of this."

He snatched a roll from the tray and seemed to think better of the hasty departure, having not expected Daryl to show up. "Two of the homeless men, the two you brought food to in the evenings are the reason why. Emilia thought they should have a job." He sipped the hot coffee, watching her for a reaction to his statement.

"Of course, a job would be nice. What does that have to do with building a house?" she asked, seeming to relax a bit.

He tossed the roll in the air catching and bowing gracefully. The perplexed expression on her gave him reason to grin. "The job is at the shipyard. The men need to live close by so they can get to work on time."

"Makes sense," she said sitting down. "So, you and Ash..."

"As well as a few other men," he added.

"Are going to build a home for these two men. You must trust them a lot." She was staring at his mouth over the rim of his coffee cup and he almost put off leaving.

"Emilia trusts them. I'm not so sure. Neither is Ash but we both decided this was a fine idea as ideas go. I've been spurred by your charity to give people a job instead of loaves of bread. Perhaps you can find some more deserving people."

She started to protest and he understood why, holding his hands in the air, "Just listen, I'm not being negative about your feeding those in need but we thought to take this one step further. If this works out, with yours and Emilia's help, we mean to provide jobs and housing for men and women who are willing to put in an honest day's work. We cannot rid Glasgow of its homeless population, but we can help a few."

"They will have to pay you back of course," she said, her sweet pink tongue enticing him as she moved it slowly across her lips before dropping her gaze to his crotch. "They will believe it is charity and those two men are proud. That very characteristic might have put them in the position we found them in."

He wondered if she knew what she was doing to him. "Of course, that is part of the agreement they have signed. The furniture we are putting in will come from Ash's home."

"Why ever not yours? You have so much more than he does."

"Because, he is hoping to wed Emilia in the next few days, and he says she should be able to redecorate his house. It has after all been furnished by a man and needs a woman's touch. In time, I hope to do the same with my homes."

He saw the rush of heat to her face, hoping that she wanted the same, would be willing to put a woman's touch on his home but it had been days since he brought up the subject of marriage. "Sounds as if the two of you have everything planned. Perhaps telling him her feeling now, might be best, rather than waiting."

"I'll be gone for as long as it takes. The more men we can gather as crew, the sooner I'll be home." Once more, he pulled her into his arms for a kiss. "I speak for Ash as well, a few loaves of bread every morning would be wonderful."

"At night as well?" she queried. "It would be nice to see you, bring you something to eat."

He stiffened, terrified she would come in the evening and trying to figure out a subtle way to dissuade her. "No, I don't want you traveling through that part of the city to the shipyard at night."

Realizing his mistake, those words were anything but subtle, "I don't want to worry about you and if what you told me about your temptation to stay behind last night is true, I would be very pleased if you heeded my wishes."

"Of course, I wouldn't want you to be afraid for me," she said, her voice whisper thin and seeming to grow more distant as she finished the sentence.

"Promise you won't come in the evening." He held his breath waiting for a response, the right response.

"What if perhaps tomorrow evening, I, we, Emilia and Justine along with myself bring food. Perhaps Munroe can come with us or you can send someone you trust. We could stay the night and return in the morning."

He was pleased she wanted to see him. He grinned then, "On one condition only because by then all of us would appreciate a meal. I'll send Sandy back to get you."

"Sandy?"

He laughed loud and long, "I really do need to get going. Ask Justine about the man and lock your door tonight."

"I will do that," she said. "Both."

He heard the words, chuckling softly as he left the room, already missing Daryl but hoping the time away would help her make up her mind about marrying him.

The ride through the city gave him time to reflect on what was said between them and what wasn't spoken. His emotions had been up and down since nearly this time yesterday when he first heard about Katrina. Now he needed to make sure the woman didn't cause any more trouble.

He heaved a large breath of air, realizing that was asking the impossible. Katrina was clearly in the city to wreak havoc wherever it would please her. He was positive now that he ousted her, some of that chaos would be directed his way.

When he reached the construction site, the house was already framed and the flooring was down. Dismounting quickly and handing the reins to his stable boy who had come along, he approached Ash.

"We've made significant progress with lots of help from the crew from one of Broc's ships. This should be finished in two days, and we can start moving in furniture." Ash beamed seemingly proud of the work.

"So, you don't really need me I see." Donal laughed, knowing Ash would probably agree with him. "Rest assured I'm not going anywhere, at least not until we see this project to its proper conclusion."

He wondered then if he was staying so he could avoid a confrontation with Daryl. It was in both their best interest to talk about what happened. Yet he felt a bit of cowardice broaching the subject.

He had to admit at least to himself that was exactly what he was doing, avoiding any type of confrontation.

"We've set our bedrolls over there. You and I are sharing a tent. The rest will take cover in Broc's ship if it rains. Otherwise everyone is sleeping under the stars as well as the village lights."

He laughed then, thinking of other bed arrangements he would prefer. "That's what I call a bit of heaven, sharing a tent with you."

"Don't ever believe it's my first choice."

"Have you set out guards," Donal paused, "In light of what happened yesterday, we should. I don't trust Katrina and she will be holding a grudge. She is obviously capable of anything."

"My guess is that she will be after Daryl, not you. As an astute woman she would understand better than anyone. I would think the best way to hurt you would be to hurt the woman you love," Ash was painting a picture Donal didn't want to see, an image that rang true in every sense.

Those were his thoughts too. A sick feeling settled in the pit of his stomach, and he was tempted to ride back to the city. He should have left someone at the bakery to guard her. For a few minutes, he walked around the empty house. Sandy was helping put the newly constructed roof structure on top of the beams holding up the house. Other men were working in more places.

Donal waited until they finished then, "Sandy, come here. I'd like to have a word with you."

The big man nodded, striding toward him. "I've a proposition for you even though I know you would rather be here doing a man's job than babysitting three women."

"What is it boss? Don't mind looking after women if they're the right women," Sandy grinned shamelessly.

Good lord, but this man was huge. He was even bigger than he was and he towered over most everyone except the bad boys. "Need to have you do a job for me in town and in my opinion these are exactly that, the right women."

"What women and what exactly do I need to do?" he asked, arms crossed in front of him, seeming suddenly wary.

"Go back into town. Make sure the ladies are safe when they deliver the leftovers from the bakery. Don't want you to come back until morning after they go to work in the kitchen. Need to have you stay with the ladies at my home. Daryl might protest, but if you get Justine to reason with her before you tell them what it is I want, the daunting task will go much better for you."

"Doesn't sound like a problem to me."

Donal laughed even while he didn't see any humor in the

situation. "You don't know Daryl. However," he paused, "with that said, they will be amenable with you tagging along when they take out the leftovers. Keep a look out for any man or woman who might be willing to earn a living rather than live on the streets."

"I can do that. Don't mind seeing Justine either. Been gone for two months now and I've missed her," Sandy said, a handsome smirk on his face, his eyes bright. "Need to have my woman in my arms and my bed seeing to her needs or I'm not pleased. No," he paused, "not pleased at all."

"Good, then I take it I came to the right man for the job." This was one less thing to worry about, yet he had this gut instinct rolling around inside him, and he didn't like the feelings.

"Perhaps we're doing this all wrong," Ash said. "There are other alternatives. I for one will miss Emilia and I'm not pleased with the scenario either."

"What?" Donal turned to listen to his friend. "Doing what all wrong" What other scenarios?"

Ashford pushed back his hat, a twinkle in his eyes. "Maybe we should close up the bakery for a day or two and bring our women here to be with us. That way we can watch them and they'll be close to us. Your fear for Daryl will be assuaged."

"You expect them to sleep under the stars? In the cold? On the hard ground?" Donal asked, thinking about Daryl and how she would react. Indeed, he had no idea how she would respond to this type of situation. He could almost feel Daryl curled up next to him in the tent, his arms wrapped around her, keeping her warm. His breath caught in the back of his throat at the thought.

"We wouldn't be worrying about anyone attacking and hurting them. I doubt if Emilia would mind sleeping in a tent with me even if it's on the hard ground. I will promise to keep her warm and comfortable. She's slept in worse places before," Ash said with a wistful hint to his voice that couldn't be denied.

"That way you could all be with your little gals," Sandy said his grin widening as the conversation continued, "And with my Justine doing the cooking, even over a campfire, our meals will be far better than cornbread and bacon."

Donal grimaced, "Either of you consider what the good people of Glasgow will say about our ladies if we bring them here and sleep with them?" Donal would feel a whole lot better if Daryl was here with him, but in his case, it wasn't feasible or realistic. If he did that, Flynt would be here and hauling them off to the church before Daryl could say nay.

They would be wed.

No way in hell was he going to force her.

Both Sandy and Ash had the good sense to look sheepish hinting on guilt. "Never thought so much about it because Emilia doesn't care what anyone thinks except me. She doesn't know anyone or have you forgotten she is living in my house with me anyway. Sleeping with her in a tent would be nothing new."

"Pretty much the same for me," Sandy said, shrugging his broad shoulders. "Justine lives in my home. Granted I'm away most of the time. We've been living together for so long most everyone believes we are wed. As with Ash, making love in a tent, my arms around Justine would be nothing new to the good people of this city."

"I see," Donal said finding no pleasure in what the men told him.

Having the women here made sense in every case except his own. Blessed hell, he didn't even know if she would agree to stay in his home instead of her apartment above the bakery. "Perhaps the two of you should think about a marriage," Donal grumbled, wishing he'd been successful in that himself. He wouldn't think twice about bringing Daryl here if they were engaged.

"Could we say the same thing for you," Sandy seemed to be a bit defensive. "Justine seems to like her life just the way it is. Says she doesn't want a man telling her what to do or how to spend her days."

Donal nearly spit the coffee he was drinking, realizing this concept seemed to be a trend with their women that wasn't going away anytime soon. At least Emilia didn't plague Ash with that newfound concept he was going to call independence. "I've been trying to persuade Daryl to my way of thinking. Not my fault if my little lady won't get off the fence and make a decision. What about you? It's been at least five years that I'm aware of that Justine's been living with you." Donal wasn't about to let these two control this. "You and Ash can get married on the same day. A double wedding would be fun and economical as well. In fact, there is a church just down the road. We could do it tomorrow."

"You could make it a trio," Ash laughed.

"Doubt if Flynt would allow that or Daryl either. Probably should get back to work."

Donal wanted to put this conversation out of his brain. Hard work and sweat might keep his mind off thoughts of Daryl in his arms, but he wasn't counting on it.

"Haven't solved our little problem yet. Am I or am I not riding into town to protect the women?" Sandy asked. "Are they staying there or am I bringing them to this little community we've established. I'm sure none of the men working on this project will care if you sleep with your woman."

Donal sighed, wishing this could be different, needing her in his arms tonight and every night after that as well. "Go on and stay there. You can bring breakfast to us when you come back to the site in the morning."

Watching Sandy ride off, he was reminded of all the things that were at stake here and at his home. Daryl meant everything to him. He didn't know what he would do if she never agreed to marriage.

He wasn't used to having his life turned upside down and gainsaid at every bump in the road. Damn it, he was the master of his life and he made the decisions. Perhaps it was well past time for him to assert his manly dominance.

He was the man after all. He laughed, couldn't help himself. She was the woman and if she wasn't happy, he wasn't either.

A cheer went up from the crew working on the house. The rooftop had been secured, the nails in place and it signaled the end of the workday. As he strode through the house, he was impressed with the progress and the quality of work as well. This would make a wonderful home for these two men and in time, he hoped, the men would be able to afford a new place, and perhaps a family.

There were two bedrooms and a kitchen. The men would have a front room where they could relax and a bathing room where a tub would be placed for their convenience. He was proud of the progress and proud that because of Daryl's work this was coming to pass. He never thought of anything like this before Daryl, yet he had the time and the money to continue this project.

"It's a good thing. All that is going on here has so much promise, don't you think?" Ashford stood beside him, rocking on his heels, seemingly pleased with himself. "What happened last night between you and Daryl after the encounter with Katrina?"

"She isn't going to let this rest, you know. I'm going to have to explain everything we saw and all Karina said, not that I mind explaining. I just wish we weren't going through this and that there was no threat to her."

He was leaning against one of the beams between the living room and the kitchen, arms crossed in front of him. He was sure he appeared more relaxed than he felt.

"I ken it. We both know what Katrina is like. Daryl has to understand the repercussion and perhaps the dangers. Do you think the woman is going to spew her wrath on you or Daryl?" Ash asked.

"By God, I pray it is me. Daryl has been through too much. I don't want her hurt again."

"Sandy will make sure she stays safe. He has a way about him and since it is not you asking her to stay in your house but Sandy, she might not argue too much." Ash laughed as he clapped him on the shoulder. "Good luck, my friend. This would be easier, gossip be damned, if Sandy transported them to us."

"You're very funny. They should be delivering the leftovers as we speak. Do you think they will have to look far for more candidates for our charitable endeavors? We've taken three of their leftover recipients and given them jobs as well as new homes."

"There will always be homeless and people without food to eat. So many need a roof over their head," Ash said, looking at the cart rumbling down the road toward them. "What do you make of that?"

"What the bloody hell is going on?" Donal asked but he knew the answer, the women won out. "Daryl and the other two ladies found a way to seduce Sandy to their side. Justine must have Sandy wrapped in knots since it's been so long since they've seen each other."

"Obviously, Sandy didn't obey your wishes. Looks like he has three ladies in the cart with him and we both know who they are. What are you going to do when they get here? Send them back or keep them?" Ashford was laughing, clearly pleased with what was transpiring.

"It will be dark soon so sending them home will be impossible and dangerous as well."

If the truth be told, he was pleased also. Now Daryl was exactly where he wanted her.

"They would have known the risks involved as well as the possibilities of gossip. They are free thinkers," Ash said. "And acted accordingly, knowing you would never send them back because of the dangers."

"Emilia and Daryl can have the tent. You and I can join the men under the stars. I hope Sandy knows he has to get up early enough to return the women to the bakery."

He didn't want to talk to Daryl right now. Hell, he wanted to make love to her. Needed to avoid her, but if she touched him... He groaned. Just thinking of her gentle caresses and smile aroused him in ways he'd never thought possible. Closing his eyes, Donal inhaled long and hard... and put a tighter rein on his own driving hunger.

Sleeping with each other in the privacy of his home was one thing, but allowing all his men as well as the crew from the ship see them going into the tent together was not tenable, yet there was no other choice because he wasn't going to risk her life.

After he helped her from the cart, she was holding her hands out as if to keep distance between them. "None of this was my doing. I told them we needed to stay and do as you told Sandy, but neither Emilia nor Justine would agree. Really, Donal, I was willing under the circumstances to sleep in your home. Now..." She threw up her hands, her brow creased. "You are angry and I had naught to do with any of this. I came along because I knew you wouldn't want me to be alone at the bakery. You should be pleased with my decision."

It seemed she could not stop talking and rambling on about the happenings.

The calm he needed to deal with this situation as well as Daryl standing next to him was eluding him. "Disappointed, not angry. Terrified too that you took that chance even though Sandy was with you." He inhaled another long deep breath, knowing the effort was just not working. "Worried more than I care to think."

"Oh."

Her smile vanished, her lips pursing in a way that made him want to kiss them.

He touched her under the chin, lifted gently so he could see into her eyes. "Not disappointed to see you. Never that."

"Then what?" She appeared confused, even disoriented a bit. "I would have thought you would be happy we brought food and I'm here. I know you haven't eaten much." She leaned forward. "Did you know that Justine and Sandy were lovers?"

"Strangely, until today no, I did not. I did ken they were friends though. I am pleased you brought dinner, but it is too late for the four of you to return to the city. You ken what it will look like to the good people of Glasgow if you stay here."

Her hand on his chest, she was shaking her head. "I don't care, never did. It won't be any worse than when I was sleeping in your bed at the country estate of yours and in your house as well."

"With no intimacy between us," he reminded her.

"No one but my family knew that, and I'm not sure Flynt believed it was platonic," she said, lifting her shoulders slightly to show her indifference. "But he allowed it because you would have it no other way."

"I do care and so you will share the tent with Emilia. Justine and Sandy have been living together for so long, so I've been told, that everyone believes they are wed. They will share the other tent." Lord, but he was having a hard time not touching her, kissing her, exploring every inch then hauling her off to the tent.

Gossip be damned.

"That's hardly fair and Donal, we still need to have that talk. There is something I need to tell you. It's very important at least to me."

One hand was on his chest as she leaned into him, her breath whispering across the bared skin of his neck, sending sensuous currents of pleasure through him.

He grit his teeth as he set his hands on her shoulders, realizing if he didn't do something to rectify this, he would be well and truly damned. "As I need to explain to you what happened the other night. Katrina is a threat to both of us. I need for you to understand that and take every necessary precautions."

"What about tonight?" she asked.

He waved a hand in the air, utterly exasperated but unable to help himself. "I'm getting another tent."

~ * ~

By the time she was nestled in his arms, darkness had fallen and it seemed everyone else had retired for the night. Her head rested on his chest, his arm around her she listened to the steady beat of his heart and slow even breathing. She didn't think he was asleep, just ignoring her and the issues between them needing to be resolved.

There had been no time to talk. This was not the right place or time. She needed privacy to tell him that she did want to marry him, that she wanted to spend the rest of her life in his arms and share whatever fortunes, good or bad came their way. Closing her eyes, she made a silent wish for the two of them.

He told her he would come home tomorrow evening. The building of the house didn't need his attention, but she did. He did not explain what he meant by that. She supposed it had something to do with Katrina, some type of retribution he believed the woman planned for one or both of them. She wasn't naïve when it came to the idea of vengeance. It seemed at one time or another each of her sisters as well as Flynt had been the subject of revenge. But she didn't understand the concept.

She closed her eyes, content for the moment, wishing this feeling might indeed last forever and there didn't need to be a day of explanations. The night would drag by then before she knew it daylight would come. She needed to be back to the bakery before dawn. Sandy was driving them and in turn they would send back a hearty breakfast.

Unable to help herself, she let herself explore his chest. He usually slept naked. Not tonight. Tonight, he wore his buckskins but no shirt. She liked the texture of his skin beneath her palm and the way his skin seemed to warm to her touch. When her fingers passed across his nipples, they tightened.

She heard the masculine groan of pleasure then his hand rested on top of hers, and with a husky passion filled voice, "As much as I love what you are doing, you need to stop. Where you and your beautifully responsive body are concerned, I only have so much willpower. Right now, I've just about reached my limit."

With the burden of her decision to wed lifted from her shoulders, she suddenly felt playful, needing to test her powers of seduction. "What if I don't want to stop? What if," she paused, "I want you to give me pleasure?" She touched one tiny nipple with her tongue then grazed with her teeth.

"You really shouldn't play with fire."

She laughed then, "I understand but perhaps I can give you your pleasure. You know like you taught me the other day. That would please you?" The sensual shiver of memory that passed through Daryl was felt by Donal as well.

"No, that would not be a good idea. We would wake the entire camp and I'm sure you don't want everyone knowing what we are doing here."

Yet it seemed he was more approachable on the subject. "But if you insist, I could give you your pleasure."

Beneath her clothing, his hand cupped her breast, touched a nipple with his thumb.

Closing her eyes, she held her breath as fire caught and was ignited by his touch, "Unfortunately, you're probably right in this. Tonight, I should not play with fire."

"Good girl," he said, lightly running his hand down her back and letting it remain on her derrière. "Neither will I but I do want you to stay in my arms. I want to hold you until it's time to leave for the bakery." He smiled then nuzzled her ear with his tongue.

"It's almost morning. Did you sleep at all?" she asked, pretty sure what the answer would be.

"Not much. I spent most of the night trying to keep from touching you and I'm sure you slept even less. You were restless just as I was. A commitment from you would certainly help with the sleep."

"I was thinking about us and what you mean to me. You are everything I've ever wanted or needed in my life." She rose above him, touched his soft lips with a fingertip, studying the expressions flitting across his face as she spoke. "I want you to make love to me. Not now, not in this tent but when you come home tomorrow night."

"I want that too but you understand my conditions. They haven't changed. Think about it, because if I do make love to you it will be with your promise of marriage." Gently he brushed hair from her eyes, studying her as if he could look beyond and see into her mind.

Nodding her head, she sucked her bottom lip beneath her teeth, her body thrumming with passion and desire for this wonderful man. He could give her the world if she would allow it. Then, "I understand completely."

He smiled but it wasn't the full-blown ear-to-ear smile she was so used to from him. The expression was gentle and sweet, holding a solemn promise. "I hope so because I'm tired of the pursuit. It's time our lives became calm and restful, past time we came together as one. Peace is what I'd like from this day forward. Can we have that, lass?"

"I want peace just as much as you. We can put all of our issues to rest. I'm sure of it and stop talking around them. I..."

"Time to go home." It was Justine's voice she heard from outside the tent. It seemed there was never peace or quiet, no time to reflect for them. "The bread won't wait for us. It's rising on the counter as we speak."

"I'll be right out." She sat up, smoothing her wrinkled clothing and refastening buttons she didn't know if she'd undone or if Donal's playful fingers unfastened them. "I'll see you tonight." She bent close kissing him on the lips. "We will have that conversation that's been in the making for two days now."

His hand rested on the back of her head, pulling her closer, deepening the kiss with the promise of so much more. An instant later, Daryl felt the deep penetration of his tongue, the velvet glide within her mouth. The heat and texture of Donal's kiss swept through her making her giddy. When he finally pulled away, "That's a promise I mean to keep."

"I'll hold you to that."

She started to leave, slowly backing from the tent and wishing she dared stay with him.

"You should fix your hair, or I can."

His grin was wide and tugged at her heart and her will power as well.

"Probably better that I do it."

She sat back and quickly she wound the length around itself, expertly tying the strands into a tight bun on top of her head. Then she smiled, "Is that better?"

"Not much," he laughed, touching one of the long curly strands that had not found its way into the bun. "Your hair feels like silken fire. It burns whatever it touches." He paused then, "You're so beautiful to me."

Riding in the cart back to the city, Daryl had more time to think about the words she would use when she finally spoke with Donal. Sandy and Justine chatted amicably, no tension between them. Emilia was quiet, keeping her thoughts to herself. She assumed the other ladies spent their night much different than she and Donal. While it wasn't fair, perhaps it was for the best.

Sandy helped each of them from the cart before following them into the bakery and locking the door behind him, the closed sign still prevalent in the window. An hour later, Sandy left with breakfast for everyone at the construction site in the back of his wagon. Hands clasped beneath her chin, Justine watched him leave.

It was then, Daryl turned laughingly on Justine, pointing a finger at her, "Who are you to lecture me and Emilia about marriage when you have refused to wed Sandy for five years or more? It is time, you know, for the two of you to make a commitment to each other."

"I never cared about marriage and ironic as it is, he never brought it up. I'd been wed once before and didn't see anything positive come from that experience except misery and pain in the marriage bed. I suppose that union was far too similar to Emilia's first marriage. So, I was not eager to have any man put a ring on my finger again. Sandy didn't seem to mind. He never brought the subject up, so I was content to continue our relationship as it was. I've always wanted to be able to walk out the door, if that was what I wanted, and never look back." She finished with a slight shrug to her shoulders. "Now, last night he asked me. Truly I was shocked and didn't know what to think or say."

"I gather he's changed his mind though," Emilia joined into the conversation. "I overheard some of your discussion on the way back. Is he really asking now? Is he sincere?"

"He has and I believe he means it. I don't think Donal or Ashford coerced him yet perhaps they put the thought into his head. Now it seems he wants marriage. Says it makes sense because he's not going to be at sea so much. Broc is going to give him other responsibilities at the shipyard so he'll remain at home."

"What did you say?" Daryl asked, pulling two loaves of bread from the oven and setting them on the counter to cool. "I know you just said you were surprised by his proposal. Did you answer him?"

"Told him I'd have to think about it." Justine busied herself, hands in the bread dough as it seemed she tried to distance herself form the conversation. "What about the two of you?"

"Do you really need to think on the subject or are you making him wait?" Emilia asked, joining the conversation and ignoring Justine's question.

"A little of both. I'm going to say yes, no question about it but I don't know when. If he had his way, we'd be married today. While I don't need a big ceremony or even a little one, I would like my friends to witness the vows."

"As you asked me, what if he finds someone else in the interim?" Daryl asked, wondering if that was even a consideration.

"Been asking myself that same question for nearly five years now. Never had an answer either. Every time he sailed into port I wondered if he would tell me to leave and that he'd found someone else he could love."

"And..." Emilia seemed eager for the answer.

With a little sigh, Justine began, "There was a time when I would have told you if he found someone else, I would be happy for him and I would move on with my life."

"Now?" Daryl asked, pretty sure she knew the answer to her question.

She was waiting impatiently, and it seemed Justine understood and was dragging this out just to aggravate her.

"Now, losing him would be as if I lost part of my soul. I want him in my present as well as my future." She smiled shyly, wiping sweat from her forehead with her forearm.

"What does he say?" Emilia asked.

"That he doesn't think he can live without my cinnamon rolls and French pastries." She laughed then, "And other things he can't live without too. Not sure if it's just the sex he wants, but he is a good lover, much better than my first marriage, when making love was not what the two of us shared."

"Good, then are the two of you going to tie the knot?" Emilia asked.

"In a few days. When the house is built. It seems Ash knows a minister nearby who would love to perform the ceremony," Justine said, looking pointedly at Emilia then Daryl.

Daryl held up her hands, shaking her head at the same time. "That's too much like eloping. Flynt and Grams would never let me get away with anything like that. Grams would like to help plan a wedding with a dress and flowers. They would have to buy the cake because I'm not making my own wedding cake."

"Get away with what?" Lacie walked into the bakery, which had just opened. "And whose wedding are we planning? I suppose it must by yours, Daryl. Other than you, I'm the only sister left who isn't wed. I'm sure Justine and Emilia would be thrilled to make your cake."

"Eloping," Justine said before Daryl could deflect the question with something else entirely that was not even close.

"I see then you've changed your mind about never letting a man control you." Lacie grabbed a roll from the counter before sitting down. "Well," she paused with an all-knowing grin. "I'm here to look at the books. Do you think you've made a profit now that you have much needed help?"

"I hope so. I certainly haven't done much to assist the situation."

When she first started seeing Donal, she never thought her life would become so chaotic. The days she'd spent in the bakery since then she was sure she could count on one hand.

"On another topic, our sisters are talking about going after the man responsible for Flynt's knife wound," Lacie said, "I've a good idea where to find him and I told them as much. Believe they are planning the excursion for tomorrow morning unless their husbands find him before then."

"Really, even after the other day when I'm sure everyone has received a lecture."

Daryl was astonished they would consider something so reckless. Yet she meant to go with them. As she told Donal the other night there was safety in numbers and she would never let her sisters down.

"Really and I didn't receive much of anything except a stern look from Flynt. I know my abilities," Lacie said. "Leslie doesn't even know what we did, and I'm not going to be the one to tell him. He's away until who knows when, so what do I care what he thinks?"

"Donal told me he could disarm me. That he could overpower a woman without even blinking," Daryl said even though she didn't believe he could do the same with five women who were pointing guns at him. "He also told me that he would show me but we've had very little time and no private time since that day."

"So, I'm guessing he hasn't done that," Lacie said laughing. "Maybe he's afraid of your prowess."

"Maybe he doesn't want to hurt me. I don't like this conversation and the direction it's heading. I have little doubt he could disarm me, but at the time I was speaking of five armed women. Lacie would have blown his kneecap off before he got even one gun away from any of us."

Daryl went back to work, trying to keep her mind out of the discussion the girls were having.

Lacie seemed to be ignoring her now, working diligently on the ledgers in front of her. She sighed. Daryl knew she was checking out the supplies and making a list as to the items they would have to buy. At least in the kitchen the women were in agreement with a few things.

The little bell at the front door chimed, announcing a new customer. The man had coal black hair and deep brown eyes that twinkled with humor. She smiled at him, watching him tip his hat and nod her way.

"Excuse me, I'm going to see who our new customer is." Daryl walked across the room, hand extended in greeting. She knew her smile was wide. Dear lord, he was handsome, maybe too handsome for his own good or hers. But she wasn't going to admit anything or acknowledge the fact.

"*Enchante*," he said, accepting her hand in his before bringing it to his lips and kissing the back. When he looked up, it seemed he saw inside her mind and knew what she'd been thinking.

"The same," she said, her heart pounding. "Why don't you have a seat and I'll bring you something. What would you like?"

"For starters, your name, pretty lady."

His voice was low and smooth, his shoulders broad tapering to narrow hips. His dark black hair was a little too long, curling just above his collar. He was a fine specimen of a man, and she was sure he knew the affect he was having on her, most likely every lady he encountered.

She moistened her lips, barely able to suck in enough air for her to put a coherent sentence together. "Daryl," she said, "Daryl MacTavish and yours?"

"You can call me Etienne. My last name is not something I want you to know."

"Etienne." She felt tongue tied and nervous. She wiped her clammy hands on her apron. "What would you like?"

"You."

"Me?" Her hand went to her chest as the tiny breath of air she inhaled whooshed out. "That isn't what I meant. To eat, what would you like to eat?"

His grin widened, and it seemed his gunmetal gray eyes sparkled even more. Then he repeated, "You."

"Food, what's over there on those," she inhaled deeply, "shelves would you like to purchase."

"If you were for sale, I would purchase you."

"Good lord." She sat down. Her eyes closed as she thought on what to say. "You're incorrigible."

He sat down next to her, sliding the chair close. "*Merci*, just thought you would want honesty from a man. I don't like playing games. If I see something I want, I take it." Once more, he held her hand in his, turning it over before tracing the lines in her palm with a fingertip.

She tugged on her hand and he let it go, his smile widening but his expression held more than good humor it seemed to promise something in return. She just didn't know what that was. "You can't have me. Now back to the question and I would appreciate a different kind of honesty. What would you like to eat and drink?"

"Hmm..." He gazed at her first then the display case and with a heavy sigh of discontent, "If I can't have you then what did you make?"

"The scones."

"I'm disappointed. I would have liked to choose something created from your lovely hands but alas those rolls with icing on them seem to be calling my name. A cup of coffee, too, and if it's not too much trouble, would you join me? Promise... well don't think I can make that vow."

"What were you going to promise?"

She stood, intending to get him his order when he stopped her, his hand circling her wrist. "Stay, sit, I'd like to talk to you more and if you leave you might not come back. I'll get the food. Would you like something?"

"A cup of tea would be nice."

She really didn't understand these strange feelings for this man. He seemed to sweep her off her feet, stealing her breath in the same instant, and she had no idea how to respond. He excited her, and aroused her. Gut instinct told her he was trouble. She should run but his eyes, the way he looked at her seemed to reel her into his web. When she thought of Donal, a bit of guilt swept through her. This man would be gone soon. He would leave the café and she would most likely never see him again. Donal was solid and dependable. She loved him, his kisses set her on fire, turning her heart upside-down. This man represented a moment's infatuation.

How would it hurt to talk with a man who wasn't going to make decisions for her? Who might listen and see things her way? She meant to enjoy his company and conversation, nothing more. In a few minutes he returned, setting her tea in front of her.

"Now, where were we?" He picked up her hand again once more slowly tracing the lines. "I remember. The lines in your palm tell a story all their own. My grandmother used to read palms and foresee the future. She had the ability known as sight."

"You?"

She was trembling, her heart racing as his thumb traced tiny circles on her wrist. If she were wise, she would leave right now before she caved into her impulsiveness and did something rash.

"No talent there but I do see us spending a little more time with each other."

His lips touched her hand, teeth nibbling on the sensitive underside until she nearly let a tiny moan of pleasure from her lips.

"What do you do?"

Her voice was whisper thin, barely audible even while she wanted to put all the sensations he was creating and tuck them away where she wouldn't feel them.

"Ah." He looked at her, "My talents lie in seducing beautiful ladies. I do that very well, I'm told. No one has complained so far. And you? Would you like to try out my talents?"

Sudden desire for him surged through her. "Perhaps you should let go of my hand."

She didn't tug it from his easy grip but watched as he picked up her other hand and continued his exploration. Teeth, tongue lips, he created an enchantment within her, one she could not deny. Yet it was not like the sensations Donal elicited in her.

"You could ask me to let go but I would have to believe that's what you truly wanted. Looking into your eyes right now I'd be hard pressed to believe you."

Slowly, he ran a fingertip up her arm then down.

She didn't think she could breathe. "You should eat now."

"I'd rather take this upstairs with you. We could explore so much more than the palm of your hand and the silken skin on your arm." He paused, studying her, "I wonder..."

"What?"

"What your nipples taste like. I suppose sweet and tart just as the lady seems to be. Are you both sweet and tart?"

"That's entirely not appropriate."

Yet she didn't pull her hand away, didn't tell him no, continued to gaze at him as if he was a beautiful god.

"Appropriate, how droll. I don't want appropriate in a relationship. I want wild and reckless, fast and slow when it comes to pleasure." Without setting her hand down he sipped the coffee and bit into the cinnamon roll. "Delicious, not as delicious as you I'm sure."

The shivers ripping through her could not be controlled. She looked down for a moment then decided her tea would bring a little moisture to her mouth. "I think I should go back to work." Yet she didn't leave, just continued to watch the brazen man who was like no other.

"So soon but I've a few questions I'd like you to answer." He licked icing covered fingers. They were long and slender and for a second, she thought about him caressing her intimately.

"Like what?" Her voice quivered and she understood he knew the affect he had upon her and was delighting in the fact.

"Do you have a lover?"

She gasped, wondering how to answer and why she should. If she had a lover was no business of his. "Yes and no."

"Awe, you are indecisive about that. He must not be very good if you don't have a definitive answer. Yes and no, what exactly does that mean?"

"We are waiting until we are married," she blurted, unable to think or form a coherent thought.

"When is the date?" he persisted.

"I haven't said yes to him."

She was confused and disoriented in this conversation. All she needed was to leave and it would be over and despite the different ways he made her feel, she was enjoying the easy banter.

"Why is that?" His gaze rested on her bodice. "You know how easy it would be to... no perhaps I shouldn't say. Would you like to go for a carriage ride with me? We could go to the river and watch a sunset."

"No." Her voice wavered.

"Then walk outside with me. If we found a secluded place, I could kiss you, taste you. I would like that, would you? Do you want to taste me?"

A part of her said yes but she realized she should be firmly saying no to this smooth-talking man. More guilt swept through, her but she was sorely tempted to say yes. Only one man had truly kissed her, Donal. Perhaps a woman should find out what others had to offer. She owed it to herself and her future as well to find out if Donal was the only man who could make her burn.

"No, no, I don't... I can't." She swallowed, trying to pull her hand from his. "This conversation is really," she passed her tongue across her lips. "It's disconcerting and bewildering. I don't know who you are or what you want."

"I thought I made it perfectly clear. I want you."

"No, you don't. You can't... Not really. You don't know me. How could you want me?"

"I won't stop trying." He smiled at her. "You should really kiss at least one more man before you marry."

"I don't see why. I've wanted Donal since, since, for as long as I can remember. He is the only man I've ever wanted to kiss."

Ninny, until this man showed up and made you feel strange and needy.

"All the more reason to see what else the world has to offer."

"Such as yourself."

"I'm a practiced lover and I would never let you down," he said, the grin growing. "Can you say as much for your man? Oh, yes and no. Has he or hasn't he. Never mind, you don't need to answer that question."

"I think you said something like that a little while ago."

She was grasping at straws and still he held her hand in his, still seducing her with the slow, gentle glide of his fingers.

"Give me one chance and if you're disappointed, I'll never ask again."

His whiskey smooth voice sent shivers of desire through her, so very different than the passion she felt for Donal. While he wasn't in any way repulsive to her and she knew he wouldn't hurt her, she also knew he was a person she should avoid. Yet the temptation of one kiss was something she was having trouble denying. Just one kiss for comparisons sake, was that so bad?

For a moment, she closed her eyes and with a long deep breath she looked at him, "If you let go of my hand, I'll go for a walk with you. But I'm not agreeing to the kiss."

"*Tres bien.*" He brought her hand to his lips, kissing the palm and sucking each finger into his mouth, caressing each with his lips and teeth before he tenderly set it on the table gently touching the back.

He stood, extending his hand to her, "May I?"

"You just let go and I'm perfectly capable of standing without a man's help."

She did just that before striding out the door and down the sidewalk, for a moment leaving him behind.

When he reached her, he bent close to her ear, whispering, "Like I said, sweet and tart. You intrigue and fascinate me, my darling. What else can you show me that is truly and remarkably just you?"

They were walking side by side, his body touching, tantalizing hers once in a while. She rubbed her arms, feeling a chill in the air. The sun was shining and she realized the chill came from her feelings for this man. He was not what he seemed, yet she wasn't able to tell him no or even send him away. For her, he was trouble, clear and simple. Her curiosity was getting the better of her, and she would have to answer for this bout of carelessness yet she wasn't going to deny herself this one opportunity to kiss another man.

She would have to tell Donal about him, and she wondered if it was important in the scope of all the words between them that were still left unsaid. Nothing wrong took place here and it wouldn't. Yet when she touched her lips, she realized she wanted that kiss, if nothing else so she could compare. Donal had multiple women he compared her with, including Katrina. Perhaps this man could teach her something.

"Where are we going?" He draped an arm across her shoulder as they turned down a narrow street. "I'm new in town. Don't know much about Glasgow and can I assume you've lived here your entire life?"

"There is a park down that way," she pointed. "A fountain where we can sit if you like."

"You want to be alone?" He smiled that all knowing smile she was starting to recognize as arrogance or maybe confidence. Who was she to put labels on his expressions? In any case, he was comfortable with women, more so than he had a right to be.

"The park is never empty," she said, wondering if he was right. The kiss was something that intrigued her. Then, "Perhaps I do want to be alone with you."

He let his head fall back, laughing. "You are a woman of many facets, yet I understand your hesitancy. What will your man say? Keep in mind I would bet he's had multiple lovers and of course you just have that indecision, yes and no."

"Not while I've been with him," she said, yet was sure he heard the hesitancy in her voice.

She thought of Katrina and by the talk about her they were supposed to have been intimate only two months ago even though he denied it. According to the woman, he was supposed to be the father of her baby. He might have slept with her during their short time together. Hadn't Justine warned her about other women in Donal's life?

"Are you sure about that, pretty lady? I see doubt in those beautiful blue eyes of yours." He stopped then. "Has your man slept with someone else or kissed someone else in the short time you've been together? Hardly fair, is it?"

They stood beneath a tree with large overhanging branches. There was no one around. "No. I don't believe so." Yet she was sure he would hear the question and hesitancy in her voice.

"A simple kiss would be nothing to the digressions your man has taken, will it?"

"If that is true, yes. Yes, you're right." She passed her tongue across her lips, anticipating the touch of his.

"Is that a yes. May I kiss you?" He paused a few seconds before brushing his lips lightly across hers, his hands on either side of her face.

Her quick breath of air was sharp and her response was to open for him. His lips were soft and moist against hers, tantalizing and coaxing. When his tongue pushed inside, her breath broke. He sucked and bit gently, sending a ripple of desire through her. He was right. He was good at seduction.

When he stopped and drew away from her, she reached out to touch him. "That was nice." It was nice, she thought but it was little else. It wasn't demanding, passionate, or filled with fever. It wasn't a kiss to cause the world to cease spinning, a caress to warm her inside and out. He did not touch her blood or reach into her limbs or into the very center of her being.

It wasn't Donal's kiss.

"Nice? Is that all you can say about the kiss? Nice?" He smiled and touched her mouth with his calloused fingertip. "Nice is too tame a description for what I'm used to, but I'll graciously accept the compliment."

There was so much to like about this man but he wasn't Donal. "Yes, but he was unique and she did want to get to know him better if only for this short walk. You taste different but it was nice."

"Nice again, not exciting and arousing. Are you wet for me? If I tossed up your skirt and touched you intimately, would your juices be flowing, getting your body ready for my entry?"

She stepped back then, swinging her hand at him.

Easily he caught it and laughed. "Not appropriate again, *cherie*?" he queried. "If you ever want more than your Donal is giving you, come to me."

~ * ~

"How did your little diversion with Daryl MacTavish go?"

Katrina and Etienne were eating dinner. She sipped some of the wine she poured earlier then looked over the rim to the man who never failed to give her what she wanted. "I suppose you didn't get the little whore into your bed. Yet perhaps that is just a matter of time. Is that what you would like?"

"Our time together went very well, better than I expected, actually. I thought she would be harder to seduce, but it seemed she was attracted to me the moment she saw me which made this so incredibly easy. One could say I captured her interest right away."

He winked at her, enjoying this woman and her devious side as well. So be it, he loved all women, devious, tart and sweet and any package they came in. His sole purpose was seeing to their pleasure and his as well. Yet this mission had taken on serious undertones and he realized he would need to be cautious. Katrina could well be pushing too hard and become a detriment to what he was sent to accomplish. He didn't want to run home with his tail between his legs.

"Really? Care to expand on what went so well?" she asked, studying him, her intentions clear to him.

She wanted him, or his body, but she wasn't going to have what she wanted tonight. He was still thinking about Daryl and her innocence.

"I never kiss and tell."

He enjoyed that kiss, thought to try for more but he would wait, patience would go far in getting him more of Daryl MacTavish. Perhaps another trip to the bakery when he knew Donal was out of town. Even though Donal Chamberlin kissed her and perhaps had even given her a woman's pleasure, her reactions to him were innocent, unpracticed and it had been what seemed a lifetime since he held an untried lass in his arms. Lord, but he did recall the last time he was in Paris and his encounter with a virgin in Margaux's bordello. He would never forget Elisa Moreau. He wondered now what she was doing and made a mental note to look for her when he finished here and returned to Paris.

"So, you kissed Daryl. Wonder what Donal will have to say about that? He's a possessive man." Katrina was tapping her crystal glass with a fingernail, rolling her eyes upward. "I can imagine..." She waved her hand in the air, "Well, perhaps I shouldn't."

"Perhaps or perhaps not. It was just a common phrase. What I do with a woman is not your business. But rest assured I could have taken this farther today. I chose to hold back, to tease and maybe create a curiosity in her that she can't deny. She is a very passionate woman. As a lover she would please me."

His brief encounter with the lass made it clear to him that he wanted her, would enjoy making love to the woman. If the possibility existed, he wouldn't deny himself.

"Good, I appreciate the help in this matter."

"I'll stay by your side as long as you need me or until you take this farther than I believe you should. Revenge is a double-edged sword, and I won't be caught in the middle of a feud between you and Donal Chamberlin."

He enjoyed Katrina and the wild abandon that spilled from her when they had sex. She was, if anything, unpredictable. Even enjoyed sharing her with other men. Sharing created a different spin on the act, still he preferred one on one.

"I don't have a plan as yet." She downed the wine then replaced it with whisky. "Need something stronger. What you're saying about the lass means nothing to me other than you are talking in circles."

"When you have a plan, I can be clear with you about my intentions. As long as no one is hurt, I can probably help you with your endeavors. After today's encounter with the lovely lass, I won't be part of anything that will do her harm. As to Donal, I'm not so picky. If he ceased to exist, I would have free rein with Daryl."

"You're smitten with the lass." Her voice dripped venom as crease lines formed between her brows, making her very unattractive. "If you took her, Donal might not want her anymore."

For a moment Etienne was taken aback by the tone of her voice then he grinned. "Never smitten, nothing like that but I do want her in my bed for as long as it pleases me. Somehow I will do my best to find a way to convince her she wants the same."

"Should I be jealous?" Provocatively, she licked her lips, tilting her head to the side.

Suddenly, he was repulsed by her blatant quest for sex and he was tired of the practiced lovers he'd been seeing for the last few years of his life. "You should," he grinned shamelessly regaining his equilibrium and hopefully the upper hand.

"So, the plan should involve Daryl I assume."

"I would like that. While I don't seek revenge and have no need for more money than I already have, the girl in my arms as well as my bed would be a nice prize, the icing on top of the cake so to speak. No, I won't force her. Don't need to in any case. I could have taken her this afternoon with little to no resistance from her."

"Why didn't you?" she shot back at him, obviously furious he didn't take the lead and bring her here.

"I enjoy the chase, relish the seduction. I want to tease her to the point she can barely breathe. Her passion and lust for what I will do next will keep her from telling me no."

Good lord, just thinking about the chase and what he intended had him hard. He schooled his features, understanding there was more to this than pleasing Katrina. Caution and collecting of information came before anything else. Katrina had been in the bed of many foreigners, some with influence, some with the soul purposes of spying against the crown. He was here for information, nothing else, he reminded himself.

"I will wait impatiently then for the results of your seduction of the lass."

"Despite her relationship with Donal she is untried, still innocent in her reactions."

Blessed hell, he remembered the kiss, her shy and hesitant reaction to him. She wanted him. He was practiced enough to understand her tentative response as well as the blossoming passion simmering deep inside.

"They have not had sex, of that I'm sure. It's been at least five years since I bedded a virgin. After the last one I made a promise to myself never again. Daryl is different, though. She is passionate. Even though she tried to deny herself she wants sex and is curious. Today it didn't matter that I wasn't Donal."

"So, why is she still safe and with Donal?"

"We have no plan," he reminded her, studying the frown lines across her forehead and the tension around her eyes.

"Since you say you can take her easily, I want you to kidnap Daryl MacTavish. While you might not need money, I do. When you have her,

I will send a ransom note. Nothing here has gone as planned, and I need the funds to leave Scotland before it's too late."

"Where will you go?" He was curious. Without giving his purpose away, he concentrated on sipping the wine she'd poured earlier. "South of France? Amalfi Coast? All nice destinations."

"Perhaps Tuscany, I've a craving for Venice and Italian lovers are amazing." She looked upward as if remembering a lover from the city with canals."

"Better than me? *Mon cherie,* you wound me. Perhaps we should recreate our first mating and you can then make a better decision."

He stood behind her now, his hands pushing the sleeves of her gown from her shoulders before cupping her breasts and teasing the hard peaks. "Do you want the sex hard and fast? Perhaps you would prefer gentle and slow."

"Both, I want you to treat me as if I'm a virgin. I need to know how you will make love to his woman."

He laughed then, "I don't think so," He walked around her pulling her into his arms. "You could never react as a virgin. I doubt if you did your first time either."

In an instant her back was on the table, her legs around him and he was deep inside her. He knew she would be ready. Katrina was always swollen and wet. Not for a moment did he believe it was because of his great sexual prowess but because that was just the way Katrina's body reacted when she saw a man. For the first time that thought disgusted him and for the first time he thought of finding the right woman and settling down.

She throbbed around his rod and he found gratification with very little time, but he wasn't satisfied. He wanted Daryl. All he could think about was having his sex buried deep inside her.

To what cost?

Chapter Seven

Another night passed before Donal was able to return to Glasgow. He found the husbands ensconced in Flynt's home and pretending the women weren't about to do something dangerous again. He spent another evening with Daryl doing absolutely nothing to curb the dangerous habits of the woman he hoped would be his wife. He put his own wishes ahead of her safety, refusing to lecture her, tell her what she could or could not do.

They had yet to discuss anything really important, and he had the distinct feeling she was now hiding something from him. It seemed to him his life had spiraled out of control. He didn't understand anything any longer. All his dreams seemed to be sliding away from him.

What to do?

She stood in the door, her hair tumbling around her shoulders, a shy hesitant smile on her full lips. "Hello. I missed you today."

To him, she never looked more beautiful. "Come, sit beside me." He needed to hold her in his arms, learn what it was she was unwilling to tell him. It did not bode well for their future if she feared him.

Slowly, she walked toward him, her hands fisted together in front of her. When she sat on the bed, he held one hand, wound his fingers between hers. "What's bothering you?"

"N-nothing." She turned a way for a moment, seemingly unable to look at him. Lifting her chin, "There is absolutely nothing wrong."

He decided he needed to let her tell him in her time. "I've misread your expression and tentativeness." He placed a finger beneath her chin. "Will you kiss me, *mo chroi*?"

She ran her tongue across her lips and nodding, "I'd like that, a

176

kiss," the tenor of her whisper frightened him.

He felt her trembling, guessed it was not passion or desire but fear or perhaps anxiety. He didn't want her to fear him, and he didn't believe that was true. So, what was she afraid of if it wasn't him? He would have to find a way to draw the truth from her without her knowing it was his doing.

Gently, he touched her lips with his, teased with teeth, tongue and lips then he deepened the kiss, his hand around her waist pulling her closer. With his other hand he ran his fingers through the glorious length of her hair.

He pulled away, "Have you made any decisions about us?" He smiled, running the back of his hand along her face, studying her eyes. Lord, he needed to know what happened today and why she felt so different in his arms. She was holding back somehow, keeping part of herself aloof from him. None of her reactions made sense.

She waited a few seconds before answering. "A lot has happened today. I guess I lied to you. Something is bothering me. If I tell you, the information could change your opinion of me, of our relationship."

His heart lurched for a second, every part of him stretched to the breaking point. "You lied?" That was something he never expected from her.

"Only about nothing happening."

One tiny hand rested on his chest. He covered it with his. Her fingers were cold to his touch.

"I know I have to tell you. It's just that..."

"Start at the beginning and I doubt anything you say could change my mind."

He sat back, bringing her with him. One arm was wrapped around her, holding her close. Her body trembled against his.

"I met someone," she began, her head resting on his chest. "He doesn't mean anything to me, but he was nice and..." she passed her tongue across her lips.

"Why would meeting someone give you reason to lie to me?" he asked, letting her go when she pushed away from him.

Her eyes were huge, moisture lodging within. If he could make everything right, he would do it in a heartbeat.

She was sitting on the bed, now crossed legged and facing him. For a few seconds she played with her skirts then as was predictable, she began to fumble with her buttons.

He grinned, wondering if she was so nervous, she would undo all of them. "I want you to make love to me. I need you to..."

"Is that an agreement of marriage?"

He forgot her nervousness and the reason, forgot that she lied to him and that might be good reason for him to listen to her more carefully than normal.

Her smile was shy and innocent and she looked at him with her huge blue eyes, "Yes."

"You don't care if I tell you how I feel about things and even try to force you to my way of thinking? I don't believe that."

He meant to lay all his feeling about marriage and relationships out in the open. He had been treading carefully around her, perhaps too carefully. "In the future I mean to tell you all I feel about the things you do that I don't agree with. You need to understand. It doesn't mean I want you to change for me, never that. I just need you to know how I feel, and I expect the same from you."

"I do care but it doesn't mean I don't want to marry you. It doesn't mean I won't respect some of your wishes."

All but two of the buttons were undone and he almost laughed. She was going to be his and blessed hell, he did want her to disrobe. It would be easier if she did it for him but not nearly as seductive.

"So, you will obey my wishes?" he queried, knowing the answer before she spoke, unable to keep his gaze from the soft curve of her breasts she revealed.

"Only when you are right."

She stared at his mouth, moistening her lips before catching a bottom lip between her teeth.

Perhaps this was what she was nervous about. "Ach, lass, I'm right most of the time and you ken it even if you won't verbally acknowledge the fact."

"Not about the other day when we captured the instigator of

Flynt's attack. You are wrong about the numbers not being in our favor. I know you can disarm me but not all of us."

So, she meant to continue in this vein. He couldn't allow that even though it might well put a damper on the seduction he planned now that she agreed to become his wife.

"Stand over there," he told her, his voice curt.

"Why?"

"I'm going to show you what could happen to you if you tried something like that with a man." He handed her an object. "Pretend that is a gun and you have it pointed at me to keep me from hurting you. Imagine also your sisters and Hope are there also with a gun pointed at me."

"All right then," she braced herself, keeping the tip directed at him.

He cocked his head watching her, memorizing her position then in a fluid move his hand came down hard on her arm and the other grabbed the gun. In an instant, his arm was wrapped around her neck and the pretend gun was pointed at her head.

He heard the cry of pain but had to ignore it to make his point. "Now, what are your sisters going to do? Shoot you? Pretend they still have the upper hand. Not sure why Sean didn't disarm you. You were lucky." He let her go, wishing the conversation had not turned in this direction.

She was rubbing her arm and looking at him with huge, moisture filled eyes. He tried to tell himself they held moisture before. "You hurt me."

"I'm sorry about that," he said taking her arm in his hand, examining the spot where a bruise was already forming. Guilt swept through him. "I'm really sorry."

He strode from the room, hating himself for his part in this charade, a lesson that needed to be learned, and he prayed Daryl took the point seriously and that it was the last lesson he needed to teach.

A few minutes later he returned. She was once again sitting cross-legged on the bed, her arm resting across her leg. She looked at him. "You didn't have to do it so hard."

"You're wrong, I did need to give you a much needed education. If I had gone easier, then that you wouldn't understand the full strength of a man." He set the cold cloth on her arm, wishing there had been some other way to show her.

"I still think you're wrong. We could have overpowered you. I would not have stood so close that you could reach me like that."

"I would have drug you through the door, keeping your sisters in front of me. Nothing could be further from the truth." He realized then she didn't believe him and let out a long exasperated sigh.

Before he sat down, he poured a glass of wine for her. She sipped, looking at him with a strange look in her eyes.

"I thought you were going to make love to me." she told him with a hint of recrimination in her voice.

"Just give you your pleasure. Making love is reserved for the wedding night. Do you want me to give you your woman's pleasure? I would do that."

"I don't know," she told him stubbornly, looking pointedly at the door. "I think you should go home."

"Since you don't know if you want pleasure, you might try buttoning your blouse so I can't see the soft curve of your breast and the dark outline of your nipples through your chemise. You shouldn't tempt a man, a real man."

She looked down and shrugged, lifting her shoulders in a gesture that he was learning meant she didn't care. "I can see your tiny nipples through your shirt too."

No doubt about it she was getting to him. "Why don't you tell me about this person you met. While you're weaving the story, you can decide what it is you want. It's up to you."

"I want you to make love to me then I want you to marry me." It seemed she deflected the question. "After you make love to me, I'll tell you about this person I met today in the bakery."

She lost the hurt little girl look, and he wondered if she used that expression to get her way with Flynt when she was growing up. He laughed then. "You think to bribe me? I will give you pleasure but the making love will have to wait. Should we wed tomorrow? Catherine and your sisters can plan an elaborate reception if they wish for later."

"No, I would like a nice wedding, with flowers and a wedding dress. I want my sisters to be in the wedding." She slipped off her shirt, her eyes on his lips then lowering to his crotch.

"You trying to seduce me?" His laughter echoed in the small room.

Desire lanced through him, tightening his body even more. His rod hardened as he watched her toy with the tiny straps to her chemise.

"Is it working?" she asked as she rose on her knees to rid herself of her skirt.

In front of him she shimmied out of it. Now she wore only the thin chemise and her stockings. He sat back against the headboard, his hands behind his head, enjoying her antics and wondering what she would do next.

"No, not in the least but you may continue. You can't seduce me into doing things your way. It just won't work." Yet it would take incredible will power to see this through. "Your pleasure or nothing at all. My mind is made up."

Blessed hell, but he wanted to come behind her, touch her, slide his hand down her body to touch her intimately. Seducing could wait. For the moment, he was truly enjoying the show she was putting on.

She stopped then, "I'm not taking all my clothes off if you are keeping yours on."

A hot shudder racked him from head to heels. His heartbeat doubled. Blood raced through him and gathered in a tempest, transforming him. His entire body hardened watching her sensual game.

He looked at himself before meeting her gaze once more. "Be my guest. I wouldn't want to wear clothes when I don't have to."

She straddled him. Her thighs pressing against his, her moist core on top his sex. He felt her heat as well as her dampness. "You're burning me alive, *mo chroi.*"

"Is that good or bad?" Her voice was thready, thin, yet now he knew her trembling was the passion heating her, arousing her and had nothing to do with fear.

"Both of course," he told her, allowing her to take his shirt off and run her hands along his chest, her nails scoring lightly on the way downward toward his sex.

She bent over, brushing her lips across his, playing with him as he did earlier. "Both..."

He cupped her breasts in his hand, teasing the nipples just as she was now teasing his with her lips and teeth. He should end this now, stop before they took this so far there would be no return. Yet he closed his eyes, allowing her access to him.

"Who is this person you met?" he asked, wishing now he could proceed without the revelation.

She sat back, pushing hair from her eyes, a wounded expression on her gorgeous face. "It's nothing really. I met a man in the bakery. I've never seen him before."

"There is nothing else to tell?" One eyebrow rose in question.

She lifted her shoulders a bit before smiling. "We walked to the park. The day was nice and he's new in town."

"Is this what you were afraid to tell me?" he asked, knowing there was more to the story. She would not appear so worried about a walk to the park.

"I didn't know how you would feel." She sighed softly. Then, "He kissed me."

She moved away from him. His brows drew together while he searched for something to say. All the desire he had for her vanished with those words. "No, I don't like that. Did you like his kiss?"

"It wasn't yours. He didn't taste like you," she told him, her voice so soft he could barely hers. "So, it wasn't as nice."

"That's not an answer."

"What do you want me to say?"

"Did you like the kiss?" he insisted.

"Yes, but not as much as yours."

Her breaths were short pants. He watched the rapid beating of her pulse at the base of her neck, the way her breasts rose and fell with her agitation.

"Did you do anything else?" His jealousy spiraled to a breaking point. "Perhaps you should have waited to tell me until I gave you your pleasure."

"We talked and it was just one kiss. You've kissed countless women and made love to them."

"Hardly countless," he muttered.

"I wanted to compare kisses. Is that so bad? We aren't engaged and I don't think that can count as cheating on you. Can it?"

"You've never been kissed except by me?"

He never asked because he simply didn't think it could be true. She always responded passionately, almost expertly, even that first kiss when she was only sixteen or seventeen. Weel, not expertly but with so much passion and the way her moist hot tongue responded to him every time nearly undid him.

"Never," she told him. "I don't know what came over me, only that when he asked, I knew I had to say yes."

"I don't like what you're telling me. What if he wants to touch your breasts or give you a woman's pleasure? Don't you want to find out how another man does it so you can compare us?"

Bloody hell but he didn't think she should be comparing him with anyone. He didn't like the fact he might be giving her ideas.

"Do you compare me with the other women you've had in your bed? Women you've touched and kissed, made love to." Her pointed questions stopped him. "Did you compare me to Katrina?"

"What kind of question is that? Of course I don't."

But did he?

"Are you sure? You've said things that have led me to believe differently. Don't you think if I'm going to commit my life to you, I should know how it feels when another man kisses me?" she told him, her chin rising in the air. "A kiss really means nothing."

"Would you want him to touch you intimately, give you your woman's pleasure as I have done?" he asked again needing the answer, nearly beside himself with the thought of Daryl in another man's arms.

She looked stunned by his words then indignant. She cleared her throat before saying, "That's hardly the same thing as a kiss and it's hardly fair of you to even bring that up in the same conversation."

"I didn't think before I said the words."

He ran his hands through his hair, frustration racing through him, had never thought anything like this would happen.

"I can't believe you think so little of me." Her anger seemed to simmer. "You should apologize."

He supposed he should be pleased by her expression. "No, no it's not the same at all. I am sorry."

"You should be, you know."

"I need to think." He rose from the bed before pulling his shirt then his boots on. "I'll see you in the morning."

"Where are you going?"

"For a walk or to a tavern, I need to punch something, anyone will do.

He was out the door before she could say anything. This was not something he could have ever anticipated. She kissed another man and she liked it. How the bloody hell was he supposed to deal with that fact? Just like Katrina, needing to sample every man she saw. The thought nearly sent him to his knees. No, she was nothing like that woman.

His feet hurt. He'd been walking so long. He doubled back, heading for the park near her home as if he could recreate the kiss, she told him about. Thinking about it was not good but her actions didn't please him, no they didn't please him at all. This was not well done. He kept on walking, finally stopping at Ashford's home when he saw the light was still on.

Ash and Emilia were sitting in the parlor. He was sipping brandy and Emilia had a cup of tea. He needed back up if he was going to a tavern. He wouldn't start the fight but he was joining in if one started.

"Good evening?" He stepped into the entry when Ash opened the door.

"What's got you tied in knots? She say no again?" Ash asked with a chuckle. "You should really try for compromise. It might work wonders with your disposition."

"Need to hit something. Thought you might go with me to a pub."

He looked to Emilia who was smiling and nodding her head. "If you get a black eye, don't wake me up."

"Of course I'll wake you up," Ash said, "It won't be to get help.

It will be to make love to my beautiful fiancée."

"No, you won't," she said. "Since we're getting married in the morning, I fully intend to remain chaste tonight. I'm sleeping alone in one of your guest rooms."

"Why?"

"It will make the wedding night more... more well, exciting." She smiled at him as she left the room. Then, "Don't wake me up. I'll be in the spare bedroom."

"She's been talking to Grams," Donal laughed.

"Weel, we will see who wins this little skirmish," Ash said, watching her leave.

Donal was chuckling inside as he listened to his friend swear. "Too bad for you, but I guess you'll be more inclined to hit something now, knowing she does not intend to welcome you into her bed this evening."

"I will but I'm not sleeping alone tonight. She's going to have to tell me no when I pull her into my arms and touch her in certain places that make her burn with pleasure."

"You're not going to respect her wishes? I wouldn't either but I'm not sure I'm getting married anytime soon."

"What happened? Thought Daryl was leaning toward saying yes." Ash said as they entered a bar and ordered a Guinness.

They were both leaning on the counter watching the scene in front of them. Much to his disappointment, no one seemed to be rowdy.

A woman sidled up to him, her hand on his chest. "You free tonight, fancy man? I've got time for you." She pushed against him, her breasts nearly spilling free from her low-cut gown.

"Not really interested," he told her yet perversely he was tempted. Tempted just because Daryl kissed a man. "Ask me later." A wave of guilt rushed through him and he was reminded of her words. That giving and receiving a woman's pleasure was hardly on the same scale as a kiss.

She moved to Ash, "Maybe your friend is more interested in a little sensual pleasure upstairs."

"I'm getting married in the morning," Ash said, "You're going to have to look somewhere else for your entertainment."

"All the better, one last fling with a woman before you're leg shackled for life," she laughed, sliding her hand down his chest until it rested just above his pants, seeming tempted to move lower but held back.

Ash moved her hand away. "Think my friend is more than willing to see you tonight." Ash laughed at the frown he shot him.

"You two don't know what you're missing." Her hands on her hips she thrust out her breasts.

"Most likely I do know." Donal wasn't sure why he was standing here drinking and looking for a fight when he could have spent the night in Daryl's bed with his arms around her.

"What cha doin' with my girl?" Some drunk stumbled into him, his hands gripping his shirt.

Donal looked at Ash, shrugged slightly before hitting the man in the jaw. The man crashed into a table spilling drinks. The two men sitting at the table stood, searching the room for whoever started this and found them.

The fight was on and Donal felt immediate gratification with each blow he landed. The few patrons still in the bar joined in, picking sides. This was exactly what he needed.

For Donal the confrontation was over too soon. He left enough coin to pay the owner for damages before he kissed the whore who approached them earlier square on the lips.

He guessed they were even now. Problem was he couldn't say he liked the kiss. Now the only kisses he wanted were Daryl's. He left Ash at the door of his home then walked to the bakery. There were no lights on in her upstairs apartment. He sighed heavily, knowing he should not wake her up. Pulling out his pocket watch to see to the time, he groaned. It was three in the morning, nearly time for her to get up. Justine would probably be in his kitchen cooking his breakfast to leave in the small warming oven.

He started up her stairs. Hand on the railing and nearly at her door, he stopped himself. He would see Daryl at Ash's wedding and he would beg her forgiveness. Caught between walking in and leaving, he pulled the key from his pocket.

Before he used it, he knocked on the door and there was no answer. His heart caught in his throat as the unlocked door slowly opened.

~ * ~

Unable to stay away from the pretty lady who instantly caught his heart and for the time seemed to hold it in the palm of her hands, he'd never before known this type of instant attraction to a woman. He would have enjoyed pursuing this, but he had a job, two jobs to be exact. He needed to figure out how to do the second one without compromising the first.

This feeling was new to him.

He was about to leave his vantage point when Donal stomped down the stairs, swearing under his breath. Etienne smiled. He guessed she told him about the kiss. No reason to make this easy for the other man. The carriage to take her away waited for them. For a moment he felt an instant of regret.

Taking advantage of their quarrel seemed a likely way to proceed with his seduction and kidnapping of the pretty lady. He knew she wouldn't fall easily, and he wasn't even sure any longer that he wanted to make this harder for Daryl, but he wanted her the moment he saw her. "It's up to Daryl to decide how this goes. I won't stop if she gives me any indication she wants me. Whatever pleases her," he murmured.

Etienne climbed the stairs to the apartment, eagerly anticipating the meeting. He inhaled a deep breath of air. It wasn't for courage. The breath was simply to give him strength to stop the seduction if that was what she wished. He hoped it wasn't though.

When he knocked, she opened quickly, surprising him then.

"Oh..." She stepped backward several times, "It's you? What are you doing here? At this hour?"

"You were expecting someone else," he grinned, his smile captivating her. "Undressed as you are?"

She looked down then back, her eyes huge. "I was..." Her tongue passed across her mouth.

"I saw Donal leave, swearing. May I come in?" he asked even though he now stood inside her small home. "I would spend a few hours with you before the sunrises."

"Yes, yes, I suppose so." She left then went into another room, which he assumed was her bedroom. When she returned, she'd put on a robe, covering her.

"You realize of course I can see more of you than you probably want me to see." He reached out, touched her cheek before running his hand along the slender column of her neck.

She looked down again. "I don't have anything else to put on."

"Your clothing perhaps. What you had on before Donal undressed you would be more appropriate."

Her hands were on her cheeks, "So hot."

"May I sit down and stay for a few minutes?" He poured her a drink then one for himself. "Come sit beside me."

"I shouldn't. I'll be right back."

He reached out to stop her, the warmth of his fingers sending gentle shivers of heat through her. "I like the way you look. You don't have to dress for me. I promise I won't look at you too closely."

"All right." She blinked a few times, pressing her hands down the fabric of the sheer robe she wore. She was nodding her head, believing him, flustered by his presence. She sipped the drink then grimaced as the whiskey burned a fiery path down her throat. "I'll stay this way if you like. I-I wasn't sure when you told me you could see all of me. I wouldn't want to be too forward."

"I assume he left angry because you told him about us and the shared kiss." His hand rested on her leg.

He felt her shiver of pleasure as he stroked her and he wondered if that was something, she would let him do without telling Donal. "I did tell him and he didn't understand. Said he had to think and left. It wasn't well done of him. We needed to talk, have things that need to be said, before..."

"Did you point out no one else in your life had kissed you or touched you other places and he was much more experienced in sensual pleasures? You wanted to have something to compare."

She was nodding again, unable to think as his hand ran up then down her leg.

"W-what are you doing?"

"Touching your leg makes me feel good. How does it make you feel?" He switched to her other leg.

"Shivery and hot." She was barely able to speak or think when he caressed her.

"Are those good feelings?"

He placed his finger beneath her chin and lifted. She was staring into dark brown eyes, eyes that seemed to mesmerize her, enchant her in every way. They simmered with passion and desire, darkening to near black while she watched. "May I kiss you again? Since I've already kissed you and you reported it to your Donal, you needn't tell him about this one if it will make your life easier. If all we do is kiss, you needn't say anything. Would you like that?"

She didn't say no but she didn't say yes either, just watched his mouth as it came closer to hers. Felt the whisper of his breath against her cheek. She moistened her lips then his softly brushed hers. His hands were holding her head as his teeth tugged gently on her lower lip before laving it lightly with his tongue, leaving an extraordinary fire shivering in its wake. Her breath caught and her heart turned over at the tender caress. She wanted more, knew she should tell him no.

"Will you open for me?" he asked, his voice raspy.

She suddenly wanted to be the aggressor, anger at Donal for abandoning her the catalyst for her behavior. Her teeth nipped his lower lip, just as he had done to her. The startled breath he gasped was the opening she looked for. Her tongue slid into the warm darkness of his mouth and began exploring intimately. This was something she never dreamed of doing.

She made a throaty sound of pleasure when she tasted him. Then and there she decided she would feel no guilt, would say nothing to Donal. It was a kiss, nothing more. Donal already knew she shared a kiss with another man. There was nothing left to tell.

"I love the way you taste," she whispered, realizing she couldn't remember if she said anything like this to Donal and yet she loved the way he tasted also. She made a promise to herself that she would become the aggressor with Donal. May chance, that was why he held back. "I love the way your teeth feel so slick and hard and your tongue is all velvet and warm. You give me shivers of pleasures."

Etienne made a low growling sound in the back of his throat. His arms tightened until he held her in a powerful warm vice. She needed to explore these new feelings and realizations. Despite her anger with Donal, Etienne offered something different and she meant to discover what exactly it was.

"You shouldn't say things like that to a man," he whispered, his lips touching hers, ready for more.

"Why?"

She pulled back, one hand resting on his cheek, enjoying the texture of his stubble so different from Donal's beard.

"You'll make me lose my head. You're burning me alive."

"Just for a while. Just for this evening I want to feel something different. You are special and I don't want to feel a moment of shame. I want to pretend that what we have between us is not a betrayal of any kind."

She was slowly talking herself out of the intimacy she anticipated with Etienne.

Before he could pull away, she shifted a little and he pulled her onto his lap. As she moved, she felt his arousal beneath her, hard and pulsing almost as if his member possessed a life all its own. It felt wonderful but she remembered the other man, the one she loved.

She recalled when she touched Donal, closed her mouth over him, bringing him to his man's pleasure. The way he tasted and the smooth texture that excited and aroused her. Etienne's sex was full, hard, ready. She could do the same with Etienne. She could give him a man's pleasure if he wanted.

She made another low sound and moved again, caressing him, knowing at some deeply feminine level this was a way of asserting her control. She wondered how long she would continue this.

No guilt. No recriminations. Just pleasure.

He tried to speak. All that came out was throttled groan when her mouth slanted over his, sipping the corners of his lips. Yet no matter how fully their mouths joined, it wasn't enough. She needed more tonight, much, much more. She didn't know when it would be too much more.

Her name was a husky question on his lips.

He stroked her urgently. "It's your skin I want to feel, not your clothing. Is this what you would like too?" Quickly he undid the ties on her robe then slipped the fragile straps of her chemise from her arms. Her breasts were exposed now for him to see, to caress if he wanted and perhaps to kiss. They were after all just kissing. Kissing wasn't wrong, she reminded herself. She told Donal about the kiss.

His fingers were cold from the night air. Daryl gasped when they plucked at her nipples. When he hesitated, she inhaled a deep breath.

"Have we gone too far?" he asked, even while he bent his head to suck one of those hard buds into his mouth.

"I don't know but I know I don't want you to stop," she whispered, frustrated and somewhat angry with Donal and his stubborn refusal to compromise.

"Doing something that will make your life difficult with your man is not something I intended when I walked up the stairs to your apartment this evening. I just wanted to see you, maybe kiss you again, taste your essence and I needed to make a decision. I should go." He put a tiny amount of distance between their lips, still she stared at him.

It seemed to Daryl that tonight everyone was leaving her. She didn't want to be alone even though the evening was passing too quickly and she would need to be downstairs in a few hours. On some primal elemental level, she wanted him to stay with her.

"Don't leave me. Donal just left and I know I displeased him. I don't ken what I've done to displease you or why you want to go." She searched her mind for everything she said and did with Etienne. "Did I say the wrong things?"

"No, everything you said was right, perfect, what I wanted to hear and feel. Yet I know you are not a woman who would give herself to more than one man. And yes, I want you but..."

His words trailed off and she understood all too well, this was not right for either of them and that she'd ventured too far in her curiosity as well as the sexual need Donal left her with. "What is it you want from me?"

For a few seconds he closed his eyes, breathing deeply as if he had a story to tell. "A very long time ago I fell in love with a woman. She wasn't the person I thought she was. I think she carried my child, but no one would allow me to see her. I left then."

"You found out different?"

Daryl sat back, rearranging her clothing, bringing her chemise to cover her and slipping the robe over her shoulders. He seemed so sad, wistful and she understood there was more to this story.

"No, I never looked back and I've stayed away for too many years. If I thought she could return my feeling, I might return." He downed the whiskey he poured earlier. "I think we might have had a baby," he said again, pensively, "No one would tell me the truth. Even now I don't know."

"Overtime you thought she would come to love you. She didn't understand what kind of person you are." Just as Donal had done earlier this evening, Etienne was drawing away from her.

"Perhaps not. By the end of the evening you won't like me either." He stood then and walked to the window, peering out into the darkness, leaving her behind. His back was rigid against the night and revealing anything more about himself seemed impossible.

"I don't understand." She spoke softly, curious now as to what he was implying. "I don't know why I wouldn't like you. You've always been a perfect gentleman."

"Well..." He turned to look at her and with a harsh laugh, "Far from perfect, I made her one last promise and I intend to keep it. After that, I'm going to return home and look for a love for myself. Putting her to the back of my mind should not be too hard. Perhaps I'll find someone more like you."

"It was Katrina. You fell in love with a woman who cares only for herself." She felt sadness for Etienne. "You deserve so much more."

"No, it's not Katrina."

"No?"

"Sadly, you won't feel that way. I was hoping perhaps you would return to me half the love you give Donal. But you can't and that fact has nothing to do with the future."

"No, I love him. What we were doing is wrong, but somehow you're important to me. I'll always care about you." This conversation had taken a direction that confused her.

"You were curious about other men. I purposely sparked that curiosity because I too was selfish. I wanted to kiss you, hold you in my arms and feel the silken fire that is your hair. If you would have given me more, I wouldn't have thought twice about taking what was offered. I would have seduced you until you weren't able to say no, until you were at that point where sensations would rule your mind."

"But you didn't." Daryl reached out to touch him, caress his face.

"Don't." He took her hand away and placed it on her lap. "It's time. You need to get dressed."

"I don't understand."

He sighed heavily, staring at her with a sad lonely look. "I made Katrina a promise I intend to keep. Now, go on into your bedroom and put some clothes on. Dress in something warm, it's going to be a long ride, and I don't want you to get cold."

"No. Only when you tell me why."

Now he was frightening her. The expression on his face changed to a harshness she'd never seen before.

"Katrina needs money. She thought to seduce or entrap Donal, but her ploy didn't work. He was too smart so Katrina set her sights on you, trusting I could seduce you. She wants revenge."

"You did seduce me."

"Not entirely. Still she needs me. I promised her one last thing and I'll see it through despite the fact I abhor what she is trying to accomplish."

"So, what does that have to do with me?" Her hands were trembling now as she tried to figure out what he wasn't telling her. She was suddenly afraid of this man and what he intended, yet her heart told her he would never harm her.

"I'm taking you away from here and giving you to Katrina. She won't hurt you, just wants to hold you until Donal pays for your safe return. He will, won't he?"

She was shaking her head then backing into the bedroom where she had her gun. She would defend herself. "I won't go with you."

"You will, pretty lady. If you don't dress yourself, I'll take you the way you are. I'm sure clothing that a man cannot see through would be preferable for our trip. Although we'll be inside a carriage then inside her home, I can't tell you who else will be there. Katrina has numerous lovers. She will want to play games. See what kind of person you are."

"Very well."

She stiffened her back, determined to protect herself. She didn't understand much of what was happening or why Etienne would do something so despicable when he no longer cared for Katrina. One last promise to be kept then he would be free of her but she was part of that promise. It did not sit well with her.

She found the gun. Then standing in the doorway, she pointed it at him. Her voice shook but she was determined. "I'm not going anywhere with you."

"You are stubborn, too much so, and you believe you have the skills to keep me, a man, at bay. You do not." He stepped toward her, his arm outstretched. "Hand over the gun before you hurt yourself." He stepped forward again.

"I'll shoot you." Her hand was trembling so hard she thought the weapon might shake from her hand. She knew using the gun on him would be nearly impossible, but she could do it. She had no other choice.

"No, I don't believe you will. Give me the gun, pretty lady. If you don't, one of us might get hurt. Do you want that? Do you truly want to shoot me?"

He was so close, she was sure she felt the heat of his body. He could take it from her just as Donal had done earlier this evening. It would not be difficult.

"No, you know I don't but I don't want to go with you either." She let the gun fall, clattering on the floor. "This isn't right. You are doing something wrong because once a long time ago you loved a woman who would have nothing to do with you."

He picked it up, turning it over in his big hands then gazing at her. "It's not even loaded."

She grimaced then resigned to make the most of this fate. "I ken it. I'll go dress." Perhaps if she lingered, the others would be downstairs and come to her aide. Donal might come back and apologize. She realized none of that would happen as the clocked chimed two times.

"If it takes more than a couple of minutes, I'll come in and dress you myself," he threatened. "Or take you the way you are."

He would too. She didn't doubt that fact for a moment. "Alright." Quickly and seeing no way out of this, she dressed.

"I'm pleased you're cooperating. I didn't want to tie you or carry you out of here on my shoulder."

She stood in the parlor now, her hands clasped in front of her. "You don't have to do this. Changing your mind would not be wrong. It doesn't matter if you keep your promise to that woman. You could go home."

"Good, I'm glad you see reason. This will all be over in a few days, and you'll be returned home to marry Donal." He opened the door for her, following her down the steps. "The carriage is waiting."

"You came here with the intention of taking me, not as you said earlier that you wanted to see me."

She felt a rush of helplessness and despair surge through her. She had been so stupid, just as Donal told her. She could not overpower a man. She could not fight him.

"What if Donal no longer wants me?"

"Because I kissed you?"

She nodded.

"Then I'll be a pleased man and we can discover what we can have together. You could come with me."

"Where is that?"

"I'm going home to France. I should have returned a long time ago. My home and the rest of my life waits for me."

"He will pay the ransom, won't he?" She'd never been so unsure of herself as she was now. "We argued and he was angry with me, walked out. What will happen if he no longer wants me?" She could not keep from thinking the worst possible scenario.

"I believe he will. Even if he has a few misgivings, he will come around. He is a good man." Gently, he helped her into the vehicle. "I'm glad you are resigned. I promise you no one will hurt you. Katrina doesn't want that either."

"Where are we going?" She sat opposite him, her hands fiddling with the fabric of her skirt. "How long will it take?"

"A few hours, maybe more. Try to relax."

He sat back, his arms draped across the backseat, his long legs stretched out in front of him.

"I don't see how I can do that," she told him while her body shook and blood pounded in her head. She didn't know if it was nerves or the damp coldness surrounding her.

"There is a blanket beneath your seat and food if you are hungry." He closed his eyes as the carriage picked up speed. "Help yourself."

"You never said where we are going." She pulled out the blanket then wrapped it around her shoulders.

"Near Langbank on the Firth of Clyde." He told her. "After we get there and you are comfortable, Katrina will write the ransom letter. I'm sure Donal will pay for your release and come to your rescue within minutes of receiving her demand."

"I don't like you much right now," she told him petulantly. "This is not well done of you."

"I ken it, pretty lady. I told you that you wouldn't. You feel betrayed and yes, that is exactly what I did. I used you to get what I wanted. I am attracted to you though. That part is not a lie. If not for Donal in your life, this would end up far differently than you could ever perceive now. I would not be taking you to Katrina."

"You're right," she told him, wishing she could sleep and wake up in her bed. This was all a bad dream and it wasn't happening.

"I'm glad you're resigned to your fate. All will go much better for you if you don't fight."

They rode in silence then. She did dream but the dream was far different than the reality. When she woke up, the sun was beginning to lighten the night sky. Shivering, she pulled the blanket closer. "Are we almost there?"

"You slept. I'm pleased. Your strength and stamina will come into play when we arrive. While Katrina promised you would not be forced or hurt, unfortunately, one can never count on her temper or a new game she might have concocted. If she doesn't like something, she will react without provocation. You must be careful and keep your wits about you. Whatever you do, don't challenge her."

"I don't know her except by what little Donal has told me."

"She is dangerous, lass, and I will do everything in my power to keep her from doing something awful. She has a foul mind and it wouldn't surprise me if she would like to play sexual games with you, ones you couldn't possibly understand, ones that might truly ruin you for Donal."

"You will remind her of her promise."

"More than that, I will stand as your champion if she is anything but gentle with you. I've the power as well as the knowledge to ruin her and she knows it." He pulled out the basket of food. "Have some things to eat, if you are interested."

Despite the fact her stomach was rumbling, she wanted to say no to anything he offered. Instead, she accepted the scones, ones she made yesterday. "You planned this since yesterday?"

"I did. As I said, Katrina wants this to be done as soon as possible, as do I. She needs to leave Glasgow and Scotland behind, but she also needs the funds to do it."

"I would have you on my side."

She shivered at thoughts of Katrina and what she might have planned for her. This could not possibly go as well as Etienne thought.

"We are here, I think. The carriage is slowing. Are you ready? It will be best for you if you do what she asks, within reason that is."

"No, if I believed I could get away from you, I would run." Her agile mind continued to look for some avenue of escape. "I won't be a docile captive."

"You know that would be a waste of your energy. You will need all of that in the following hours. Docile is the only type of captive you should be." His voice was gentle and a bit wistful.

She was shaking her head, confused and frustrated with

everything he told her. "One moment you tell me nothing will happen to me. The next you warn me that Katrina is unpredictable and I should be on guard."

"I do and that is to keep you thinking and resilient. If she does something I cannot agree with at least in part, I will abandon her cause and side with you." He leaned forward, stroking her cheek. "We can sit here for a few more minutes if you would like."

"Or we can meet the lioness in her den," she said, inhaling a sharp quick breath. "Best to get this over with."

"Or we can greet the lioness and show her just how strong and indomitable you are." He smiled then and it was the first time since he told her his plans. "You will beat her at her games. Stay strong."

"I'll try."

He helped her from the carriage. While she gripped his arm, they strode to the front door.

"I see you did as you promised. I was beginning to wonder if you would fail me," Katrina said, her voice dripping venom. "What took you so long?"

~ * ~

They followed Katrina through the house to a room overlooking the Firth of Clyde. The chamber was on the third floor. Etienne knew she could never escape this place, and he also knew there were peepholes in the walls for anyone to observe what was going on in the room.

His gut tightened when he realized Katrina would implore him to take her virginity and she would watch. He wouldn't do that. Daryl made it perfectly clear she wanted nothing more to do with him sexually. If he made love to her, Donal might never take her back. He choked on that thought. If he wouldn't take her back, it could only mean he didn't really love her.

He could seduce her and she would not say no, but he promised himself even if Katrina asked, he wouldn't do such a deplorable thing, not to Daryl. In such a short amount of time she'd come to mean a lot to him. It was a feeling Katrina would never understand.

Katrina held up a sheer gown, one he understood was meant for sensual pleasures. "She's to put this on. If she refuses, I want you to see to it."

"No," he told Katrina, understanding she would continue to insist and afraid some other man would take his place if he refused. He needed to proceed one second at a time and evaluate the situation, making changes in his disposition as needed.

"I have another man who will take her virginity if you don't want to," she told him smirking. "You like the little bitch too much. It's affecting your judgment. It's either you or another man."

"No, we discussed this before I took Daryl and there were promises made by both of us. You cannot change your mind now and expect me to stand beside you." Even though he'd foreseen this, he was furious with her, his anger simmering just beneath the surface. "Daryl is not willing. No one will force her. If it pleases you though, I will make sure she puts on the gown."

Katrina cleared her throat, looking Daryl over. "We will see. I know you and you can easily seduce her. You have that magic touch when a woman's pleasure is your goal."

"No man will touch her save Donal. I made a promise to her. You vowed no one would be hurt or forced. I've played my role in this scenario. Now it is up to you to accept the ransom and hand Daryl over when the time has come."

"Seduction is not force," she reminded him, pointing a finger at him and smiling. "I want to watch the ruin of Donal's woman, unless you've already taken her. Have you?"

He was tempted to lie but knew Katrina would find a way to discover the truth. "She is still a virgin."

"Don't suppose he will want her if she isn't. At least that's the way he was with me. Take her into the dressing room and make sure she puts on the gown. You can have her or this one can," she nodded toward the other man, Leod, who was stepping into the room. "What will it be? You can always give her the choice."

"While she is changing, you'll write the ransom letter. You do want the money. Think about what is happening here. If he doesn't want her, or suspects she's been violated, you won't get the money. You know he's a hard man. One you couldn't deceive before. Do you truly believe you can do that now?" Etienne was wracking his brain to find a way to change Katrina's way of thinking.

"Something to contemplate," Katrina said then tapping her chin in thought, "Put her in the gown. I'll make my decision after the letter is written."

"The right conclusion is to make sure Daryl remains a virgin. What I know of Donal Chamberlin is that this won't end well for you if you come to any other resolution. He will find you and bring the law into this. You could hang or find yourself on a prison ship headed to Damien's Island. You need to tread carefully."

Etienne watched as she left the room before turning his attention to Daryl. He hoped he made his point with her. "Pretty lady," he began, "this is an example of how we should choose our battles with Katrina. For some reason she wants to humiliate you as doing so will hurt Donal. Donning the gown will do that. You must play the part. Don't try to stand up to her or pretend you are not embarrassed by what she is doing. Not courage but humility is what you need."

Her voice catching in her throat, "There are different degrees of humiliation. I ken that. Doesn't mean I like it."

"We are agreed? You will put the gown on and present yourself to her and whoever else she chooses to bring into this."

He held her by shoulders, looking into her huge blue eyes. If she was anyone else, if she had not found a way to touch his jaded heart and give him hope for his future, he might have gone along with Katrina's wishes. Yet he understood, seducing an unwilling woman was catamount to force. That was never his way, at least he prayed he'd never taken a woman against her will or through blatant seduction.

"We are agreed then. It is only you and Katrina who will see me?" she asked, placing her hand over his. "It would be unbearable if there were other men in here."

"I can't make any promises. Only that I will stand by your side. You saw the other man when we entered the room and while he left with Katrina, there is no guarantee he won't return or more with him."

He placed a quick chaste kiss on her forehead.

"Hope, my brother, Flynt's wife, has told us stories of the harem where she grew up, tales of women who were brought to Arie and his father. They were humiliated in much the same way. Hope is Broc's sister. She was born in captivity but their mother survived her kidnapping and was stronger for it."

Daryl tilted her chin up, defiant yet realizing this was not perhaps the persona she should pursue.

"Then you will follow my lead. If there are other men here to look at you, then you will keep your chin high and pretend you are somewhere else. Whatever happens here today, tonight, I'm sure Donal will help you get over the trauma."

She left to change and when she was gone, two men entered. It seemed just a few nights ago he was in bed with Katrina and these men. Disgust swept through him and he wondered why he stayed with the woman for as long as he did. She was nothing to him. Had never been. He'd learned as much as he could from her a long time ago. He supposed he must have been bored with nothing else to do except return to France.

"What are you doing here?" he asked as the men poured drinks.

One smiled and said, "We were told we can look and if the lady agrees we can do whatever is acceptable to her."

"You may not seduce or force her in anyway."

Etienne poured himself a drink, staring hard at the men and hoping the tone of his voice would tell them how he felt and that he was the one who was giving the orders not Katrina.

"That's not what Katrina said."

"She's getting her money and she might share the ransom with the two of you but only if Daryl is left unscathed and still a virgin. If anything happens to this lady, she will receive no money."

"Who is going to stop us?" the other asked, a smirk on his face.

"I suggest you find your pleasure with Katrina or you might not live to see tomorrow."

His threat was strong and he saw the two men believed him. One stood, leaving the room.

Katrina returned with the note, handing it to him.

Donal,

It is too bad you did not believe I was pregnant with your child. Now you have to pay. Well, no your dear fiancée or is she your fiancée yet, will pay. Etienne has been very good with teaching her how a real man kisses. He will seduce her tonight and make love to her, taking her virginity for himself. This is something I've understood you have waited for the wedding night to claim. Next time you see her, she will no longer have her maidenhead.

Too bad.

Ah, what can you do to keep this from happening? Etienne is more than willing to teach her the ways of love. However, he's told me you should have a chance to rescue your would-be bride. Bring me ten thousand pounds sterling not Scot and I will let her go unscathed. Of course, I only have Etienne's word that he has not made love with her already.

Meet me tomorrow at six o'clock at the rocks just north of the beach house your friend, Cam, I think that's his name, owns. When you hand over the money, I will give you the MacTavish lass.

You might want to send me a message as soon as possible that you will do this for her. I'm not known for my patience and I would truly like to witness her deflowering.

Your one-time love,
Katrina

Chapter Eight

"Daryl," he called out. "You in here?" He strode through the parlor and into the bedroom. Her pistol was on the floor. "Daryl!" He rushed down the steps then into the bakery. Blood pumped hard through his veins. A deep shattered sound rushed frantically from his lungs. "Where the devil are you?"

Darkness enveloped him as he plowed through the bakery, searching everywhere, upending tables and chairs in his haste. "Daryl," he called out again and again, but no one answered. It was too early for anyone to be at work. Bloody eyes, no one was going to be there today. The bakery was closed. Ash and Emilia were getting married along with Sandy and Justine. Where the blessed hell was she?

He walked back to her apartment, searching for any clue that might tell him what happened. The gun had not been fired and was not loaded. Blood rushed to his head. The room swirling around him, he sat down in the sitting room, his head in his hands. When he looked up again, two glasses sat on an end table. They'd been filled with Whiskey.

Leaving her this evening had been a huge mistake. He regretted it already. She could have gone to Flynt's home or even to the country. He hurt her tonight, had left her alone after she told him about the kiss. It was not well done of him. Why did he care so much that she kissed another man?

She was all right. She had to be.

Flynt would have taken her in, given her solace, let her sleep in her old bedroom and cursed him for whatever Daryl told him he did. He hoped she did not pour her heart out to her brother. Prayed she would talk to him first because he loved her. Fool, you've never told her how you feel.

And why would she do that after the way you treated her? Why would she even want to talk to you? She would need to seek solace. For that she would go to her sisters, or Catherine. He pounded his fist on the table, the glasses rattling.

He picked up the two pieces of crystal from the floor, wondering if perhaps she left him for this man who kissed her. She did not tell him his name. Ah, but if he'd been more understanding, she might have confided something that would have told him how she felt. Might have given him a name.

As it was, he had no ideas, no clue as to where she went.

It didn't take long to ride to Flynt's home. The night was still dark but he pounded on the door. "Flynt. Flynt! I need to talk to you now." Then, "Daryl! If you're in there let me know. I've a lot I need to say to you."

A light came on then the door swung open. "What the devil is going on?" Flynt stood in the entrance. "Do you have any idea what time it is?" Hope walked up behind him, sleepy eyed and fastening her robe.

"I know exactly what time it is. Is Daryl inside? She has to be here. Where else would she be?" He pushed his way inside, looking up the steps and hoping he would see her standing at the top.

"Daryl is not here. Why would you think... Did you look in her apartment? Well, of course you did." Flynt turned to Hope as if she might have some answers.

"What has happened?" Hope asked with no answers for either of them. "You can't find Daryl? That's not like her to disappear."

"I may have said something she took exception to. We argued. I need to find her and apologize. She might have gone to my house but I doubt it. Going to ride out to the home in the country," he said even as he realized she would not have ridden in the dark. His gut churned with apprehension. Sweat beaded on his forehead as more fear pounded inside his head pulsing uncontrollably.

"Wait. Let me get dressed. I'll go with you. You're not in any state to do something like this by yourself," Flynt said.

"Sit down," Hope gestured toward a chair. "Take a few seconds to think. You might figure something out."

Donal paced instead, roughing his hair with his hands, fear for Daryl growing. If it hadn't been for the two glasses and the pistol on the floor, he wouldn't be this worried. More was going on here than Daryl in a snit, leaving for the country. They had plans today, and he didn't think she would miss the wedding of her friends because she was angry with him. That wasn't like her.

"She would not have gone to the country today. Something has happened to her." He pounded the door with his fist. "It's my fault."

"Of course, it's your fault. Now tell me everything," Hope said, her voice soothing.

Yet the tone really had little effect on him. "I really don't want to talk. Suffice it to say we had an argument. I said... made her feel... as if she'd done something wrong. This is about Katrina, I'm sure of it. What has happened to Daryl has the stink of something that woman would do." Leaning on a windowsill he stared into the darkness for a few minutes before sitting next to Hope.

"All right then," Hope placed a hand on his knee. "Tell me about this Katrina and why you think she might be behind Daryl's sudden disappearance. I've never heard you mention the woman. Perhaps patience would do best in this situation rather than running haphazardly all over the countryside."

She seemed to be a calming force in all of this yet with each second that passed the terror grew. A bead of sweat slipped down his cheek or was it a tear? He knew what Katrina could do if she was confronted and backed against a wall. She would lash out. The object of his fury would be Daryl simply because she meant to get back at him.

He sighed long and heavy, wiping the moisture from his face. "I believed that I loved Katrina once a long time ago and recently she claimed she carried my baby. It wasn't so and I proved to her that I kenned she was lying. She was angry and she's capable of anything. She would want to hurt me and what better way than kidnapping the woman I intend to wed." Still it seemed he couldn't say the words.

"So, you think she's done something with Daryl?" Her voice was the only reassuring element in the room.

"Yes." He clung to those words understanding everything Hope said was right.

"We should proceed in that vein."

"Of course, I'm sure you are right."

"If what you say is true, it would be a waste of time for Flynt to ride to the country. I will send the stable boy to your home just to make sure Daryl is not there. He's run that errand on occasion, and I'm sure he will be up by now. Even if he isn't, Flynt will wake him."

"Thank you." Donal cleared his throat, trying to say more but unable to form the words. He felt a pawn in this horrible game Katrina played. She toyed with his heart and he would make sure she paid the price.

"Now where else could she be? Do you think she might have gone to your townhouse?"

"Anything is possible. I found two glasses in the living room apartment then her pistol on the floor in the bedroom. I tried to teach her last evening she wouldn't be able to hold a gun on a man. If she tried, she could be hurt. The gun had not been fired and it wasn't loaded either. There was no sign of a struggle."

"What do you believe happened?" Her cook brought them both a cup of coffee. "Thank you. You must have overheard us talking."

"You're welcome, I'll bring something for you to eat. It is too early for anyone to be up, so I suspected you would need your breakfast earlier than usual."

"Back to the question, tell me what you think happened and we will proceed from there." Hope spoke as Flynt strode into the room.

"Katrina sent a man, one of her minions, to seduce her away from me. She either refused and that man took her or she agreed and left willingly. Because of our argument I've no idea."

"Kidnapped?" Flynt asked as he drank from his wife's coffee cup. "We will have to wait for a message. Daryl would not willingly leave with any man except you."

"You're sure of that? I wish I was," Donal said, remembering the argument and the way he abruptly left her.

"What time did all that happened," Hope asked listening as the clock chimed five times.

"I left her a little after midnight. Told her I had to think. I walked for a long time then Ash and I went to a tavern, looking for a fight. Thought I'd feel better if I hit something. Never expected anything like this."

"Did you find one?" Hope asked, a tiny smile forming. "I hope it made you feel better."

"No, when I returned to Daryl's apartment the door swung open. She was gone. Vanished."

He didn't lock it, he recalled. The man might have walked inside and found her sleeping.

"Go." Hope turned to Flynt, "Have the stable boy ride out to his country home then you should go to his townhouse. We need to know where she is not before we can figure out where she has gone, willingly or not."

"I'll stop by and round up Cam and Broc. Leslie is still out of town. Is there anyone else?" Flynt asked before leaving.

"Don't say anything to Sandy or Ash. They are getting married today. While they need to know what has happened, I don't want to ruin the day for them and their soon to be brides," Donal said.

"I assume they are expecting you at the wedding, you and Daryl?" Hope asked. "They will be more concerned if you do not show up and they do not know why. You must tell them and elicit their help. They will not be pleased if you leave them out at a time when you need all your friends." She nodded at Flynt who seemed to understand her silent message.

"Rest assured, we will find her," Flynt said before he left.

Find her yes, but would Daryl be unscathed, even alive when they finally located her?

"We need to be patient now and wait to see if Katrina has any demands. The sooner you give Katrina what she wants, the sooner you will get Daryl back. She will be fine, I'm sure of it," Hope said, touching his hand, a simple gesture but it did give him a bit more confidence in the outcome. "Do you think this man who might have taken her is a friend or a foe?"

"I've no idea. I left the door unlocked so he could have walked inside without a confrontation, but the two glasses on the end table tells me she didn't ask him to leave, at least not right away. There was no sign of a scuffle, and she did willingly kiss him the day before."

"She did what?" Hope asked, her eyes suddenly wide with questions. "I don't believe... she let him kiss her? Is that what you were arguing about? If so, I understand a bit more. You need to realize you don't own her and even if she does become your wife, you still will not own her."

He was shaking his head. In any case he really didn't understand what Hope tried to tell him. "I didn't believe her at first either. She said she had never kissed anyone but me and she wanted to know what it was like to kiss someone else. That is truly ridiculous." He still was unable to come to terms with this idea.

"His words not hers," Hope said. "He's a smooth talker, that one. So, he came back in the middle of the night to try his hand at seduction again. The only reason to do something like that would be to take her. Perhaps because of that kiss, he will have a soft spot in his heart for her and keep her safe."

"She will need a friend when it comes to dealing with Katrina. He must be one of the men I saw in bed with her the day Ash and I confronted her about her possible pregnancy." Now that he was beginning to think, he was recalling more things.

"So, where did you find Katrina and her lovers?" Hope asked.

"Ash and I visited her at her parents' home. I really doubt if she would be there now. She would find some out of the way spot to hold Daryl until she wanted to let her go."

"Think back, does she own a place away from the city or do her parents?"

Slowly Hope was bringing up things, jarring his memory but in this case, he could think of nothing.

"There is no place that comes to mind. I haven't seen her in years, and the little ploy she concocted to leg shackle me was two months ago. I remember very little about that time with her because she drugged me."

Cook brought in a platter of food and more coffee. Hope dished up food for both of them before covering the platter. "You don't recall the location? When Flynt gets back, we will return to your townhouse. We can monitor from there. It seems to me Katrina would send any possible messages there, certainly not here."

Then he remembered, "It was by water, the Firth I believe, but it could have been farther away, closer to the ocean."

He was wracking his brain for anything and everything but he was coming up empty. He did remember the carriage ride there but not why he agreed to go with her. The drugs must have been in the wine she gave him before they traveled. He still didn't understand or remember why he agreed to see her."

"We've eaten and we don't need to wait for Flynt. In any case, we'll pass him on the way to your home if he returns here. Or he'll figure out why we are not here," Hope said.

"You could leave a message with your cook."

"Yes."

At his home Ash and Emilia met him, Emilia with hugs and Ash with deep concern etched in his face. "You have to go ahead with your plans. I don't want you to put your marriage off another day."

Emilia waved her hand in the air before pointing at him and shaking her finger, "Nonsense. Our ceremony would hardly be a celebration if we were worried about you and Daryl. We will wait for a happier time." She turned, "Right Ash?"

Donal looked to Ash for conformation and was rewarded with a nod of his head. "We will wait. In any case, I need you as my best man, wouldn't be the same without you standing by me."

"As will we," Justine and Sandy walked into the room. "We want you and Daryl as witnesses to our marriage as we want to be at yours. Of course, you have to convince her to become your wife first."

Donal felt his heart sink at his friend's words. Yet he was proud of them and relieved. They were there for him as well as Daryl. He and Ash had always vowed to be friends for life. "I know Daryl will want to be at the ceremony. We don't know what happened to her, have only guesses, but we think Hope and I any way that Katrina is at the root of her disappearance. The woman appears to be seeking revenge."

"I've heard rumors she's in need of money," Sandy said then he shrugged seeming to notice skepticism on his face. "Men talk. Sailors talk more. She's gives herself freely to most any man she can solicit. There were many on the docks who have been in her bed."

"Which would explain why she tried to make me believe she carried my child."

Donal walked, staring out window, his nerves stretched into one. His thoughts and fears centered on Daryl.

"And why this might be a plan to extort money from you," Hope said, "She is using Daryl to force your hand. We need to give her whatever she wants. If you don't have enough money at your disposal, we will all help."

"I'm sure I'll have enough. She won't ask for more than she knows I can get my hands on in a moment's notice but thank you. If she does ask for too much, I'll take you up on it. You all know I will do my best not to let her get away with her plans."

The hours drug by. Justine fed them all lunch, a tasteless lunch for Donal, and he wondered if Daryl was getting something to eat. Surely Katrina wouldn't torture her. No, she would want her to play sexual games, games she liked to play with men. She would want to watch.

Hope reached out to him again, a hand on his shoulder. "If she has been violated, what are you going to do?"

"I don't know."

His heart seemed to launch to his throat. It was not something he wanted to think about.

"You have to figure this out. From what I've heard of Katrina that is how she would exact her revenge against you. She will not think twice about having one of her many lovers force Daryl into an intimacy she doesn't want."

"I have thought on that but how it affects Daryl and me, I don't know."

He felt the bastard for saying that. He loved her and why would something she had no control over change how he felt?

Because she kissed the man and she'd done it willingly. Might she not let that man make love to her also? She is still innocent and could be easily seduced. Hadn't he done just that when he coerced the kiss? The main difference was that he stopped himself before urging her farther.

"You must remember she is more a victim than you. Stop thinking of yourself as the victim. You will have to give her unconditional support when she returns. Blaming her for any of this is not acceptable and agreeing to one kiss is not agreeing to sex."

Donal had to think over what Hope said. Until this moment this had been more about him and his feelings than how Daryl might feel when she was returned to him. None of this was her responsibility, but he felt as if she would come home less than she was when she was taken.

Why did he think that way? He was not a virgin as she pointed out to him. But damn it, he was a man. Men didn't want used women, but women profited from a man who knew how to give a woman, his wife, her pleasure.

"Cam and Chelsea are here," Ash announced as he welcomed them. "Broc and his wife should arrive soon."

"How on earth did our little sister get herself in so much trouble?" Chelsea gave Flynt a quick kiss to the cheek and Hope a hug.

"Ask Donal," Flynt said scowling at him. "He seems to have done something incredibly stupid."

Donal looked away. What Flynt said was true, yet, "Daryl has a mind of her own as you all know, but she met someone and trusted him. That was her only mistake. At least that is our guess."

"The sisters are all too trusting," Cam said, shooting Flynt a disparaging look. "You raised them."

"They are women. Women are trusting creatures," Flynt said defending himself to the men he called friends.

Hope frowned at him, shaking her finger at her husband. "Only if they have been raised that way. The women in the harem trusted no men. They could turn against you at any time. Because of the way they were raised, they trusted no man or woman for that matter."

"You don't trust me?" Flynt asked, his brows drawing tightly together in concentration.

Hope gifted her husband with a long drawn out sigh. "This is not about you. We've got to stick together. Daryl is not at fault in any of this except that she trusted someone she should not have."

"We don't know any of that to be true either," Donal reminded them. "We are guessing and making up stories to try to figure out where Katrina might have taken her. We don't even know if that part is true, at least not yet."

Broc and Bliss strode through the door. "Katrina is not at her parents' home. We stopped on the way here. Her parents were in residence. Said they just returned from a trip to Italy." Bliss hugged her sisters and Hope.

"Did you think to ask them if they knew where their daughter might be?" Donal asked.

"No, I didn't want to upset them, but they seemed to hear the urgency in my voice and volunteered a location," Bliss said focusing on Donal.

"Where?" Donal was on his feet, his hands fisted ready to retrieve her and have this over with.

"They own a home near Langbank. The father said it was one of her favorite places to visit as a child. We should check it out," Broc said, his eyes narrowed in concentration.

"All of us?" Donal wanted to race the wind to get there but if she was not...

"Blessed hell," Bliss said. "You need to think with your brain and not your heart. You cannot all go racing after a rumor."

"We still have to wait for the ransom message if one is coming. I would guess it should arrive soon. We've been here for hours, enough time to ride from the village," Cam said.

"I don't know what to do."

Donal sat with his head in his hands, near to tears, frustration and anger simmering in the pit of his stomach. He wanted to hit something, needed to take action yet nothing he could think of doing was practical. He couldn't race to Langbank only to discover she was on the other side of the island.

"You have enough friends to explore different scenarios. Unfortunately, you need to wait for the ransom note if there is one," Ash said then looking to Sandy, "Sandy and I will go to the beach home and find out what we can. One of us will get back to you."

"Did Katrina's parents give you directions?" Sandy asked. "The home could be anywhere."

Broc rumbled off the route they should take and a few minutes later Donal heard the steady beat of their horse's hooves as they left.

"Now we wait some more," Donal said, staring out the window as if he could bring the message to them. "I'm not good at waiting."

"Now you comprehend how women feel when they are left alone at home to wait for their men," Chelsea said. "Staying and wondering about the safety of the one you love is not an easy task."

Once more the clock chimed the hour. Donal poured himself another drink. When he sat down, he closed his eyes, remembering the feel of Daryl in his arms, the way she felt and her taste, so heady and sweet. He would die if anything happened to her, but first he would make sure Katrina paid dearly.

The knock on the door came a few minutes later. Donal's breath caught in his throat. He leapt to his feet, rushing to the door. The boy handed over a sealed note. "Donal Cham—"

Donal grabbed it from the boy and tore it open, reading it. A strangled desperate noise flashed from his throat as he dropped the letter to the floor. When he looked up, "She wants ten thousand pounds sterling and I'm to bring it to the rocks near your beach home, Cam."

"I will go with you," Cam said, taking his coat from the stand. "Do you have the funds and are they accessible on this short notice?"

"I do. I believe so."

Yet he hesitated, trying to figure it out. He never paid much attention to his liquid funds. He always had enough for his needs but ten thousand pounds sterling was a great deal of money.

Bliss stepped forward then, "I will go with you. You can get money from my bank and while I'm pretty sure Broc can take the money out without me present, I'm not positive. I've more than enough just sitting there with nothing to do. I was going to invest it in something, might as well be my little sister."

"You don't have to do this," Broc said.

"No, I don't but I'm liquid and I've a feeling the two of you as well as the rest of the men in this family are not. So, shall we take the carriage? You can put two horses behind the carriage or perhaps four would be better. You might want to change up a couple of times so you can get there quicker."

The ladies watched them go then Hope read the letter to Daryl's sisters. "We should all pray."

~ * ~

The evening was chilly, the sun was yet to set and when it did, Daryl thought she would surely freeze. Katrina chose to keep her in the see-through gown. Etienne stood by her through the ordeal, and while she was humiliated beyond what she ever thought she would have to endure, she was alive and untouched. She just prayed Donal would come for her and that she had not angered him to such a degree he no longer wanted her.

One of Katrina's lovers was the man who forced Emilia and hit her that day she was delivering bread. The other was a man who claimed to know Graham, Donal's brother. He claimed Graham stole from him. The man wanted revenge but that seemed impossible.

Now they waited for Donal to come and there was a question in her mind. Would he and if he did would he still want her to be his wife? After all he could assume happened to her, he might consider her a whore.

Looking to the horizon she could see nothing except the encroaching darkness. Waves splashed the rocks at her feet. She had an uneasy feeling about this. The look in Katrina's eyes was wild and seeming a bit unhinged. Daryl knew anything could happen, and Etienne encouraged her to be on guard.

For the moment Etienne stood by her side, his horse waiting for him nearby. He would leave soon, would have to in order to stay out of jail. "I will stay with you until we see Donal. Don't want to risk being captured for kidnapping you. A trip to the hangman or Damien's Island on a prison ship is not something I see in my future. Now be strong for a bit longer. Ashford and Sandy have said Donal is willing to pay the ransom. He should be here soon."

"I wish you luck, Etienne. You've been good to me. If it had not been for you..." She shivered from the wind buffeting her. It appeared a storm might well be on its way.

"Ah, pretty lady, I would lend you my coat if I dared. Katrina has lost all sense of compassion these last few days and this afternoon I barely recognize the woman. She is touched in the head.

"It's alright. I'll survive. Coupled with the spray from the ocean waves and the buffeting wind, I feel as if I'm frozen to the bone."

They had better come soon. She closed her eyes, hoping when she opened them again Donal would be racing toward her.

He took his coat off anyway, placing it around her shoulders. "Suppose I'll deal with Katrina sooner than I wanted, but I won't let you freeze to death."

"She doesn't ken you're leaving?" Daryl laughed softly. "Are you afraid to tell her or just don't feel the need."

"Afraid of what she will do to you when I tell her. Now, I want you to memorize this."

He gave her two addresses, one in Edinburgh and one in a small town in the Bordeaux wine region. Now say them back to me."

She did. "Why?"

"You have to commit them to memory. Promise me you won't forget." He looked over his shoulder toward Katrina.

"I promise, but why?"

"If for some reason Donal no longer wants you, come to me. I'll be in Edinburgh for two weeks then I've made arrangements to go home. You can come anytime. I will welcome you with open arms." He smiled briefly. "I would make you my wife but only if that's what you would like."

"Thank you, that's very kind but you have to look for a woman who can love you as much as you love her. You told me as much." Still shivering and with her hands tied together, she tried to brush damp hair from her face.

He helped her, placing the strands behind her ears. "He will be here soon. I know it just as I know you will be fine and will marry the man you love."

"You can't promise something like that. You've no idea if he will even want to rescue his deflowered woman." She choked on the words, believing he would think of her in that light.

"Don't talk like that. You are still a virgin and when he finally decides to make love to you, he will discover the truth. Tell him the truth but don't beg. Stand proud of the fact you survived this. And pretty lady, I would tell you the same even if you were no longer chaste."

"What are the two of you talking about now?" Katrina stood beside her, hands fisted at her sides. "You need to stay quiet and if you're plotting some way to save her, Etienne, you cannot. Nothing will save her."

"Stand by your promise, Katrina," Etienne said with a snarl. "You swore to me that if I delivered her to you, she'd come to no harm."

She bumped into her slightly and Daryl was sure she tried to push her off the rocks. "Nothing, we're not plotting against you, if that's what you think."

She focused her attention toward Daryl. "The way you were staring into Etienne's eyes did not look like nothing to me. You cannot have him. I would kill you first." Her words were filled with malice and a deep-seated hatred. "Perhaps I will kill you so you cannot have Donal either. They are both mine."

Etienne laughed outright. "Neither of us is yours. Donal left you years ago and I'm leaving you today. Won't have you bring me down to your level although you nearly succeeded."

Her anger seemed to boil over and she slapped Etienne. His eyes darkened with what Daryl assumed was rage, but he held back even while he stepped between her and Katrina.

"Don't try to do that again."

His threat was met with hysterical laughter.

"I will do what I please, always have."

She tossed her head back, laughing again, her long black hair floating in the chilling wind. Then she pointed to the east, "Someone is coming for you. Do you think it's Donal or perhaps he wouldn't rescue you and it is only your brother and his friends?"

When she looked toward the forest, she saw six men. One surely had to be Donal because she counted Donal, then her brother, her sister's husbands then Ash and Sandy. Perhaps she would survive this night after all.

A large wave crashed against the rocks, soaking her through to the skin. Etienne's jacket did little to keep her warm now that all of her was drenched, her skirts dripping. With the wind beginning to howl, she was sure her lips must have turned blue but she stood her ground.

"You must go now. I know where to find you if I need help for any reason. Go, don't let those men catch you. They will hold you responsible along with Katrina. Your horse is fresh. If any give chase, I'm sure you can out run them."

He kissed her forehead then, "Stay safe, pretty lady."

"Take care, Etienne."

She watched him leave, galloping southeast across the flat land before disappearing into the dark forest. The soft sigh she felt was for a man who treated her well, kissed her, a man who she might have given her heart to if it weren't for Donal. He risked his life for her. Now she prayed he would escape untouched.

Two men branched off as if to give chase but when Etienne disappeared into the surrounding hills, they turned around. She knew he was safe from her rescuers as well as Katrina. She said another silent prayer for him.

The ransom would be delivered, and Katrina would let her go so she could escape. She wondered if the men would allow that."

A bolt of lightning slashed through the sky, casting light across the land. A few seconds later thunder battered the space around her then another slash of lightning. She would give just about anything to be warm and dry. Now rain pelted from the dark clouds above. It seemed she could no longer feel her fingers and toes.

The men were nearly to the rocks. She held her breath, watching as Donal and Sandy dismounted, striding toward Katrina with the satchel of money.

"Well, I see your Donal did come for you." She placed her hands on Daryl. "You aren't going to be in his arms anytime soon."

"Just take the money and leave," Daryl told her, watching as the valise was set on the ground. Sandy and Donal stepped back, seeming to wait for Katrina to let her go or come forward to take the money.

"Bring Daryl here and the ransom is yours," Donal called out.

Katrina cackled then her laughter became shrill and terrifying. "You would just chase me down. No, I've changed my mind. Etienne is no longer here to defend your woman. You know I watched them make love then I gave her to those two men, Leod and Troy." She pointed at the others.

"It doesn't matter," Donal said, his body stiffening. "Nothing that happened while Daryl was in your captivity makes a difference to me."

Daryl would give anything to be able to see his eyes, his expression. If she could see, she would ken if he believed Katrina and if she could believe his words as well. She understood the only way he would know the truth is if he would make love to her, and she also knew she would have to figure out a way for that to happen.

"She enjoyed it, moaned with the pleasure Etienne gave her. Your Daryl is a very passionate woman, and it seems she doesn't care who it is that is inside her."

"The money is here. Release Daryl and it's yours."

Donal's voice was strong and sure yet she still didn't know what he was thinking.

"She cried out his name. Etienne, she cried then begged for more as they rutted like animals." Katrina did appear to want the money, for a moment she was stepping forward.

"Let me go," Daryl whispered, praying Katrina would do the right thing. "They won't follow you. You can get to Tuscany or wherever it is you want. Just let me go. I beg of you."

"I've another plan." Katrina's laughter sent a shiver as well as fear straight to her soul. Something demonic resonated around her.

"Just take the money. Let me go or it will not end well for you."

She understood how empty her threat was. Something needed to happen soon or she would freeze to the rock she was standing on.

"Like I told you, I've a different idea, another plan for you." With that said she pushed Daryl hard.

The slippery rock coupled with the wind, Daryl lost her balance, plunging into the ocean. "Donal!" she cried out before the water surrounded her. Help me please. Don't let me drown.

The waves battered her against the rocks as she fought to push her head above water. Her hands tied she could only kick with her feet. Finally, she broke the surface. Her gasp for air was met with a combination of ocean as well as oxygen, filling her mouth and lungs. Kicking hard, she tried to propel herself to the rock but couldn't.

Once more she went under. No. She felt herself tugged from below as currents swirled around her, sucking at her legs. Kicking again she forced her body above the waves and a strangled breath of air.

She was going to die here. It seemed she found two more gulps of air and salt water before exhaustion and coldness began to consume her strength. For a moment she dreamed she was in Donal's arms. She saw his face as she closed her eyes, giving into the power of the ocean. She floated now unable to struggle against the currents or fight for her life as the water continued to draw her deeper.

When she opened her eyes again, she knew she was dreaming. Donal's arms were wrapped around her and he was looking down, a tender smile on his face.

"I've got you," he told her.

Yet her body still shook, the cold seeming to reverberate from the inside out.

She tried to speak but only a tiny moan of pain filled the night surrounding her. He's got me. She closed her eyes then, hoping this wasn't a dream and he really did have her.

Her eyes opened as he let go of her, handed her over to someone who then, in a few seconds, gave her back to Donal. Her hands had been untied. She tried to touch his face but her arms didn't move.

"We're going to be at Cam's beach house in a few minutes. We'll get you warm and all will be fine."

She knew her lips moved or at least she tried to speak. Still nothing came out but a tiny croak. She believed then this wasn't a dream. Etienne was right. She would be fine yet her fingers and toes didn't move and she couldn't feel them.

When she tried to nestle close to Donal, she discovered he wasn't any warmer than she was. He was wet, drenched through to the skin just as she was. His body was terribly cold. They were riding now and he must be holding her. She needed to ask what happened to Katrina, but words didn't come. Closing her eyes, she gave in to the moment, allowing Donal to take control.

To Daryl it seemed as if hours passed before they stopped. He gripped her tight as he swung his legs from the horse and dismounted. She felt the jar when they hit the ground. Then he was striding quickly. She knew the moment he reached the stairs and strode into the house.

"Don't try to talk. First order of business is for the two of us to get warm. Cam rode ahead and he told me there would be a warm bath waiting for us. Not too warm because that would not be good either. Chelsea is here to help."

Inside the home, she knew the rooms would be warmer but the heat didn't permeate through her frozen body. When they reached the bedroom, Donal quickly stripped her of the gown before carrying her to the warm water waiting for them. He gently set her in the tub.

A tiny bit of warmth filled her yet still she shivered, her body not reacting to the warmth. He joined her, captured her in his strong arms, holding her. His heartbeat was strong and steady. She smiled.

"Are you any warmer, *mo chroi*? he asked, voice soft, filled with tender concern.

She tried to tell him yes, she was warm but it wasn't true. The coldness was still a part of her. From the inside out she was still frozen, the constant shivering enveloping her in its shroud soul deep.

"Wrap your arms around me. Let the heat from my body permeate through you as the water will."

Warmer water was added to the bath.

She did and it seemed like hours and she was not quite as cold. He held her fingers in his hand, and they began to tingle, the feeling as well as the warmth slowly returning.

"Do you need more hot water?"

It was Chelsea there, in the room with them, bringing a bucket of warmer water again. She felt embarrassment. Her sister was seeing her naked with Donal. Yet it was better than Cam seeing them.

"Yes, it will be fine. She is warming albeit slowly. You should bring two more buckets in about five minutes."

She felt the heat of the fresh water surround her, knew the warming of her limbs yet her core still seemed so very cold. This time when she tried to touch him, she felt the softness of his beard.

"Yes, bring up more hot water. This should help warm her faster than anything else."

His hands cupped her breasts, his thumb roaming across the tips and she wanted to laugh.

"If I give you your pleasure you might warm faster."

He grinned, tracing the line of her jaw with his finger and she understood he was teasing. Yet what he said was true.

"I might want that," she was finally able to speak. "If I could move my hands, I could give you a man's pleasure. Alas they are still so numb I cannot."

"Hush, your lips are still blue." He pushed hair from her eyes, his own shimmering in the candlelight. "Do you have any idea how worried about you I was, still am? You could have died. When I watched Katrina push you into the ocean, I was filled with rage as well as terror. I've never been so horribly afraid, afraid I would not reach you in time."

She nodded, resting her head on his chest as he tenderly stroked her, "You are still cold also."

"Here is more water," Chelsea said as she emptied one of the buckets. "The second one is for her hair. There are three towels when you are ready to get out, and the fire will be built up while you sleep. You should wrap one towel around her head to help dry her hair. I know how long it takes for Daryl's hair to dry.

"It's enough. In a few minutes I'm going to take Daryl to the bed and finish warming her body."

"And you, are you warming up?" Chelsea asked, clearly concerned for both of them. "Your swim in the frigid water could not have been pleasant."

"I'm fine now. I wasn't cold before the frosty dip as Daryl was.

Who knows how long she had been standing on that rock exposed to the elements?"

"Don't let her sleep. It's important to keep her awake until her body is completely warmed. If she sleeps now, she might not wake up."

Chelsea's cautioning words stunned him. He had not thought about anything like that. Had believed sleep would do her good.

"You have any thoughts on how I can do that?" he asked, wondering what they could talk about.

"Perhaps you could enthrall her with your past indiscretions," Chelsea laughed softly.

He wondered if Chelsea heard about his argument with Daryl. If she had, her answer struck him in the heart. "I'll consider your advice. Perhaps we could both learn something about each other's past life."

"Don't stay in the water when it starts to get cold," she said as she left the room.

He didn't intend to. They were alone now. "You heard your sister. I have to keep you awake."

She moved against him then, his body hardening with the innocent gesture. Here he was, naked with this woman who was so precious to his heart and it was platonic, could not be anything else. "I understand. What do you think we should talk about?"

She buried her head in his chest, not wanting to think of things to speak of, there was little he didn't know about her.

Not the kiss you shared with this man Etienne. "We will think of something, I'm sure. Are you ready now?" After rinsing her hair with the warm water, he stood then helped her from the tub.

Grabbing one of the towels Chelsea brought to him, he wrapped it around her then a second towel to wrap around her wet hair. He toweled her off, making sure she was thoroughly dry before putting her in the bed naked. Turning his attention to himself, he used the towel then climbed in bed.

Pulling her close, he nearly groaned when he felt her soft rounded curves against his hard angles and planes. This was not the time or the place to let his body react to hers. He prided himself in his control, now it would be put to the test.

"Should you do this?" she asked, touching his face with her hand. "Should you let me?"

"Probably not, but you feel so good next to me, and I am getting warmer."

"You are still cold though and yes, this is the best way to warm you up. Now all I have to do is keep you awake."

"You could tell me something I don't know about you?" she told him, her voice a sleepy softness.

The sound of her voiced alarmed him, "You could tell me something I don't know."

"Anything I'd have to say would bore you to tears. My life has not been that exciting until now."

He thought about all the tears he shed for her since he found her missing. "No, no tears and even if they were tears of boredom that would please me. So, tell me something I don't know about you."

"Why don't you go first?"

She moved in his arms, her cold hands now around his back. His shiver gave her reason to grin.

"What would you like to know about me?" he asked, wondering at her answer.

She hesitated a moment, "Honestly?"

"Nothing less than honesty."

He couldn't fathom why she would ask that, thinking there had always been honesty between them.

"I don't know," she paused, her hesitancy surprising him. "Who was your first kiss? Or when?"

He laughed, understanding here curiosity. This was because of his reaction to her when she kissed someone else, "I don't remember her name but I used to walk her home from school. Her family lived just down the street. They moved to New York shortly after."

"Did you like it?" she asked, frown lines forming on her face.

He could barely think now, her nipples were hard and pressing against his chest. Each time she moved, he grew harder and hotter. He supposed that was a good thing, because his heat would warm her more quickly. Gazing at her, "Your lips are no longer blue and your hands are warmer. She ran one foot up his leg. "Your feet though are still freezing. Can you feel your toes now? Perhaps wiggle them a wee little bit."

"Avoiding my question?" she asked, repeating what she asked earlier. "Did you like the kiss? Your first kiss?"

"I was a young man, thirteen or fourteen, can't remember exactly. Of course I liked the kiss. I'm a man, or at least I thought I was one at that time."

He laughed then, thinking of his newly burgeoning feelings for girls.

"Was that all you did? Kiss her?"

He sighed heavily, "The first time yes, but eventually we found a private place and I had sex with her. My father found out what I had done. I guess he decided it was time for lessons."

"He punished you?"

She was idly running her fingers through his hair, acting as if she didn't care.

"Not exactly. Father took me to a widow he knew. She taught me how to give a woman her pleasure. There was no punishment. He was proud of me but knew there were a lot of things I needed to learn."

"She was older, experienced," she said, "You were young and naïve, perhaps trusting. So, the lady seduced you."

"I suppose but I wanted her to seduce me. Enjoyed every minute." He laughed at the expression on her face. "Now it's your turn."

"A boy did try to kiss me a long time ago. It really wasn't a kiss. I turned my face away and it was more like a slobber on my cheek. I didn't like it at all."

He roared with laughter, his hands roaming along her body, caressing all her soft curves. "You are beginning to heat up. Perhaps in a little while you will be able to sleep."

"Don't want to sleep, want to learn something else about you."

She placed tiny hesitant kisses across his collarbone. Wanted him to make love to her and find out she was still a virgin.

"So, what would you like to know?" he asked smiling, pleased with the fact she was no longer freezing and was now choosing to stay in bed with him.

"I suppose how you became a bad boy. You are younger than Flynt, both you and Leslie."

"Only a year," he laughed, pulling her closer, hoping this would eventually end up with sex. "We all met at the university. A few classes together here and there. The land in America and Bordeaux," he shrugged, "it seemed we liked each other and had a lot in common."

"You all like women."

His voice took on a solemn tone, realizing all her questions returned full circle to the way he treated her concerning the one kiss she told him about earlier. "True and we dubbed ourselves the bad boys."

~ * ~

Wind raged and the ocean churned in anger. Ash watched from a short distance. Instead of walking to retrieve the ransom, Katrina cackled then shoved Daryl into the ocean. His breath caught in his throat as his blood throbbed through his veins, anger taking over all other emotions.

The bellow of rage he heard reverberated in his body rushing out as he took action. Donal raced to rescue Daryl, stopping long enough to pull his boots off before diving headlong into the ocean.

Ash ran behind him, tackling Katrina before she could leave.

Hitting her so hard they flew through the air, she landed awkwardly on her back. He heard the air rush from her lungs then she didn't move. Ash pulled away, placing a finger on her pulse. Nothing.

He expected her to wake up, to fight him, but she was dead. He killed her. Still he didn't trust what he saw. "Watch her," he called to Sandy. "If she's not dead, tie her up."

He left her, striding to the edge of the rocks where both Daryl and Donal disappeared. Peering over the boulders he watched for any sign that either or both would surface. He saw Daryl's head poke above the waves before she disappeared then Donal. Donal looked at him briefly before diving under again.

His heart in his throat it seemed as if hours passed before Donal finally surfaced with Daryl, one arm circling her chest. He was breathing hard, but Daryl appeared limp.

"Is she alive?"

"Take her. Yes, but weak and very cold."

Ash reached out, grasping her under her arms. Once she was safe and on dry ground, he returned for Donal. Helping him from the churning water, Donal laid on the ground for several seconds, seeming to catch his breath, his face pale from fatigue. He stood up then, a grim expression on his face.

"Help me get her on my horse."

Without saying anything else, Donal carried Daryl. Striding quickly, he reached his horse and with Ash's help he mounted then set her in front of him. Ash expected some orders something about Katrina but with a forbidding look on his face, Donal rode.

"Katrina is dead, isn't she," Sandy stood over Katrina. "Good riddance to her. Pray she goes to the devil for what she's done."

"You should get the constable. I killed her and I'll take all responsibility." Ash ran his hands through his hair. "Didn't mean to though. I would have just as soon seen her convicted and hung. This death was too easy for her."

"There are witnesses if it comes to that. We will all testify in your defense. After what happened here, no one will believe this wasn't to protect Daryl," Sandy said as Flynt and Broc walked up to him.

"They are on the way to Cam's beach house. He had servants sent there when we knew where Daryl would be found. They will have everything they need. Cam and Chelsea are there also in case."

"Don't like the way that sounds. Daryl wasn't in good shape when we pulled her from the ocean. She could have drowned, could still die from the cold."

Ash was nodding, trying to absorb everything that happened and praying Daryl would survive. It seemed to him she'd been underwater a long time. When he placed her on the rocks to help Donal, she was breathing though. When he helped her out of the ocean, he felt her breath against his cheek as well as the frigid temperature of her body.

She would be fine. For Donal's sake she had to survive. He didn't think Donal would forgive himself if she didn't.

Sandy clapped him on the shoulder. I'll stay here with you. You shouldn't be alone right now; besides it doesn't take more than one person to fetch the constables."

"I'm going to take two of the horses and ride home. Her sisters should know what happened. Afraid if I don't go, they will all show up here. Broc, you should go home, too, after all the loose ends are tied up. Nothing you can do here. Cam and Chelsea can take care of them."

Chapter Nine

"Donal." Daryl ran her hands along his chest, hoping to keep him here not sure how to tell him she was still a virgin. Yet she understood the truth needed to be told. "Nothing happened to me. I wasn't..." She couldn't finish the sentence. In any case, she couldn't summon the courage to talk about what happened.

Beneath her fingers she felt him stiffen, his body shaking with what emotion, she wasn't sure. His breath seemed to catch in the back of his throat. "You can be honest with me. Katrina told me you were forced. Well, she told me how much you enjoyed the other men. I knew it was all a lie."

"I wasn't though, wasn't with other men. Etienne protected me from that," she spoke softly, afraid of him leaving or worse being disgusted with her and what he thought happened.

"You can be honest with me. I understand. Hope talked to me, helped me figure this out. It doesn't matter to me what happened when you were a captive. I thought your virginity was something I needed, something that was important. I realized this wasn't about me. You were a victim, the only victim in Katrina's evil plans." He sighed, long and deep closing his eyes as if in pain.

"I'm telling you the truth," she persisted, realizing as Etienne told her he would find out when he did make love to her.

If he chose to do so.

She had to find a way for him to break his promise to himself and her. If he didn't realize now, he might decide not to marry her. How ironic now that she decided she wanted a husband. "Make love to me, Donal. I don't want to go another second without you. I need you, need to feel the warmth from your body around mine. I want to feel alive and whole again."

"You're too weak and fragile. I don't want to hurt you." For a moment his voice wavered.

She felt him pulling back from her. He wasn't going to change his mind about this, but he would most likely change his mind about marrying her. Why would he want her if he believed she had been violated by another man and in this case more than one? The most precious gift she had to give her husband was her virginity and because of Etienne, she could do that now. While she went through this ordeal unscathed, Donal chose to believe Katrina over her.

The thought did not sit well with her.

"I want to feel you inside me. Need to show you I'm telling the truth, not Katrina. Your trust would be better," she whispered. "Her words were lies to seed doubt in your mind and you are letting her get revenge. Why would you do that? Why would you believe that woman over me when the truth will come out when you make love to me?"

He made a deep broken sound and rolled them both so she lay beneath him. His weight warmed her even more as he pressed her into the mattress. "I do want to believe you. It's just that..." he paused as if searching for the words. "Your virginity no longer matters to me. I don't care about it."

"You believe I can be that easily seduced. Only by you, only you can arouse enough passion and desire for me to say yes to something all my life I've been programed to say no to. Trust in me, believe my words. Forget what Katrina told you, a woman who lies as easily as she breathes."

"Will you marry me then? I don't want to break my vow unless I have your promise," his voice was gruff, filled with the promise for their future.

"Yes," she spoke with no hesitations

"Are ye sure? You have said no so many times."

"I would be foolish not to accept your proposal, stupid to pretend my life would be better without you in it. I will marry you as soon as we can find a preacher if that is what you would like."

"Yes, as soon as possible. After tonight you might well carry my child." Above her he was smiling, his hands threading through her hair.

"Our child."

"Will you let me inside?" he asked as he stroked her, caressed her, explored her body with his calloused hands while she couldn't stop the sweet cries of pleasure only he could elicit.

The scent of him gave her pleasure, pure masculine and enticing, arousing her fully, touching her, bringing her to incredible passion. She remembered everything they'd done before and she wanted to caress him, taste his rod, give him a man's pleasure just as he taught her. He gave in then stroking her deeply. She felt liquid fire spill through her while her body reacted to each simmering, heart stopping caress. She tried to say his name but couldn't. He had stolen her breath as well as her heart.

"Wrap your legs around me, *mo chroi*." He helped her then groaned when she lifted her hips to meet him. His body against hers touched her with fire, filled her with newfound hope and seemed to burn her alive. The inferno and the tempest he created swept through her.

With his sex, he rubbed against her core. She shivered with pleasure and returned the caress, sliding over his hungry flesh. Slowly as if he was afraid he might hurt her, he guided himself to her, testing her readiness. As he stretched her, the intimate heat of their bodies joining spilled through her.

"Really, Donal, I'm still a virgin," she whispered the words to him, hoping they would penetrate.

"You don't have to plead your case," he told her. "As I said before, it doesn't make any difference to me."

Without hesitation, his body corded. He sank into her as far as he could go. He drank the cry of pain she made with his mouth over hers before it traveled any farther than her lips then he stopped himself. She tried to hold back the tears of pain both physical and mental. She couldn't.

"I'm sorry. I should have done this differently." His body shook with sensual need and his control vanished. "You're sweet and innocent response should have told me the truth."

"I'm not stupid. I knew it would hurt but what hurts more was that you believed Katrina over me." Moisture filled her eyes.

It was not well done of him and he knew it.

"I could apologize a thousand times and another thousand times as well, but the words would not take away your pain or my betrayal. Let's move on from here, forget the past and start a new future."

"Forgetting is hard but I want to do just that."

Her hips moved again, seeming to accept him now that the pain vanished. The movement seemed to overcome his control. He suddenly drove inside her, his thrusts, faster, harder and deeper into her.

Overcome by the incredible sensations swamping her, Daryl tightened her legs around him, and her hips moved to meet each thrust, urging him, as she became more and more awakened.

"I want to slow down, but I cannot. You have enchanted me. Forgive me."

"Don't stop, please don't stop now."

She clung to him, praying he would not leave her even now that he understood the truth. Her nails sank into his thighs as she twisted to meet him. The night came apart around him in a series of deep, wrenching pulses that left him shaken and light-headed, fighting for breath.

With uncertainty Daryl held him, stroked him, gently kissed his forehead and eyelids and lips. "What happened? I thought there would be pleasure, well more than this. Is it different when you come inside me?"

After a long time, his breathing slowed and he lifted his head looking down at her with shimmering eyes. He regretted what just happened, needed to make it up to her.

"I'm sorry, I hurt you," he told her, his voice gentle yet filled with self-recrimination. "No, it is not different when I control myself, when I have command over my body. You should have pleasure too. This was not well done of me."

"I knew there would be pain. Hope explained everything to me," she said unhappily. "I just didn't expect you to... You sounded as if you were dying. I was afraid it was something I did."

"No, you didn't hurt me, that was my man's pleasure and it was so intense..."

"I'm glad I didn't hurt you because of something I might have done wrong."

"You did everything right."

She hesitated before she asked, "Do you believe me now?"

"Believe you? What are you talking about?"

Once again, she hesitated so unsure of herself, "That I am..." she stroked her lips with her tongue. "That I was a virgin until a few minutes ago."

"I believed you from the start. Katrina has never told the truth. I knew when she tried to goad me and persisted."

She breathed in a long sigh of relief. Her prayers had been answered. "Alright then, where do we go from here?"

"I still have to give you your pleasure. A woman's pleasure, your pleasure should always be a part of lovemaking. I've been terrified for nearly twenty-four hours. I needed you desperately, needed to feel your life pulsing inside me. I ken that's not a very good excuse for what I just did, but it's the truth and I believe I would have made love to you even if you didn't agree to the marriage."

She let out a long breathy gasp of air. "I forgive you as long as you don't leave now. As long as you still want to marry me."

"Change my mind about something I've wanted for so many months I've lost count? Never."

"Why does it seem as if there is something you are regretting?"

Her breaths were ragged as she looked into his eyes. There was remorse in them.

"I feel guilt about your first time only because I've never before lost control like that. I'm truly sorry. Yes, I'm ashamed that I lost control." He brushed hair from her face, studying her. "Are you feeling well now? Are you warm?"

"If you're asking me if I'm still cold, the answer is no. An inferno seems to have encompassed me, still encompasses me. You've warmed me from the inside out, set a fire in my blood." She laughed then, holding his face between her hands. "I want to taste you, all of you. I need to kiss every inch of your body."

Groaning, he started to roll from her. "At least you are warm now," he said roughly. "I should put more wood on the fire."

Her legs locked around his hips.

"You told me you believed me. From the start?" she whispered not understanding why she pursued this when she should be more than eager to put it behind her. "Did you ever think Katrina was telling you the truth?"

Donal caught her face between his hard hands, staring into her eyes, trying to read the thoughts behind them.

"I believed you when you told me and I still want to marry you if you'll agree," he said distinctly. "I will repeat those words as many times as necessary. You excite me as no other woman has, ever. I want you in my life until I kick up my toes."

"Then why are you going away?"

"Because I'm crushing you and there are no guarantees your sister won't walk in on us just to make sure you are still alive."

"What if I don't care?"

Smiling, she rocked her hips against him. The hot, burning emotions that sizzled through him at each movement made him want to hold her even closer, deeper.

"You're playing with fire."

"You're not crushing me," she laughed softly. "You're keeping me warm from the inside out. That's handy since I almost died from freezing to death. Would you like to remain my blanket?"

He made a strangled sound and lowered his face next to hers on the pillow. "My God, what you do to me in your innocence."

"Donal, what's wrong?"

He laughed and all the promises he made over the last months to himself and her. "Nothing is wrong and it seems everything is right. You make me want to... need to..." He couldn't say the words.

His voice unraveled. He couldn't explain the complex emotions seething just beyond his control.

"What are you trying to say?"

"I don't want to lose you," he said finally. "I don't want to lose you, to wait for you to do something stupid, to fall in love and become more vulnerable than I've ever been. Yet it seems that is what is happening to me."

"It's alright," she whispered fiercely. "I'm going to learn to obey your wishes, at least I'm going to try. Nothing else is going to happen to me or us. The rest of our lives will be boring."

"You promise?" he asked raising one eyebrow. "I could live with that and be a happy man. There is nothing wrong with boring, nothing at all."

"Yes, I promise that and so much more." As she spoke, her hips moved with a sensuous need that was unmistakable to Donal.

She still wanted him to make love to her, needed her pleasure too. He laughed inside, pleased. Her need shouldn't surprise him. After all he initiated her into the finer points of lovemaking.

A hot tremor beset him from head to heals. His heartbeat doubled. Blood raced through him and gathered in a tempest, changing him for all eternity. His entire body stiffened against her. He filled her until she overflowed.

"Whatever you do, don't stop," she whispered softly, her words feathering across his chest. "That feels wonderful and now there is no pain. Will you give me pleasure this time?"

Her hips moved in counterpart to her words, stroking him and pleasuring both of them.

"Daryl."

"Mmm?"

"You're burning me alive," he said roughly.

"Is that good or bad?"

"Ask me again in a few minutes."

"What?"

His answer was a kiss that filled her mouth as thoroughly as he was filling her body. He didn't stop until she was breathless and twisting against him hungrily, seeking the delicious ecstasy she would soon know.

He rose above her for a few seconds, gazing at her with more passion and desire than he'd ever felt for anyone before.

"Wait," Daryl said urgently, reaching blindly for him. "Don't go away."

"I'm not leaving you. I'm as hungry as you are. I just want to look at you. You are so very beautiful, and I want to gaze at every inch of you."

Moonlight ran in pale streamers over her silken flesh as she lay on her back, her skin a normal color now that she had warmed. Still, her body was sweat sheened from the passion between them glistening against the night. He touched a nipple, then the other.

She reached out and touched him, "I suppose I didn't truly notice before," she whispered, "Was all that inside me?"

Donal made another odd sound, laughter or pain or both at once, he couldn't be sure.

"Every bit of it," he said in a low gravelly voice.

Even the darkness didn't conceal the widening of Daryl's eyes.

"That's hard to believe," she told him.

"You will know and understand this time and every time after. You liked it, *mo chroi*. You twisted up against me as if you were a cat seeking warmth, wanting more, but I lost control before I could give you everything you need. I won't let that happen again."

She reached toward his hard arousal before she stopped, gazing up at him, her long sultry lashes lowering for a moment. "I know we did this once before but may I touch you?"

He was sure his grin reached from ear to ear as he looked at her, acknowledging her desire for him in every way.

"Go ahead, touch me, kiss or taste me anywhere you want," he said roughly anticipating her fingers closing around him. "Would you mind sharing the blankets again. Even with the fire in the hearth, it's getting cold out here."

The blankets lifted as she scooted to one side and let him beneath the covers. Only a moment passed and Donal was underneath the blankets with her, holding her close. She lay on her side, facing him. At first his skin was cooler against hers. Once more she felt deliciously warm next to him.

Slowly, thoroughly, he gathered her close, putting the naked length of their bodies together, reveling in the feel of her soft inviting curves. This time it was not platonic, not meant for her to survive the night but to make love. His blunt arousal lay against her stomach, seeming to have a life of its own.

"My God," she breathed. "There is an awful lot of you."

Though he made no sound, his shoulders moved in silent laughter, pleased she was impressed.

"No more than there was before," he finally whispered against her lips.

"As I said before, it's hard to believe."

"It's hard period."

"I saw."

"That's why women are so soft," he murmured.

"As in the head?" she whispered tartly. "So that we'll let men put that great hard thing inside us?"

Once more his shoulders shook with laughter.

For several moments he made no sound.

"Your head is harder than mine," he whispered after a few seconds.

"Ha!"

"If you don't believe me..."

His fingers closed around hers. He pulled away just enough to guide her hand down his body. "Do you remember how to do this? What I taught you?"

Daryl's breath came in with a startled sound as he stroked her fingers from the smooth blunt head of his erect flesh to the hot thatch of hair at the base.

"See?" he asked huskily. "Not so hard after all."

"You are hard as stone."

"Stones don't have heartbeats." He wrapped her fingers around him. "See, I do. Feel my life pulsing beneath your fingers."

Her breath shook as if she realized all he was saying. Curiously, she explored with her fingertips the flesh that was both rigid and alive. She recalled it all from before but today there was more meaning. Dear God, but she could have died tonight.

"Sleek satin here," she murmured, caressing his tip, "and so different down here. Not rough. Just... different."

As she combed gently through his den of hair, it seemed she discovered another way that men were different from women. She curled her fingers around the tightly drawn spheres and at the same time smoothed her palm over the heartbeat hidden within stone.

His breath came in on a husky curse and a ragged prayer.

"Are you sure you want me to do this?"

"Damned sure."

Still she hesitated.

"Do you want to do this?" Donal asked.

His hand slid down between her legs. He threaded through the hot nest of hair and found the slick, aroused flesh beneath. Deliberately, he circled the sultry opening, waiting for her response.

Her breath broke.

"Do you like this?" he asked.

"You must be joking," she said, her voice trembling. "You know how good this feels to me?"

"I mean to make it feel even better. Is that fine with you?" He loved watching the myriad of expressions that crossed her face when he touched her intimately.

"Dear God, yes."

"That's how it feels to me," he told her. "Astonishing, dazzling, nothing can compare. It's going to get even better."

He parted sleek folds of skin and teased her until she made a broken sound. Silky heat licked over his hand, the moisture telling him she was ready to take him inside, but he wanted to prolong the moment.

"Pure fire," he breathed. "God, I love feeling your response. Why did I ever want to wait? I should have made love to you that first day we were together."

"It might have been your manly pride stopping you. Once you make up your mind, you rarely change it."

"This is one of those times."

Daryl didn't say anything more. She sucked in a gasp of air as his thumb rubbed against the coiled knot of her passion.

"Tell me if I do anything that hurts," he whispered.

She would be open and vulnerable to him. He needed to make

sure he respected that fact.

"Donal, I—I'm open for you and you..."

Her voice broke.

His fingers were teasing her, and he delighted in the tiny sounds she was making while he plucked, caressed, probed the depth of her response. Her hips were rising and falling beckoning to him to enter into her.

"Give me your mouth," he whispered.

Blindly she lifted her face to him.

"Now," he said, against her lips, "give it all to me."

He felt her pleasure as it seemed to stab through her. She arched against him. At the peak of it, Donal stroked deeply, increasing the pressure and the speed.

Daryl shivered and he absorbed her cry into his mouth. He ruled her mouth as surely as he ruled her body. The knowledge sent a shudder of raw emotion pulsing through him. The need to give her complete fulfillment overruled all other thoughts.

The feeling was a wild freedom that came from a man's certainty about his woman. He knew he would protect her while she was helpless in his arms, just as he had protected her when she lay shivering and exhausted from the evening's ordeal.

He knew pleasure speared through her when she arched reaching for more. He could give her more. At the peak of it, Donal stroked deeply, increasing the delicious pressure in her most feminine places. Then his thumb moved and he felt the pleasure shimmering, and smolder through as it burst into a fire that ravished her. The heat swept from her into him. Spasms seemed to claim her body as she reached her climax.

He drank her broken cries, muffling them so none went beyond the blanket they shared. Slowly, reluctantly, he released her silky, sultry core.

She protested in the only way she could, arching her hips toward him.

With a throttled sound he gave her what she was asking for, whether she understood it or not. He pushed his rigid, hungry flesh into her. When he couldn't get enough of her that way, he rolled her onto her back and drew her legs up around him beneath the blankets.

He sank into her completely.

The feel of her all tight and hot around him made his whole body clench with pleasure and an elemental hunger that shocked him. He needed her with a primitive need he'd never felt before.

Vaguely, Donal understood he should be afraid of the fiery, living need consuming him: but as it had been for Daryl, at that moment the lure of ecstasy within their interlocked bodies was greater than fear.

"I wish we were on the top of the house, gazing at the stars above," he said in a husky voice he almost didn't recognize. "Are you cold? I could stoke the fire."

"All I know is you, your heat, the living fire you created within me."

He looked down at her. Her eyes were closed and her face was taut with what could have been pleasure or pain.

"How do I feel to you?" he whispered.

"Amazing."

He let out a long breath and reined in the savage urgency of his body.

"Now, so there's no confusion about it," he said, "put your hand between us."

Her eyes opened and moonlight turned them into a gleaming mystery.

"Go ahead," he whispered. "Do it."

"Like this?" she asked, pushing her hand between their chests.

"Lower."

Her hand moved down to his belly."

"Lower still," he urged.

Her hand inched lower. Her eyes widened suddenly.

"Yes," he whispered so close to her lips he could taste her still. "All of me, every inch of me is inside you. Still scared?"

"Astonished."

She moved as she was still unsure.

He stifled a groan of pure pleasure at the sensations she elicited with that tiny movement.

"You're not too big," she breathed against his cheek. "We actually fit."

"Blessed hell, yes."

He bit her lips delicately and was surprised by the quick, broken rush of her breathing. He knew she found her release just seconds before. He didn't expect her to want more sensual play.

Yet there was no mistaking the instinctive tightening of her body around him and the gentle pulses.

"I'm going to make love to you again if you keep doing that," he whispered close to her ear while nipping lightly.

"What am I doing to you?"

"Stroking me all over, deep inside your core."

Again, Daryl caressed him without moving her hips. He felt her shiver at the sensations that cascaded through her with each hidden clenching of her body around his sex.

"Like that?" she whispered. "I can do that to you?" she sounded surprised as well as curious.

"Yes, you don't have any idea what you're doing to me."

"The way..." she caught her lip between her teeth, staring at him. "I don't want to stop."

"Will this feel good too?"

Donal moved his hips sinuously against her. He barely covered her mouth with his in time to muffle her surprised, sensual cry. He twisted against her again and again, exciting her even more with each powerful movement of his body.

Her nails scored heedlessly down his back and dug into his flexed hips. The sensations set fire to him more than any tender caress could have. He was too completely aroused to feel a gentle touch. He had to have something as primitive as the urgency cording his body until sweat glistened over every bit of his skin.

She gave him what he needed, all but fighting him for the embrace, demanding that he give her everything he had in turn.

Nothing was out of reach. It was all around him, inside her, light and darkness shattering into endless colors, melding together in a vibrant dance as primal and as old as time.

He continued to move against her, driving into her, feeding the ecstasy until he felt her shiver while tremors throbbed within her. With a hoarse cry, he gave himself in turn, repeatedly, blindly, knowing only the golden fires of ecstasy burning him all the way to his soul.

It was a long time before either of them moved or could speak. They simply held each other hot and close, gentle and fierce, hungry and sated, stripped naked and basking in the searing, tender fires of satisfaction.

"My god," she whispered finally. "Is it always like this? I didn't think I would ever be able to move."

"My sentiments exactly," he breathed.

He brushed her lips with his own, tasted her, felt her sweet tasting of him in turn. "You should rest."

As he remembered she had nearly died tonight, a wave of guilt passed through him.

"As you should, too." She stretched against him before curling her body around his. "I never knew how much more wonderful making love could be than what we did before."

"You understand you have to marry me now. I won't take no for an answer." He grinned, kissing her lightly on the lips. "I nearly lost you tonight, and I don't want to live any longer than I have to if you are not mine."

"We shouldn't think about that. I don't want to remember anything about that part of tonight."

"No, but every time I look at you now, I see your head disappearing beneath the ocean. I feel the sheer terror when I watched Katrina shove you into the sea."

She placed a fingertip on his lips. "I don't want to talk about that."

~ * ~

She found then that she was exhausted. Her eyes closed, enjoying the warmth of his body against hers of his naked male strength. Drained of energy but not sleepy, she decided.

"What do you want to talk about then? His fingers stroked

through her hair. It seemed sometime during the last hours, the towel slipped from her head. "We should get your hair dry." His voice was a soft murmur.

"Mmm..." She didn't want to move from the heat and the sensual play of his hard body against her softness. This seemed like heaven to her. "Suppose you might be right."

"You don't want to get sick," he reminded her, rising then from the bed, his body in full display for her to admire. "I'm sorry," he said. I should have taken better care of you. We both know this was my fault and I take full responsibility."

"What do you mean?"

She sat up, pushing hair away from her face, the covers falling around her thighs. It was then she saw the blood. Her breath caught in the back of her throat, and for a few seconds she stared at the red stain then back to him. "I understand, but this is normal."

"Hope told you everything," he said, his voice flat as if he was angry.

"Yes." Her eyes were wide and her breath shaky.

"Perhaps but it's proof I hurt you, again." He dipped a cloth into the cool water still left in the tub. A moment later he sat on the bed, cleaning her tenderly. "I won't ever hurt you again."

The guilt in his eyes stabbed her in her heart. She lifted her shoulders and for a moment was unsure of what she should say. "It wasn't your fault. You and I both know the first time would have hurt no matter what you did."

He looked to the fire, sitting on the hearth, "Come, let's dry your hair then go to bed. The morning will come soon enough, and I'm sure we'll have to answer far too many questions from your family and their spouses. I don't know what happened to Katrina, but Ash was sitting over her when I carried you to the horse. I didn't stop to find out."

"Do you think she's alright? Honestly, I don't think I care. If Ash killed her, there should be a celebration. If not, she should hang."

She knew the bitterness in her voice was not well done of her. She hated that woman. She had never hated anyone in her life. For a slender moment, she felt a stab of guilt. She'd always been told hatred was poison in the soul, a foul emotion at best, but she couldn't help how she felt.

He spread her hair around her shoulders. "When I stepped over her body, she didn't seem to be alive. At that moment I didn't give a damn, you were all that mattered to me. Ash would take care of the forthcoming events. Perhaps Cam would know but I think he was here along with his servants a long time before us."

"I suppose you're right. We should try to get my hair dry since it is still damp. I don't like to sleep with wet hair."

She rose then, naked and somehow surprisingly feeling no shame or shyness. He had touched and kissed every inch of her.

He found a robe and wrapped it around her. "You need to stay warm. This must be Chelsea's and I'm sure she won't care if you borrow it for one night." He paused, seeming to think, "Where do you suppose they are going to sleep?" he asked, laughing. "At least for tonight, I would be hard pressed to give up this bed for anyone."

"Probably on the roof. There is a bed there and they look at the stars. My sister is gaining quite the education on the solar system."

Daryl laughed with him, sitting by the fire, soaking up the heat and remembering the frigid cold of the sea. She sighed heavily, looking over her shoulder at Donal.

"What is wrong?" Donal asked as he ran her comb through the wild, heavy length of her curls.

"I gave up on life. When I was in the ocean, I quit living, just quit." She swallowed then turning to face him she touched his beard. "I didn't have the strength to keep fighting. Before you found me, I discovered a dream world where everything was a beautiful life and there was no pain or heartache."

His breath caught. "I'm glad I found you when I did. When I pulled you out of the water, I feared deeply for your life. I don't think you were breathing."

She grimaced when he found an unruly knot of hair and tried to drag the comb through it. "I should do that."

"I pulled your hair. That wasn't well done of me, but I love it though the strands are so hot, silken to the touch. I will never tire of running my fingers through it." He sat back then, watching her comb run through her hair as it slowly dried.

"A glass of wine?" he asked not waiting for an answer, pouring two glasses and bringing one to her. "We should probably eat. When was the last time you actually put food in your stomach?"

"I don't remember."

He tenderly cradled her in his arms, carrying her to their bed. "The wine will go straight to your head. Perhaps you will be able to sleep. Food and sleep, that's what you need."

"If you say so," she laughed at the expression on his face.

"Is this your attempt at obeying?"

He ran a fingertip along her mouth. She opened, sucking the tip inside and biting gently.

She grinned, delighted by his husky groan she now knew was one of pleasure not pain.

"No," she told him. "Will you stay by my side?" He could still leave her and why she had this strange fear was something she didn't understand. He proved himself this evening. She should trust in him.

"All of tonight, but tomorrow I have to find out what happened to Katrina. If there are any lose ends, I will have to see to them. I don't want Ash blamed in her death if indeed that is what happened." Leaning against the headboard, he pulled her into his arms.

"Now that you know I'll survive, you want to leave me." Her voice was whisper thin and fear still swamped her. "I wish you would stay."

"Only because I need to know what happened out there and if Ash has been left unscathed. From the corner of my eye I saw him throttle Katrina. They flew through the air. It might not have gone well for her."

"It would be justice if something happened to her but again, I don't want to dwell on Katrina." She paused, "What to do, I'm not sleepy."

With heavy lidded eyes, he watched her for a few moments, then "Why don't you tell me something else about yourself I don't know?" One arm was wrapped around her shoulders, the other held his glass of wine.

His lashes lowered slightly and she wondered what he thought about now.

"Only if you will return the favor."

She moved away from him, sitting across from him then, cross-legged, holding her wine glass in both hands.

"Of course."

She smiled slightly thinking of all those times she shared with her sisters. "We, my sisters and I, used to swim in the river near our house. There is a place where the water pools and the current is not swift. We would skinny dip." Wide eyed she watched for his reaction. "Are you shocked?"

"No, but I'm trying to figure out how Flynt never found what you girls were up to." He held a strand of her hair between his fingers, seeming lost in his thoughts. "So silken."

"Flynt was busy with his own life. If someone saw us..."

She stared at his grin and she didn't want to believe what he was thinking. "I suppose they would have told him. Lucky for us, no one ever rode on that part of our property."

"If someone saw you..." He encouraged, seeming well pleased with himself. "You believe they would have told Flynt."

"If we had been seen, they would have reported our misbehavior to our brother." She suddenly didn't sound quite so sure of herself. "Wouldn't they? Why are you grinning like a fool?"

He chuckled then downed his glass of wine. "Would you like a berry tart?" he asked as he leaned far enough to reach the food, brushing her shoulder with his arm as he did so.

"You saw us." Her breath left her lungs in a rush at the realization. "You saw me naked."

"I did and today you look much different. And since I already knew that little secret you will have to think of something else, I don't know about you."

"Why didn't you tell Flynt?"

He shrugged broad masculine shoulders. She resisted the urge to caress them and see where it would lead.

"Didn't want to see any of you punished, and I knew you would be. It's what I would have done if I had sisters."

She allowed his words to shuffle through her mind. He protected her from her brother and punishment, yet she couldn't get the one thought from her head. "You saw me without clothing."

"True." He smiled before nonchalantly popping a grape in his mouth. "All your sisters."

"I don't know what to say. That wasn't well done of you."

"I was merely riding from your house to my property. It was the most direct route, if you think about it."

"Still..."

"If I recall, you were..." he said pausing in thought, "must have been barely thirteen. You had no curves whatsoever. No waist, no beautiful bubbies as you have now. You were a child at the time."

She scowled at him and he laughed. Quickly, before she could back away or protest, he placed a kiss on her lips.

"I... it was not well done of you," she repeated. "We should have known someone was watching."

"I'm not a voyeur. Would you have been pleased if I announced myself? Would you be happier if I told Flynt and ruined your fun?" he asked, seeming totally relaxed and thoroughly relishing his thoughts.

"No, but Bliss and Chelsea had curves and breasts. They were older." She wanted to know what he had to say about that.

"I wasn't interested in them..."

"Donal."

"Hush," he placed a finger on her lips. "Nor was I interested in you at the time. You were still too young for me, for any man to be interested in." At her look of chagrin, he chuckled. "I did however find you intriguing, your hair anyway. It wasn't until our first kiss that I realized you were growing up and that with a modicum of patience I could wait for you."

In a slight huff, she crossed her arms over her chest. "I'm not pleased."

"You thought a man should be interested sexually in a little girl?" he asked sounding shocked at her thoughts.

"Of course not." Yet she still felt wronged somehow, and she wanted to surprise him further. "Well, you wouldn't know this. From the first time I saw you... I thought I was in love with you."

"Really?" He seemed pleased. "Perhaps we should pursue this train of thought farther tonight. You thought you were in love with me when you were thirteen. What about now?"

He leaned over, brushing her lips with his own, smiling at her when he pulled away, his hands still caressing her.

"If you're leaving me tomorrow to pursue knowledge about Ash, we still have the rest of the night for us. We can do anything you'd like," she told him, her voice taking on a prim edge.

White teeth flashed briefly against the ginger color of his beard. "The thought pleases me and tomorrow while I'm gone, you can sleep. If I can find the stamina, I'll keep you up all night."

She ran her finger down the center of his chest, following the caresses with tiny nipping kisses.

"There are certain kinds of, uh, things that a man can't do more than once or twice a night," He said still chuckling.

"What kind of things?"

She turned her attention to his tiny male nipples, smiling when a slow groan rumbled from his chest.

"You can't guess?"

Her grin grew even wider and stretched deliciously against his naked male muscles, hoping that with her newfound sexuality she could persuade him, seduce him to make love to her again.

"Does that mean I can stroke you and touch you intimately now and have you fall asleep peacefully in my arms," she asked, running a nail down his chest again, stopping just short of making contact with his sex.

He nuzzled against her neck, yawned, and rolled onto his side, taking her with him. She felt his hard-erect flesh against her belly.

"Whatever you like," he spoke very softly. "At least until I do fall asleep. A man has to get his rest sometime."

"You just said we had the rest of the evening to pursue pleasures, perhaps other things," she said as she ran her fingers through his hair, arching against him, letting her breasts float across his chest.

She would take advantage of this while she could. No one could ken what tomorrow would bring. Anything could happen, she thought as she remembered last night and all that happened to her since.

Daryl kissed Donal's neck, his shoulder, the hard hand that was cradling her cheek. She tasted the salty sleekness of his skin, tested the muscular resilience of his biceps with her teeth, caught the hair on his chest between her lips and tugged.

There was no teasing in her caresses, no seduction, no demand. She simply was experiencing his textures in every way she could. Slowly she worked her way down his big body, turning her face from side to side, smoothing her cheeks over his chest and belly, inhaling the elemental scent of man and woman and completion.

The line of hair that arrowed down from his navel to his groin intrigued her. It tickled her lips in a way that made her smile. She was still smiling when her mouth brushed against firm male flesh that was becoming increasingly familiar.

His sex was increasing period.

Her head lifted until she could look at his face. He was watching her with a smoldering intensity that even candlelight couldn't conceal.

"Is this a permanent state with you?" she asked softly, perplexed, thinking he'd just told her he wouldn't be able to make love again. "I thought you said a man could only do this a couple of times in a night. Did I misunderstand you?"

"Never was before."

"Before what?"

"You."

"Alright. Is that... good?" she asked, tilting her head sideways. Every second that passed she was learning something more about this man.

"I can't say, good or bad. It's never happened before. But I'm looking forward to figuring it out with you. What else do you have planned for my poor man's body?"

Daryl rested her cheek against his belly. Her breath sighed out over his swelling arousal.

She kissed him. Ran her tongue across his swollen member,

desperately hungry for him.

He let out a long shuddering breath of air. "I wonder if I've died and gone to heaven instead of the hell I've always assumed waited for me."

Quickly she looked up. "Why would you think that?"

"What? Did I say something?"

"You said you thought hell might be where you are going when you died. Why?" she asked.

"Guess I was thinking out loud. Shouldn't do that with you around now should I?"

"That doesn't answer my question."

She needed an answer and didn't mean to let it go.

"It's just a man thought. I've had mistresses as you pointed out, done things I'm not proud of. Created trouble when there should have been none. Nothing to lose sleep over or other sensual pleasures that might await us in the present."

"Guess you just told me something I don't know about you. I don't like it. You should stop thinking that way."

Her stomach twisted in knots at his words. Somehow, she needed to change his mind.

"I think it would be much more pleasant for us to get back to what you were doing to my manly parts before they forget what you were about."

"You want me to kiss you again?"

He nodded as her lips found his heavy arousal. The tip of her tongue drew a line over the pulse that beat so heavily in his rigid flesh.

"Like this?"

"It's good, very good. Your tongue is drawing a line of fire over me. It's so damned good I can't believe what you're doing is real. Could this all be a dream, or perhaps a magical enchantment? If it is, I don't want to wake up."

"My God, I hope not," she said, her voice soft. "You are real and very hard. I want you inside me again," she told him, her voice so soft and compelling he understood he would do anything for her.

"As soon as you are ready," he said.

"I don't want this to be a dream either. Need to wake up with you by my side and know you are very real."

Daryl continued caressing and exploring, touching places she was sure she never touched before. His hands wound into the strands of hair that had fallen over him.

"We can do this until. dawn but I promise you I'll return for more as soon as possible."

Daryl closed her eyes, praying their marriage would take place tomorrow or even the next day. Until they were wed, she would never feel secure, so for now, this moment needed enough to last her a lifetime.

"Until dawn then," she said. Then so softly that she hoped he couldn't hear, she whispered. "I love you, Donal."

He cleared his throat before he tried to speak. Instead of words it was a raspy noise as she closed her mouth over his erection, sipped with her lips and stroked with her tongue.

"Blessed hell, but I've lost the ability to form a coherent thought."

She wanted to give all of herself to him, show him how much she loved him minus the words. For a few seconds she held her breath, unable to breathe in any case. She reached for the power and the strength that embodied Donal and she clung to the sensations.

He drew her to him then, settled her on his shaft. She rode him until there was no breath left in either of them and their bodies were limp.

She wondered if he did, prayed that he didn't hear her words of love.

~ * ~

Chelsea opened the door to the master chamber. She hoped her sister had recovered and needed to see for herself.

In a whispered voice, "Daryl? Donal? Is everything?"

Cam's hands on her waist surprised her. She found herself pulled back against his hard chest. He pulled the door to the bedchamber closed behind them.

"Hush." The one heated word swept across her cheek. "They are making love. Do you want to interrupt them?"

"No." She shivered at the thought. Somehow, she had not expected that scenario. "They are not wed."

"Does it matter to you? Are you going to rush in there and pull them away from each other?"

"No and no."

"Then what were you doing poking your nose into their business when you could be with me in the rooftop bed?"

His heated words whispered against her neck, sending erotic sensations down her spine. His lips sipped kissed and teased down the long column before exploring across her collarbone.

"How do you know that's what they are doing?" she asked even while she found herself against the opposite wall her legs wrapped intimately around him. Unable to help herself, she arched against him, her hips moving.

"Because I heard the same tiny little mews of pleasure that you make when I'm deep inside you." He kissed her ear then nibbled the lobe worrying it until the sounds he'd just spoken of rippled up from her lungs. "I want to be deep inside you. Do you want me there?"

She heard the noise he was talking about come from her throat. "What are you going to do?"

"Make love to my wife." His voice was a low growl, his hands around her waist. "If she wants, I'll make love to her again."

"Right here? In the hallway?" She wanted to sound shocked, but nothing Cam did surprised her any longer.

"If you like." His attention shifted to her mouth as he covered hers with his, his tongue running across her bottom lip then. "Open for me. I need to taste your sweetness as well as the tartness I've come to love so well."

His hands ran along her thighs and she felt his hard arousal against her belly. "No, I don't think that would be a good idea. Not here, the servants might..." Her breath caught in the back of her throat, stopping her.

"Why?" Once more he was kissing her neck then her collarbone, lower to her cleavage, as he tugged fabric to the side so he could reach a nipple and worry it with his teeth.

"Do you think Daryl is alright?"

She pulled him closer tried to rub herself against him.

"I think she is probably burning from the inside out just as we are going to be in a few minutes."

"Not here. We need a room."

"What's wrong with right here? Don't know if I can wait long enough to find an empty room. Unfasten my buckskins and I'll be inside you."

"No, one or both of them could walk out and see us."

His grin stretched across his face. "What would they see? You've all your clothes on and your skirts will cover anything we're doing. Except for this one breast..." He nipped at the sleeve of her dress as if he tried to move it down her arm.

"Not if you pull my bodice down to my waist," she said indignantly, trying to wriggle from his grasp.

"You have such lovely breasts and I want to look at them, kiss the tips, hear more sounds of pleasure. My chest would cover you so no need to worry about anyone seeing your top half."

"Not here." She was adamant, pounding ferociously on his chest.

"Very well," and with a heavy sigh, "then where?"

She stroked his face, reveling in the rough stubble of his beard. "On the rooftop. I want to see the stars and hear the ocean."

"There was a storm." It seemed he protested and that surprised her.

"You didn't open the doors, did you?" she asked perplexed.

He growled low in his throat. "Of course, don't want to wait that long. Need you now."

She let her legs slide down his. "I'll race you there." She ran knowing he would catch up to her before she made it down the steps.

When she was half way, he gathered her in his arms, gently cradling her. "Sorry, you're just too slow."

Carrying her outside and up the stairs he set her down long enough to open the small room that housed a bed with dozens of pillows.

Before she could think, he was inside her and she climaxed with him. "I love you, Colin Angus Monroe. Next time can we take this a little slower?"

He sat up then, pulling her to him and seeming to notice the surroundings. "I love you too. I see you planned this though," he told her as he poured them each a glass of wine. "Food too, that was well done of you, but you should have told me."

"Spoil the surprise? Never."

Chapter Ten

Two weeks later, inside the Presbyterian Church, Donal paced nervously, waiting for his bride, Daryl MacTavish, to walk down the aisle. The men were in a large meeting room and as far as he knew his bride and her attendants were at the MacTavish townhouse.

He inhaled a long deep breath, hoping the air would ease the nerves that seemed to be splitting him in half. Emotion splintered through him, shaking him. He could not live without her, had nearly lost her only a few weeks ago.

Over the days he tried to be patient even when he knew they could have wed the day after she almost drowned in the Firth of Clyde. They made love for the first time in the aftermath warming her so surely, he prayed she'd never feel the cold again.

Sandy and Justine were married as were Ash and Emilia the next day, but he had to wait. They should have ridden to the nearby church and bade the preacher there to do the job.

Catherine wanted to plan a grand wedding. She'd not been able to do that with Bliss or Chelsea. Their grandmother wanted everything to be perfect, and it would take time to have dresses created for the occasion. Daryl promised her wedding gown would be created from his clan's dress plaid. She also promised to leave her hair down but he wagered her sisters would override that promise.

He wore a kilt of the Chamberlin dress plaid as well as a sporran. His jacket was double breasted and made of velvet and in addition wore a lace jabot and lace cuffs. Never before had he been dressed so elaborately.

Flowers and a cake had to be chosen. This all took time, Catherine told him, and she was rushing things just to accommodate him so she didn't' want to hear any complaints.

Catherine went on to say he was lucky she was only making him wait two weeks and that she paid extra money to have more seamstresses brought in to sew the gowns.

The wedding cake was easy. Emilia volunteered to bake it and Justine promised to cook all the food for the reception afterward. It would be his favorite French cuisine from the sea as well as other foods that might be preferred over mussels and oysters.

Roughing his hair then pulling out his pocket watch, he gave a huge sigh of discontent at what he saw there. Only a few minutes had passed since last he looked. The minutes were running too slow.

His palms were sweaty. The rest of the men needed to arrive soon. He wanted someone, some sane person, any person to talk with.

He didn't plan on staying at the reception only long enough to cut the cake and have one dance with his new bride. She might have other ideas and it would take some time to return to the MacTavish townhouse where the reception was planned.

Cut the cake. Justine told him the cake would be five tiers high. They had a lot of family and friends who needed to be invited and fed.

That was something else Catherine presented him with, the invitations. They both needed to make a list and the invitations would be sent. This was all in such a short time, Catherine scolded him, not all would be able to attend.

And he replied he didn't care. As long as they were wed, that was all that mattered to him. Gretna Green or the church between the Firth of Clyde and Glasgow would have done just as well as this ceremony in this church.

He chuckled then, one thing he was sure of was that they would eat well. The food would be amazing. Justine promised to send a goodly amount of food to the ship as well so they would have something when they got hungry.

Be patient, Bliss told him with a smile. You will appreciate the wedding more if everything is as it is supposed to be. That was a week ago. There was not one tiny iota of patience left in his body.

And Hope told him he should be thankful for all God graced him with. Of course he was thankful but the sooner Daryl was him, the sooner he could relax.

A huge sigh escaped his lips as he paced the confines of the meeting room. He stopped at a window to lean on the sill and gaze over what he could see of the city.

He reached ecstasy that one night with her in his bed, lying beside him and now he had trouble sleeping without her by his side. Several times he thought about sneaking into the MacTavish townhouse and her bedroom so he could spend at least a fraction of the night with her in his arms. Flynt had been angry at first, but he had little room to cast insults. His relationship with Hope had not been stellar. When Daryl decided to stay at the bakery apartment, both Catherine and Flynt had said no.

In truth he didn't understand what perverse idea kept him from sneaking into her bedroom.

The list of unsolicited advice went on, each sibling with guidance he didn't want to listen to. Flynt and Catherine even kept him away from her for the duration except for the tiny amount of daylight hours he could see her.

He only saw her when she was at the bakery. Going every morning would have been preferable to staying away but he had business to conclude even spending one week in Edinburgh with his brother, Graham.

In the week that followed and before they left on the honeymoon, certain things had to be done here in town. Leslie could have taken care of most everything if he'd been in in the city. He supposed he should be happy he was in Glasgow with Daryl not some place far away. No one even knew Leslie's whereabouts.

Now he waited for her to walk down the aisle, waited to kiss her and hold her in his arms again. Waited for the preacher to announce them and Mr. and Mrs. Donal Chamberlin.

The men walked in, finally joining him. All were dressed as he was in their dress plaids and sporrans, knee high socks to match. The wait would be easier now. At least that's what he told himself.

Flynt clapped him on the shoulder, laughing, his grin wide. "You nervous? You understand the wedding won't take place for another two hours. She most likely has just risen and is taking a bath."

He groaned, in his mind, seeing her naked, water lapping over her soft breasts and hard budding nipples. Even the image in his mind tempted him, aroused him.

That night after her recovery had been a celebration of life.

"I see I managed to create a persona for you, one, I might add you shouldn't have until after the wedding night. Unfortunately, I wasn't diligent enough in watching my sister. Chelsea and Cam allowed you to have your way with her before you were wed."

"No, you were more concerned with Broc's sister, Hope. Seems you were newlyweds then, and your only thoughts were for her. Daryl could have walked off a cliff and you wouldn't have known," Donal said.

Broc strode into the room, with Guinness, Cam behind him with food. "Time for a drink and a toast to the dashing groom."

"So, you're actually going on a honeymoon. The rest of us didn't have that opportunity," Cam said, thought you had one a couple of weeks ago at my beach house. Chelsea almost walked in on the two of you."

"You shouldn't have allowed that," Flynt said.

"Don't see how anyone could have stopped what happened in that bed. Your sister needed warming. Would you have wanted one of us to do the honors?" Cam laughed.

"Of course not."

"You would have left her to freeze to death?" Donal said, his hands fisted at the absurdity this conversation just took.

"Of course not but..."

"What I did was the only way to save Daryl's life. She was frozen to the bone," Donal said. "You should be pleased not tossing out recriminations.

"Suppose a change of subject might be in order."

"You say Chelsea walked in on us? First I've heard of that."

A protective wave washed over him. How dare anyone walk in on them?

"I saved the two of you from Chelsea's curiosity. Rest assured she didn't see anything," Cam said, grinning. "We enjoyed ourselves on the rooftop. No harm done."

"Drink up, let's put the past behind us. It's the future we all have in front of us," Flynt said. "Now I only have one sister left to get married."

"Might happen sooner than you think, if Leslie ever returns." Donal was pretty sure though, the two were already married. According to Daryl, they wed the night he left but never consummated the marriage. No one could be sure because Lacie wasn't talking.

"At least Daryl isn't about to give birth," Broc said laughing and gazing out the window as if he remembered the day Bliss gave him his adorable twins. "We barely said our I dos before that moment."

"That was not well done of you," Flynt said. "A gentleman doesn't run away from the woman he impregnated."

"All that is in the past," Broc said. "If Bliss can forgive me my transgressions, then her big brother should be able to do the same."

"Sit down and relax," Ash said handing him a glass of Guinness. "In a few hours you won't have time to think let alone breathe."

"I just want this to be over with." Donal drank long and hard, thinking about the night to come. They would be on board one of Broc's ships headed to France. Then he wasn't sure how he would spend the next few months. Perhaps figuring out where they wanted to live or if she might want to divide her time between Glasgow and the states.

He hoped by the time they reached Paris, she would be pregnant with their child. Perhaps she was now. They had spent most of that one night making love and if he had his way, they wouldn't leave the cabin of the ship for the duration of the trip.

The thought pleased him.

Yes, it pleased him greatly.

It was too early to tell though, yet he was beginning to suspect the possibilities. He wasn't at all prepared to confront her about the most blatant physical realities.

Broc clapped him on the shoulder, laughing. "Your mind's in the clouds, soon to be brother-in-law. What are you thinking about besides the wedding night? Perhaps that this is the end to your bad boy days?"

"My bad boy days were over almost two years ago. You all

remember the encounter with Flynt's sisters? One of the last times we got together for a game of cards and manly gossip coupled with drinking. The sisters invaded the space, and we all gave chase. I kissed her that night."

"Blessed hell, Daryl was only sixteen then," Flynt said, seemingly outraged even though they all understood he had no reason for that emotion.

Donal shrugged, giving him a sideways glance. "I know but that's all it was, a kiss, nothing more, but that night and with that one kiss she touched a part of my heart that had never been touched before. It was only a few months later I got rid of my mistress."

They all laughed. "We all pretty much went through the same thing that night," Cam said. "You just had to wait longer than the rest of us. Chelsea was older and I didn't have to wait as long so I could court her."

"I wasn't even there that night," Broc said. "Was busy in the cottage with Bliss. Crazy thing was, I didn't realize it was Bliss until Flynt confronted me. Shocked me so bad, I ran away. Wasn't well done of me. Bliss points it out whenever I make a mistake."

"You've been celibate since that night?" Cam asked in clear disbelief.

Donal looked away not wanting to answer, and in any case, his celibacy was no one's business but his own and maybe Daryl's. Then he grumbled, "The wedding should have been this morning. We would be married now if it had been planned differently, and I would be on the ship with my new wife as company not the bad boys giving me an equally bad time."

"Too bad we're missing Leslie. He's the only one left who's not leg shackled. I'm sure Lacie would love to see him," Donal said in a feeble attempt to change the subject, remembering then a few things Daryl told him in private.

When Donal closed his eyes, he imagined his soon to be wife in his arms, realized her scent was so sweet and pure almost always of vanilla and cinnamon. He laughed inside recalling the memory.

She always smelled like cookies.

"Have you told her you love her yet?" Flynt asked. "A man's got to do that you know."

"Told her what?"

"That you love her. It's tradition you know, to marry someone you love," Broc laughed clearly amused with his statement.

"It's also tradition to not say the words," Ash added.

"That's true, didn't tell Justine until we'd been together for over five years. She broke down and cried when I did say the damn words," Sandy said, roughing his hands through his hair. "Glad I did finally tell her. How about you, Ash? Have you told Emilia how you feel about her yet?"

Ash frowned, "Can't say that I have. She's hard to understand. Sometimes I believe she married me just for the security and protection I provide."

"Does that matter to you?" Donal asked.

"Can't say that it does. I like having a woman in my life," Ash answered. "It would be extra nice though if she did love me."

"None of us thought love even existed until we fell hard for the MacTavish ladies," Cam said, glancing out the window in the direction of the townhouse where the ladies would be getting Daryl ready to walk down the aisle.

"Love doesn't exist. It's just a romantic notion dreamt up by poets and writers so they can earn their money at other people's expense," Donal muttered before swigging his beer.

Why did he have this damn feeling that he couldn't live without her. Was that love?

"Don't be so jaded," Flynt said. "You're about to embark on a new journey, and I'm pretty sure you're going to change your mind about love."

"Of course love exists," Broc slapped him on the back, his beer sloshing in his glass as Donal's words seemed to surprise him.

Donal wiped the leftover Guinness from his clothes. "Maybe it does, maybe it doesn't. She told me last night she loved me, but she didn't want me to hear the words."

"Who said the words first, you or Bliss?"

"Damned if I know," Broc muttered. "Bliss is stubborn as hell. She would hold out until I told her I felt that way."

"Same with Chelsea," Cam said. "I can't remember but I'd wager I was the one who said the words first."

"I didn't think my Justine cared one way or the other," Sandy said, seeming disgruntled. "She told me she didn't want to get married when she did. Contrary women."

"And Daryl would do the exact opposite anytime I asked her to do something. Got her figured out right away."

"She said yes then because you told her you didn't want to marry her?" Flynt asked. "Sounds highly unlikely."

"No, but I think rescuing you, Flynt, when you had the knife wound, was one of the things that convinced her as well as the fact I wouldn't make love to her until she agreed."

"So as soon as she said yes, you tossed her skirts," Flynt scowled, his brotherly reaction did not go unnoticed.

"You realize of course it didn't happen quite that way."

"We all took advantage of our women in some way," Broc said as he tried to be the peacemaker. "I was probably the worst."

"You were the worst," everyone said, amidst the laughter.

"Actually," Broc said, "I don't want to share the sentiment. I said the words but now I'd just as soon move on to another topic. I hope I've made up for my mistakes one thousand times over. I was a fool and don't deserve her forgiveness."

"You have it though, don't you," Flynt said. "Bliss forgave you far sooner than she should have."

"Forgiveness," Cam held his beer in his hand. "Let's all drink to forgiveness. Heaven knows none of us are perfect."

"Here, here," they all agreed, laughing and jesting more with Donal.

The rowdy conversations continued and it seemed they each had to defend some act.

"I see we are all here and ready to witness the marriage vows of Donal and Daryl," Catherine stepped forward smiling, giving hugs to everyone. Then, "I'm so proud all of you have become part of my family."

"Welcome, Catherine. Does this mean Daryl is ready and she's waiting in the church?" Donal asked, inhaling a stiff breath of air.

As far as he was concerned this was long over do.

"Not yet, they are putting the finishing touches on her wedding finery. Perhaps a half hour more and they will be on their way." Catherine stepped close to Donal, placing a hand on his cheek. "You will, I promise, look back on this day with fondness. The memories will always be yours to hold in your heart."

"I'm sure I will, but at the moment," He ran a finger around his collar, nervous energy consuming him. "I just want this to be over with."

"The stories you can tell your children, god willing," she said, "will have them enthralled."

"On the edge of their seats with wonder in their eyes," Flynt laughed. "I'm sure they will appreciate that Donal risked his life to save their mother."

"All of you should be a bit more empathetic in my mind," Catherine said, her gaze traveling from one young man to the other. "You've received precious gifts in your wives. Don't ever take them for granted. Keep them close and love them dearly. Life is far too short to forget how much you love each other."

"Or we will have to answer to you?" Cam asked with hint of laughter in his voice. "I wouldn't have life any other way."

"You will indeed. Now have you practiced what needs to be done when Daryl arrives?" she asked as the preacher strode into the room bible in hand as if the ceremony was about to begin.

"We just have to stand up for him, don't we?" Sandy asked, looking sheepish and a bit out of place. "Never done anything like that before. Stand up for someone getting married."

"There's always a first time," Ash said," laughing as Sandy looked as if he wanted to run from the room. "I'm sure you will survive and Justine will be proud of you."

"All you have to do is walk out of the back room which we will go to soon enough then take your place next to the man in front of you. When the ceremony is over, you will escort Justine from the church then to the reception. So, let's practice so we don't make too many mistakes."

"I'm ready," Donal said suddenly feeling the nerves escalating. Adjusting the lace at his throat and unexpectedly realizing it itched, he braced himself for more discomfort. He supposed anxiety had to come before pleasure.

"Let's go. Then, "Follow me." She headed to the room behind the church area.

When they reached the waiting area, Catherine continued, "Now there is the door. Line up in this order. Donal, Flynt, Broc, Cam, Ash, then Sandy. Can you do that?" she was laughing, clearly amused at them. "This will not be the demise of any one of you," she told them. Suddenly there was a commotion. A hollering in the front of the church. Catherine poked her head out the door, waving the man toward them.

"Hurry! You've just made it in time.

Once inside, Graham slid to a stop, roughing his hair from his face. "You could have given your brother a bit more notice."

"What? Were you having too much fun in the city?" Donal asked.

"You might say that." He winked and fell into line.

Donal didn't feel anything at this moment in time was the slightest bit humorous. The amusement was not well done of Catherine. Now that his brother showed up out of the blue, the couples were uneven. At least Graham was dressed properly and not in his buckskins.

As if they were still school children, they lined up in the proper order. "Now what?" Donal asked, feeling more impatient and nervous by the second. "Can we practice now? Doesn't seem like walking into a room, in order, needs to be practiced by grown men."

"You will all walk out that door, turn and face the entrance to the church. Again, do you think you can do that without mishap?" Catherine asked, her deep blue eyes shimmering with humor.

"Suppose it's simple enough," Sandy said, shifting from one foot to the other. "Don't know why we can't."

"Like I told you, pull this off without a hitch and I'm sure the rewards will outshine anything that is awkward," Ash repeated his earlier words of wisdom.

"Good, let's practice, but I will go after the minister. When the door shuts behind me, all of you can make your entrance. Understood?" Catharine asked.

"Understood." they all said."

~ * ~

Daryl stretched lazily on the bed. Slowly opening her eyes while breathing deeply, she relished the moment then she sat up, covers slipping from her. The realization filled her with happiness.

"Oh my, it's my wedding day. Today I'm getting married," she murmured, her heart catching in her throat. "I've barely seen Donal for the last two weeks. What do you suppose he's been doing?"

Lacie stepped from a back room. "So true, this is your wedding day and he's probably getting ready for the wedding just as you are." Lacie was smiling, seemingly pleased. "I was just going to wake you up. Your bath is ready and the others will be upstairs in about fifteen minutes to help you dress."

"Good lord, but I need more than fifteen minutes just to dry my hair," she ran her hands through the length. "Donal wants me to wear it down. Do you think that's appropriate?"

"Well, that's one wish he won't get today," Lacie laughed, the sound infectious. "Your sisters and Hope will make sure your unruly mass of gorgeous red hair is not flying all over the place. He can wait until he has you alone to do with it whatever pleases him and you, of course."

"I thought he was absolutely crazy for asking. If I left my hair down, it would be in my eyes and will catch in things. I can't even imagine the horrid way it would look by the end of the ceremony," she said, laughing with her sister over the image that she conjured and was sure Lacie saw the same.

Lacie's shoulders rose an inch and with wisdom she shouldn't have at her young age said, "He's a man and of course he wants to run his fingers through the length, but one doesn't do that kind of thing at a wedding. That sort of caressing is for the bedroom."

"I see your short relationship with Leslie has left you wise to all types of things," Daryl laughed softly, rising from the bed, understanding she should not speak of such things when the topic was so difficult for Lacie.

Lacie didn't seem to like where she was taking the conversation, and with a long drawn out sigh she said, "No time to soak in the tub as you just said if it's going to take a while to get your hair dry. We'll have to tell the others to wait a few more minutes before coming upstairs. You get in the hot water and I'll go tell them."

Daryl watched her sister hurry out the door before undressing and stepping into the tub. She settled down so the water reached the tip of her chin. Closing her eyes for a few seconds, she took the moment to think about today and the way it would change her life. She loved Donal and should tell him, but he might not return the sentiment. And, she reasoned, he might have heard her words last night.

The door opening and closing behind her caught her attention, reminding her she needed to finish the bath and wash her hair as quickly as possible.

"I'm back," Lacie called from the outer chamber as the noise of her entrance reached through to the other room. "Do you need rinse water for your hair?"

"Give me two minutes," Daryl smiled, washing her hair, the scent of vanilla rising from the tub. "I used up a bit of my time day dreaming. Don't think Donal will run out on me if I'm five minutes late. How long do we have until we have to be at the church?"

"Three hours give or take a few minutes," Lacie laughed, "I know what you're thinking."

"You do?" Daryl asked. "How is that?"

Lacie stood by the tub hands on her hips, "Yes, I do. You don't understand how it's going to take three hours to dry your hair, dress then get ourselves to the church on time."

"Well, of course I don't understand, but I trust you will tell me or I will learn as the morning passes by." Daryl looked over her shoulder at her sister. "I'm ready for the rinse."

Twenty minutes later her hair was dry and the rest of her sisters, Hope and Grams, joined her as well. Daryl was dressed in a chemise and corset, her wild red hair streaming down her back.

"Here it is and we are lucky such a beautiful dress was made in so short a time," Grams said as she shook out the gown before she hung it up. "This is absolutely lovely, and I know Donal will think you the most beautiful woman on this earth when he sees you in it."

Her dress was created using the Chamberlin dress tartan and trimmed with Belgian lace. The off-white lace decorated the top of the corsage as well as the bottom of the dress and sleeves.

"It's beautiful, Grams, and all of you are also gorgeous. I'm a very lucky girl, I suppose."

There was a chorus of thank you around the room.

Justine entered, Emilia behind her with cinnamon rolls, scones and muffins along with several bottles of wine and a carafe of tea. They were both dressed in gowns designed with their husband's tartans in mind.

"Before we get you dressed, I want you to take a few seconds to eat. Too many hours will pass before you can put something else in your stomach," Grams said, smiling tenderly at her. "We don't want anyone to faint while they are standing at the altar. That wouldn't do. No, it would not be well done at all."

Daryl gave her grams a quick huge hug then, "I don't know how I could have done this without you." She waved her hand in the air. "All of you. After all my hesitation about marrying, I didn't want or care if I had a nice wedding." Moisture filled her eyes. "I just wanted to marry Donal to make sure he wouldn't change his mind."

"Now, now, don't cry. At least it's happening before we get the makeup on your face. Donal would never change his mind, of that I'm sure," Grams said.

Hope poured each a glass of wine, holding it aloft, "Here is to the bride. May all your wishes come true?"

"And," Bliss continued, "Your business will continue to profit so you will not need his money."

"Here's to monetary independence, even though I don't have it," Chelsea added with a sigh. "Perhaps we could all put our heads together and come up with some monetary enterprise for me. First, we have to figure out where my talents lie."

"I'm sure Cam has an idea about your talents." Bliss laughed before giving Chelsea a quick hug.

"Here's to my sister. I love you very much and may you learn to keep your books better. I noticed that since you've been back, they are much more disorganized than they were when Justine and Emilia were making notations," Lacie said with a wink and a nod in the direction of the two other ladies.

"I'll try," Daryl laughed. "But you all know I lack skills with numbers."

"You must learn to use the note board we created for you," Lacie said directly at Daryl. "All you need do is write down what has happened."

"To my beautiful granddaughter," Grams said, changing the subject at hand. "I'm so pleased you are not with child on your wedding day."

Daryl felt the blood drain from her face. She suspected that might not be true. "Thank you everyone."

A few hours later, Daryl was dressed in her wedding finery. Another glass of wine was poured. A few more toasts were said as they drank in celebration.

"It is to help your nerves," Grams told her, still smiling only this time there was moisture in her eyes. "I remember my first wedding day as well as my second as if it was yesterday. Hopefully, you will have only amazing memories of this day."

"Thank you, Grams. As long as Donal shows up, I'm sure everything will be more than wonderful." Daryl's voice caught in her throat.

"You must have at least one dance with him before you leave, although I know the two of you are eager to get on with the honeymoon," Bliss said, raising her glass again.

"And smear cake on his face," Lacie laughed. "I've always wanted to do that," her smile was wistful almost nonexistent. "Although if you do it, I'm pretty sure he will retaliate."

Daryl knew she was thinking that she would never have a

wedding such as this. Leslie, in male selfishness, took that away from her. At the moment she couldn't say anything having been sworn to secrecy.

Near to tears, Daryl took Lacie's hand in hers, "I'm sure will have a beautiful wedding one day soon. I will personally make it my mission to see that it happens for you."

It was difficult to encourage Lacie when no one else knew she was already wed to Leslie. Even though it had not been Leslie's wish to keep the secret but Lacie's.

"Thank you, but I'm sure a wedding is not going to happen in my immediate future," Lacie said, blinking back the unshed moisture in her eyes.

"Nonsense, Leslie will be home soon or as soon as he can find a way to get here," Grams told her. "We will all put our heads together and make this happen for you as well. He is a duke after all, and he must live up to the standards of royalty."

"Let's give the wedding gifts," Chelsea said, happily changing the subject to one that would put smiles on everyone's faces instead of tears in their eyes.

The gifts were given, something new, something blue and something borrowed. After that the girls were off to the church on Cochran Street. The trip seemed to take hours when only ten minutes or so passed before they arrived.

Daryl felt every emotion possible as she watched the buildings pass by. All the while Lacie held her hand, encouraging her.

"You are supposed to smile and be happy," Lacie whispered.

Grams' husband, Nial, was at the carriage door to help the ladies from the vehicle. Lacie and Bliss held Daryl's dress from the ground to keep the beautiful fabric from getting dirty. They stopped into the church's foyer to make sure everything especially her hair, was set in place.

Daryl felt the urge to laugh, knowing within seconds the wayward strands would tumble around her face once more.

"There you go, are you ready?" Grams asked. "You are a very beautiful bride. The loveliest I've seen since Hope was wed and your other sisters before her."

"More so than I ever thought I would be," she smiled looking down the aisle to see the church filled with family and friends. She smoothed her skirts with shaking hands.

Until this moment she had not felt the nerves collide and shatter within her. Now, however she could barely breathe, felt as if her throat constricted. If this continued, saying the wedding vows might be nearly impossible.

"You're trembling, lass," Nial said, holding her hand. "That's normal. I'm sure your groom is more nervous than you. The ceremony will not take long. Try to enjoy it and recall everything that is said."

"I'm sure that will be nearly impossible."

"Perhaps," Nial spoke softly. "The task might keep the nerves at bay."

She watched as the preacher walked from a door at the front of the room, Catherine following.

When had Grams left? She didn't notice.

Grams sat in the front pew as Donal walked from the door and the other men followed, ending with Sandy.

Her heart caught in her throat when she saw Donal dressed in his kilt and velvet jacket with his sporran and knee socks. He'd never been more handsome, except perhaps... she let the thought drop. Inhaling a sharp breath of air.

When the men were assembled in front of the alter, music began to play. Organ and bagpipes left a haunting sound yet the tune changed to something more uplifting. Daryl's knees felt weak, and she wasn't sure she could walk down the aisle.

This was about to happen. She was going to become Donal's wife, something she vowed would never happen. He persisted, never giving up on her. Until a few weeks ago she had continued in saying no. Yet she couldn't imagine spending one more day without him by her side.

Bliss was first to go, walking slowly and holding the hands of her twins as they dropped flower petals on the floor.

Chelsea followed, carrying her son as the pillow that held the rings was positioned on her baby; after that, Lacie, Emilia and Justine.

Nial squeezed her hand that rested on his arm. "You can still run away. If that is what you want, I will help," Nial said with a chuckle, "but you've never run from anything your entire life."

"I'm not running now. I can barely put one foot in front of the other to walk," she smiled at him. "Shall we?"

Once more, the music changed, and as she grew closer to Donal, she saw the smile on his face, his eyes shimmering with the passion she'd come to recognize. When Nial stopped in front of the preacher and the question was answered, he left her to sit by Grams.

Her trembling hands were placed in Donal's. "Don't be nervous, lass," he whispered.

She inhaled a shaky breath, staring into his eyes and understanding the truth. Indeed, there was nothing here to worry about. While they gazed into each other eyes, the preacher read from the bible. She wasn't sure what he said. All she knew was she wanted to be with Donal for the rest of her life.

Then, "Donal, you told me you had something you wanted to say."

He nodded then a deep breath of air, "I'm honored this beautiful lass has agreed to become my wife. Throughout our lives she has intrigued me, fascinated and infuriated me along with terrifying me. She first came to my attention when she was a young girl swimming with her sisters."

Blessed hell, don't tell everyone now she and her sisters were skinny dipping in the river.

She let out a long slow sigh of relief when he continued talking leaving out the embarrassing part. Good heavens, no one except the two of them should know that little and very damning piece of information. Her lips seemed to quiver as she pulled her lower lip beneath her teeth in an attempt to stop it.

Once more she looked into his eyes, held back the need to touch his face, feel the softness of his beard.

"We encountered each other another time. Once again, she fascinated me and charmed me. I came to the realization I needed to know her better but she was too young. I understood I would have to wait. Over the years I prayed she would not find another man to love. Luck was on my side."

The congregation chuckled, seeming to listen to every word. A ripple of whispered conversation ran the length of the church.

Donal cleared his throat, looking at his friends and family before beginning again, his gaze resting on her once more. "When she was old enough to court, she was quite amicable. She wanted to go places, do things with me, but she made it perfectly clear from the very first day that she wouldn't ever wed me or anyone else. It was left up to me to convince her otherwise."

She closed her eyes, remembering those first times she saw him and how charming he was. How he coaxed a raw hunger from her, inflaming all her sense but would not make love to her, recalled the vow he held over her head until they both finally gave into the passion and desire simmering between them.

"Guess I got lucky again."

Once more laughter rippled around the room.

"One could say, she led me a merry dance. In any case, I want, no, need to spend the rest of my life with you, Daryl. I find I cannot live without you by my side."

A few moments of silence followed.

"Daryl, did you want to say something."

She nodded before looking at Donal's smiling face.

"I never knew I could feel this way about another person, care about a man more than my life. I saw that with the way my sisters and Hope as well felt about their husbands, but I never thought that emotion would fill my heart and encompass my soul."

Donal gently squeezed her hands, a different light shining in his eyes. It seemed she was falling in love with him all over again.

"I'm not sure what else to say, but he has touched me in an unfathomable way. There are things I would say to him in private but not here." She lowered her lashes as a soft chuckle swept through the church.

"Do you have the rings?" He looked to Chelsea's little boy who was brought forward with the ring pillow and handed it to Donal.

More vows were said and promises made then, "I now pronounce you husband and wife. You may kiss your bride."

As their lips met, she had the fleeting thought that it would have been nice if the preacher had said, "You may kiss your husband."

She almost laughed at the incomprehensible thought, yet to her the idea was not unfathomable. They were equal is so many more ways than most.

His lips brushed softly across hers and for a fleeting moment, she thought he would deepen the kiss, but he did not. When he drew away, looking into her eyes, he whispered, "You are my life and my heart, *mo chroi.*"

She swept her tongue across her lips tasting him, a hint of Guinness on his lips, recalling the feel of his soft beard on her face. *I love you.* "You are my heart also." Still she could not say the words aloud.

Perhaps in time.

Then, to his congregation, "Please welcome Mr. and Mrs. Donal Chamberlin."

Hand in hand they walked down the aisle to the clapping of those present, their attendants following. They stopped in the foyer to greet those family and friends wishing them the best and good luck.

To Daryl it seemed an eternity, but Donal kept an arm around her, keeping her close to his side. Warmth and confidence spread from him into her. Her body began to respond to the subtle suggestion from his dancing fingers.

Finally, they were inside the carriage and on their way to the reception at the MacTavish townhouse. He pulled her onto his lap, kissing her nose and her eyes, and everywhere except where she wanted him to kiss her.

It seemed he still teased just as he had when they stood in the receiving line. When she stretched and moved on his lap, he grinned as if he knew how much his small touches aroused her.

"You will warm my bed tonight, Mrs. Chamberlin," he teased. "It seems an eternity since I've even kissed you."

His hand now running up her leg, stopping at the top of her stockings, "You can't mean to take anything off. Not here."

"Ah, lass, I can do anything that pleases us. If you don't want me to remove anything, tell me."

"Donal," she sighed his name, convinced the man had magic in his fingers. "Please."

"Please you until we reach the townhouse? I certainly intend to do just that."

She realized suddenly what she said and what he was doing. "I don't, no. We have to wait." She pushed at his hands.

They fell away.

She blinked a few times, wondering why he gave up so easily. His hands lay on the seat, but his grin was broad and all-knowing.

"We are here, or should I say we've arrived at the townhouse. Would you like to go inside or would you rather explore opportunities here in the carriage? It is after all, your choice."

Smoothing her dress, "You are a very wicked man, Donal Chamberlin. How could you tease me so?"

"Are you wet and ready for me?" he asked with a wink.

"You know I am."

"Then the sooner we dance and cut the cake the sooner we can ease your little problem."

"And yours," she challenged him. "I'm sure your problem is growing larger as we sit in here and speak."

He let his head fall back and roared with laughter. "You have become quite the little minx."

"You trained me well."

Epilogue

Thirty-eight weeks from the first time the couple made love, their son, was born. He was the most beautiful baby he'd ever seen, his hair threatening to be red and his eyes a gorgeous shade of blue.

Holding the baby in his arms, Donal was overwhelmed with emotion and love for his wife as well as the newborn. Still, he couldn't believe how tiny the lad was even though he knew the child would grow.

Their lives had been perfect. Now, they were better. He sat down beside his wife, handing her the child so she could feed him. She was just as beautiful and intriguing as before the baby.

"You have given me the greatest gift possible," Donal said. "Sometimes I hold my breath until I have to take a long draught of air just to make sure this isn't a dream.

"As you have done the same for me. I've loved the dance between us, dancing with Donal," she murmured. "Do you remember all the wicked things you did and said before we hardly knew each other? she murmured.

"You did leave me a merry dance, and I regret having never told you how much I love you."

"I love you too."

"Do you think it will always be this way for us?" Donal stroked the baby's cheek, so soft and delicate.

"I pray it will be and that we will have many fine sons and daughters." She leaned her head on his shoulder, stroking his arm.

"I would say our life to this point has been more like dancing with Daryl," he laughed then, setting the child in his wife's arms and watching intently as she bared a breast to feed his child, his heir. "I had to take delicate steps around you before you would agree to marry me.

"Yes, dancing with Donal," she murmured as he bent to kiss her lightly on her forehead.

They did go on to have another son. Both boys looked just like his handsome father, with the ginger hair and silver blue eyes. Their daughter was more like her petite mother, quick to smile her blue eyes flashing with merriment and her thick red hair flowing wildly around her head. Of course, she was independent and opinionated thinking her answers would most likely be the correct ones.

Donal and Daryl spent the rest of their lives laughing and loving, enjoying their children as well as those of the other bad boys and the MacTavish lasses, including Hope who had become more and more like them as the time passed.

Coming Soon
by
Christine Young
at
Rogue Phoenix Press

Loving Leslie

Chapter One

Winter 1825

Leslie Stewart, Duke of Southcliff, stared out the open window in his family's chateau just north of Bordeaux, France. The water that filled Gironde estuary shimmered with a silvery hue, sunshine sparkling off the ripples. Egrets and other birds took to the air in a silvery cloud of wings. Today was beautiful the clouds having cleared early this morning. The rain cleansed the air, leveling any smoke or dust.

He was going to his home tomorrow, back to Glasgow and his new wife, Lacie MacTavish Stewart, the Duchess of Southcliff. The last words he said to her were stay put. He wanted her to remain in his townhouse in the city but the more he thought on it, he realized doing that would be devilishly uncomfortable for her.

She'd been just seventeen when he wed her, something he felt he needed to do before he left on his final mission for the government and Drake Montgomerie. He wanted her to have the protection of his name and title. The commitment, he felt, was essential. Lacie had been in his thoughts from the moment he first kissed her when she was all of fifteen, the same age as his sister was now. At this time, he regretted his hasty departure, taking leave of his wife without consummating the marriage.

It wasn't right of him to take advantage of an underage lassie and making love to her at such a tender moment in her life would have been exactly that. Yet he needed to bind her to him before setting off on what he'd told Drake Montgomerie was his last and final mission. Drake had a hell of a time taking no for an answer, but he finally convinced him that he was the only one with the skills to succeed in this particular assignment. The ridiculous thing was that he believed Drake.

"You're leaving?" Jolie, his mother, waltzed into the room with her usual flamboyant style. "I hope you have every intention of begetting an heir sooner than later. It's what your father would have wanted, nay expected. If I'm honest, I suppose I want that too, a grandbaby to hold and spoil."

Leslie let out a long slow exasperated breath of air, taking his gaze from the window to turn it toward his mother who had a way of annoying him even when she was being sweet. "You do know I've wed. She will just be turning eighteen when I return. I'm not going to rush things with my new and very innocent bride. That's why I've stayed away from Glasgow these last few months when I could have left earlier. I've no intention of terrifying my wife."

Jolie waved her hand in the air, grinning at him. "You are too stoic by far, Leslie, and I suppose some of the fault lies with me, certainly not your father. He would have seen you play all day and night with every skirt that wandered past your nose. You should take a page our of your brother's book and have some fun before you have children to raise and a wife to keep amused."

"I take my responsibility seriously and by the way, weren't you just talking about me begetting an heir. Playing with each and every pretty bit of muslin that comes along will not have the desired result. You don't want any bastards, neither do I." He sighed again, the air leaving his lungs slowly. This was the same conversation he had daily with his mother. "And we all understand the ways of Link. That isn't for me."

"Of course you take your obligations well in hand, it's what you've been tutored to do since you were born. We both understand the responsibilities that go with the title. Is your new wife up to those requirements? Will she make our family proud?"

"I'm sure she will do fine," Leslie said, turning his attention back to the scene outside as well as thoughts of Lacie.

"Brandy? Or perhaps an aperitif, dinner will be served soon." His mother effectively changed the conversation to something less annoying. It seemed his mother knew just how far she could push him.

"You choose." His thoughts returned to Lacie, then, "Actually, I've no idea how Lacie will handle the duties. She's always been a handful for her guardian, impulsive in nature, a bit like Merry. We all understand the kind of innocent trouble my sister can get herself into without even blinking."

"If it's left up to me, I'll have a brandy now and an aperitif later." Jolie found the brandy, pouring them both a glass before she sat down. Her gaze riveted on him as if she was trying to see into his mind, ferret out his plans for his future. Sometimes, Leslie was sure she saw too much, more than he ever intended for anyone to see.

He sipped, once more turning his attention back to the view he'd been admiring earlier. From his vantage point, he could see the ship that would return him to Scotland. On board were several cases of wine. One was filled with Sauternes, a sweet wine he was sure Lacie would like. The other cases were filled with varying Bordeaux wines, red as well as white. Even from this vantage point, he could see the hustle on board his ship. He was eager to get on his way, excited to see his new bride.

"Your last night here, you could pay me a bit more attention." Jolie sighed dramatically as she waltzed across the room to stand next to him. "I won't see you for months, I'm sure. Should I join you in Glasgow when your child is born? I believe I'd enjoy a diversion."

He turned, leaning nonchalantly against the windowsill, his eyes narrowing. "You don't need me to pay attention to you, mother. There are others in this household who do that." He paused thoughtfully, "Please don't come to Glasgow until you're invited. Your appearance would only serve to make Lacie nervous. She has sisters who will help her if she needs anything, and of course she will have me."

"Doesn't mean I don't enjoy it when you do pay attention to me. Thank God you don't want me to help out. Crying babies are not my forte." Jolie smiled prettily, lowering her lashes for a moment. "Changing the subject, my son has become very handsome and debonair. You never told me if your wife will be able to perform her wifely duties. If she is so young..."

Leslie wondered what was behind the smile as well as her attempts to pry into his life. Nothing she asked was appropriate here. "Because it's none of your business, mother, and I'm not really sure what duties you're speaking of."

"Really, Leslie, do I need to get specific. The most important duty of begetting an heir, of course, can she perform or is she a cold fish in bed?"

He choked back a laugh. "That will happen in due time. I'm sure as to the others, Lacie is a quick learner and she will please me. Have you seen my brother? He's due here. We have important subjects to talk about." Like how he is a walking scandal even though he's the most handsome and amenable devil to ever show his face in Bordeaux.

"Don't tell me you intend to lecture him on his dalliances," she said, sipping the brandy and looking over the rim at him as if she disagreed with his intentions. "You should take at least one page from his book. He's enjoying life to the fullest."

"Need I remind you that Link is the second son and has very few responsibilities in this world. He can afford to be carefree and lighthearted as well as tardy whenever it suits. His constant dalliances are different. He will bring shame on our family name if he keeps this up."

"Your words are all true. I'm sure in time he will settle down rather than finding the most beautiful widows to entertain in the evenings." Leslie sat down on his desk, swinging one leg while wondering how he could ever convince Link to change his ways. It was, he decided, most likely an impossible task.

"You know he doesn't like to be summoned. So, I'm sure he'll show up when he feels like it and not a moment before," Jolie laughed, staring at the door as if he was about to walk through it. "I do appreciate your younger brother. He is, you know, a breath of fresh air in an otherwise stagnant pool of dead air."

"You're referring to me as the stagnant pool I suppose," Leslie said dryly, a dark brow arched intuitively. "Doesn't suit you to take favorites, especially when I control the purse strings."

"Neither of you are a favorite child. I love you both as well as your charming unique ways. I'm merely pointing out the differences."

"Nonetheless, Link and I need to talk and I would prefer to do that in privacy, if you understand what I'm trying to say. Pour yourself another brandy then go visit with your daughter. I'm sure she could benefit from your years of wisdom and motherly advice." He slanted his mother a pointed look, which he was sure she would ignore. "That means when he arrives, I need to have you leave."

She waved a hand in the air, seeming to stay put, "Balderdash, you can't keep anything from me. Between the gossip of the servants and your sister's penchant for blurting the truth, I learn everything. I would quite enjoy listening to the forthcoming lecture to Link."

"Hate to admit it, but I'm sure you're right. It's just I'd like to have a few minutes alone with my brother before I leave for Scotland. I've something important to talk to him about as you well know. At the moment, I'd rather the conversation be man to man."

"Well, I can find something to do. Perhaps teach your sister a bit more about being a lady. She does have a penchant for climbing trees and running around the properties like a little hoyden in her britches, which she seems to prefer over dresses." Once again, Jolie stared at the door as if the object of her words would waltz through and plop herself unladylike on a chair just to prove her point.

Leslie held back a burst of laughter. His sister was a breath of fresh air. Merry had been named well, but her nickname was the name that stuck. Everywhere she went she left people feeling good about themselves while laughing. His mother was right, however, she would need to learn how to be a lady and soon. Angelica Louise was almost fifteen, the same age as Lacie when he met her and kissed her.

He'd been unable to resist the young woman who beguiled him with her smile and tender sensibilities as well as the bit of the hoyden inside her. Even then her eyes simmered with what he was sure was passion or wickedness. He smiled then quickly cleared his throat, hoping his mother would not see the expression and comment on it.

Suddenly, Link burst into the office, windblown, smelling of leather and horse as well as the sunshine, alive as the wind, showing lots of white teeth, very nearly on time. It was only five minutes past the hour.

After all, Link was nearing an ample age himself. He was very almost twenty-five. He should consider settling down and starting a family.

"I've been summoned. I'm here." Link stepped through the door then quickly hugged his mother. "What is it you want to talk to me about?" He poured a brandy, his gaze focused on him. "Thought you two would have been drinking some of the Sauternes before dinner."

"Mother wanted both a brandy then an aperitif before dinner. Was willing to oblige her in this." Leslie regarded his brother who had grown into a devilishly handsome man over the years he'd been living in Scotland. Perhaps he should have come home more often. If he had then mayhap there would not be so many bastards to take care of.

The two of them should stick together in this. "It's time for you to find Merry, don't you think?" He pointedly addressed his mother, arching an eyebrow for emphasis.

"Very well, I shall leave the two of you to discuss, well... things, men things." She didn't move from the chair. It didn't appear Link had any qualms about discussing his entertainment with his mother in the room.

"Lord, but it's a beautiful day. I was riding with Suzette along the banks of the estuary. Nothing like it, I tell you," Link began with a wink directed toward his mother.

"That's nice." Leslie meant to remain patient in this, yet his brother was making it devilishly hard. He had no qualms where it concerned women and bedding them. What he always had a hard time understanding was how there could be so many bastards when he always chose widows and women of experience. The women he knew personally that Link bedded never conceived.

"I'll take a brandy," Link said, sitting down, relaxing as if someone in the room would serve him before providing his brother more of his white-toothed smile, seeming to ignore what he must know the conversation would revolve around.

"That's nice," Leslie said, dryly, disregarding his brother for the moment. "No one's waiting on you. Did you mange to stay on your horse or take a side diversion to some place private?"

Link laughed, the sound rolling pleasantly off his tongue, "Just wanted to test you." He rose then returned with his drink, smiling more widely. His eyes, upon closer inspection, appeared somewhat vague.

He had the look of a sated man, a look the duke was becoming quite familiar with the longer he remained in Bordeaux and in the company of his little brother. "We need an accounting," Leslie began. "An update on all your children."

"Well," Link said after another moment of silence, "If you insist upon these meetings every time you're in town, I must do something to make them worthwhile."

Leslie turned to Jolie, nodding as if this time she would understand what he wanted. She smiled, sipping her brandy. "Don't mind me. You two go ahead and talk. I'll just sit here and not say a word. Won't even listen."

"Mother?" The pointed question should get the desired results, but she still wasn't moving. "If you don't go, we will. There are plenty of rooms in the chateau as well you know."

"Very well," she said in a huff, flouncing from Leslie's office as if she'd been insulted. "Dinner will be at seven. The two of you don't be late."

Leslie had been waiting for their mother to leave. When she did, he turned to Link, "But Suzette? Why her?"

"The widow is quite soft and sweet smelling, brother, and she knows how to please a man. Ah, does she ever do it well. Also, she'll not get caught. She's much too smart for that, my Suzette. There will be no bastards coming from her."

"She sits a horse well," Leslie said, hard pressed not to smirk or laugh. "I'll admit that much. And I suppose she won't cry foul and demand marriage if by some perverse chance she did conceive."

"Ach man and that's not all she sits well," Link laughed again, thoroughly enjoying life, his life, while putting Leslie's lecture away as something inconsequential.

Only through intense resolve did Leslie keep his grin to himself. He was the duke; he was the head of the far-flung Stewart family. Even now there might be another Stewart growing despite Suzette's intelligence. Link didn't seem to care that he was siring bastards in almost every part of Bordeaux as well as Paris.

"We don't have all night," Leslie said impatiently, but Link continued as if there was nothing he had to apologize about. He must have seen the twitch of his lips because Link laughed outright one more time.

"Yes, we must proceed in ways that make us the happiest. There are better things waiting for us around the corner, so to speak, don't you think?" He raised the glass of brandy toward Leslie. "Here's to all women and the sweet pleasures they share with us the male species."

"Now," Leslie continued reading the top sheet of paper in front of him and trying his best to ignore Link's toast to women, "I need to confirm some things. As of this meeting you have three quite healthy sons, four quite healthy daughters. Pour little Jacque died during the spring. Julia's fall doesn't appear to have had lasting injury to her arm. Is this up to date? Or do you have more children to be accounted for?"

"I will have another baby making its way in February. The mother appears hardy and healthy. So, in a few months I will have another precious child. They are very important, you realize and they must be taken care of and given every opportunity in this life."

Leslie sighed heavily, staring at the floor for a few seconds before continuing the conversation. "Very well. Her name?" As Link replied, Leslie wrote. He raised his head. "Is this now correct?"

Link lost his smile and downed the rest of his brandy. "No, Roger died of the ague last week. He is no longer with me, poor fellow."

"You didn't tell me." Leslie thought he should be informed sooner than later, but Link had his own timetable he followed.

Link lifted his shoulders in a nonchalant shrug, "The poor baby wasn't even a year old, but so bright, Leslie. I knew your were busy, what with the trip home to your new bride, the mission as well. Didn't want to bother you with something like that even though I knew it was important."

"I'm sorry," Leslie said again. Then he frowned, concentrating, thinking he must be missing something. "If the babe is due in February, why didn't you tell me when I arrived home?"

Link said simply, "Because I didn't know until recently. Can't tell you something I don't know, now can I? The mother didn't tell me because she feared I wouldn't wish to bed her any longer." He paused looking out the same window at the estuary that fascinated Leslie earlier.

"Silly woman. I wouldn't have guessed she was with child, although I suppose I should have conjectured. She's already quiet big with the baby. She might well give me twins. Wouldn't that be splendid? Two blessed children instead of just one."

Link turned his gaze from the window before swigging more brandy, unable to fathom what seemed to drive his little brother.

"I forgot, Leslie. There is also Sadie."

Leslie dropped the paper. "Sadie who?"

"Sadie Arbuckle, the draper's daughter on St Jean Street. She's with child, my child. She will have it in May, my best guess. She was all tears and woes until I told her she needn't worry. The Stewarts take care of their own. It's possible she might even marry a sea captain. It doesn't seem he cares if she's carrying another man's child. He loves her, you know. So, we most likely won't be accountable for the baby or the mother, although I would dearly love to see it when it is born."

"Well, that's something." Leslie picked up the paper he dropped and tallied the numbers on the sheet. "You're currently supporting six children and their mothers. You have impregnated two more women and their children are due early next year."

"I believe that's right. Don't forget the possibility of the twins or the likelihood of Sadie marrying her sea captain."

"Can't you keep your damned rod in your pants?"

"No more than you can, Leslie."

"Fair enough, but why can't you remove yourself from the woman before you fill her with your seed?"

Link flushed slightly, a rather strange occurrence for him considering, and said, his words defensive, something else unlike Link. "I can't seem to keep my wits together when I'm inside a woman. I forget everything except the pleasure, the damn pleasure. There is no rational thought in my muddled brain except the sheer pleasure of it all."

"You need to figure this out, Link," Leslie said. "It's not up to you to singlehandedly populate the entire world."

"I know it isn't much of an excuse, but I just can't seem to withdraw once I'm there, so to speak when the lady is all warm and willing to have me there. Her sultry core quivering with desperate need." He stared hard at his brother then. "I'm not a damned cold fish like you,

Leslie. Your mind never runs off its track. Doesn't it ever turn into vapor when the pleasure of it all takes over? Don't you ever want to just keep pounding and pounding in the velvet warmth and the consequences be damned?"

"No."

Link let out a long slow breath of air, thrumming his fingers on the arm of his chair. "Well, I'm not so well disciplined as you. Have you not wanted to lose control and everything else could rot?"

"No, can't say that I've ever felt that way. I've controlled myself my entire adult life. As far as I know there are no illegitimate children. Now, your lust becomes more costly by the second," he said after a moment. "Damned costly. You really must do something about this infatuation you have with sex."

"Stop your frowns and your posturing, Leslie. You're bloody wealthy, as am I. Where money is concerned, we've nothing to worry about even if I sire another ten children."

"Doesn't matter, this is not well done of you. I'd like to see a stop put to it in the future. Perhaps in the future you could sire legitimate children."

"You're always saying our bastards are our responsibility and so I agree with you. I also agree with this plan of yours, the meetings you know. It ensures we don't miss any children. I would have quite forgotten about Sadie if you weren't here to remind me. That would not be well done of us at all."

Link was chuckling when the door opened. He looked up to see their sister dart quickly into the room then stop, watching them. A hoydenish expression on her beautiful face.

"Ah, if it isn't Merry. Come in, our meeting is nearly finished. Leslie has already reprimanded me about my bad boy behavior. I'm sure he will find something to lecture you about also. What have you done wrong in the last few months, I wonder."

Leaning against the door with her arms crossed, Merry seemed amused at all that was happening. Leslie was sure she knew everything that was said by the all-knowing smirk on her face. She was far too intelligent for her age. He would have to be wary of her from now on. She was, after all, nearing the age where she would have to be chaperoned. He groaned at the thought of Link taking over those duties.

Then turning to Link, Merry asked, "So, how went the meeting? Mother told me you kicked her out and that she has every intention of getting even."

"The smirk doesn't become you, brat."

"Now, Link. I'm young, true, but I've grown up around the two of you. I'm not stupid or innocent. With the two of you as older brothers how could I be uninformed about the ways of men?"

Shocked by what Merry said, the small sip of brandy Leslie just imbibed spewed from his mouth. Leslie wiped the drops off his pants with a handkerchief, staring at his little sister, wondering if he knew her at all. *Ways of men?*

"Forget what you think you know, Merry. These things we're discussing are not for the ears of someone your tender age."

Merry grinned at Link, "How are all your beloved ones?"

"They all do very well, thank you."

"I won't say a word," she said then grinned at him, blew him a kiss before walking toward Leslie who was still sitting on his desk.

He didn't like the expression on Merry's face any better than Link's countenance. She was up to something he knew he would dislike.

Holding his breath for a moment, he eyed her critically. "What are you up to, brat? It isn't enough that I have to put up with your brother but now you have that same look in your eye."

She laughed, staring at the brandy glass as if she was about to partake before she turned her attention back to him. She clasped her hands in front of her, appearing sweet and innocent, lowering her lashes a trifle, something she could do very well when she put her mind to it. Now, Leslie was sure he wasn't going to like what she was about to say.

"I'm going to Glasgow with you. Mother already gave me permission. My bags are packed and on the ship."

"Blessed hell, you can't... Jolie can't... none of you are serious." Chaperoning his little sister was not going to be a duty he was prepared for. Thoughts of Flynt MacTavish and his horrible attempts at guardianship of his four younger sisters spread through him too fast for him to contemplate thoroughly. Lord, he was wed to Flynt's youngest sister and the man wasn't even invited to the hasty wedding.

"I'll either go with you, Leslie, or I'll book passage on another ship. Would you like that better?" That smirking look she did so well was plastered on her beguiling little face again. Then she lifted her shoulders slightly, the smug expression still there, "It's your choice."

"It's a hell of a choice," he told her, like being caught between two evils. "I'm leaving first thing in the morning. If you're not on board, I won't wait for you. You should also know the weather isn't the same as here. There is no sunshine, only rain. It's dreary and won't suit your sunny disposition."

"No worries about that either, I'm going tonight. Holcum, you do know the man, the chateaux's butler. He's taking me in the carriage right after we eat, which I assume is in a few minutes." I won't be a problem, I promise. You won't know I'm even there. The weather will be a welcome change for me, something different."

"I'll hold you to that, brat," he said, understanding the whirlwind of problems he was about to face.

~ * ~

Lacie bent over the ledgers at her sister's bakery, her mind in a cloud. Making sense of Daryl's figures on a good day was difficult, but today her mind was in the clouds. She couldn't think, couldn't concentrate. There were just too many things swirling around in her head. It seemed Leslie was coming soon. He'd written that he would arrive within the month. That was two months ago, she thought letting go with a heavy breath of air.

It seemed she felt Daryl's gaze on her back. The more receipts and numbers she scratched out, the harder her sister stared. She sighed, long and deep, wishing she could escape somewhere, find a hole to climb into where she didn't have to get out.

Daryl's scribbling was always hard to decipher. The ledger was nearly unreadable, except for the ones Justine made which were neat and precise. But Daryl wanted to take on all the responsibilities here at her business, and she was doing just that.

Once again, though, nothing made sense.

Lacie put this off for as long as she dared. She didn't want to stay here, in the bakery or even the city any longer than she had to. "Justine, can you come over here for a second and look at something for me?" Lacie really needed someone to explain this last notation.

"Of course," Justine replied, wiping her hands on her apron as she left the kitchen to sit down beside her. "What do you need? Ah, I see you're trying to make heads or tales out of this ledger. Sorry for that."

Heads together, Justine pointed out different things and explained what her sister wrote down as well as the items she purchased that cost the listed dollar amount. She wanted to tell her sister not to touch the board, but she didn't have the heart to hurt her feelings.

"Thank you. I might need your help again. Don't go too far," Lacie said as she pushed flyaway hair from her eyes that seemed to be crossing when she looked at the numbers in front of her.

"Not until the shop closes and that's hours away. Hopefully you will be done by then," Justine laughed, heading for the kitchen. "The boys are delivering left over goods today. They tell me they don't need us."

"I would have turned the job down anyway," Lacie said, unable to swallow the painful memory ricocheting in her head. She no longer wanted anything to do with the deliveries, always found some excuse to keep from joining.

"You could have asked me for help with this. It's my fault, after all, that everything is such a mess for you." Daryl sat down beside her, clearly annoyed at her.

"True." She didn't want to tell her sister just how absurd that idea was. Daryl would never be of any help where this was concerned.

"True? That is just not very well done of you," Daryl said, eyeing her critically then exasperated she puffed out a breath of air, "I want to learn how to do this the right way, and I did believe I was doing a better job."

"You are doing better, but it's still devilishly hard to decipher your writing and while I could have asked you, when I do, you never seem to be able to recall what isn't written down. Asking would have been a horrible waste of my time as well as yours."

"I see, you don't want me to do any of this," Daryl said, standing before starting back to the kitchen in an obvious huff. "Perhaps you are right. For the good of the bakery, I should only bake."

"I didn't say that," Lacie said to Daryl's retreating back then looked to see if Justine was watching. Perhaps it was true.

She turned then, "You didn't have to. You're my sister and I can read your mind. I'm going to stay in the kitchen for the remainder of the afternoon. At least I can bake and no one criticizes me except to sing my praises." She continued, back stiff, striding into the kitchen.

Lacie sighed heavily, understanding nothing was going her way. Well, what did she expect? She had spent time trying to teach her sister the ways of making all the numbers make sense as well as readable. As usual, those teachings eluded her sister. Numbers were foreign to Daryl and that was that. Her mind just would not wrap itself around numbers and where organization skills were required, Daryl had none. Her brain was so scattered.

Abstract, nothing in sequence.

The numbers seemed to blur in front of Lacie, and all she could conjure in her head was what happened nights ago, too many to recall exactly, the terrifying feel of the man on top of her as she lay sprawled on the hard ground. She didn't believe anything could erase that memory from her head. He smelled; remembering his yellowed teeth made her nauseas even now. Her body shook as the memory collected in her brain.

She touched her breasts, still feeling the pain of his teeth as they closed over them. Suddenly, she ran to the back of the kitchen, reaching the door to the outside just before emptying the contents of her stomach.

"No," she moaned, "Not again." She closed her eyes, wishing all thoughts to evaporate into the day's sunshine. Facing her future seemed distant and bleak.

Breathing was nearly impossible as was walking and talking. She cleaned her mouth, drinking water then made her way into the kitchen. Justine didn't say anything, just handed her a cup of tea and a cookie.

"Thank you," she said then went back to her table and the work that was in front of her. Still, concentration on something that was usually so easy for her, now eluded her. Her stomach rumbled again, but she didn't have to make a mad dash anywhere.

The tea must be doing its job.

This could not go on indefinitely. The nightmares as well as those images ransacking her brain during the day had to stop. She didn't know how to go about it though. No one could tell her how to make the nightmares all go away. Daryl told her with time she would no longer remember. She didn't believe a word.

Despite her best efforts in the following weeks that had passed since the incident, she could not get the horrific night as well as the images out of her head. She breathed in a deep breath, filling her lungs with new air yet nothing helped. Closing her eyes made the horrific pictures clearer. She had not slept, barely ate.

Daryl sat down beside her with a gentle smile, placing a hand over hers, "I know I've done a horrible job with the books, ignored most of what you tried to teach me, but losing your meal over my ineptness?"

Lacie wanted to laugh at her sister's attempts to make her feel better. Nothing helped her forget. She didn't even believe time would ease the pain as Hope, her brother's wife, also told her it would.

Hope knew things though, things no one else could comprehend, at least none of her friends or family. She'd had lived in a harem where women had no rights, were abused on a daily basis. The knowledge didn't help her. She doubted if it helped the other women either. But Hope knew how to listen in ways her sisters did not. When the images became too real, she would visit her sister-in-law. The time spent would give her some optimism for the future.

"You know why I lost my breakfast. It wasn't your insufficiencies with numbers. I'll figure this out, but you really need to let Justine take care of the ledgers from now on. She is very good, you know. This business is yours. So, it is your right to delegate the responsibilities. It's just stubborn pride that keeps you doing something you can't."

"I don't like thinking I'm stupid," Daryl said, leaning back against the chair, looking at the ceiling as if that would give her the answers or teach her how to overcome her issues with computations and organization.

You're not stupid, Daryl. Numbers have always puzzled you. Nothing has changed. There is no reason to deny that fact. It's the same for me with cooking. I burn everything or what I make ends up like mush and tasteless. I can't read a recipe to save my soul. We all have the things we are good at as well as the things we don't do so well."

The little bell over the shop chimed as Bliss entered with her twin boys, Garret and Grant, in strollers. They were walking now and the mischief they caused always gave Lacie a reason to smile and forget her troubles. They were heaven sent in her world that was fraught with nightmares and fear. The twins looked so much like Broc. Even at this tender age, it nearly stole Lacie's breath.

Bliss bent over so she could see their cute little cherubic faces. "See, there is Aunty Lacie and Aunty Daryl sitting at the table, poring over the numbers. If you ask nicely, maybe they will give you a cookie."

"They don't say very much yet," Daryl said. "Let me hold one and Justine will bring each a cookie."

"Can't help but try. They do say da, da, a few other words as well. Haven't gotten either one to say ma, ma and Broc holds the fact over my head on a daily basis even though I tell him if he keeps it up I will withhold his nightly privileges. When I do that, he just smirks at me with the grin that tells me he knows ways to get around my threats."

Lacie wanted to tell her sisters they could say whatever they wanted because she was married too, but she didn't feel comfortable telling them. Yes, she married Leslie with only the minister, his wife and Kelly as witnesses then he left. She hadn't seen him since.

It wasn't well done of him. He did write though. She had to give him credit for that tiny bit of consideration.

Then, "Really, you don't have to pretend with me. It won't be that long before I'll know everything you're speaking of. Perhaps I'll learn something I can make use of in the future. You tell me all about these nightly privileges and why withholding them would be a punishment."

"Well, Leslie should marry you as soon as he gets back from whatever it is he's doing and teach you himself. I don't understand what is taking him so long," Daryl said to her, assuming an angry edge that matched Lacie's feelings.

"Lacie is not yet eighteen. Maybe he is honoring that magical birthday and he won't return until January," Bliss pointed out. "I for one have never quite understood that number or the magic. We all know women who have wed before eighteen."

The thought made her smile. For some reason, at least for the self-proclaimed bad boys, they didn't touch a woman who was under that special age. So, perhaps that was why he was still gone. Her birthday was a couple months from now.

"He might be like Cam and refuse to even kiss you," Bliss said. "Chelsea was so angry and frustrated. She didn't know how to tell Cam she would never tell Flynt if he kissed her."

"Leslie has kissed me so I suppose the age limit doesn't apply to kissing," Lacie said with a small smile, remembering the few times yet with that memory the nightmare returned.

"We all know kisses lead to other things and it's those other things they forbid themselves," Daryl said with and all-knowing smile.

One of the little boys tugged at her skirt, looking at her with gorgeous aqua colored eyes just like his mother's. He's going to be just like his daddy," Lacie said, grinning at the little boy and ruffling his hair.

"And how is that?" Bliss laughed, seeming to know the answer before Lacie could say the words.

"He's a charmer and totally irresistible. All he needs to do is look at me and I want to give him anything he is asking for," Lacie said. "Including all the cookies he can eat."

"He probably wants his diaper changed," Bliss pointed out.

"Well, he won't get a diaper change from me. I'd most likely botch the job. Believe that's your department, big sis. Comes with having children, which I don't."

"Probably should learn sometime," Bliss said. "If you're still thinking you might want to marry Leslie someday."

"Did you know anything about babies before you were married?" Daryl asked, a smug grin on her face.

Bliss laughed, "Of course not, it wasn't one of the things we were taught at home," Bliss said.

"Who would have taught us?" Lacie pointed out.

"Flynt was the only one available. I'm sure he didn't know the intricacies of diaper changing," Daryl said laughing.

"A bad boy knowing how to change a diaper...? Who would have ever thought such a thing?" Lacie asked, wondering if Leslie was just as ignorant about babies as she was. Then with a sigh, it didn't really matter anyway. After what happened to her that night, she didn't want anything to do with men or babies. She supposed he would have to seek an annulment to their hasty marriage.

"Hardly," Bliss said and the conversation lagged for a moment, Lacie going back to the myriad of numbers in front of her with Daryl and Bliss chatting about their husbands.

She had a husband she barely knew, a nonexistent husband for that matter. A husband she wanted to remain nonexistent because she didn't know if she could bare his touch. The irony didn't escape her.

A few minutes later, the little bell chimed again.

"Grams," Lacie rose to give her grandmother a big hug. She wished she could confide everything to the woman who helped Flynt raise her, wished too she could tell everyone she was married. Grams had always been the person to listen, to wipe tears away in bad times and to laugh with in good ones.

"How are you doing? I've been worried about you. My, I still can hardly believe I'm a great-grandmother. I feel just too young." She gave the twins each a hug and a kiss on the cheek before she sat down next to her then turning to Daryl, "Could I get a cup of tea and a ginger cookie?"

Lacie grimaced, looking at her grandmother once again thinking this would be so much easier if she could tell everything. Yet Leslie had never said not to mention their marriage and had expected her to stay in his home. Maybe she was the only one who didn't want anything to be mentioned about the quick vows. "I'm taking one day at a time."

"Are you able to sleep at night yet, without the nightmares?" Grams set her hand on Lacie's, squeezing gently. "I could stay at the townhouse if that would help. I'd be happy to do that."

"I just want to get away and be alone. Nothing is going to help accept time, at least that's what Hope is telling me. But how much time?" Lacie needed to scream and pound her fists on something hard. Needed to ride across the fields and let the wind sift through her hair, until she couldn't remember. Perhaps that was all she needed, the wind on her face as well as a little alone time.

"I think everyone is different in this," Bliss said as she watched the boys toddle their way into the kitchen.

Daryl rose to go after them.

"Stay here and relax, I'll go after them," Grams said, standing and heading toward the kitchen.

Justine brought them out, one in each arm, laughing as she set them on the floor near their mother. "Look what I found in the kitchen. I believe they want a second cookie. They are so adorable."

"Don't you dare," Bliss said. "They are incorrigible enough without the sweets. If they eat too much food like that, they will be awake all night and Broc will spend the hours frowning at me wondering why there is no peace and quiet to be had in our household."

"See, I'm learning all the time," Lacie sipped the tea while ignoring the cookie. "I would bet that with one year old twin boys there is never alone time despite what they eat."

"Speaking of food, you need to eat more," Grams said, "You are growing too thin."

"Really, you haven't noticed her bosom lately then," Daryl said. "She is growing daily, nothing thin about that part of my sister."

Lacie felt the heat rise to her face. Her large bosom was not something she needed to be reminded of. She was painfully aware of the fact, second by second, her breasts were still getting larger. They were a source of embarrassment to her and even the good-humored jests didn't make her feel any better.

"So, when did you decide to move back to the country?" Grams patted Lacie on the hand still appearing concerned. "It's not an impulse decision is it? You'll be all alone since everyone is in town for the winter months."

"In a week or so. I've really nothing more to do here as long as Justine keeps the ledgers. I'll pack up my things and have Ashford help me settle in. I'm sure Flynt and Hope are getting ready to welcome a baby into this world and don't need someone else in the house to get underfoot. They need their privacy. In subtle ways I'm reminded of that fact daily."

"Well someone should help you pack and move," Daryl said, looking into the kitchen. "Donal probably won't mind lending you Ash for the day, that is if Emilia will also let him go."

Lacie picked up Grant who was once again tugging at her skirts. "Are you after my cookie, little man. Can't give it to you unless your mother gives the go ahead. What do you think? Should we ask her?"

The little boy gurgled something unintelligible as he reached a pudgy hand for the desert.

"Don't you dare," Bliss said again this time a bit more sternly. "One cookie is enough. Now where is Garret?"

"He likes the kitchen." This time Emilia brought the little boy out. "Maybe he's going to follow in his aunties foot steps and become a chef." She set the boy in his stroller then to Lacie, "Of course Ash can help. If he doesn't, he'll be relegated to the couch for the week."

Bliss laughed, "There is nothing like keeping men in line by telling them no when they ask for their husbandly rights."

"You can do that? Tell them no?" Lacie asked, filing away that bit of information for the time, if ever Leslie comes home.

"Of course you can, at least we can," Daryl laughed. "When you finally marry Leslie, you'll have to figure it out for yourself. There will be ways. I'm sure you can let him know he's gone too far with his manly demands and righteous airs."

"It depends on the man. I couldn't tell my first husband no. If he wanted me, he took me and he never cared how I felt," Emilia told her with a heavy and long drawn out sigh. "Ash isn't anything like that. I don't think I would ever have a reason to tell him no. I like the way he makes love to me, the way he feels next to my body when we are in bed."

"As do I," Bliss said, laughing. "Broc is a wonderful lover just as he showed me time and again before we married. He doesn't let me forget. Has an ego bigger than anyone's, but again I love the fact that he is so confident."

This time when the bell chimed, Hope walked in. "Can I get a cup of tea, strong with a little milk and lemon," she asked before she sat down across from Lacie.

"Coming right up."

"How are you feeling?" Grams asked, pointedly looking at Hope's swollen stomach.

"Now that I'm no longer throwing up I feel fine." She reached for one of the cookies on the platter in front of her.

"Ginger cookies are supposed to start labor. How close are you?" Grams asked.

"Still a month to go." She nibbled on the cookie. "Wouldn't mind having the baby early as long as he's healthy. I'm exhausted and tired of not being able to see my feet."

"He?"

"Flynt is positive it's a boy so I humor him."

"That is hard to get used to. Broc is already talking about more children. I keep telling him to bite his tongue. The twins need to be more self sufficient before I go down that path again."

"And when will that be?" Hope asked.

"Another year or so, praying there are no mistakes. He has a horrible time withdrawing from me, and he says he doesn't want to use a condom, so there we are."

"What about you, Daryl? When are you going to have children?" Bliss asked. "Shouldn't be too much longer before you become pregnant if you aren't already."

"I'm late. I know," Chelsea rushed in breathless, her baby in a stroller.

"We're all here then," Bliss said grinning.

"I can't seem to get anywhere on time."

"Babies will do that to you but back to Daryl. Are you expecting yet?" Grams asked.

"No, I don't believe so. Perhaps it's too early to tell," Daryl said with a shrug.

"You've only been wed a few months. Of course it's too soon to tell for sure, but I'm guessing you have an idea," Bliss said, watching her younger sister very carefully.

Lacie didn't think they should be prying, but they'd always wanted to know each other's business. "You all should leave her alone. After all this issue is between the newlyweds, don't you think?"

Good Lord, but she'd been married longer than her older sister and she'd yet to have her husband make love to her.

"Any news on when Leslie will make an appearance?" Chelsea asked, picking up the baby from the stroller. She stood by the table, swaying while she gazed at the child.

"Haven't heard anything from the man for several months," Lacie murmured. "I'll probably know when he shows up. Doesn't seem to believe in schedules. Told me he'd be here but that was over a month ago." She paused, "But then he has no real reason to apprise me of his whereabouts. We've no commitment to each other." What a bunch of nonsense. She was his wife, or had he forgotten that fact?

~ * ~

A few months earlier

The duke was beyond anxious. He felt in his gut something was going to happen, something he wouldn't like. But he didn't know just now what it was. Yet he had volunteered for this mission. So, here he was, waiting for something to blow up in his face when all he wanted to do was go home to his wife and make love to her.

He hated feelings like this. They made him feel helpless and that was something he didn't enjoy. He should have stayed home and taken his chances with Lacie and her brother. He knew he would have never been able to keep his hands off her until she turned eighteen. So, sparks would have flown.

Damned age, why was it so important? It was only a few months. So why couldn't he wait that long? For that matter, why did a month or two make so much difference?

Leslie dismounted from his stallion, slowly striding to the edge of the surf. The water unhurriedly rolled onto the sand, inching higher as the tide seemed to be coming in. Wind swept the waves higher and spewed ocean water into the air. He sucked the salt air into his lungs, felt it gritty and wet against his face. The breeze was strong and sharp, blowing his hair about his head, making his eyes water. The day was cloudy, a dull gray just like his mood.

He cursed, wishing this was not the job assigned to him, but he wanted out of the country. So, Montgomerie sent him to France, his home away from home. Because he was fluent in the language, Montgomerie told him. Because of this he could move about with out anyone being the wiser. And an added benefit, his mother lived there.

Two days passed. Leslie was bored and restless. As it turned out, he received his instructions from a one-legged beggar who sidled up to him and poked a thick packet into his coat pocket.

He read the letter twice, memorizing the precise instructions then carefully studied each of the enclosed papers and documents. He was in disbelief at what was expected of him. Shaking his head, he folded the papers into their packet, once again wishing he had declined the mission.

It was obvious hours had been spent formulating a plan to rescue this woman, this Caroline Dubois. Montgomerie never explained the reason for this. Leslie was beginning to think it was a ruse to give him what he wanted, an escape from Glasgow for as many months as he needed.

Now after reading the documents, it was becoming increasingly clear the woman he was supposed to rescue was the mistress of Jean Laurent. She had been stolen a few months ago. He didn't completely believe that particular story, but the evidence was pointing in said direction. So, some of the tale must be true. Laurent was important to the working political scene in France.

Now after chasing leads, he found General Denis Caron and the location of Caroline. If all the stories were true, she was now the general's whore. He sold her to the highest bidder, pimping her out to make money. Sometimes she was the wager in card games. He didn't understand the motive in this scenario. He assumed comprehension was not imperative to rescue Caroline.

He was playing cards with Denis who possessed the key to the room where Caroline was kept prisoner. To Leslie the game seemed rigged in his favor. Perhaps the general enjoyed giving her to men. Now he was handed the key, told he could perform sexually with this woman since he won and that he was to be pleasured by her. This time it was free but if he enjoyed himself, he would have to pay the going price for further encounters.

He said the wench loved threats and a bit of pain, liked the sex rough. Then the bloody fool decided to shadow him. "Because," he said as they climbed the stairs to the third floor," she isn't exactly trained fully as yet. She's a novice, if you get my drift." Leslie watched the man unlock the door and stride inside, hoping and saying a few prayers as well that the man was not intending to watch.

He followed, saying nothing. It was a spare room with only a bed and dresser and one small circular rug in the middle. There was only one occupant, a single woman standing in the middle of the room wearing what appeared to be just a robe. Was this Caroline Dubois? He assumed so. The general grinned drunkenly at her and said with a flip of his hand. "Strip off the robe, Caro. Lord Stewart needs to see what he's going to be enjoying tonight."

The woman hesitated then complied. He'd expected someone younger, though why he should have he didn't know. No, she wasn't really a girl, Leslie thought, looking at her more closely, rather a woman in her mid-twenties. She was obviously scared and she was lovely, despite her pallor, the shadows beneath her eyes were very dark. She was overly thin.

The man waited silently until she'd stripped to her shift. Then he lurched toward her, grabbed her chin in his fingers and kissed her, fondling her breast with his other hand through the thin lawn. Suddenly, he grabbed the front of her shift and ripped it off.

He laughed, saying over his shoulder to Leslie, "I wanted to see if you approved of her. A bit thin for my taste, but she does have nice bubbies." He pushed her onto the bed, leaned over her, and said low, "You see this man, my girl? You do everything he wants you to do or... you know the punishment, don't you? I would like to stay and watch, but I'm tired." He straightened and turned to Leslie. "You are quiet. Don't you think she is lovely? Not a virgin, but not overused either. She belongs to me, and now, because she isn't stupid, she obeys my every command. So, you may enjoy her but as I said, just for tonight."

The man stumbled out of the room. Leslie moved after him, listening as his footsteps receded along the corridor then down the stairs. He listened to another door open and close on the second floor. Then he turned back to face the woman.

She was standing now by the bed, trying to cover herself with her hands. Leslie couldn't believe his good fortune, but he wasn't about to doubt it, not for a moment.

His voice was urgent as he strode to her. "Is your name Caroline Dubois?"

She was tiny, very fair, her hair falling straight down her back nearly to her waist. She had light blue eyes, very blond brows and lashes. She was lovely.

"Are you?" he asked again.

She nodded, taking a tiny step backwards.

"Don't be afraid of me. I'm here on behalf of Jean Laurent. He wanted me to find you and bring you some place safe, somewhere out of the general's reach. He seeks revenge for your kidnapping."

She was cowering in front of the bed, speechless and Leslie was losing patience with her. He wasn't about to do anything here that would send the general after him. This was the woman he was sent to rescue. He would see her safe even if she decided she would be better off with the general.

"Do you know Jean Laurent?"

She nodded, still obviously afraid of him, not believing for a moment despite the flare of hope he'd seen flash through her eyes.

"You need to dress, quickly. I am here to take you away, to Jean. We must hurry."

"I don't have any gowns."

Leslie looked around the room searching. "A cloak, anything. Come we must hurry."

"Why should I believe you?" So, there was some spirit left in her. She was nearly strangling on her fear but she still kept talking. "I know that he gave me to you. He said so, and I know why he did it."

"It's because I won a wager."

"Oh, no, not that," She became even paler. Her rouged lips parted then closed. She shook her head, saying in a rush. "He wants me to find out what you will tell me about the government when you return to Paris. He's worried also that you are a spy and will deceive him. If you try to take me away from here, he will discover it and kill us both. He told me I must discover the truth or he will kill my daughter. He says he has her and she won't continue to live."

"Ah." Leslie smiled down at her and gently began to run his hands up and down her thin arms. So, the general hadn't been drunk after all. The game, the wager, his loss, it had all been the generals plan to trap him. Not bad. It was nice of Caroline to inform him.

He felt the usual surge of excitement in this adventure, wondered if he would be happy living without it. "Easy now," he said absently, trying to calm her, all the while thinking furiously. "Where is your daughter? Once we get out of here we will get her and bring her with us. I promise she won't be hurt."

Caroline started. "She's at the farm, two miles from St. Emilion to the north. He says he has a man there watching her and that the man will kill her if I don't do as he orders."

If I know Jean, he's already taken care of any guards at the farmhouse. Truly my job here is to save you. Jean will save your daughter. Now let's get you dressed in something. I am taking you and your daughter to London where you will be protected until Jean can come to you."

"London," she said slowly, her dark eyes wide with surprise. "But we only speak French. I wouldn't know what to do or say?"

He waved his hand, dismissing her fears. "It doesn't matter. Many people speak French in London and you will learn. Jean lives in the city much of the time and he can teach both you and your daughter the language."

"But—"

"No, I can say no more. We can't linger here any longer. Jean wishes me to take you to London, so that is what I will do. You will be safe there until he returns to fetch you. There are chores he must attend to in France before he can leave. Will you trust me?"

She looked at him, worship and trust shining from her face and said simply, "Yes."

"Good. Now, listen to me. Here's what we will do. First, we will find something for you to wear even if I have to wrap that bed sheet around you." Leslie wondered as he stared down into that pale tense face that she held such trust for him, why people in general and females in particular believed him to be some sort of Saint George. He hated it but at the same time he found it amusing. He thought of Jean Laurent and fervently hoped she would remember him in her thoughts. After all, he was a married man now.

Other Books by Christine Young
Available at Rogue Phoenix Press

My Sweet Broc
Bad Boys Book One

He's a bad bad boy...

Broc Wallace is a fun-loving rake who never thought any beautiful woman could melt his heart. He lives life in the present enjoying the camaraderie of his friends and the pleasures of his mistress. When Bliss races into his life, he is ill prepared to deal with her secrets or give up the tenor of his life. When the truth is revealed, he finds himself unable to forgive and forget the betrayal.

...but she's sweet for him

Bliss MacTavish knows she's playing with fire when she refuses to tell this bad boy her name. He tempts her with sweet whispers of seduction knowing her innocent nature will be unable to refuse all he yearns to give her. Deciding to follow her heart, she finds the repercussions more than she bargains for when she gives herself to this bad boy.

Crazy for Cam
Bad Boys Book Two

He's a bad bad boy...

Lord Cam MacEwen, Viscount of Rosehill, tries his best to be proper and court the lady of his dreams in the acceptable way. The feat proves impossible when the lady in question uses every means at her disposal to tempt him. He fights his jealousy for another man as well as the need to make her his own, finally giving in to her irresistible passion.

...but she's crazy for him.

Chelsea MacTavish wants the bad boy she fell in love with and kissed just before her eighteenth birthday. With feminine wiles and irresistible allure, the sensuous lady plans to best Cam at his game of hearts and make him forget his need to court her properly.

Falling for Flynt
Bad Boys Book Three

He's a bad, bad boy...

Fascinated by Hope's loss of memory yet haunted by her sultry beauty, Flynt is irresistibly drawn to the stoic miss—and into her troubles with the sultan who wants her for himself. When he discovers she is the sister of his best friend, his pride keeps him from pursuing her and making her his.

...but she's falling for him.

Raised in a harem but now penniless, alone and without her memory, Hope must discover a way to remember all that she has lost. She finds a way to continue with her life as a servant in Flynt's home. The first sight of Flynt steals Hope's breath as well as her heart. Can she overcome her fears and give herself to the man she fell in love with.

Foolish for Piper

The pickpocket...

Piper has spent her life surviving the streets of St. Giles Parish in London, a den of iniquity and crime. Masquerading as a boy she escapes the whorehouses the young girls are sent to as they come of age. The day she encounters Brett MacLachlan begins the same as every other one. When she picks his pocket, she has no idea her life is going to change irreversibly.

...and the mark

Handsome aristocrat Brett MacLachlan has come to London for his amusement only to find his world turned upside down by a thief and her dog. From the moment he spots her, Brett knows there is something intrinsically wrong. In his arms, Piper discovers passion and joy. Yet secrets of her past haunt her, and a scar will tell the true tale as well as her identity.

Taylor's Destiny

She traveled to another time and place to change destiny...

Enjoying a day of sailing, Taylor Maxwell never expected after a suffering a concussion she would wake up in another century. A resilient independent woman in the twenty-first century, the blond beauty is ill prepared for life in the 1800s. Her first sight of the naval captain who rescues her makes her heart stop, giving her hope for her future.

His life is transformed by a woman who appears from nowhere...

Born to a life of ease, Reid Stewart defies the dictates of those born to aristocracy and chooses a life of adventure in the navy and as a spy for the crown. When he discovers a nearly naked woman on the bow of small sailing ship, his heart warms. His love for Taylor and his need to protect her from a man who pursues her might cost him his life as well as hers.

Caitlin's Duke

She played a fiddle in an Irish pub....

Caitlin O'Shea Is the most beautiful woman Roc Leighton has ever seen. With her blue violet eyes and long black hair she captivates him. In turn he mesmerizes Caitlin. Caught in the power of his gaze as he watches her, she is wise enough to know he desires her but will never give his heart to her. Caitlin has vowed to never be any man's mistress.

And fell in love with an English Lord...

Roc knows the first time he watches her play the fiddle and dance around the pub, she will be his next mistress. Despite her protest, he will find a way to convince her that her place is with him. While Caitlin's determination to keep her vows, fate takes a cruel turn and she is forced to seek refuge with Roc.

Catching Meara
Book One in the McKenna Clan Series

Meara Thorton was a feisty, world-class computer hacker—cornered by the FBI and shockingly given the chance to be their newly acquired technical analyst. Brilliant and intuitive, yet aching with the loss of everyone she has cared about, her restless heart led her to discover a love she fought and a world she didn't know could possibly exist.

Sweet Sexy Sadie
Book Two in the McKenna Clan Series

From the first time Sadie's eyes met those of Brody McKenna in the hot Sierra Madre Mountains, theirs was a potent attraction—not gentle, slow, and easy, but hot, hard, and all-consuming. The daughter of a dysfunctional family, Sadie had dreams no man could wrench from her with hot sex and an all-consuming passion. She'd challenge this alpha male with all the strength she possessed. But her red hair, fiery temperament, and indomitable spirit obsessed Brody...and he knew he had to find a way to show her he was more than he appeared and convince her to make a life with him.

Sweet Misbehavin'
Book Three in the McKenna Clan Series

Cast adrift after fleeing the home of Jokul, the ice demon, Atantsi, a firestarter, grew to womanhood as she moved through time to keep the demon from finding her. Though stubborn and courageous, she was ill prepared to use powers she had not been taught. Her first sight of the intoxicating Carr McKenna left her breathless, and her second encounter gave her hope for a future she never thought she had.

A playboy, a second son and a shifter, a man who thought his life would be carefree, Carr McKenna was shocked to discover the woman he'd paid as an escort is a firestarter who is running for her life. He is the leader of all the McKennas around the world and that he has multiple powers. His passion for Margo and the need to defend her might cost him his life as well as hers.

Sweet Talkin' Sugar
Book Four in the McKenna Clan Series

Lyonesse McKenna, was dreaming or was she? From the instant Lyn saw

Deacon McClain across a black jack table in a crowed Las Vegas casino the unmistakable attraction sent Lyn's senses flying into overdrive. Her family of shapeshifters believed in soul mates. She'd always been skeptical yet she couldn't help but question the way her heart sped when he looked at her.

When Deacon appeared in Las Vegas he knew his first job was to save Lyn from a Sea Demon, but the next order of business was to convince her he would someday mean more to her than she'd ever expected. But her stubborn nature and unbendable spirit consumed Deacon...and he had to chase away all the demons real and imagined in order to win her heart.

Sweet Surrender
Book Five in the McKenna Clan Series

Ripped from her family at the top of Infinity Cliff, Kimi McKenna finds herself thrust somewhere into the future. Dark elements threaten to destroy the earth unless Kimi can work together with the white witch to stop the destruction. Confused by her mate's role in the conspiracy, she refuses to acknowledge the connection. But amidst raging fire and attacks on the people she is coming to hold dear, she allows Maska O'keefe into her heart.

Maska O'keefe has loved the beautiful shapeshifter for years. Unable to save her life years ago, he vows to watch over her as he is given a second chance to convince her that even though he is a witch and not a shifter, they are indeed soul mates. Kimi's divided loyalties between her family and the cause she is now a part of will determine their relationship. Only the part she plays as the messiah can bring this to a conclusion in the final battle.

Dakota's Bride
The first book in the Lakota/Pinkerton Series

When Emma St. John received her brother's letter imploring her to escape her stepfather's vengeful scheme and to trust Dakota Barringer with her life, she was willing to chance it. But the handsome, brooding riverboat owner Emma found in Natchez a danger of another kind. For Emma soon found herself surrendering to an unrelenting desire.

Raised by the Sioux when his parents were killed, Dakota had been betrayed once before by a white woman. He wasn't about to trust another, especially one claiming that her stepfather, a powerful U.S. senator, had framed her as a murderess. But he couldn't let Emma's intoxicating effect on him. Now Dakota would risk his very life to protect the innocent beauty who had seduced him with her tender love.

My Angel
The second book in the Lakota/Pinkerton Series

A BEAUTY IN BUCKSKINS
When her father decided to send her to a finishing school back East, Angela Chamberlain refused to be confined to stuffy drawing rooms. Instead, the daring spitfire who could shoot like a man and ride like the wind longed for a life of adventure and romance—and she knew exactly who could give it to her. Devil Blackmoor was a hired gun with a dangerous reputation. But Angela was willing to go to the ends of the earth to capture the handsome devil's heart.

A DEVIL IN DISGUISE
He'd come to America looking for excitement, but Devil Blackmoor got more than he bargained for when he encountered a beautiful rebel who answered his kisses with a wild innocence that touched his very soul. Yet standing between them were more obstacles than either ever dreamed. For Devil had strapped on a gun for the wrong man. And that made

Angela his enemy. Now he'll have to choose between his duty and the woman he loves more than life.

The Locket
The third book in the Lakota/Pinkerton Series

The year is 1894. Seeking revenge for crimes against his family, Misha Petrovich follows a path that leads straight to Ariel Cameron's boarding house in Mist Harbor, Oregon. A family heirloom in Ariel's possession leads Misha to believe she is guilty. The locket has been handed down to the oldest girl in the Petrovich family for generations. Ariel is innocent of wrong doing, but her father is not. Misha is torn by his feelings for Ariel and his need for restitution against her father. Knowing that the relationship between them is fragile, Misha does everything in his power to protect Ariel's father. His efforts are to no avail when her father is shot. Ariel comes to realize Misha's steadfast courage and determination to protect her and her father despite what has happened to his family. Ariel's love and devotion heals Misha's heart.

The Talisman
The fourth book in the Lakota/Pinkerton Series

Running from a marriage that lasted one night, Dr. Moriah McKeown discovers the land she has settled on is coveted by determined and lawless men. Yet the proud young woman who once vowed never to abandon her home has second thoughts when her adopted children are threatened. Her only recourse is to enlist the aid of a dark, dangerous gun for hire.

Haunted by the past and a betrayal he will never forgive, Ian Civanovich uses his fast gun and his reckless courage to forget the faithlessness of a woman in his past. He will trust no female—nor will he rest until the threat hovering over Moriah McKeown is put to rest.

Forever His
The fifth book in the Lakota/Pinkerton Series

Struggling to come to terms with the part she played in Jacob St. John's death, Etta Barringer resigns from Pinkerton Agency and seeks peace and solace in a Rocky Mountain Cabin.
Jacob has vowed to discover the reason Etta has betrayed him, sold him out to his enemy and left him for dead.

Isolated in their cabin, they discover their love for each other and learn to trust. But the trust is shattered when Jacob learns she is married to his sworn enemy; the man who left him in the desert to die.

Allura's Secret
Twelve Dancing Princesses Book One

Allura McClellan is horrified by her father's decision to take out an ad in the Times awarding her to the man strong enough and smart enough to win her hand and uncover her secrets. She's an intelligent young woman who takes great delight in the freedom allotted to her by her father. She's well aware that marriage would effectively curtail the adventures she's shared with her sisters and cousins.

Hunter Gray is nothing like the other men who've arrived to vie for Allura's hand in marriage and everything that goes along with it. However, he is the first to refuse to concede defeat and pursue her despite her attempts to disguise her true appearance. It's her temperament that is of more concern to him than her looks. Hunter has worked all his life with the hope of someday owning his own land. Now that it looks like there's a very real possibility that everything he's ever wanted is within reach nothing is going to deter him – including Miss Allura's disagreeable disposition.

Amorica's Wager
Twelve Dancing Princesses Book Two

Amorica Hepburn was sent to London to find a husband. Finding a man was the last item on her agenda. With her two cousins, Amorica wagers she can dissuade her suitor before the others. Despite her efforts she discovers a chemistry that cannot be denied. Suddenly she is the arrogant man's wife, pledged to a marriage neither desire. But swept off to his ancestral home above the Dover cliffs and into his strong embrace, Amorica is soon possessed by a raging passion for the husband she had vowed to despise…

Damian Andrews couldn't afford to trust the emerald-eyed spitfire who happened upon his secret. Amorica's hatred of all men of his kind only inflames the war that rages between them. Still, he can not control the intense desire his stubborn bride inspires, or make her surrender to his will until he has conquered the headstrong beauty on the battlefield of love…

Ravyn's Marriage of Inconvenience
Twelve Dancing Princesses Book Three

A REGAL BEAUTY
When the duchess decides to wed her to a wastrel and a fop, Ravyn Grahm takes matters into her own hands and declares her engagement to another man. Instead of fessing up and telling her great aunt what she has done, she goes through with the pretense. Ariec Lakeland is the bastard son of an earl and has a dangerous reputation. But Ravyn is willing to do most anything to keep the duchess from discovering the lie.

A DEVIL-MAY-CARE SMUGGLER
He'd bought land in America, looking to put down roots and end his life of adventure, but Ariec Lakeland got more than he bargained for when he encountered a beautiful heiress who made a promise she didn't want

to keep. But the promise could not be undone and standing between them were more obstacles than either ever dreamed. Ariec had made plans to spend the rest of his life in America and that was at odds with Ravyn's plan of living in England and running her father's estate. Now, he'll have to choose between his dreams and the woman he loves more than life.

Christel's Sunrise
Twelve Dancing Princesses Book Four

He Made Her An Offer...

Life has thrown Christel McClellan some experiences that could have devastated a less determined woman. Beautiful, self-assured and fiercely independent, she is trying to forget the loss of her stillborn child. But is the child alive?

She Couldn't Deny...

Life is carefree for Ryder MacLaren who loves to see what is on the other side of the sunrise. Laird of Clan MacLaren, he is wealthy, handsome and happily unencumbered...until stunning Christel McClellan enters his life. When he hears her story, he believes the child she thought dead has been sold to a wealthy buyer.

Storm's Passion
Twelve Dancing Princesses Book Five

SHE MADE A PROPOSAL...

Life strikes Storm Graham a shattering blow when she learns her father has bartered her to a man she detests. Storm is beautiful, self–assured and fiercely independent, and refuses to be a pawn in her father's schemes, yet she can find no way out of this bargain made in hell. Going on the offensive she asks the wealthiest man on the eastern coast of England to marry her, never believing she might fall in love.

HE TRIED TO REFUSE...

For Hadden Johnston life has provided everything he ever wanted, including a sanctuary for homeless children. He is wealthy, handsome and happily unencumbered...until stunning Storm Graham marches into his life and proposes a marriage of convenience. Yet this type of marriage to a woman who inflames his senses is far from acceptable. If he's going to be tied down, he will move heaven and earth to have this woman warming his bed.

Gotta Have Fayth
Twelve Dancing Princesses Book Six

A regal beauty with raven hair and piercing blue eyes, Fayth Graham is unwilling to parade herself in front of the wealthy Lords of England during the season. Seeking a means to dissuade any man wishing to wed her, she seeks a way to ruin herself for marriage. When she unexpectedly meets a man with sparkling gray eyes and an infectious grin, she decides this is the man who will keep her from agreeing to obey.

He returned from six months at sea, looking for a few nights of pleasure with a willing lass, but Jarret Kinsley got more than he bargained for when he met a beautiful debutant who responded to his kisses with a wild innocence that touched his heart. Yet the obstacles looming between them might rip them apart. Both had vowed never to marry, so when consequences of their dalliances got in the way, Jarret would have to choose between the life he's always desired and the woman he loves more than life.

Ella's Pleasure
Twelve Dancing Princesses Book Seven

A WHISPER OF PLEASURE

Ella Hepburn was an auburn haired debutant from the harsh Scottish coastline—a wild innocent to be seduced and tamed. A spirited beauty, she captivated Drake Montgomerie's jaded heart—while succumbing to the smoldering desire she felt for her unyielding suitor.

A WHISPER OF DANGER

In Drake Montgomerie's glittering world of money and privilege, young Ella discovered passion and desire could overcome everything she'd been taught to resist—entangling Drake, the heir apparent, in a lethal coil of aristocratic family intrigue. But grave peril would only nurse the sparks of a love that knew no limits and a magnificent ecstasy that would not be denied.

Eveleen's Seduction
Twelve Dancing Princesses Book Eight

A WHISPER OF SEDUCTION

A brutal attack on Eveleen Hepburn's cherished island off the Scottish coastline leaves her shattered and bewildered. Learning a man she once trusted can kill as easily as he can breathe even though the deed saves her life, creates questions that need answers. An innocent beauty, she enchants Logan Maxwell's cynical heart—giving in to the raging passion she feels for her mysterious suitor.

A WHISPER OF INTRIGUE

In Logan's Maxwell's world of espionage and privilege, young Eveleen discovers truths about herself she never expected, and a need for passion and love can overcome all her fears if she learns to accept certain truths. She finds herself entangled in a lethal battle for land that was once owned by French nobility, taken from them during the revolution and sold to Maxwell. But grave peril would unleash the flames of love that simmers, creating a magical union that cannot be refuted.

Tavia's Deception
Twelve Dancing Princesses Book Nine

WHISPERS OF DECEPTION

When her father decides to send her to London for her season, Tavia Hepburn resolves to see the world instead. The raven haired beauty decides to disguise herself as a lad and find employment on a ship bound for Barcelona as a cabin boy. But she never bargains on finding passion and love to a red haired sea captain who rescues her from certain death.

WHISPERS OF MURDER

For James Macmurra, the world is black and white until he meets a young debutante, who turns his world upside down. He's unable to deny Tavia's intoxicating effect on him. In a match tense with obstacles, unwillingness to divulge secrets, and unforeseen peril, irresistible desire and passion grows into undeniable love. James would risk his life to shelter and protect the innocent debutante who seduces him with her sweet love.

Larena's Fascination
Twelve Dancing Princesses Book Ten

WHISPERS OF FASCINATION

Fiery, free spirited Larena Graham never wanted to marry a duke. She is thrilled to be in love with the fourth son of an aristocrat, Gavin Broon. But when it seems Gavin ignores her, she set her sights on politics and bettering human life. Unsuspecting intrigue and a plot against her, she continues her dangerous plans despite Gavin's wishes.

WHISPERS OF TRUST

Gavin has every intention of properly courting the beautiful Larena until he must leave the city in order to put his affairs in order. Returning to London, he finds the woman he means to make his own is embroiled in political protests that could lead to a prison ship. Larena must learn to trust the handsome Scotsman whose most pressing mission is to protect her and keep her from harm.

Tira's Education
Twelve Dancing Princesses Book Eleven

WHISPERS OF EDUCATION

Learning how to build ships is Tira Hepburn's only dream until she meets Jamie Lundin and her world is turned upside down. With her raven black hair and vivid green eyes, she tempts Jamie and pushes him to defy his vows. She never bargains on finding an irrevocable love and a passion to a man who cannot fulfill her dreams despite his burning desire for her.

WHISPERS OF A BARGAIN

Arrogant and self-assured Jamie is brought up short when Tira captures his heart. All his carefully made plans are put to the test when he decides to teach her the art of ship building if she will spend a week with him alone on his ship. He is unable to deny Tira's intoxicating effect on him. When Tira leaves him behind unwilling to live with him without the benefit of marriage, he races after her. Jamie will risk everything to shelter and protect the innocent debutante who seduces him with her sweet love.

Aidan's Love
Twelve Dancing Princesses Book Twelve
Whispers of Love

Aidan McLellan has loved since she first set eyes on him as a young girl. Spontaneous, wild and eager to grow up, Aidan haunts his waking thoughts day and night, insinuating herself into his life. With her fiery red hair and sparkling sapphire eyes, she seizes Blade's heart even while he tries to resist the innocent child until she becomes a woman.

Whispers of Courage

Blade has waited what seems a lifetime to claim the woman who captures his heart as a little girl. Claiming his inheritance before his younger brother takes what is rightfully his, Blade must convince Aidan of his sincerity after years of avoidance and wed her before his father dies so he can return home, securing his rightful place. Everything is put to the test when his life as well as Aidan's is threatened by the man who once called him brother.

Twelve Days to Love

When Archer Steele shows up at Calanthe Durand's failing plantation with an alligator over his shoulder, Cali thinks she's never seen a more handsome man. During the war she had to defend herself and her servants from both union and confederate soldiers. Independent and self-sufficient, she vows to never marry.

But Archer Steele has different ideas. The first time Archer sees Cali in town, he feels an instant attraction. He decides he will do everything and anything to convince the beautiful Miss Durand he is worthy of her love. During the weeks leading up to Christmas, he gives her twelve gifts in hopes she will fall in love with him. Yet they are faced with challenges they must overcome before Cali can commit to a marriage.

Door to Heaven

Jessica Lawrence is the stepdaughter of a woman born in the twentieth century transported back in time to the year 1868. An acclaimed suffragette, she raises Jessica to believe in the equality of women. Jess Law believes everything she was taught, and when the time is right she becomes a private investigator. Courageous and impetuous, Jess finds danger in her quest to save all women from white slavery. Her passionate mission results in a wedding to Roc Newman, a man she knows can steal her heart...

Roc can't trust the sapphire-eyed spitfire who invades his home in search of secret papers and knocks him flat with her karate moves. Jessica's refusal to obey his wishes serves to inflame the war between them. Still, he cannot control the intense desire his reluctant bride inspires, or make her surrender her independence, until he has conquered the headstrong beauty on the battlefield of love...

Rebel Heart

HER REBEL SPIRIT DEFIED HIS OUTSIDERS SOUL...She was velvet and silk, eyes the color of a summer storm and amber hair. Victoria DeMontville, because of a promise and a codicil to her father's will, was forced to marry one man to protect her from another. She hated Cameron Savage with a fierce passion. But to hold on to her genetic research and find a cure for the deadly Signe virus, she must pretend to love the enemy at her door, come with weapons of fire to melt her icy heart...

HIS OUTSIDERS TOUCH IGNITED RAGING PASSIONS...He wore a mask, disguised as the Phantom, a true legend come to life. Even as war and debate over new genetic research engulfed them all, he would find his greatest adversary in the beauty who'd branded him an outsider and barbarian, the woman he was born to possess, his soul mate.

Safari Moon

Solo St. John, a wildlife photographer, is preparing for a trip to Alaska. Suddenly, Solo finds women of all sorts invading his privacy, his home and his office, all cooing nonsense words and blatantly throwing themselves at him. Solo doesn't know why, and he has no idea how to rid himself of the persistent women. He finally decides to beg a favor of his best buddy Nyssa Harrington.

In love with Solo for the past ten years and knowing he doesn't return her feelings Nyssa doesn't want to talk to Solo. She knows if she accepts his phone call, she will not be able to resist the temptation to hope again.

Straight to Heaven

Running from demons, Alexandra McMurdie stumbles into Forbidden Ground where up is down and elements of nature are contested. Though a strong independent woman in the twenty-first century' she is unprepared for life in the 1800s. Her first site of the formidable James Lawrence makes her heart skip a beat, giving her cause to reconsider her desperate need to find a way home.
Born with a silver spoon, James' life was torn apart during the War Between the States. Moving west he vows to put the life he once knew in the past. When he discovers a half-frozen woman near Gold Hill, his heart begins to thaw. His love for Alexandra and his need to keep her from a man who has pursued her through time might cost him his life as well as hers.

A Valentine's Anthology

The Lending Library-a fantasy by Christie L. Kraemer

Faeries try to fit into the human world when the forest where they make their home is destroyed by a mysterious enemy.

Chasing Rainbows-a contemporary romance by Genene Valleau

An eccentric aunt, an inventive uncle, a mother who wears poodle skirts, and a brother who wears pearls provide a hilarious backdrop for the courtship of a young woman who yearns for a "normal" family.

The Gift-an historical romance by Christine Young

A man and a woman on opposite sides of the Civil War get a second chance at love after one final battle returns soldiers to their war-torn homes to rebuild their lives.

A St. Patrick's Day Tale

Christine Young, C. L. Kraemer, Genene Valleau

Tumble through time…

…to Ireland in 1817, when tensions are high between Protestants and Catholics and fae people guide the fate of villagers. A lovely Catholic lass stumbles upon the weakly ritual fisticuffing between Irish lads. She falls into the lap of a handsome young Protestant. Family ties, grudges, and two conniving faeries threaten their budding love. But the faeries outsmart themselves when they hijack a time machine that has mysteriously appeared in their forest and are whisked to…

…Eugene, Oregon in the 20th century, amid a property feud between the local faeries and night elves. The conniving faeries from Olde Ireland try to stir up more mischief. However, a warrior gnome convinces the magic folk to control their own destiny, and forces the intruding faeries to take refuge in the time machine again, spinning their way toward…

…A modern day castle in western Oregon. An eccentric inventor is determined to reclaim his wayward time machine and save his beloved wife from her latest misadventure. If only they can travel safely past the black hole…

a May Day Anthology

Christine Young, C. L. Kraemer, Rosemary Indra, Genene Valleau

Highland Miracle — Christine Young

HURTLED THROUGH TIME, Sean Michael Sterling, landed in the midst of a May Day celebration he didn't understand, assuming the role of Laird Sterling.
ILLIGITAMATE CHILD OF NOBILITY, Reagan Douglas searches for a way out of her half brother's house.

Defying the Odds — C.L. Kraemer

The night elves on the hill aren't happy without their magic. They concoct a plan to punish those who were involved in the act that rendered them almost human. Meanwhile, Uther, the rogue night elf, has returned to woo the Librarian to be his eternal mate.

Love in Bloom — Rosemary Indra

When childhood friends reunite it takes two fairies and a matchmaking daughter to help them admit their true love for each other.

No More Poodle Skirts — Genie Gabriel

After drifting for years in the innocent age of the 1950s, a woman struggles to join today's world by finding a career and a new love, with some help from her zany family.

Once Upon a Christmas Moon

Christine Young, C. L. Kraemer, Genene Valleau

TWELVE DAYS TO LOVE

When Archer Steele shows up at Calanthe Durand's failing plantation with an alligator over his shoulder, Cali thinks she's never seen a more handsome man. During the war she had to defend herself and her servants from both union and confederate soldiers. Independent and self-sufficient, she vows to never marry. But Archer Steele has different ideas. The first time Archer sees Cali in town, he feels an instant attraction. He decides he will do everything and anything to convince the beautiful Miss Durand he is worthy of her love. During the weeks leading up to Christmas, he gives her twelve gifts in hopes she will fall in love with him.

BOOTS AND BLADES

An ancient evil from the old country has arrived in the high desert of Oregon. Gnome children are vanishing then re-appearing, showing various stages of traumatization. Tiamoon, warrior gnome, will put her skills to use alongside Killian, a handsome warrior, also in need of a cause.

CHRISTMAS PAWSIBILITIES

With their world destroyed and their space ship malfunctioning, the dogizens of Planet Canid have little choice but to crash land on Earth. They face tortuous experiments at the hands of the Geeks in Green...or they can trust an eccentric inventor and his zany family to deliver the Canine Queen's puppies and help them celebrate new lives.